CU00944290

Victoria J. Price lives on England's breathtaking south coast. She loves fairy tales, myths and legends, and grew up creating stories both in words and pictures. When she's not writing you'll find her exploring with her husband and their two dogs, searching for beautiful hidden places and secret picnic spots.

www.victoriajprice.com

Follow on social media:

Instagram @victoriajprice

TikTok @victoriajprice

Facebook @authorvictoriajprice

Books by Victoria J. Price

A Legacy of Storms and Starlight

Daughter of the Phoenix Series

The Third Sun

The Eternal Dusk

The First Dawn

VICTORIA J. PRICE

A LEGACY OF POISON AND LIES

Copyright ©2023 by Victoria J. Price

All rights reserved. No part of this publication may be reproduced, stored in a retrieval system, or transmitted in any form or by any means, electronic, mechanical, recording or otherwise, without the prior written permission of the copyright holder.

This is a work of fiction. Names, characters, businesses, places, events and incidents are either the products of the author's imagination or used in a fictitious manner. Any resemblance to actual persons, living or dead, or actual events is purely coincidental.

Editing services provided by Melanie Underwood

Cover and title design by Franziska Stern

Map by Andrés Aguirre Jurado

ISBN: 978-1-9163540-6-7

www.victoriajprice.com

For anyone fighting their own monsters

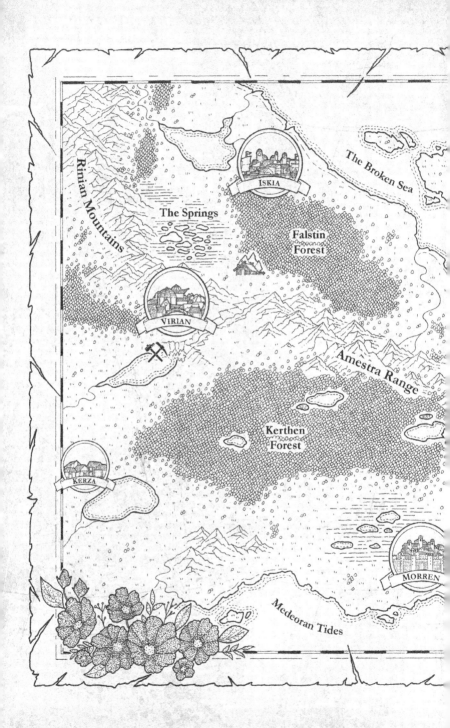

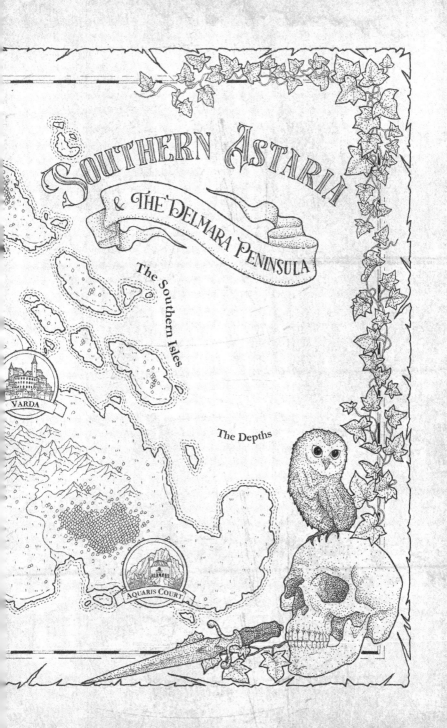

SOUTHERN ASTARIA

& THE DELMARA PENINSULA

The Southern Isles

VARDA

The Depths

AQUARIS COURT

Murderer.

The word echoed on repeat as Zylah inspected the coins in her palm. Three measly coppers were all she'd managed to make at the market, standing in the bitter cold.

The people of Varda had little coin to spare, but Zylah needed to eat. She reached into her apron and pulled out a vial, popping off the cork with her thumb. It was a tonic of her own making, and she'd seen it in use enough times to know it worked.

But it wasn't healing her as it should have, only quietening the burning sensation that seemed to blaze through her, day and night.

The stall owner beside her started arguing with a customer, but Zylah drowned out the sound. She sifted through images of everything she'd eaten in the Kerthen forest, questioning, not for the first time, whether she could have mistakenly identified a plant for something else.

But there was no chance of that. She knew her plants too well to eat something she shouldn't have, and besides, she'd left Kerthen three months ago.

And worse than that worry, she suspected the sickness was a side effect of the knot on her spine, the little lump she'd had for as long as she could remember.

Not a lump, she corrected herself. The vanquicite. A black stone that hindered magical abilities—Fae abilities—and one she'd unknowingly lived with for her entire life until just a few months ago.

"Arnir was a plague upon Astaria, we're better off without him." The stall owner seethed. Zylah was inclined to agree.

King Arnir flopping face first into the dirt repeated over and over in Zylah's thoughts as the customer muttered under her breath, slamming the candles she'd been about to purchase down onto the table and marching off into the market.

A dark speck darted through the air just beyond the woman's head, and Zylah held out a hand for her owl. He dropped a small drawstring bag into her hands before flying off amongst the market stalls. The bag was light, because the owl was tiny and could fit in her palms, but also because the locals barely had any money to part with.

Zylah sighed. Another slow day. She watched Kopi's tiny frame as he flew to the far end of the market, collecting the coin that was owed to her. He wasn't really *her* owl. But it was easier to let people think that. If she had a copper for every time someone had asked her if he was Pallia's owl, Goddess of War and Wisdom, she'd have a considerable amount more money for her dinner than the few filthy coppers she was staring at.

Gods, what she'd give for a canna cake. She shoved the coins into her apron, taking a step back as a boy huffed past with a cart. Vendors were already beginning to pack up for the day, dismantling their stalls with swift efficiency, vibrant colours draining from the market and leaving a dusty brown in their place.

Zylah had often wondered if Varda was the poorest town in Astaria, and yet the vendors always had the brightest stalls of any she'd seen. It was just her bad luck that she was stuck there for the winter. She reached for the cloth covering her table, rolling the vials and poultice pouches into a bundle.

When she'd dreamt of seeing the world, becoming a travelling apothecary was not how she'd imagined she'd get by. But Zylah made it work. She had to. Varda was just her stop-over for the winter, and the moment it was over, she'd be moving on to the next town.

The fish cart rolled by, and Zylah discreetly sniffed at a besa leaf to cover the stench. The ocean was over a week away pulling a loaded cart—probably closer to two—and it turned her stomach thinking about how rotten the fish would be. But the cart was always empty by the end of market day, another telltale sign of how desperate her neighbours were.

She tugged at the coarse crimson fabric that draped above her table, assembling her bundle as if it were a baby, and wrapped it over her shoulders and around her waist. It wasn't a long journey back to her cabin for the night, but only a fool went anywhere in this town with their hands full and their guard down.

Kopi touched down on her shoulder just as she tugged up the hood of her cloak. An old habit, though it was certainly cold enough to need it. A wave of nausea hit her, and she wondered if Kopi could sense it now—he was always with her whenever

3

the worst of the sickness shook through her. She reached out for an empty stall to steady herself, grinding her teeth until the feeling passed. She didn't know which was worse, the nausea or the pain, but didn't dare pull on her magic to try and heal herself. All magic left a trace, and Zylah needed to remain hidden.

She pressed on to her first stop, barely at the end of the market and glanced up to meet a pair of jewel-blue eyes that reminded her of... Zylah sucked in a breath and reached for her necklace.

"You still haven't heard from him?" the old woman asked as Zylah approached. No matter how many times Zylah explained it, she wasn't waiting for anyone. The *him* the old woman was referring to was dead.

But of course, Zylah hadn't shared that part. She'd only said it to herself, in the quiet of the forest with nothing but the trees and the sprites to hear her.

Zylah reached for two coppers in her apron and dropped them into the old woman's hand. "Has he been good to you this week, Sasha?"

The old woman cupped her cheek. "Not a peep since last week, my dear girl. Gods bless you." She tucked the coins into the folds of her dress and smoothed over the patched fabric. "Got a fresh loaf from my eldest boy today if you need any for your supper."

"You hold onto it, Sasha, just in case one of your boys stops by for lunch tomorrow." Zylah smiled as she toyed with her necklace. There was little chance one of the old woman's sons would pay her a visit again so soon, but Sasha needed the food more than Zylah did.

"I found another book for you," Sasha began, pressing it into Zylah's hands before she could protest. "He's coming you know; I can feel it in my bones. And old Sasha's never wrong." She tapped her head and then her heart, offering a toothy grin.

Zylah bit the inside of her cheek. It had been the same conversation every week, and far too much time had passed now for her to be able to explain herself. So she let the old woman believe someone was coming for her. She thanked her for the book before waving goodbye, cutting down the back alleys she'd committed to memory in her first week in Varda.

Grey clothes that were once white hung on lines above, crisscrossing from building to building and blocking out the last of the daylight. The aroma of spices filled the air, and in one of the nearby houses, a couple argued about money. All the arguments in Varda were either about money, or who the rightful ruler of Astaria was.

Zylah cared for neither, and so many times she'd wished she could evanesce back to Virian to see her friends and her brother, to sit quietly with them all even just for a moment. But the same fear that stopped her from healing herself prevented her from evanescing, from using her Fae abilities to travel through the aether to visit the people she loved. She would not be discovered. She would not put her friends at risk again.

Her thumb traced the spine of the book Sasha had given her; another to add to the growing collection in her cabin. Sasha didn't know it, but the old woman had inadvertently taught Zylah more about the world in a few months of handing over books than Zylah had learnt in her entire life, her knowledge of plants the only exception.

5

Sailing the Southern Isles. She shoved the book into her apron as her eyes passed over the tattered remnants of posters plastered to the wall beside her. A coronation notice, a man wanted for stealing a large sum of money, fighters wanted for an event all her regulars gossiped about every week. But none of the posters were of her, not this far from Virian, and she allowed herself to feel a morsel of relief at that knowledge.

The new king certainly wasn't the rightful ruler of Astaria, that much Zylah knew for certain. But Astaria was a vast sprawling continent, and it was foolish of any man, or Fae, to think he could rule over it alone. *King Marcus.* The bastard must have been loving the title. Zylah didn't care that he was a king *before*—whatever birthright he thought he held claim to—he was a monster for orchestrating his own son's death.

She paused to listen as she stopped outside a splintered green door. Two heartbeats thumped steadily in the room beyond, one louder than the other. *Good.* That meant the drunk that also lived here hadn't yet returned for the day. Zylah might not be able to use her magic, but there were still some benefits to being half Fae that she could utilise, like the heightened senses that she hadn't known were because of her Fae heritage until she'd escaped King Arnir's prison.

She raised a hand and paused. A small shrine sat beside the entrance—the goddess Pallia, hands clasped before her, her little owl perched on her shoulder. The goddess who was not a goddess, but a Fae, just like the rest of the gods Zylah had been raised to believe in.

What would the humans of Astaria do if they found out? Would they find something else to believe in?

Would they throw out their old gods in favour of something new?

She rapped her knuckles against the door, and it opened a crack. The room beyond was dark, but Zylah could see plenty. The young woman cowering in the opening balanced a child on her hip, and her eyes widened at the sight of Zylah.

"He'll be home any minute now," the woman murmured, eyes darting left and right down the street. Her lips were cracked and split, and a bruise swelled under her eye.

Zylah dropped two coppers into her hand and reached into her apron for a vial. "For the bruise."

The woman's lips formed the words *thank you* before she gently clicked the door shut, leaving Zylah and Kopi alone on the street. Zylah lingered long enough to hear the familiar sounds of floorboards being pulled back to hide the money—just in case the drunken husband stumbled home and discovered it.

The young mother needed twenty coppers to take the boat from Iskia across the Broken Sea, back to her family, and the first day Zylah had seen her wander through the market, she'd promised she'd get it for her. She pressed on down the street, wary of the fading light. There were still a few more stops to make; her last two remaining coppers and a few vials and poultices.

Kopi shifted on her shoulder as she glanced down an alley to her left, catching sight of a priestess and her acolytes making their way to whatever evening activities they liked to interfere in. Priestesses were not an uncommon sight back in Dalstead, and Zylah had seen a few back in Virian. But over the last few months in Varda, they seemed to be everywhere; perhaps its citizens were more… malleable to their lies.

Zylah's stomach grumbled as she made her way in the opposite direction, Kopi settling, happy with her decision. She sidestepped a filthy puddle, one hand pressing another besa leaf against her nose to cover the stink, another grasping at her necklace. The necklace Raif had given to her. She may not have been the one to kill Raif, but she'd led him to his death, just as Marcus had. And that made her just as much a monster as Marcus. A curse to those she cared about.

She hadn't thought it possible for her heart to hurt as much as it had in the days after Raif's death—her nights alone in the Kerthen forest had given her time for little but thinking and surviving. She'd been warned about the monsters that lingered there, and on many nights, she'd asked herself if she was one of them.

A dangerous creature, the definition she'd read once. She fell into that category, without a doubt.

Zylah sighed. Every night she came to the same conclusion: there was no going back to the person she was before Raif's death, and all she knew for certain now was that she couldn't stomach the reflection staring back at her in the mirror each morning.

Her feet brushed against something, dragging her attention to the cobblestones. Another advertisement for the fighting ring. She slid the besa leaf into her pocket and reached for the poster, smoothing the parchment between finger and thumb. Winning fighters received a hefty prize. One that would see anyone here through a difficult winter.

She frowned, shoving the paper into her pocket.

Candles began to flicker within homes. There were no orblights here. There were barely any traces of Fae at all, something Zylah had been careful not to draw attention to. She tucked her necklace inside her tunic, the blue stone warm against her skin.

Kara's story books had it wrong. There was no happy ending. Only a continuation. One foot in front of the other, one day to the next. Zylah wondered what her friend was doing now; if she still served in the palace after Arnir's death, and prayed that she didn't. The thought of Kara anywhere near Marcus was enough to make Zylah want to evanesce back at once every time she thought of it. But she couldn't.

She placed a vial on a doorstep, knocked once and walked away. The boy within wouldn't come to the door until she was gone. These back streets were always empty; only the residents that were stuck with these sorry excuses for a home passed through them. And though she'd considered offering up her cabin to those who needed it more, it was too dangerous to risk it. If anyone found out she was half Fae she'd be thrown back into a prison cell, where this whole sorry mess had started. Only this time, she wouldn't be able to evanesce herself to safety.

"And they all sang 'three coppers for a kiss, four for something more…'" A group of revellers laughed between the lines of their song in a nearby street. Zylah kept her head down. They were headed to the night's fight most likely, and there would be more than a few sore heads in the morning.

By the time Zylah had finished her rounds, darkness had fallen, clinging to every filthy corner and crack. Her cabin was on the outskirts of town, nestled in the forest that lay beyond. Quiet. She'd had to sell her horse to pay for it, but the horse had a better chance of surviving the winter this way. It had barely survived Kerthen.

Kopi hooted softly, pushing off from her shoulder to sit on the roof of the cabin, his spot for the night. He stayed with her during the day, but he often snoozed like a cat on her shoulder. And though his presence sometimes drew unwanted attention, Zylah let him. He was all she had left now, and she didn't think he would leave her even if she told him to go.

Tired wooden steps creaked underfoot as she made her way to the door, pulling her key from her apron and pushing it into the rusty lock. She hadn't dared to ward it, hadn't risked using any deceits to disguise her hair. Once the last of the erti root dye had faded, she'd left her hair to its natural shade of blonde, but she still wore her eyeglasses to conceal her eyes. Violet was not a common shade in Astaria, but hardly anyone looked her in the eye in Varda.

She preferred it that way.

The door groaned open, and the familiar musty scent of her cabin hit her. It wasn't much, but it was hers. She shrugged off her load, lit a candle and unstrapped her bracers, throwing them onto the kitchen counter just as another wave of pain burst through her.

Zylah steadied herself, taking in the sight of her little cabin until the feeling passed. It was a small space: not unlike the cabin her friend, Holt, had taken her to when he'd helped her escape Arnir's men. The cabin they'd been staying at when—

She couldn't finish the thought.

Six months she'd been away, and her intention had been to see the world, to travel all over Astaria. She'd studied her map night after night in Virian, thinking how vast the world was, only to discover it wasn't even half of it. A bitter laugh escaped her at the thought. How far she'd thought she'd come until she'd seen a map framed in a tavern on her first night in Varda. At first, she'd felt a fool, but then the sting of hurt had settled under her skin as she'd realised her father and brother, her adoptive family, had never told her the truth, never taught her, and that sting quickly turned to simmering anger.

She'd spent her evenings during the last few months trying to fill in many of the gaps in her knowledge, the history of humans and Fae, of a time they were at peace, the times they were not. What she had been taught to be an uprising around the time of her birth was another effort on the part of the humans to keep Fae numbers under control, led by King Arnir. She'd read how the humans loved the lesser Fae for a time, but simply for the spectacle of them, treating them as pets, as attractions, as *things* to be tamed.

Pain fluttered like moths' wings across her back, and Zylah focused on her cabin, on the moment, anything to keep her from curling into a ball.

The fire needed building, but the embers were still smouldering at least. The threadbare lounger she used for a bed stretched out before it, beside it the worn wooden table and its two benches, one overflowing with books Sasha had given her.

All were written by humans, and all had a sickening perspective: Fae were an abomination, not of this world and not welcome in it.

She leaned against the workbench sucking in deep breaths as her eyes roved over the covers and spines. The Fae were monsters to humans. That was what she had been raised to believe in Dalstead.

And with everything she'd done, she couldn't think of a worthwhile reason to prove them wrong.

Zylah reached for her pestle from the counter behind her, focusing on her task to silence her thoughts. It could barely be called a kitchen, but it held everything she needed to get by. Everything she needed to make her poultices.

She'd found an empty house the day after she'd left the Kerthen forest. The interior had been thick with dust, and Zylah had torn up the bedsheets and used the pestle and mortar from the kitchen to make her first few poultices using the knowledge she'd learnt from years of working in her father's apothecary, of the things she'd taught herself, and even a little from her time at the botanical gardens in Virian. She'd intended to make her coin as a travelling apothecary of sorts, always moving, selling in markets. Never stopping for too long. But things hadn't worked out that way.

The truth was, she was too sick to travel through the winter, and if she couldn't heal herself with plants and natural medicine, she wasn't sure she'd see the spring. She could feel her body trying to heal itself, trying to push out whatever toxin had seeped into her. But without using her magic, plants and anything she made were her only chance of recovery until she could find a skilled healer she could trust.

Kopi quietly *hooed* outside, as if he'd heard her thoughts. It wasn't his warning cry, just a gentle reassurance that he was with her. Zylah brushed her fingers over her necklace again, reaching for the knife she kept tucked in her boot.

She had brought this upon herself. Raif, too. Upon Mala and Asha, two of the Fae who had been working for the uprising back in Virian. Her father. They'd be alive had it not been for her.

Murderer.

She hadn't been the one to end their lives, but she'd as good as handed them over to their fate.

On the wall opposite, a tattered poster was pinned to the wood. Zylah hurled her dagger, and it hit its mark; right between the eyes of the face painted onto the parchment.

This was her punishment. Their lives for hers. She pushed to her feet, running her fingers over the poster where it had split, smoothing the parchment until the pieces met. The likeness was always unsettling; the artist had captured her face perfectly. *Calling all Bounty Hunters. Fugitive Fae wanted for the murder of Prince Jesper. Highly dangerous. Use caution. Bonus rewarded if the subject is brought to the king alive.*

The king was dead, and the prince was very much alive. And Raif… Zylah unfastened her necklace and hung it on the hilt of the dagger, the blue stone glittering in the firelight. She should have just kept running. Should never have got involved with the Fae uprising, should have ignored that stupid desire to be a part of something. Her selfishness had caused all of this.

Raif was gone because of her, and Zylah deserved whatever fate she was to be delivered.

2

A week later, Zylah dragged her feet to another market. She'd woken in a sweat, to the sound of someone calling her name. It had been the same every night for weeks, and she'd put it down to whatever sickness had settled within her.

On the first night, she'd thought it was Raif. For so long in the Kerthen forest, all that had held her together were her memories of him. But memories were fickle things, a friend had told her once. After a while, all Zylah had been able to think of was how she hadn't told Raif she'd loved him. How he'd asked her to stay and she'd run.

Her stomach growled; the mushroom broth she'd had for breakfast had done little to quell her hunger, but at least there was enough for later. She'd spent the last week foraging and drying out what she could for the colder months, dividing up her finds between what she could use to make poultices and what she could feed herself with. There wasn't much for either, and Zylah knew it was going to be a long winter.

The knot in her spine, the vanquicite lump, ached if she stayed in any one position for too long, sending bursts of pain through her body and waking her in the night with fever dreams. She needed to find someone to remove it, and soon.

"Come, sister. Let the loving hand of Pallia feed you and clothe you, do not fare the winter alone." A priestess.

Zylah looked up to meet her brown eyes and wondered how she hadn't heard the woman's heartbeat. Kopi flew down to her shoulder as the priestess took a step closer, her robe so light it made a swishing sound as she moved.

Zylah frowned, even in her layers the cold bit into her cheeks.

The priestess was unperturbed, eyes roving over Zylah like she was a shining jewel in the market for purchase. "An owl. You truly are favoured by the gods. Come, let us care for you."

Nothing about the woman struck Zylah as caring.

"I must make it to the market." Zylah smiled as sweetly as she could. "My father relies on the coin to pay off his debts. But thank you for the kind offer." The lie was easy—Zylah had always had a knack for it.

The priestess offered a tight smile, her acolytes joining her from the depths of the market. "There are whispers of a witch in Varda, of healing poultices being left on doorsteps. What goods do you sell?"

"Witches don't exist." Zylah held the priestess's gaze as she reached into her cloak, tucked a hand into her apron and pulled out a vial. "Tea and spices. Father's a trader."

The tight smile didn't leave the priestess's face as she nodded in response.

"I don't want to make you miss the morning rush." She inclined her head in a bow, turning her attention back to her acolytes. Zylah resisted the urge to look over her shoulder as she walked away, certain that the priestess's gaze would be fixed upon her.

She'd read about witches in Kara's storybooks, but it wasn't the first time since leaving her old life behind that she'd heard them mentioned. She'd grown up in a village overshadowed by Dalstead, the old king's city, where any talk of magic and the Fae were punishable by death. Witches, Zylah supposed, if they were real, would fall into that category.

The scent of macana hung heavy in the air, the milky hot drink they seemed to favour in Varda to stave away the cold. It was too strong for Zylah's liking and left a bitter aftertaste.

The streets were full, busier than she'd seen them, and everyone seemed to be selling something. How many would bet their coin on the fights instead of saving it for the winter months? Too many. But Zylah was counting on it.

Witch. The priestess's accusation wasn't entirely strange, but something had been a little off about her. Kopi had seemed to agree, and that alone set Zylah on edge. She kept one eye on the edge of the crowds as she made her way to her stall, looking for any signs of trouble. The truth was… she wouldn't know the truth, even if it was standing right in front of her. Because for months now she'd been turning over the same questions every quiet moment she got: why had her father and brother hidden so much from her? She'd been raised to believe King Arnir's lies… but if Zack knew the truth, her father must have, too… so why lie? Why keep it secret from her? Why let her grow up so naively?

When she'd finally made it out of the Kerthen forest she'd been called a witch in the first village she'd found. There had been no true reason for the villagers to fear her, but after months alone in the forest she supposed the sight of her must have given them a fright. None dared enter Kerthen, she'd discovered, not unless they had a death wish.

She hadn't decided whether to thank her friend Holt for that or to throttle him if she ever saw him again. The dark creatures she'd encountered there made a street fight in Varda sound like a tea party to Zylah.

She reached her stall, unravelling her bundle just as a group of acolytes walked by. There was no priestess leading their group, but that meant one was likely nearby. The same one from earlier perhaps, but no—Zylah caught sight of the grey robe, a different woman, hands clasped together a few stalls away, waiting for her acolytes to reach her.

Zylah paid her no heed, setting up her table as swiftly as she could and handing Kopi his first vial for the day. He liked to snooze, but he worked hard for his naps. A struggle broke out at the table beside the priestess, and Zylah held a hand over her wrist, ready to pull a blade if she needed it. She never went anywhere without her dagger in her boot and one in each bracer.

Although tonight she'd have to forgo the blades, no weapons were allowed, but that didn't bother her. She watched the stall holder scuffle with a thief, a drunk, who Zylah had always kept a close eye on, and waited for the priestess to intervene. She didn't. And Zylah couldn't draw any more attention to herself.

"Pallia teaches us to use our words, gentlemen, before we employ our hands." It was the priestess who had spoken. Her hands were still clasped in front of her, her head inclined in the same gesture exactly as the other had done.

Zylah suspected that Pallia, wherever she was, would hate the way the humans used her name.

She was no goddess.

She was Fae, just like all the gods Zylah had spent her whole life praying to until she'd learnt the truth.

And yet, in her darkest moments in Kerthen, she'd still whispered quiet words to Pallia regardless.

The stall holder and the thief peeled apart from each other, cheeks flushed and chests heaving as they took in the priestess. The woman murmured something to them, and the pair nodded. Wisps of red hair blew in the cold breeze, eyes darker than emeralds. She took a hand from each of them, murmuring again in what Zylah could only presume was a prayer to Pallia.

The acolytes behind her seemed to whisper the same prayer, but Zylah couldn't hear their words.

Kopi descended through the crowds, and Zylah, at last, drew her fingers away from her bracer to hold her palm open for the little owl. He dropped a small pouch into her hand before darting away to resume his position on her shoulder.

When she looked up, the priestess and her acolytes were already away through the crowd, the stall holder back to serving customers and the thief nowhere to be seen.

>>>>> <<<<<

The rest of the day passed without incident. Zylah had only sold three vials, two sales made by Kopi to their regulars. She needed to leave early if she was going to make her rounds and get to the fight on time, but the crowds were already thinning by late afternoon.

18

A cart rolled by, its owner huffing with the weight of the goods he hadn't managed to sell, and for a heartbeat, Zylah could have sworn she'd scented acani berries in the air. But that wasn't possible; she hadn't seen any acani berries on this side of Astaria since leaving Virian.

She packed up her table and made her way to Sasha, the old woman's smile wider than ever as Zylah approached.

"Today's the day, Liss, old Sasha has felt it in here." She tapped her chest, her toothy grin lighting up her face. Liss was the name Zylah had used when she was hiding in Virian, and it had become a habit to give it to humans instead of Zylah. Her true name seemed nothing but a burden.

Zylah placed the coppers into Sasha's hands. "You'll be at the fight?"

The old woman tucked the coins into the folds of her skirt and smoothed down the tattered fabric. "Wouldn't miss it for the world."

The hairs on Zylah's neck stood on end and she looked over her shoulder. Nothing unusual stuck out to her in the crowd. Kopi hadn't given a warning, but that didn't stop Zylah's stomach from twisting.

There were a few more rounds left to make, so she moved everything she needed to her pockets. There wasn't time to make it back to her cabin, and Sasha was the only person in this godsforsaken town she trusted not to pawn her belongings.

Zylah unsheathed the blades from her bracers as discreetly as she could, rolling them up inside her cloak with her apron, and bundled it all into the cloth from her stall. She'd retrieve it after the fight; it would be safe with Sasha.

Sasha reached out her hands for the bundle, and Zylah helped the old woman fasten it to her back.

"Is he staying with me, too?" Sasha asked, motioning her head in Kopi's direction. He'd rested on the perch above her doorstep, eyes closed.

Zylah raised an eyebrow. "You know as well as I do, he does what he wants." Besides, she'd never risk him getting injured on her behalf.

Sasha reached into a basket at her feet, unravelling something from a piece of cloth. "You'll need your strength tonight, girl. Take this." It was a knishi, a local meal made of meat wrapped in pastry. Knowing Sasha, it was likely rabbit inside. Zylah's stomach rumbled at the sight of it, and with a small laugh, Sasha pressed it into her hands.

"I can't take this," Zylah said. Gods knew how much it would have cost Sasha to buy the pastry. Coin she certainly couldn't afford to part with.

"I'll be happier watching tonight knowing you did." Sasha held Zylah's upturned palms. "I know what you're thinking. But my boy gave me some butter and flour. I've one for myself, too. See?" She inclined her head to her basket, and sure enough, another bundle sat wrapped up inside it.

Zylah smiled. It was far more kindness than she deserved. "Thank you." She said her goodbyes to Sasha and continued her rounds through Varda, not wanting to waste any time.

Had it not been for the vanquicite weakening her body, she'd have had no concerns about the fight. She'd trained with two Fae princes, seasoned warriors, and she'd continued her training on her days alone in the forest and every day since.

She was relying on her opponents being nothing more than half-starved citizens looking to make some coin for the winter. Just as she was.

She took small bites of Sasha's knishi, savouring the feeling of real food in her belly as she made her way to her first drop-off. The shrine to Pallia seemed to stare up at her as she approached the green door, the goddess's eyes burning into her own. *Not a goddess*, she reminded herself.

Zylah had tapped her knuckles on the door once when she heard the second adult heartbeat inside. The permanently drunk husband. *Shit.*

He opened the door a crack, eyes widening a little as he took her in. "I thought I told your lot to fuck off. We don't want to buy anything." The door slammed in her face.

Zylah bit her lip, weighing up her options. She had two coppers in her pocket for the young mother, and she couldn't risk the husband taking them, or worse, his temper if she tried to give them to his wife. She couldn't risk taking them to the fight either. Zylah glanced left and right down the street, crouching beside the shrine, and tucked the two coins underneath the statue of the goddess. At least they would be safe until her next visit.

She finished the rest of her rounds without incident, the streets starting to fill as darkness fell. Half the town seemed to be on their way to tonight's fight, but that would only work in her favour.

The more bets, the more coin the victor took home.

She could already hear the noise from the structure they called the arena, a sorry looking ring surrounded by benches and towering stacks of hay on the far side of town. Exhilarated voices and oddsmakers called out to the crowd.

Zylah's skin prickled with anticipation, a knot of apprehension settling under her ribs. She sucked in a breath and stroked a finger across Kopi's head. "Time to go, buddy. I don't want you too close for this." He hesitated for a moment and then flew on ahead. Zylah smiled. He made straight for the arena, to find a place to watch, no doubt.

Zylah glanced behind her, feeling eyes on her amongst the crowd, but saw nothing but groups making their way towards the venue, none paying her any heed. With a frown she made her way to the side entrance, checking the tightness of her braid and pulling the strips of linen she'd prepared the night before from her pocket, wrapping them around her knuckles.

A bouncer stood before an open door, thick arms folded across his broad chest. "Spectators that way." He didn't even look at her as he spoke. He'd been in his fair share of fights judging by his face—marred with scars, a broken nose, a missing tooth.

"I'm here to fight." Zylah stood tall and looked him right in the eye. She'd had plenty of practice at hiding, but she knew how to hold her ground. How to ooze confidence even if she didn't feel a shred of it in her bones.

The bouncer's gaze met hers, eyes sliding too slowly down her body to her wrapped hands, and back up to her face again. He shrugged, the corner of his mouth twitching. "Shame. Your funeral."

He stepped aside to let her in, and Zylah's eyes adjusted to the darkened room beyond. No time to slide a besa leaf into her mouth to calm her nerves, not with four pairs of eyes watching her from the shadows.

"And who the fuck are you?" a tall, skinny man asked.

Zylah slid her hands into her pockets and did her best to look bored. "Here to fight."

The man scoffed. "Got a name?"

Zylah shrugged. "Call me whatever you like."

Another man stepped up to her. He was almost as big as the bouncer outside, but he moved awkwardly, and Zylah suspected the muscles were just for show. "I've seen you in the market, with that owl of yours." His breath was foul, his stench suggesting he hadn't had a bath in weeks. "Folks can't decide if you're a witch or Pallia in disguise."

Zylah didn't baulk as she stared up at him. "My name is Liss."

The skinny man rubbed a hand against his chin. "We'll call you Little Bird." He pressed a hand to the other man's chest to usher him back a step. "Four fighters. Six fights to begin with, then we'll see how everyone's faring after the first round. Got it?"

Zylah nodded. Where she'd found her resolve, she didn't know, but she said a silent thanks to Pallia, nonetheless.

The wannabe bruiser sneered at her. "We'll try not to touch the face, won't we, fellas?" The two remaining fighters laughed along with him.

Zylah didn't care.

She'd been hit in the face enough times. She didn't expect to come out of this unscathed and this was her only hope of making enough coin to survive the winter.

Outside in the makeshift arena, the crowd clapped their hands, shouts filling the air as they began stomping on the ground, faster and faster.

Just like her racing heart.

In the dim light, Zylah saw Raif's death play over in front of her eyes. The way Jesper's fangs sank into his neck. The way he slumped to the floor. She met the stares of the three fighters, eyes fixed on her, trying to intimidate her.

The truth was, she gave away whatever coin she made and food she found because she felt it was her tithe to pay. Truth was, she didn't think she'd walk away from this at all.

3

The first fight had been over almost as soon as it started. He'd been nothing more than a trader, and it had taken Zylah only a few well-timed moves to get him on his back, begging for her to release the arm she'd twisted back.

The crowd had roared at her success, the sulking trader pulling out of the remaining fights, muttering that he wasn't made for violence.

The two remaining fighters had eyed her warily after that.

She circled the ring, doing her best to ignore the cheering crowd. Some whistled and shouted Little Bird, but Zylah blocked it all out.

Rain had begun to fall in fat droplets, splattering into the dirt. But Zylah wasn't worried. She was short and light on her feet, and it would only work to her advantage.

Her opponent was the mouthy one who'd taunted her earlier, the wannabe bruiser with muscles she'd suspected were only for show. She missed the name the ringmaster had called out for him, the sound of the crowd drowning out everything but her heartbeat and her ragged breathing.

Wannabe grinned as he wiped rainwater out of his eyes, slicking his hair back to his head. "I said I'd try not to touch your face. But I make no promises."

He lunged for Zylah, and she ducked, swinging away from his outstretched arms. She swiped a leg at his feet, but he'd been ready for it, rooting himself to the spot. Mud coated her hands, and she wiped them against her sides.

"Come now, Little Bird," Wannabe taunted. "You'll need to try harder than that."

She ran for him, all the breath rushing out of her as he slammed her into the ground. Eyes closed, she could smell his rank breath on her face and rolled out of his grip, pushing herself to her feet.

The rain came down harder, and Zylah welcomed it. She landed a blow behind his knee, one beneath his ribs.

He caught her cheek with an elbow as she spun away from him. But she was biding her time.

She spun again, waiting for his anger to spike.

Wannabe spat a wad of phlegm to the ground, smearing mud across his face with the back of a filthy hand.

"I thought you'd be more of a challenge," she said with a smirk.

That was enough to rattle his ego. Wannabe ran for her, but his steps were less sure in the mud. As he reached for her, she ducked, but instead of pivoting away, she slid through his legs, springing to her feet to land a kick on his back before he turned around. He fell to his knees, fighting for purchase in the slick mud. The brute fell on his face and Zylah circled, waiting for him to haul himself out of the mud as she stood before him. It was too pathetic to watch. He managed to push himself back up to his knees, just as Zylah landed a kick right between his legs. The crowd cheered as he fell, chanting Little Bird over and over.

Zylah barely had the chance to catch her breath before Wannabe was dragged out of the ring, replaced by the last fighter, announced only as the Wolf. Gods above, the ringmaster must have been from out of town with his taste for theatrics. If Zylah had known she was walking into such a spectacle she might have reconsidered.

Of the three fighters, the Wolf was the only one she'd been concerned about, and he eyed her now as if he knew it. She imagined how she must look to him, gasping for breath and covered in mud, a wild look in her eyes that he might have mistaken for fear.

He'd have had no way of knowing she'd taken more than one life. No way of knowing what she was responsible for… that it wasn't a young woman standing before him, but a monster. They circled each other, and she observed the way he held himself, the way he turned to his right, his strongest side, the way his eyes roved over her, conducting his own investigation.

More than half of his head was shaved, fine tattoos running in lines from his hairline, down the sides of his face, over his ears and onto his neck. His hair was like knotted rope, fastened high at the back of his head, thick strands spiralling over each other and down to his back. A smirk tugged at the corner of his mouth as he continued his assessment.

The crowd seemed to hold their breath, their cheers easing. Or maybe it was just the rain quelling their enthusiasm. Her opponent moved at the same time she did, and Zylah sucked in a breath, stomping down on the shred of apprehension that had begun to push its way to the surface. *After*, she told herself. After, she could worry all she wanted.

The Wolf swung a punch at her, but she dodged it easily. *Did he just wink at me? Gods.* He was leaner than Wannabe, a little shorter too, but he was light on his feet. He seemed less like a starving trader and more like a skilled fighter who moved from town to town to fill his pockets. As he swung for her a second time, Zylah had a feeling that was precisely what he was.

Her foot collided with the back of his knee and his fist drove hard into her ribs. She staggered back but he yanked at her sleeve, landing another blow to the side of her face.

The Wolf circled her as she pressed a hand to her ribs, searching for an opening. If he wanted to play dirty, so could she. She feigned right, then spun to her left to grab hold of his sleeve, swinging up onto his back and clamping her legs around his neck. He threw her over his shoulder with a deep laugh, and as Zylah slammed into the mud she could have sworn dark shadows swarmed towards her.

She rolled out of the way, mud coating her soaking clothes. "Cheat," she breathed, wiping at her mouth.

Not only would he have been pulled out of the ring for cheating, but magic was not something to reveal in these parts of Astaria. But he'd done it subtly, so no one else but her would have seen it. It was how he intended to win.

The Wolf gave her a toothy grin, and for a heartbeat, Zylah wondered if he was Fae. She hauled herself to her feet.

"So what if I am?" the Wolf asked. His eyes were so dark they looked black through the rain, not a splash of colour remaining.

"Bastard." Zylah still had her dagger tucked inside her boot, but she'd be disqualified if she pulled it on him. She swung for him again, and more of those dark shadows spread from his fingertips, but Zylah didn't care, she launched herself towards him, her fist connecting with his jaw so hard it sent pain rolling through her body, right to the vanquicite lump in her back.

The Wolf stared down at her in disbelief before swinging at her, and they quickly became a tangle of limbs as Zylah slammed herself against him, grabbing hold of his shirt to duck out of his blow.

His shadows had felt like wards... but Zylah didn't have time to dwell on that. She pivoted away from him, swinging a kick into his lower back and he staggered forwards into the mud. Her lip had split in their scrabble, her head was throbbing. He'd landed more blows than she cared to admit. More shadows shot towards her, pulling at her limbs until she was kneeling in the mud as if she'd merely stumbled.

The Wolf loomed over her, one hand fisting in her hair to yank her head back. He leaned close to murmur above her head, rain falling off his face onto hers. "I don't know how you did that, but I'm fucking tired, and I want to go home."

Zylah weighed her options as the rain came down, and the Wolf seemed to pause for dramatic effect. If he was willing to cheat, she'd wager he was willing to do more than just a few knocks and scrapes. Kopi cried out again, and it was all the encouragement she needed as she felt more of those shadows creeping towards her. She reached for her dagger, yanking herself up against the Wolf's arm until the tip of her blade pressed into his ribs.

His eyes widened as she looked up at him. "You just had to be a show-off, didn't you?" she murmured, holding her blade firm.

Arms pulled her back, the ringmaster dark-eyed and soaking wet between them. "The Wolf wins by default. Little Bird is disqualified for bringing a weapon into the ring."

The crowd booed and Zylah was vaguely aware of small objects hitting her back. Rotten vegetables, if she had to guess. The Wolf held her gaze. *Cheat.* She shrugged out of the grip of whoever was holding her, sheathed her dagger in her boot and swung her braid over her shoulder as she glared at him.

The crowd continued booing, but Zylah didn't care. Didn't give a shit what they thought of her. Tomorrow they would all have forgotten, heads heavy with hangovers and the beginnings of a chill from the rain.

The Wolf winked at her as she stormed out of the ring, wiping her wet hair from her eyes. She pushed past the bouncer, who took a step back as she passed through the room that led to the street.

"You fought well," he said, following her.

She glanced up at him, one eye already swelling. "Shame I'm a fraud though, right?"

She didn't wait for his response as she shoved open the door to the street. Rain ran thick and fast through the gutters, puddles forming across the dirt. Zylah swore under her breath. She was covered in wet mud. Everything ached, and she didn't know where to press a hand to first as she glanced out at the rain. Kopi flew down to her shoulder and hooed softly.

"Let me through," a voice called out from behind her. "Liss!"

It was Sasha, unfastening Zylah's belongings from her back.

Zylah sighed. She couldn't handle the old woman's disappointment.

Sasha fastened the bundle onto Zylah's wet back and rested a hand on her cheek. "What did I tell you, girl? Old Sasha doesn't miss a trick. That sneaky bastard will get what's coming to him." She ran her thumb across the mud Zylah knew was caked to her cheek, the gesture making her eyes burn.

Zylah tried to smile, but the split lip turned it into a grimace. "You saw him cheating?" Sasha didn't seem like she was Fae— but there was the possibility she was hiding, too, just as Zylah was.

"I did. Now get home, before the crowds find you." She patted Zylah's arm gently, ushering her out into the street.

Zylah didn't have it in her to argue. She staggered back through town, one hand pressed to her ribs, glancing over her shoulder every few minutes with that feeling she couldn't place, like someone was lingering in the shadows, chasing her all the way home.

She tried not to think about how long it would take for her injuries to heal. She'd prepared plenty of poultices and vials of tonic, but the more she used for herself the less she'd have to sell… and that meant she'd have to find other ways to make money over winter. As the traders earned less, people had less money to spend, and Zylah doubted she'd be permitted back into the ring after tonight.

She sucked in a breath, white hot pain shooting through her and slicing up her back from the vanquicite lump, reminding her that her wounds would not heal so easily. She'd been a fool for thinking this could work… reckless… but she couldn't deny the exhilaration she'd felt in that ring. It was the most alive she'd felt since before Raif's dea—

Zylah couldn't finish the thought. She deserved every ache and bit of broken skin. She had to find a way to make money for Sasha and the others. She would come up with something.

The forest was quiet as she made her way out of town, buildings giving way to trees. With her heightened senses and the rain that had yet to ease, all she could hear were the usual sounds of the forest at night, nothing out of the ordinary. She knew Kopi would warn her of any trouble, anyway.

As soon as the cabin was in sight, the little owl flew up to the roof. But Zylah stopped as a familiar smell carried to her. She stumbled up the steps, her eyes falling to the brown paper bag at the foot of her door. A pathetic whimper escaped her as she scooped up the soggy parchment one-handed, the wet paper falling away from her fingertips.

It was a canna cake.

She spun around, canna cake clutched to her chest as she searched amongst the trees.

She felt him before she saw him, the raw, ancient power that rolled from him just like the first time they'd met.

There.

The Fae stood watching her, arms folded as he stood beside his horse, his familiar green eyes visible even in the darkness.

Zylah's voice came out in a whisper. "Holt."

4

Zylah staggered forwards a step, and in less than a heartbeat Holt had closed the distance between them, pulling her into an embrace despite how wet and filthy she was. She threw her arms around his waist, leaning her weight against him as she fought back tears, a sob lodged in her throat.

"Hi," she murmured into the hardness of his chest. He towered over her, strong arms enveloping her in his familiar scent— acani berries and a musky, earthiness that settled something inside her as she breathed him in.

Holt touched a hand gently to her hair, his chin resting against her head and Zylah willed herself not to cry. Not to break right there and then in front of him. The rain came down harder, but neither of them moved.

His voice was hoarse as he said, "Hi," pulling her tighter for a heartbeat.

Zylah couldn't speak. Could do nothing but stand there and let him hold her.

He eased back, one hand softly brushing her hair from her eyes, the other moving to her cheek, a muscle feathering in his jaw as his gaze settled on the wound the Wolf had inflicted. Zylah felt the warm tingle of his healing magic as it passed between them, knitting her split lip back together. "Come on, Little Bird, let's get you inside."

"You saw?" She punched his arm, instantly regretting it and clutching her hand against her chest.

Holt gave her a rare smile. Gods, she'd forgotten how beautiful he was. Even with the rain plastering his hair to his face, it was no wonder she'd thought him a god when they'd first met. She frowned, thoughts drifting to darker memories, and Holt's smile faded.

He took her hand in his, more of his magic pouring from him as he healed her bruised knuckles.

"But aren't you worried?" Zylah began.

"I've learnt a few tricks in the last few months," he said quietly, releasing her fingers one by one.

Zylah's brows pinched together again. "That's why I couldn't hear you." And the magic... all magic left a trace. It was why Zylah had been too afraid to heal herself or to evanesce. But the last time she'd encountered a spell to conceal sound and scent, it had led to her capture. And if Holt had learnt that spell, maybe he'd learnt to conceal his magic, too.

He took the key she pulled from her pocket and opened the door, standing to one side in the rain to let her in. "I found the bounty hunter that took your brother."

Zylah kicked off her boots, pressing a hand to her ribs and taking short, shallow breaths. It was her fault, all of it. She looked up at Holt and he caught her arm gently, pressing a hand lightly to her ribs to heal her broken bones. The sensation was strange but soothing, and she resisted the urge to lean into his touch, exhaustion pulling at her bones, mud caking her skin.

She peeled off her tunic, let it fall to the floor with a wet thwack. "I'm having a bath, and I want you to explain everything."

"Neither of those things surprise me," Holt said, gathering her tunic from the floor. "There's hot water in the bath for you."

Zylah didn't need to ask him how. He'd explained once, precisely how he could call things to him in the same way they could evanesce to other locations, but Zylah had never quite managed it. And it wasn't the first time he'd filled a bath with warm spring water for her.

She let the bathroom door fall shut behind her, leaning against the wood as a silent sob shook her shoulders. She'd been alone for so long, and it felt wrong to be happy about Holt's arrival. To feel anything good.

Monster, a voice whispered in her thoughts. But there was worry there, too. Worry that she'd only draw him into her trouble.

Her reflection stared back at her from the partially steamed-over mirror, dark circles under her eyes, stark against her pale skin. Hair soaked through with rain and mud. But her face was unmarked. Holt must have healed her eye, too.

She unravelled the strips of cloth around her knuckles, peeled off the rest of her clothes, and stepped into the bath with a hiss. Everything still ached, but she pulled her knees to her chest out of habit. "Holt," she called out.

"Can I get you anything?" His voice carried from the other side of the door almost immediately.

"Will you sit with me?" There was nowhere *to* sit in her tiny bathroom. But she wanted his company. Needed it. Hadn't realised how much she'd needed a friend these last few months. And she had questions—like what he was doing there and how he'd found her after all this time.

The door pushed open, Holt's gaze fixed on the floor as he sat beside the tub, back facing her to offer her some privacy, despite the fact that they'd shared a room for months back in Virian.

"Pass the soap?" Zylah asked quietly.

He held out a hand and the soap appeared in it.

"Show off."

She caught the smile that tugged at the corner of his mouth, but he tilted his head down to hide it. He was still soaking wet, his scar peeking out of the top of the shirt clinging to his back and neck. The scar Marcus had given him.

Zylah dipped the soap in the water, trying to shove Raif's father from her thoughts. "So you watched the fight? Any pointers?"

"You did well, until that Fae cheated you at the end."

"You noticed?"

He nodded. He seemed tired. Haunted. As if the last six months had taken as much of a toll on him as they had her. He was playing with something in his hands, but Zylah would have had to lean over the edge of the tub to see what it was, so she didn't.

"I hung back for the three men that followed you," he said.

She clutched the edge of the tub, water sloshing as she leaned towards him. "What men?"

Holt frowned. "They had hefty bets on you, and you lost their coin."

It wasn't something in his hands. It was a piece of leather at his wrist. The bracelet she'd given him at the festival of Imala.

He rolled the tiny bell between finger and thumb as he spoke, the one she'd had the pin removed from. "They followed you for a few streets, but they won't bother you again. I hung back to make sure there were no more."

Zylah rested her cheek against the edge of the tub, watching him. Stubble peppered his jaw, and even from this angle, she could see he wasn't just tired; he was exhausted, as if he'd been travelling for days without rest. "You killed them."

He turned to meet her gaze, green eyes darkening. "Yes."

Zylah couldn't say she was sorry, a very vivid image of what their idea of reclaiming their losses might have looked like threatening to take over her thoughts. She held his stare as she said, "Good."

A heartbeat passed before Zylah cleared her throat, pushing off from the side of the tub. Holt turned away from her again, and she set to scrubbing the mud off her arms. "Tell me about the bounty hunter. His name was Cal, if I recall."

Zylah hadn't forgotten his name. Or the way he looked, or the sound of his voice. She'd killed Oz, the bounty hunter who took her, concealed their whereabouts with a spell and then lashed her, but she'd always promised herself she'd find Cal one day—the hunter who took her brother and delivered him to King Arnir.

"He was reluctant to tell me about the spell," Holt said, still toying with the bracelet as if it were an old habit.

"I hope you made him suffer for it."

"I did."

Zylah smiled as she rubbed the soap into her hair.

"After Arnir had used the same spell, I had my suspicions. Cal confirmed it. It was Marcus who taught them."

Raif's father. "Marcus… why?"

"Part of his long game. Aurelia and Jesper. Arnir. Marcus has been pushing all the pieces around the board for years." Raif's mother, who they'd long believed to be dead but wasn't. The prince. The dead king. Their paths were so tightly woven thanks to Aurelia and Marcus. Raif's parents had always wanted more power, Zylah had been told back in Virian. To be High Queen and King.

"Aurelia… is she… a vampire too?"

"No. She just learnt how Ranon and Sira made them, and she made Jesper. And now Jesper is making an army for *her*. For Marcus."

The hairs on the back of Zylah's neck stood on edge. Ranon and Sira were two of the original Fae to come to Astaria, but when they hadn't liked what the other seven had planned for this world, they'd broken away and created creatures of their own. Dark things, monsters, like the vampires. They'd used humans, their experiments having a thirst for blood that Ranon and Sira had hoped would cull the human population quickly. But they soon developed a taste for Fae blood, and lots of it. Zylah had seen first-hand what that thirst looked like, a shiver dancing across her skin at the memory.

Which could only mean… "An army for what?" she asked, her voice small, quiet.

"To reclaim what they believe to be theirs. To become High Queen and King. To obliterate the humans once and for all. To control the remaining Fae and bend them to their will."

Zylah hugged her knees to her chest, her voice falling to a whisper. "Why?"

"They always craved power. Always."

She saw Raif's death, over and over, Prince Jesper ripping into his neck like it was nothing, Raif falling to the floor. Raif was strong, but Jesper, he had been unnaturally powerful. An army of them… of vampires… it filled her with dread.

"What does Marcus want with me?"

Holt blew out a breath, as if he were debating his answer. For a moment Zylah thought he'd make some excuse, try to reassure her, but instead, he said, "Marcus covets Fae with unique abilities."

"Covets…" Zylah frowned. Marcus knew she could evanesce, and she'd been warned on multiple occasions not to do it in front of others, not to let any Fae see that she possessed the ability. Her eyes widened as realisation settled in. "He wants to turn Fae with powers that are of use to him into vampires. For his army."

Holt nodded.

Raif's sister, Rose, had warned her Marcus was coming for her. Had she known why, too? Zylah had been in no state to ask… her departure from Virian felt like a bad dream, and she'd been reeling from Raif's death, too far gone to stop and question any of it.

"Part of me wondered if Rose made it up, just to be rid of me after… after what happened." Zylah couldn't finish the sentence, coward that she was.

Holt dragged a hand through his wet hair. "Rose keeps many things close to her chest. But this… this time she was telling the truth. You caught Marcus's interest the moment you evanesced from the gallows."

"Aren't you worried he's going to have Jesper try to turn you?" She didn't know the precise details of Holt's relationship with Marcus, only that he seemed to be working off a debt that Marcus had tricked him into. At least with the spell, Marcus wouldn't be able to track Holt, but the thought did little to quell her worries.

"He'd have done it months ago if that's what he had planned for me. I can't be found here." He cleared his throat. "The water must be cold." It was. Holt uncoiled to his feet, making for the door, his wet shirt plastered to his broad shoulders.

Zylah watched him go, willing the last dregs of her energy into holding herself together, to not allow herself to unravel completely in front of him. "Thank you. For sitting with me."

He tapped the door frame as he left, and Zylah stepped out of the bath carefully. Her back ached from sitting for too long, and a spike of pain shot through her as her foot landed on the floor.

"Everything okay?" he asked from outside the door.

"I'm fine," she said through clenched teeth.

He still hadn't explained what he was doing there, how he'd broken away from Marcus this time. She dried quickly, pulling undergarments and an oversized shirt from the drawer and slipping it over her head before stepping out into the cabin.

Holt was at the sink, his back to her as he wrung something out in the water.

"That better not be what I think it is." She rushed over to the counter where he was washing her filthy clothes by hand. "What happened to rule number one?" *No touching Zylah's undergarments.*

Holt arched a brow, a corner of his mouth lifting momentarily. "It's nothing I haven't seen before."

Zylah flicked water at him before reaching for her soggy canna cake and settling down on the lounger. She watched Holt wring out the clothes and hang them around the fireplace, the fire already blazing. She'd missed the way he moved, missed sharing a room with him at the tavern. She'd missed having a friend.

"That shirt looks familiar," he said, taking a seat on the floor opposite her, his eyes dipping to the garment for a moment. It was his.

Zylah shrugged. "There haven't been many opportunities to go shopping for clothes." The truth was, wearing his shirts had been a comfort, and on some nights, she'd convinced herself his scent still clung to them.

He was toying with the bracelet again, waiting for her to finish the canna cake.

"Tell me everything I've missed," she said through a mouthful of cake. Gods above, she'd missed cake. If she didn't know any better, it tasted like one of his own making.

"I'm sure you're well aware by now that Marcus took Arnir's position."

King Arnir. Jesper's father, the man responsible for sending her to the gallows, the man she'd escaped from after she'd killed Jesper. Or rather, *thought* she'd killed him. And Marcus was far worse than Arnir. "The coronation posters are unavoidable. We replaced one tyrant with another," Zylah murmured.

"He's posing as a human," Holt said. "Told the masses he's Arnir's cousin on his mother's side and rightful heir to the throne."

The prince couldn't claim it, not after the world had mourned his death. Alone in the Kerthen forest, she'd promised herself two things: she was going to kill Jesper. And then she was going to kill Marcus, no matter what it cost her.

Marcus had sent Jesper after her. And though Jesper had delivered the killing blow, it was Marcus who had orchestrated Raif's death. She blinked the image away as she stared at the fire. "Are you going to tell me why you're here?" Her back ached and she tried to hide her wince, aware that Holt was watching her every movement, but as she looked up to meet his gaze he looked away.

"Rose had a vision." His brows pinched together. "She saw you were sick. Because of the vanquicite."

Not dead, sick. Zylah could feel the effects of the vanquicite, like it was taking something from her, piece by piece.

Her tithe.

She was a curse; she'd told Raif as much the last time they were together. A monster just like Jesper.

"Rose had her vision, and I couldn't risk leading Marcus to you, so I went after the remaining bounty hunter. It's old magic, and Marcus must have a source."

"How long ago did Rose have the vision?"

"Soon after you left. Cal was difficult to track with the spell covering him."

Zylah opened her mouth and closed it. It had been six months since she'd left him on the outskirts of the Kerthen forest. Six months since the bounty hunter had whipped her and dislodged the vanquicite in her back, weakening her, and making her sick.

"I need to know more about what we're up against," Holt continued. "Saphi thinks the vanquicite in your back was put there with old magic, and we'll need something to counter Marcus with."

Zylah nodded. Rose's partner Saphi was Fae too, but something about her always struck Zylah as different. And it was no surprise Holt sought something to oppose Marcus with. "To balance the scales," she murmured absentmindedly. "You think we can find someone to remove it?"

"It's worth a try, isn't it?"

Zylah sifted through her thoughts. She'd spent most of her life believing she was human, and though they hadn't been kind to her in the time since she'd discovered she was half Fae, she couldn't stand by and let Marcus and Jesper attempt to wipe them out. And if old magic was what it would take to remove the vanquicite from her back... maybe she could get to them both, take them by surprise.

"I've been using my position to learn as much as I can about Marcus's movements," Holt said when she didn't reply. "I want to speak with some allies. See who I can recruit to our cause. If Marcus and Jesper have been making an army, we'll need every advantage we can get against them."

Zylah blew out a breath. "And all along, Arnir thought Marcus was his pet."

"That was thanks to Jesper's compulsion." Anger coated his words, and he didn't meet her gaze.

Zylah's stomach twisted at the thought of Jesper. "This has been going on for so long. Saphi warned me Marcus plays a long game." She wanted to ask him then, about whatever hold Marcus seemed to have over him. She knew a little of the life debt he owed Marcus, a deal Holt had struck in a failed attempt to save his sister, and that he couldn't hear of any harm coming to the new king… but there had to be more to it than that.

"We've been busy back in Virian. Calling on old allegiances. Building our numbers, developing what we already had with the Black Veil."

The Black Veil: the human allies to the Fae back in Virian. Which meant… "You plan to fight?"

His eyes raised to meet hers, something fierce burning within them. Something that felt like hope. "I can't harm Marcus, but that doesn't mean I can't put an end to whatever he's planning. It doesn't mean I can't build an army to match his." He cleared his throat as if there was more he wanted to say but didn't.

They needed numbers if they were going to take on an army, and though they had the Fae hiding back in Virian, the humans of the Black Veil, the numbers didn't amount to an entire army.

They wouldn't stand a chance without a solid opposing force, but she knew that wouldn't stop Holt.

He held no regard for his own life, and something told her, whether his allies helped him or not, he'd carry out whatever plans he had regardless, no matter what it meant for him. And despite her fears, she understood. Her life wasn't worth saving, either.

He looked at his hands, turning them over as if he were looking through them. "What I learnt from Cal feels weak. I haven't evanesced yet, I'm not certain the spell is strong enough to conceal it. Evanescing is strong Fae magic, but it leaves a different kind of trace to those who know how to look for it. Like an echo."

Zylah studied him. His hair had begun to dry, a few strands falling across his eyes, that haunted look from before falling over him again, and she wondered if the same bad dreams that had plagued her these last six months had kept him awake at night, too. "But how did you know where to find me?"

Holt frowned. "I recognised Varda from Rose's description."

He pushed off the floor and walked over to the poster on the wall, tapping a finger to the dagger she'd left right in the centre. He pressed his fingers to the centre of the parchment, the pieces smoothing together to reveal her face. How many nights had she practised, alone?

The necklace Raif had given her hung from the weapon's hilt, and she caught the way Holt's gaze dropped to it and back up to the picture of her face. "Zylah." It was the first time she'd heard her name in months. Since they'd said goodbye. He turned to look at her, and not for the first time since she'd met him, she couldn't read his expression, but she thought she saw a trace of anger in his eyes for a moment, and then it was gone. "Can I see it?"

The vanquicite.

Zylah bit down on her lip, choosing her words. "You won't be able to heal it. I've tried." She turned away from him, pulled her shirt over her head and held it against her chest, waiting.

With anyone else, she'd have hesitated before standing in nothing but her undergarments. But she'd always felt safe with Holt, from the very first day he'd found her, running from Arnir's men, tired and afraid.

Zylah had no idea what the lump looked like now. She'd only tried to heal the effects of the vanquicite once, out of desperation. Before she'd finalised her tonic. And she'd spent the rest of the night running until the grey light of dawn had broken across the horizon, for fear someone, or rather, *something*, in Kerthen, would find her. And of course, Zylah knew there was no healing it, only removing it. She felt Holt step closer; heard his intake of breath.

"The lashes didn't heal." There was an edge to his voice, a pulse in the air as if his power had flexed from him for a moment.

"My body healed enough for me to travel, but the wounds broke open on more than one occasion, and I couldn't risk using magic."

At first, she'd thought she was too tired to heal herself, too exhausted, but then she'd realised Oz, the bounty hunter who'd taken her, must have dislodged the vanquicite somehow when he'd whipped her, and there would be no healing.

"I would never have sent you into Kerthen—"

Zylah spun to face him, shirt clutched to her chest where she still hadn't unhooked it from her arms. "It's not your fault, Holt." His eyes burned as he held her gaze. She knew he would do anything for his friends. Knew precisely what he'd done for Raif and Rose, how responsible he must have felt for everything that happened. She looked away. "It's mine."

"Turn around. Please." His words were clipped, and he didn't object to her admission of fault. Maybe he blamed her. Maybe he saw how the responsibility fell with her alone.

She did as he asked, the warmth of his calloused hands seeping through the back panel of her bralette to her skin. She felt the pulse of his magic, and though it diminished the ache, the vanquicite was still there. Despite herself, she couldn't help the quiet sigh that escaped her as more power flowed from Holt's fingertips and the ache lifted.

His fingers grazed the vanquicite lump for a moment before he pulled his hand away, and Zylah shrugged the shirt back over her head.

"That helped a lot more than I'd expected it would. Thank you." She slumped back down onto the lounger, feeling lighter than she had in months. "My turn to offer you my bed." *Shit.* "I'll take the floor, I mean, because you gave up your bed at the tavern," she added quickly. Gods, she hadn't meant it to sound like an invitation.

Holt's mouth twitched. "I'll take the floor." He turned away from her, pulling his wet shirt over his head and hanging it by the fire. Firelight danced off thick muscle, his bronzed skin marred only by the scar that ran along his arm and up to his neck.

Zylah looked away, tugging at one of the blankets that rested over the back of the lounger and resting it on the floor for him. The cabin hadn't come with a bed, and even if she'd had enough coin to buy one the space was too small.

Despite Holt's magic, exhaustion gnawed at her bones. She could still feel the lingering effects of the fight on her body, the softness of the lounger beckoning her to close her eyes as Holt moved to the floor beside her. Seeing him outside her cabin brought everything to the surface, everything she'd tried to bury since making it out of Kerthen. And Zylah knew she couldn't face it all, not now, not when it threatened to break her apart. Shutting it all out was better. Easier.

"How's my brother doing?" she asked, hoping he'd mistake the shake in her voice for exhaustion.

"Zack's fine. Rose and Saphi too."

She leaned over the edge of the lounger to look down at him. He was lying on his back, one arm resting above his head—the same position she'd seen him fall asleep in so many times back in Virian. He hadn't changed into another shirt, and seven gods, again she was struck by how beautiful he was. "Holt?"

Green eyes met hers. "Yeah?"

"The spell needs work. I knew someone was following me."

Holt's brow pinched together again. "When?"

"You were in the market, weren't you? Before I spoke to Sasha, my friend. And on my way home from the fight. I could feel someone was there. So we'll need to work on that."

One eyebrow raised a fraction as he held her gaze, the haunted look from earlier replaced with something like wonder before he shut it down. "Yeah. We do." In his eyes, honey-coloured flecks turned golden in the firelight, shadows dancing across his face.

She wanted to thank him. For keeping his promise. *I'll find you.* But she couldn't find the words. Instead, she said, "Goodnight, Holt," and shifted back onto the centre of the lounger to settle down for sleep.

"Goodnight, Zylah."

It was only then that she let the tears fall, silently, keeping her breaths steady. She hadn't let herself break since leaving Virian, but now she was no longer alone, she couldn't help it. The last of the pieces holding her together shattered completely.

5

There had been a time in Zylah's life when the most she knew of the Fae was what she read about in the books Kara had stolen for her. When they were nothing but stories of preternatural beings finding their mate and saving each other from whatever dark fate awaited them; always a happy ending. Too bad it didn't work out that way in real life.

She was still sprawled out on the lounger, listening to Holt's quiet breathing after a night of sleeping more peacefully than she had since leaving Virian, when the sound of shuffled footsteps outside marked someone nearby.

Holt was on his feet, making for the door.

"Wait," Zylah said quietly enough for his Fae ears to hear her. "It's Sasha." Zylah would recognise the old woman's hobbling gait anywhere.

Holt still wasn't wearing a shirt, his dark brown hair tousled and messy from sleep.

He angled his head to listen. "Stay down and out of sight. If she sees you without your injuries, it's going to raise some questions."

He had a point. Zylah sank into the lounger, listening as Holt opened the door.

Sasha clapped her hands together. "Seven gods, look at you. I told her you were coming for her, but she didn't believe me. How is she?"

Gods. Zylah pressed a hand to her face, her cheeks heating.

"Sleeping soundly." She could hear the amusement in Holt's voice, could picture the dazzling smile he was giving Sasha, arms folded across his chest. That was shirtless. *Oh, gods.*

Something rustled. Paper. The scent of pastry wafted into the cabin. "Give this to her. She'll need to keep her strength up."

Zylah felt her skin would set on fire with embarrassment as Holt huffed a quiet laugh. "I will, thank you. We're leaving soon to visit her brother. Liss wondered if you'd like to use her cabin while she's gone. You'd be doing her a favour, really."

It was exactly what she'd intended to do, and a smile tugged at her mouth that he'd thought of the same thing.

"In Pallia's name! Old Sasha would be honoured. Take care of her, won't you, my dear?"

Gods. She was never going to hear the end of this.

But Holt's voice had no trace of humour as he said, "Always. The key will be above the door waiting for you."

"Gods bless you."

The door clicked shut, and Zylah threw her arms over the top of the lounger. "I feel like I should explain."

Holt handed her the knishi and pulled his shirt from the fireplace, tugging it over his head. "It's fine, Zylah. She meant well."

But he didn't look at her as he said it, and Zylah could have sworn there was a hint of sadness in his tone. She bit into the

51

knishi as he filled the kettle. "Would you like some?" She could barely stomach a few mouthfuls.

He held out his hand, a brin fruit appearing in it and he took a bite. She waited for him to say something but when he didn't, she asked, "We're leaving today?"

"Unless you have another fight booked in?" He looked at her through long lashes as he took another bite of his brin fruit.

Point taken. Zylah held his stare as she forced down another mouthful of the knishi, legs folded on the lounger. For a moment he seemed lighter, as if whatever weight had settled over him had lifted. But then the kettle whistled, and Holt pushed to his feet in one smooth movement, silently moving around the kitchen. She grabbed her clothes from around the fire, glancing around the cabin and making a mental note of what to take. Not that she had much. The sword he'd given her, a few other weapons. Her pestle and mortar were too useful to leave behind, even with magic on their side. She'd have to leave her books, but most of them were Sasha's anyway.

Zylah flexed her fingers, anticipation turning the pastry over and over in her stomach at the thought of being able to use her magic again. To practice, at last. She'd never truly had the opportunity back in Virian, and yet... A thought tried to push its way to the surface, but she shoved it down and snuffed it out before it could fully form.

Holt handed her a steaming mug, the smell of alea blossom and honey drifting around the cabin, his gaze roving over her stacks of books. "We'll need to travel light, but if there's anything that's too much to carry, I can send it back to Virian when I send a note for your brother."

"I still need to learn that trick."

"I can teach you, if you'd like."

"I'd love it if you taught me everything about magic. My knowledge is… limited." Raif had always hesitated when the topic of magic came up, as if he were keeping her at arm's length. She traced her thumb around the rim of her mug, unwelcomed memories rushing in.

"Raif's magic always haunted him," Holt said, as if he'd read her thoughts. "He could take the very essence of a person and turn them to ash."

It was the first time she'd heard Raif's name in so long, and she willed herself to keep breathing at the sound of it. "Can you do that?"

Holt drained the last of his tea. "I've never tried. That kind of magic takes its toll over time, but it's like a drug… You want to feel the rush the more you use it."

Zylah was quiet at that. Raif had explained to her once, at the festival of Imala, that his magic cost him.

"I was taught that all Fae magic comes from the original nine," Holt told her, as if he knew her thoughts had carried her somewhere else. "Much of it was raw, savage. Dark. But it's been diluted over the centuries. Some of it is still good."

"I thought you didn't believe they were Fae?"

"I never *wanted* to believe it. That they were the reason for so much suffering." He toyed with the bracelet. "But that is the narrative my parents wanted to be a part of."

Zylah tried to recall what he'd told her back in Virian; that he'd refused to believe the original Fae watched their people suffer.

That they'd never come to his aid or to any who needed them.

"My mother could evanesce," he went on. "She taught me everything I know about Fae magic and like most High Fae, she favoured abilities rooted in nature, but only those that gave something back."

"The roots and vines," Zylah murmured.

Holt dipped his chin. "They were her favourite. Raif's magic was a combination of Marcus's and Aurelia's abilities—it's common amongst the royal lines, that one child inherits the parents' gifts. Marcus uses his lightning; Aurelia merely has to channel a drop of her power into the palm of her hand and her touch is paralysing."

Zylah's breaths came heavy. "Your scar. It was because of both of them. Marcus and Aurelia."

Holt's silence was answer enough. "Raif was young when he realised what he could do. It was a sprite, of all things, when we were together in the forest one day."

"Because they follow you," she said absent-mindedly, as she thought of Raif's magic, of how he could turn someone to ash with his touch.

"I was trying to teach him to harness the power of nature the way my mother taught me, and a group of sprites kept swarming us. Raif kept losing his focus. His temper flared. After he killed the sprite, he dug his fingers into the ash, and I could see the war going on behind his eyes. Half of him couldn't believe what he'd done, the other half was excited by it. And those two thoughts chipped away at him. No matter what we practised, he couldn't channel his abilities into anything else. Couldn't manipulate what was around him the way my mother had taught me." He frowned at the table, like he was seeing the memory play out before him. "I failed him that day."

"You didn't, Holt. His parents failed him. It wasn't on you to teach him."

Holt's shoulders rose as he took in a deep breath. "My mother's magic was so wholly rooted in nature, but my father's abilities were forged in combat. He was fifteen when he first went to war. He shielded himself first, an impenetrable layer he soon learnt to expand to protect his allies, too. He taught himself to wield that shield in reverse; a blast of power that he could use one-on-one as he fought. He didn't seem to realise it was aether he was drawing on, energy itself, the very heart of everything in this world, in nature. But it caused so much destruction. He was haunted by how many lives he'd taken."

Aether. Drawing on energy. The ripple of power she'd so often felt from him. Zylah finally understood the weight of the power he held.

He turned his hand, inspecting it as if he might see some traces of the magic there. "Whilst my father could only wield a single blast of power in one-on-one combat, I can release it like a wave, but it takes out everything in its path."

"That's…"

"Terrifying?" Holt swallowed. "That's not even the worst part." A pinch of his brow, and his eyes met hers. "The worst part is that in the moment I… I understand how Raif felt all those years ago."

How Raif had continued to feel, every time he'd used his magic. *I feel it take something from me every time I use it. Like a little piece of me is chipped away,* he'd said. She remembered the way the shadows had danced across his face. The way she'd told him he was good inside. But she hadn't told him she loved him. Why hadn't she told him?

Murderer. Monster.

The words tumbled over themselves.

She drank the last of her tea and padded to the bathroom, tipping what remained of the previous day's water pitcher into the sink. She stared at her reflection in the mirror, violet eyes staring back at her. Zylah couldn't stand to look at herself. She didn't know how Holt could either, knowing that Raif was dead because of her. She splashed water at her reflection, and then over her face, shoving all the feelings down until there was nothing but a muffled silence, an empty hollow inside her yawning open.

"I have a favour to ask," she said when she came out of the bathroom. Holt had already tidied up their mugs, straightened the lounger and folded the blankets. She didn't want to ask him—hated asking for help, but she'd made promises in Varda to the few she was helping. "There are a handful of people back in town…" she began.

"I left ample coin for each of them last night."

"So you *were* following me?" she asked, fighting back a smirk.

He folded his arms across his broad chest, the movement so familiar to her she hadn't realised how much she'd missed it. Missed him.

"I had to make sure there was no chance I was pursued before I made contact with you. Marcus will be waiting for the slightest hint of a slip-up."

The words were there unspoken. What he was risking by being there, for her. "Thank you," Zylah said quietly. "For the coin."

"Don't say what I think you're going to say, Zylah."

"I'll pay you back. For all of it."

"I told you before how to repay me."

Live your life, he'd told her. *That's repayment enough.* But it wasn't. It would never be, for all that he'd done for her. Zylah cleared her throat and began gathering her things. She retrieved her dagger from the poster, tucking the necklace Raif had given her into the front of her apron, the blade into one of her boots. She wasn't going with Holt so she could get the vanquicite removed. But he didn't need to know that. She was going with him for a chance at Marcus and Jesper, no matter what it took. They'd both played their part in Raif's death, and she had every intention of making them pay for it.

She looked up to meet Holt's gaze.

"I'll need to burn that," he began. "Unless you're particularly fond of the likeness."

Zylah forced a smile. "Go ahead." She watched him throw it into the fire, thinking about how the young woman on the poster wasn't who she was anymore. How for a while in Virian it felt as if the layers of her old life had peeled away, leaving something new. Something filled with hope.

She didn't know what she felt now. Only that the person she had become deserved whatever fate the vanquicite in her back had in store for her.

She gathered the rest of her things—the bow and quiver she'd taken from a corpse in the Kerthen forest, the sword Holt had gifted to her during the Festival of Imala. She fixed the sword to her belt, fastened her bracers and cloak and took one last look at the cabin. She couldn't say she'd miss it.

Kopi flew down to her shoulder as Holt whistled and a horse trotted out from amongst the trees.

"No saddle?" she asked.

"I borrowed this horse."

Zylah didn't question him. She'd done her fair share of stealing when she'd made it out of the Kerthen forest. Gods, even inside the forest she'd stolen. But she doubted the dead missed their possessions.

"We'll have to pick up supplies in the next town." Because it would raise too many questions in Varda, Zylah presumed. "Anything you can't carry will have to wait in Virian until then." He patted the horse's neck, checking it over.

Zylah didn't mind. She'd gotten used to living with little in Kerthen. She handed Holt the quiver and bow along with the bundle she usually wore on her back, his mouth twitching in amusement as he watched her slip some supplies into the pocket of her apron. The contents of her apron had kept her out of trouble on more than one occasion.

"After you, Kopi." Holt gestured to the owl, and Kopi flew up onto the horse's head, waiting.

Zylah took one last look back at the cabin, something telling her she was leaving another version of herself behind. With Holt's help, she pulled up onto the horse's back, and he swung up behind her, urging the horse on into the forest.

They rode until the pain in her back had stars dancing in front of her eyes. Not nearly long enough. When the horse traversed a stream, Zylah swallowed the pained sound that threatened to escape her.

As the sun began to dip in the sky the thick forest fell away, and the road became more defined, lined with the occasional shrine to the gods. *The not-gods*, Zylah told herself. It was a hard fact for her to swallow, that the gods she'd grown up praying to were not gods at all.

Carts and riders passed them, none paying them any heed. In the cold weather, most wanted nothing but the warmth of a fire or a body pressed against them, and Zylah was grateful for Holt's warmth despite her layers. They'd need warmer clothes for the days ahead.

This was farther south than Zylah had ever ventured. What remained of the Amestra Range was passing by them: lush foot-hills and thick forest, and a handful of small towns and villages dotted amongst them.

Kopi remained on the horse's head as they approached tall wooden gates, and Zylah instinctively tugged at her hood as they passed the guards stationed on either side, but none looked their way.

The town's newness meant it was not as poor as Varda, the streets busier with trade and shops still open despite the late hour.

They stabled the horse at a tavern, and Zylah waited outside as Holt arranged accommodation for later.

"Let me guess," she said as Holt returned. "Better to appear as husband and wife?" She tried to make the question sound light but failed to will the humour into her voice, and instead, it came out as an accusation.

Holt frowned. "It won't raise as many questions. Marcus has eyes everywhere." He gestured down the street, and Zylah followed. Questions about Marcus tumbled over themselves in her thoughts. But louder than that was the warning Raif had once given her. *We try not to speak about our father, for fear that it summons him.*

They passed a florist, baskets of cloud violas hanging on either side of the door just like the Bloom florist back in Virian. Zylah had shared a kiss with Raif just outside it. She pressed a hand to her stomach, focusing on Kopi's tiny weight on her shoulder to ground herself.

"Zylah?" Holt asked beside her.

"I'm fine." The lie was the easiest option, though she knew he'd assume it was the vanquicite, and there was truth to that part. She'd need to better school her reactions around him, to keep her face neutral. Zylah had lived with the pain long enough, and she had a few vials of her tonic should she wound herself again. Whatever it took to keep herself alive until she could get to either Jesper or Marcus. She brushed her fingers over the back of her hand where her wound had been, remembering it wouldn't have been her tonic that fully healed it, but Holt's magic.

Getting close to Marcus and Jesper would be next to impossible but… she held on to the shred of hope that an opportunity would present itself.

They purchased their supplies without incident, Holt leaving her in the market to browse while he went to make some enquiries. Zylah was assessing a table of herbs when she overheard a priestess uttering their usual speech about sinners and turned to find an engrossed crowd watching her.

Two members of the crowd broke into a fight, and just like back in Varda, the priestess broke it up. But this time, the gathered crowd applauded and cheered, the two men who had fought hugging as if they were nothing more than squabbling brothers.

The acolytes handed out pieces of parchment, and the townsfolk took them with warm smiles and handshakes. Zylah wasn't convinced. It looked like the recruitment days she'd often witnessed back in Dalstead, and something about the sight unsettled her.

She felt Holt's presence behind her, and his eyes found hers the moment she spotted him in the crowd.

That spell of his really needed some work. She tilted her head up to look at him as he joined her, a pair of saddlebags thrown over his shoulders like they were nothing but pebbles.

"Ready?" he asked, his eyes never breaking away from hers. He'd always been so good at hiding his feelings, keeping his expression neutral, but she'd always seen a warmth in his eyes when he looked at her, some of those hard edges softening.

Zylah cleared her throat, peeling her gaze away from his to wave a hand at the bags. "I'm sure there's a joke here somewhere about a donkey."

Holt angled his head, his mouth quirking as he tried to hide a smile. "I thought you were going to say something about how good I looked in leather."

"Pallia bless you," the same priestess from moments before said brightly as she passed so close to Holt that the hem of her dress swished against his legs. He didn't acknowledge the woman, but Zylah met the priestess's gaze, the woman's cold smile sending a chill down her spine before she forced herself to look away, all the lightness from moments before obliterated.

They returned to the tavern as darkness fell, the revellers within already full to the brim with ale. A drunk staggered across their path, eyes widening as he took in Holt's size. His gaze fell to Zylah, but she had no energy to bark at him, easing past Holt instead to make for the stairs.

"Couldn't get the coat she wanted? Better show her a good time up there, aye?" the drunk said as she carried their things to their room.

She found the wooden door with the same scratched mark as the one on their key, the lock rusty and old. The room was small but pleasant, patterned rugs layering the floor and faded tapestries hung on the walls in the same autumn shades as the curtains. One bed, no lounger. A small table and two chairs. No orblights here, just candles, and she took to lighting them with the flint box, one by one.

Holt returned a few moments later, a tray of food in his hand, two bowls of watery stew side by side. "It was all they had left, but it's hot."

Zylah didn't feel like eating. She unlatched the window, eyes roaming over rooftops to search for Kopi, but he'd flown off earlier on their way back from the market. He was nocturnal after all, but he spent so much time with her during the day Zylah often forgot the fact.

She emptied the contents of her apron on the bedside table and turned to Holt.

"You take the bed tonight," he said before she had a chance to speak, watching her carefully.

Zylah frowned.

"We can swap next time," he said gently, as if he knew how much trouble she was having holding herself together. He set the tray down on the table, the saddlebags beside it and took a seat.

Zylah nodded. Holt didn't say anything else, and she didn't feel like talking. Didn't feel like doing anything, the emptiness that had cracked open pulling her down, down, down. She shrugged out of her cloak and apron, kicked off her boots, and climbed into bed in the rest of her clothes, her back to Holt.

Raif's necklace stared back at her in the candlelight, the azure stone glittering and winking at her. She reached out and turned it over. Scrunched her eyes tight and willed sleep to claim her.

But it was never that easy, her insidious thoughts whispering to her, swallowing up anything good until exhaustion finally pulled her under.

6

"You still talk in your sleep," Holt told her the next morning as she stepped out of the bathroom. He sat beside the window, stroking Kopi on the head, two mugs steaming beside him.

Zylah frowned. "Anything interesting?"

"Something about priestesses." He took a sip of his tea, the scent of honey and alea blossom drifting from it as he watched her.

Zylah thought back to the first day they'd met, when she was running from Arnir's men. He'd made her honey and alea blossom then, told her she was half Fae. Another version of herself, the human one, chipped away. She took the seat opposite him and Kopi nuzzled her hand. "I've seen them more and more in the last couple of months. And yesterday it looked like they were recruiting."

His forest green eyes fixed on hers. "Isn't that what they do? Indoctrinate the masses into believing in false gods?"

Zylah looked away, out of the window across the rooftops. Ice glittered in a few places the sun hadn't yet touched. Soon it would remain until spring. "It just felt *off*." She wished now that she'd paid them closer attention back in Dalstead, but back then she'd had nothing to suspect. Nothing to fear. She reached for Raif's necklace, but it wasn't there. She'd left it beside the bed, upturned.

Zylah could still feel Holt's gaze on her as he said, "You didn't eat anything last night. Would you like breakfast?"

"Just the tea is fine. Thank you." Out of the corner of her eye, Zylah could see the momentary pinch of his eyebrows, the way he rubbed at his jaw. She was hungry. But the gnawing in her stomach was just distracting enough to drown out the roaring in her head, to stifle the emptiness that had yawned open.

Holt loosed a breath, whatever words he was going to say fading away in the space between them. "Evanescing is still too great a risk, so I've secured a second horse for us. Is there anything you'd like from the supplies I sent to Virian?"

She wanted to tell him what it meant that he'd come for her. But the words lodged in her throat, tangled with everything else she wanted to say. Should have said. "My pestle and mortar. Actually my bundle might—"

The bundle of cloth appeared on the table between them, a canna cake in his upturned palm, and something that might have been a plea settling over his features as he held it out to her.When Zylah didn't take it, Holt rested the crinkled paper beside her bundle, frowning at the cake. "Rose and Saphi went out with a team of scouts to recruit allies. We're stretched thin in Virian, but we're making it work."

There were extra vials of her tonic in the bundle, and with them, she wouldn't need to ask for Holt's help to ease the pain from the vanquicite.

She reached into the cloth and discreetly slipped a few into her apron. "Who's manning the safe house?"

"Zack. He's our liaison between the Fae in Virian and the Black Veil."

Zylah nodded, scooped up the canna cake and picked at a crumb. It made sense. Zack had been the King's Blade before all of this started. He was well suited to leading troops, to training soldiers. The thought almost made her smile, her brother amongst that great hall filled with Fae.

"We'll leave as soon as you're finished eating," Holt said. Zylah tilted her head to study him. Back in Virian she'd hated how she could never read him—never knew what he was thinking, and yet it struck her now that she'd missed the moment when she realised she could, the clipped edge to his voice now as he spoke: concern.

She rose from the table, pocketing the canna cake in her apron and wiping away the crumbs. "I'll just gather up my things."

"I could have wrapped that for you."

"It's fine, Holt. I've eaten far worse than a crumbling cake in the last six months."

She could have sworn the air crackled for a moment, but he was quiet as she collected her things, and it suited Zylah. There had been a moment when he'd arrived outside her cabin that she'd allowed herself to be happy. But it felt impossible to hold on to that feeling. Like it was a betrayal to Raif when they lived and smiled and he didn't.

Zylah fastened her cloak, Raif's necklace safe in the pocket inside it. She couldn't bear the weight of it around her neck anymore, or the feeling of her fingers brushing against it in her apron. She hadn't told him how she felt. What he meant.

"Zylah?" Holt called to her from the open doorway.

"Mmm?"

"Ready?"

She glanced at Kopi, waited for the little owl to fly up to her shoulder, and silently followed Holt out of the tavern.

Even with two vials of tonic, the ride had been excruciating. But on her own horse, it was easier for Zylah to hide her discomfort. The new cloak was thicker, and though she preferred her old one, wrapped up in one of their saddlebags, she knew she was going to need the warmth in the days ahead.

"What do you know of Marcus's source?" she asked Holt as they rode side by side through the dense forest that covered most of the fells, the horses unperturbed by the constant change in incline. Zylah was certain sprites watched them as they passed, but her father had always taught her that they were guardians of a sort, protecting the land, the waters, the little pockets of nature they resided in.

Marcus was old, ancient. Could his source be another Fae? If he and Aurelia were using Jesper to make an army, if they truly wanted to wipe out the humans living across Astaria, surely they'd be recruiting allies of their own, just as Holt was now.

Holt followed Kopi's path through the trees, his eyes searching the shadows. "Very little," he said at last. "I'm hoping an old acquaintance might be able to tell me more. Saphi suspects witches."

"Witches?" Zylah straightened. *There's whispers of a witch in Varda*, the priestess had said to her. Had it been true?

"Not just a thing of stories." He knew her knowledge of the world was different to his. Not just because of the years he had on her, but because she'd been raised in Dalstead, where King Arnir had ruled with a heavy hand. Where even her father and brother had seen fit to keep her sheltered from the true nature of the world.

Her back throbbed as the horse missed a step, and she tightened the grip on her reins. "You truly believe they'll be able to remove the vanquicite?"

"Saphi seemed hopeful if no one else has a healer skilled enough."

Zylah was quiet, wondering just what Saphi had witnessed to make her believe that. It didn't matter whether she had the stone removed or not. If she had a run-in with either Jesper or Marcus, Zylah doubted she'd survive the encounter. But she vowed to make the meeting worth it, no matter the cost.

"Travelling apothecary by day. Brawler by night. Are you going to tell me how you ended up in Varda?" Holt asked when she didn't reply. There was a teasing edge to his voice, and she knew he was trying to pull her from her thoughts. Knew he knew her better now than probably anyone else.

"You mean you hadn't heard of the Little Bird in Virian?" she asked, raising an eyebrow.

The breeze picked up, twigs snapping under the horse's hooves as they walked. Zylah could hear every insect and bird, but a shiver ran down her spine despite her reassurance.

Holt eased his horse to a stop. "We're being watched."

"Seems I lost the bet," a voice called out from somewhere above them.

Three males swung down from the trees, all pointed ears and sharp eyes, bow strings pulled back and arrows pointed at each of them. Zylah reached for one of the pencil-thin daggers at her wrists, but Holt held out a hand.

"We're here to see your High Lady." Holt had lifted his deceits, his pointed ears poking through his unruly hair. Raw power seemed to pour from him as the veil lifted, two of the males baulking under the force of it.

High Lady. Zylah knew they were searching for allies but hadn't known what to expect. "What bet?"

The male who'd spoken before hid his hesitation better than his companions as they shared a glance, sheathing their arrows. "That we'd be watching you for hours unnoticed," he said with a smirk. "Come. More Fae are a welcome sight."

Another pulse of Holt's power hummed in the air.

"Was that the Fae equivalent of a dick swing?" Zylah murmured, one eyebrow raised at Holt.

She caught his smirk as he urged his horse onwards to follow the others.

The males made their introductions, and Zylah listened in silence as Finn, the only one of them who'd spoken and made the introductions, told her and Holt about their small community. They made their distaste for Marcus known early on, quelling some of the anxiety that had unsettled Zylah's stomach.

A few times she noted nastura leaves but didn't think she could manage to dismount more than once in front of a crowd, so she told herself she'd go back for them later.

Her knowledge of plants had kept her alive in Kerthen, and though she'd read extensively back in Dalstead, it was her father she'd learnt from. Hours and days and weeks spent in his apothecary as a child had ignited her love for plants. But he was gone now, too. *Because* of her.

In the beginning, she hadn't known how to grieve for them both; her father and Raif. Their deaths had been days apart. But in the dark nights of the Kerthen forest, it hadn't mattered. She'd let the grief swallow her whole.

Sprites tracked them as their horses pushed on, but Zylah paid them no heed. The sound of rushing water drew her attention instead.

The falls.

"You must bathe before you can enter," Finn said as they neared the waterfall, a clear blue pool at the base.

Zylah discreetly sniffed at her cloak, not for the first time since she'd met the Fae.

"The water is spelled," Holt murmured beside her.

Finn grinned. "He misses nothing, this one." One of his companions handed him two bundles. "Wear these."

"You just carry these around the forest, waiting for visitors?" Zylah asked as he handed her a robe. The air was damp with spray, but the water was fresh.

"We were notified of your arrival." Finn waved a hand as Kopi flew down from the canopy, landing on a rock beside the pool. "Your friend will show you the way when you're ready. We'll take your horses."

Holt dismounted without argument, but Zylah wasn't convinced, regardless of whether Kopi had led the three Fae to them. "You're okay with this whole *go take a bath whilst we steal your horses* situation?"

"These are traditional robes, Zylah. This is a welcome, not a warning." Holt waved the bundle of fabric at her, before handing the reins to Finn.

Allies, Zylah reminded herself. All too aware of the four pairs of eyes waiting for her to dismount, she took a moment to prepare herself for the pain, hoping they'd mistake it for hesitation over their offer.

She took a deep breath, just as Holt clapped a hand to Finn's back. "Tell me, my friend, how is it that the townsfolk know of these falls?"

The other two stepped closer to Holt and Finn, arms folded as Finn offered up his explanation, their attention no longer on Zylah. She slid off the horse on the side farthest from the males, clenching her teeth as her feet hit the ground, but she didn't falter.

Holt caught her gaze as she handed the reins to Finn, and she hoped he could see the silent thank you she offered him.

"See you on the other side," Finn said a little too brightly for Zylah's liking.

They walked through a gap between water and rock, disappearing behind the spray within moments.

Zylah cast her gaze across the pool, steam rising from the water and swirling in the cold air. "This feels weird," she said as Holt stepped up beside her.

"Weirder than keeping plants in your pockets?"

"I do that with good reason."

"And cake?"

"Also with good reason." She held out the robe. It was for someone far taller than her. Which would have been most people, Zylah supposed.

Holt had shrugged out of his coat, folding his things in a neat pile beside the pool. He didn't carry a weapon, though she knew he could summon one to him should he need it, not that he required the assistance of a weapon to aid his fighting.

Zylah turned away as he pulled off his shirt, unfastening her cloak and sword belt. "I missed Finn's reason about the townsfolk."

Water sloshed as he stepped in, and she shrugged off her trousers and tunic, resting them on top of her apron and her other belongings. Holt had seen her in her undergarments enough times, back when they shared a room in Virian, and tradition or not, she wasn't about to strip any further.

His back was turned as she stepped into the pool, and she closed her eyes as the warmth and the weightlessness eased the ache in her back.

She felt a ripple of power, from the water or Holt, she wasn't sure. When she opened her eyes, Holt was watching her, his hair dripping wet, steam rising from his shoulders, and she willed her gaze not to lower.

He inched closer as if he couldn't help himself, and then paused. "He said some come to offer tributes, to have their wounded healed by magic."

"And do the Fae here comply?" she asked, taking a step back, for fear that if she didn't, she'd take a step closer to him.

Holt shrugged, water beading off his sculpted chest and along the scar that ran from his arm to his neck. "I suppose we'll

72

find out when we go inside." He turned away again, offering her some privacy.

Zylah closed her eyes, relishing the roar of the waterfall behind them as she held out a hand in the water.

"What are you doing?" Holt asked quietly.

"I wanted to see if I could feel the spell, like I can feel wards." She kept her eyes closed, but she felt the swell of the water as he moved closer to her.

"Spells and wards are different to our magic."

Water sloshed as he spoke, and she wondered if he'd done it so she knew he was near.

"I wouldn't know," she murmured, eyes flicking open to meet his.

He moved around her in the water, just out of reach of her hand. "You can heal. You can evanesce. Those are rare gifts. Most Fae have abilities rooted in nature, the elements." Like his, or what she'd witnessed. He reached for her upturned hand beneath the water and lifted it above the surface in his own.

Beads of water danced above Zylah's open palm, and she sucked in a breath. "Tell me how you did that."

"It's the same feeling as the evanescing or the healing." He turned her hand, and a stream of water danced around it. "I call to it, and it follows."

Her gaze shifted from her hand to his face, to the way he was concentrating, the way the water dripped off his hair, and for a moment the roaring in her head silenced. Then his eyes found hers, and she saw herself reflected in them. Zylah tugged her hand away, sinking her shoulders beneath the surface, her gaze fixed on the waterfall as the dark thoughts rushed back in.

She wrapped her arms around herself and suppressed a shiver.

"We should get going," Holt said quietly. "The High Lady of this court can be… difficult." In the back of her mind, it sounded almost like an apology, but the words were distant as she stared into the water rippling away from her.

What if they knew? The Fae who waited beyond the waterfall. What if they saw her for what she truly was? *Murderer. Monster. Curse.*

Holt held out her robe as she stepped out of the water, and she couldn't meet his eyes. Didn't understand how he could bear to look at her.

She fastened the robe and secured her sword belt over the top of it—because Holt might not need a weapon, but she did—and scooped up her bundle of belongings.

For a moment, Zylah felt like that old, human version of herself. Running from the king's men, afraid and alone.

Only she wasn't alone now. Holt glanced back over his shoulder, throwing her a reassuring smile as he followed Kopi behind the waterfall, spray misting the air.

Zylah silenced every thought, snuffing them out until the roar of the waterfall filled every hollow space inside her chest, following her friends into the dark.

7

It wasn't the first Fae party Zylah had attended, but it might as well have been for what a spectacle it was. The moment they passed under the waterfall, Zylah felt the wards bend and flex around her, pressing at her skin before they released.

The sound of the water had soon been drowned out by music, the darkness giving way to glittering orblights illuminating the way. Zylah had insisted they put their clothes back on, no matter the tradition, but felt thoroughly underdressed the moment they stepped out of the passage beneath the waterfall.

"Seven g—" The old words fell mute on her tongue. Nothing would mark her as different here more than exclaiming to the gods who were not gods.

She stopped to take it all in, Kopi perched on her shoulder, her robe thrown over her arm. She registered Holt's silence beside her, surprise flickering across his face for a moment before he shut it down. Though they'd walked behind a waterfall, they stood before other waterfalls cascading into each other, rock pools flowing from one to the next with stepping stones between them. More passages like the one they'd come from seemed to branch off from the rock, Fae passing in and out of them and paying no heed to Holt and Zylah.

Zylah tried not to gawk. Where there was no water or rock, springy moss blanketed everything, jewel bright against the water. Three trees stood in the centre of the falls, rope walkways crisscrossing between them, orblights hanging amongst branches and tucked along their trunks.

And at their base, faeries danced, ate, waved wine glasses and laughed. No one stared back at them or asked them what they were doing there, too engrossed in enjoying the moment.

A band played lively string instruments, faeries clapping in time with the beat. A mix of High Fae and Lesser Fae, Zylah noted. Some of the Lesser Fae had wings, some had scales, some had skin the colour of Zylah's eyes. But all of them wore pointed ear cuffs to mimic the High Fae amongst them.

"They're concealing all of this from the outside world?" Zylah asked Holt just as a green-skinned faerie walked past with a tray of food in her hand, plump fruits and cheeses, piles of nuts and berries almost spilling over the edge.

Holt frowned. "So it would seem. Old magic seems to have had something of a revival."

A group of High Fae approached them. Among them was Finn, and beside him walked a beautiful High Fae with a headpiece threaded into her silver hair, jewels dipping down onto her forehead. Her pale skin was flawless, her eyes an unusual shade that reminded Zylah of the water in the springs, somewhere between blue and green. Claw-like rings sat at the tip of each of her fingers, fine chains connecting them to bangles at her wrists. Zylah suspected they were for a display of power, but the sight of them reminded her of the Asters—monsters, and the thought made her want to recoil.

The Fae pulled her full lips into a pout as she approached, towering over Zylah, not that it was difficult. "Prince of the Forest. It has been too long since I have laid eyes on you."

Zylah had all but forgotten Holt was royalty; hadn't considered what allies he'd spoken of.

But he showed little of the warmth the female showed for him, and under that neutral façade, Zylah could feel him tense beside her. "Maelissa."

Maelissa stepped so close Zylah had to tilt her chin up to see the female's face. The Fae pressed a hand against her chest, fingers grazing the low cut of her neckline and brushing her bare skin. The scent of cloud violas and plumeria drifted from her skin. "What happened to just Mae?"

Oh.

More than friends then. Zylah's skin prickled, and she willed herself not to fidget with her cloak, despite how hot she was underneath it.

"Your court is thriving, as always," Holt said, waving a hand to the party around them.

Court. They'd all been destroyed, as far as Zylah knew.

"And you are welcome in it for as long as you wish. You and your… companion." Mae's gaze dropped down to Zylah's for a moment, then back to Holt expectantly.

"This is Zylah." They hadn't talked about using her real name, but amongst Fae, Zylah supposed it wouldn't matter. Holt's hand hovered near her back as he introduced her, Mae's eyes tracking the movement.

Zylah cleared her throat and looked up into those strange eyes. "Nice to meet you." Even without Holt's earlier warning, without the razor-sharp jewellery, Zylah already knew there would be nothing nice about the Fae before her.

Mae's gaze travelled down, slowly, before meeting Zylah's again. "Finn tells me your companion found him. Such loyalty is a rarity in today's world. Please partake in whatever appeals to you. My court is yours for as long as the Prince of the Forest wishes to stay."

She dipped her head in a bow, her eyes lingering on Holt's face for a moment longer before she turned away, her entourage already whispering into her ears as they left.

Zylah held her head high, her gaze fixed on the largest of the falls, watching the Fae pass in and out of the curtain of water at the bottom.

"I didn't believe Mae's gossips when they spoke your name." Zylah turned to the male voice that had spoken.

"Thallan." Holt hesitated for a fraction of a second, so quickly Zylah almost missed it, before he grabbed the Fae's outstretched hand and clasped his forearm in greeting.

"Good to see you, my friend," Thallan said brightly, patting Holt on the back enthusiastically as he pulled him into a hug.

"You as well," he said, though Zylah knew he didn't mean it. He shot her a warning glance before he said, "Zylah, meet Thallan."

Thallan's grey eyes met hers, and though on the surface they were warm and welcoming, something about them set her skin crawling. Holt bristled beside her, and Kopi ruffled his feathers as she held a hand out to the Fae. "Hi."

Thallan held her hand in both of his, and Zylah felt a wall of magic press against her as if she were stepping through a ward, but instead of feeling it outside her body, she felt it in her mind. The Fae's expression was friendly, inquisitive, but as Holt's fingers brushed her lower back as if in warning, Zylah forced herself to think of Arnir's vanquicite throne, of the cuffs that had bound her wrists for days and the endless black of gazing into them.

Thallan blinked rapidly and released her hand at the same time Holt pulled away. "Forgive me... old habits are difficult to shake. You have an unusual air about you." He looked at Kopi as he said it, his smile still warm.

Zylah tilted her head, the image of the vanquicite still firmly in her mind. Holt had warned her once about mental attacks, and the sensation she'd felt... despite Thallan's smile, felt like something she needed to shield herself from. The vanquicite was the only thing she could think of.

Thallan brushed a blond curl behind a pointed ear and took a deep breath. "I have to ask... how is she?"

"Rose has been better." Holt's jaw squared, but he held Thallan's attention.

Thallan's face seemed to crumple for a moment, his face blanching before he had time to hide it. If she hadn't just met him, Zylah would have said his concern lingered on obsessive, and she tried not to let her surprise show as she realised who he was. Rose's mate. Who Rose had rejected. And it had driven him mad, Raif had told her.

The Fae's hand slid over his heart, elegant fingers curling into his white jacket. "Is she hurt?"

Zylah bit her lip. Looked away to the waterfalls again. She felt Holt's attention on her before he said, "Raif is dead."

The words echoed on repeat in Zylah's thoughts as she fought back the sting in her eyes.

She heard Thallan's intake of breath. Caught the way he reached for Holt out of the corner of her eye. "I'm sorry." His voice thickened. "Sit with me, we'll raise a glass to him, talk about what brings you here."

Zylah followed them silently, wanting nothing more than to leave. To go back to the quiet of the pool outside and sink under the surface, with only the constant rumble of the falls to fill her head.

Thallan gestured to a bench at the end of a table of fairies, mountains of food covering most of the surface. He poured them both a glass of wine as they took seats. Zylah pinched at a pile of seeds and nuts, dropping them on her shoulder for Kopi. She wondered if he would leave her soon, fly amongst the trees for some rest, but he didn't.

"To Raif," Thallan said, his voice catching slightly as he raised his glass.

Zylah couldn't speak. Just took a sip of her wine and placed it back on the table. She wasn't certain if Thallan could sense her feelings as well as look into her mind, so she focused on the image of the vanquicite, polished and gleaming, hoping it would be enough to block him out.

Thallan downed his wine and poured himself another glass. "So what brings you to Lady Maelissa's court?"

Polished. Gleaming. Black. Nothing.

Nothing.

Holt rested a plate in front of Zylah before taking one for himself and began filling their plates with food. "It was Mae a moment ago."

Thallan winked, filling a plate of his own and letting Holt's remark linger.

The band finished their song, faerie laughter filling the pause until they started up again. Only when Holt had piled Zylah's plate with more food than she could possibly eat in three sittings did he answer. "News of Marcus's new position has travelled here, I assume?"

The air was stifling. Zylah pushed off from the table, and Holt raised an eyebrow at her in question. She glanced at Thallan, his glass hovering before his lips. "Please... continue without me. I'd like to find Kopi a quiet spot before I eat. He hasn't slept today." He'd hopped onto the table to peck at the seeds, head now twitching left and right between them.

Thallan seemed convinced, but she caught Holt's frown as he looked at his plate of food, also untouched.

She shrugged out of her cloak and left it on the bench beside him, Kopi resuming his position on her shoulder. "I'll only be a moment."

Zylah hoped Holt would understand. She couldn't sit and listen to him explain how Raif died; couldn't bear to relive every tiny detail. She bit down on her bottom lip almost hard enough to draw blood as she walked towards the nearest pool.

A group were gathered beside it, three males and a female. One male sat in a chair with wheels the likes of which Zylah had never seen before. Beside him knelt a... at first glance, he looked like another High Fae, but something about him struck Zylah

81

as odd. He moved with feline grace, passing things to his companion in the chair. Plants.

Zylah's curiosity was piqued, and she walked closer.

"I'm hopeful this will ease Frea's headaches," the male in the chair said. His dark sepia hands held a besa leaf, inspecting the fronds carefully. Besa could help with headaches, but not as much as—

"Nastura," Zylah said, as she passed the group. "Nastura has stronger anti-inflammatory properties than besa. I saw some in the forest on my way here. It always grows beside cap mushrooms, which are far easier to spot. I'd be happy to bring you some."

"You have my thanks," the male in the chair said, dipping his head in gratitude. He also had the pointed ears of a High Fae, but like his companion, Zylah couldn't shake the sense that they were deceits, magic disguising their true identity.

Zylah nodded and offered a tight smile, but she had nothing left to give to the conversation. She made her way to the far side of the pool, seating herself on a rock and pulling a handful of seeds from her pocket for Kopi. Her gaze drifted to Thallan and Holt's table, and she noticed Holt still hadn't touched his food. They were still talking about Raif, she assumed.

She could see the tension in Holt's body, the way his elbows locked, hands clasped together. He looked up and caught her gaze, as if he'd felt her attention on him, his features softening for a moment. Thallan rested a hand on Holt's shoulder, and the softness was gone, a frown creasing his brow.

"My mate and I wish to thank you for your kind offer," a male voice said, and Zylah looked away to see the two Fae who had been on the other side of the pool a moment before making their way towards her.

The female beside him waved with a smile but said nothing. She was beautiful: black braided hair heavy with jewels and gold rings, deep brown eyes that were soft and warm. She wore a floor-length dress in the same shade of pale green as her mate's clothes, the straps thin and the neckline low against her umber skin, the fabric almost weightless where it clung to her body. Golden bangles adorned each arm, so many Zylah wondered how she ever went anywhere silently.

"The nastura is for my mate's sister," the male said. "I'm Ellisar. This is Dalana." He was as beautiful as his mate, who still had not spoken. His pale green suit was fine but understated. Small, knotted buttons ran down the centre of his jacket, the hem dusted with embroidery a shade darker than the suit. A few braided coils of hair fell across his eyes, and he swept them away, revealing a fine tattoo inked into the tawny skin around his eye. They both had a softness to them, a warmth that took the edge off Zylah's dark thoughts.

"Zylah." She pushed to her feet, brushing the seeds from her hands as Kopi returned to her shoulder.

"Something troubles you. Dalana wishes to know if she can make your evening more pleasant," Ellisar said with a warm smile.

Zylah looked at the female. "I'm fine, thank you. How..." She bit her lip. "How are you communicating with him?"

Dalana smiled and tilted her head to one side.

"You've never met a mated pair before?" Ellisar asked.

"No."

Ellisar took Dalana's hand and looked into her eyes as he spoke. "Lana has no voice of her own, but we speak down the bond. I hear her voice as if it were my own. And even if I couldn't, I would still feel her presence. I know when she walks into a room, I can feel her anywhere."

Zylah shifted her attention to the water.

She and Holt had talked about mates once. She'd thought it cruel.

But when it works—when it all falls into place—that's a powerful thing, Holt had told her.

"We share our thoughts, feelings, even what little magic we both possess should we need to," Ellisar added, his tone cheerful as he explained. But then he turned to Zylah, his smile fading. "Forgive me. Lana says we have made you uncomfortable."

"No, I… I'm just tired." She looked over at Holt's table again, to where Lady Maelissa sat beside him, a hand on his arm, laughing at something, and squashed the ugly thoughts that were working their way to the surface.

"Any friend of Holt's is a friend of ours," Ellisar added.

"You know Holt?"

"There are few here who do not." Ellisar followed her gaze to Holt's table, where Maelissa leaned across him to reach for a handful of grapes, her body pressing against his as she moved.

"So I see." Kopi hooed quietly on her shoulder as if prompting her to change the topic. "This place… old magic keeps it well hidden from the humans."

A half-truth wasn't as bad as an outright lie, and though Ellisar had said they were friends with Holt, Zylah was yet to see any evidence of that.

"We were uneasy at first with Lady Maelissa's… developments. But we've become accustomed to them. The court thrives within the confines of these rocks, and though we miss our old home, this one has grown on us."

Zylah considered how much she should press them, whether she should admit what little knowledge she had of her own people. The rulers of the courts had been murdered, she'd thought. "Have you lived this way for very long?"

"Since a few years after the last uprising. Our Lady might not make the best first impression, but she is very… *fierce* when it comes to her court."

"But you wish to live beyond it?"

Dalana and Ellisar exchanged another look. "We wish to walk through this world freely," Ellisar said softly.

The unspoken words hung between them: despite Arnir's death, Astaria was still not safe for the Fae. Not with Jesper's army, and whatever sick games Marcus was playing. But the desire to live free… Zylah understood that all too well, and all she could offer in response was a tight smile. She took in the court around them, the laughing faeries, the music. And already the air pressed against her skin, already she felt trapped.

Her back throbbed, but her vials of tonic were in her saddlebags, wherever they were. Kopi hooed softly at her shoulder in reassurance.

"Lana asks if she may touch him," Ellisar asked.

Zylah hesitated for a moment, fighting her natural instinct to put space between her and others. But Dalana's smile seemed genuine, warm. "Hold out your hands." Zylah shifted her shoulder towards the Fae's upturned palms, a slice of pain cutting through her as she moved, but she ground her teeth together to conceal it. Dalana's face lit up even more as Kopi hopped into her palms, making a little noise, not unlike a purring cat. Zylah rolled her eyes at his dramatics, returning the smile Dalana offered her. She looked over the Fae's shoulder to see Lady Maelissa watching Holt as he made his way over, her cloak clutched in one hand, the other tucked into a pocket.

"Lana. Ellisar. It's good to see you," Holt said, stepping in beside her.

Both Fae bowed their heads. *Bowed.* Zylah pressed her lips together to make sure her mouth didn't hang open. Kopi flew back up to her shoulder, and Lana's hands began moving quickly, signs and gestures moving from one to the next so fast that Zylah barely registered them.

Holt huffed a quiet laugh, resting Zylah's cloak on his shoulder and moving his hands like Lana's as he said, "We're friends."

Zylah's cheeks flushed.

"We've had a long day. Perhaps we could catch up over breakfast?" Holt asked, his hands moving again as his attention moved between Lana and Ellisar.

"Of course," Ellisar beamed. "And until then, Lana will never let me hear the end of it if I don't offer you our home for the night."

Holt glanced at Zylah, as if *he* was asking. She felt the attention of the two Fae on her, waiting for her decision. Zylah nodded. "Thank you."

They followed Lana and Ellisar past a group of faeries and across a pool, Kopi flying off into one of the trees. His home for the night, or merely a perch from which to observe and eat. The court wasn't what Zylah had expected, but then, she hadn't known what to expect at all. More faeries than she could count wandered in and out of the space, disappearing into the rocks and amongst the falls and up into the trees, but what lay beyond or how far the court reached, Zylah couldn't be certain.

They made their way through a passage behind one of the falls and up a winding staircase, and for a moment Zylah thought of Arnir's prison. The stifling air, the lack of natural light, and it struck her then—how Lady Maelissa's court was trapped. She pressed a hand to her chest.

"Zylah?" Holt asked beside her.

"It's fine. I'm just tired." Another half-truth. Wooden doors branched off the passageway they'd entered, and Ellisar kissed Dalana's knuckles as he stopped beside one of them.

"I'll go check on the children," he said to his mate. He looked from Holt to Zylah, bowing his head. "Goodnight."

Lana smiled before continuing down the stone passageway, the rush of the falls following them everywhere. Orblights lit the way, though plenty of cut-outs in the rock let in light from the court beyond… even though it was night-time.

Lana signed something again to Holt, and this time Zylah recognised the word. Friend.

Friend, Holt signed back, his hands still moving. "It's fine. I'll take the floor. Thank you."

The Fae opened the door to a room with a bed big enough for five people, another cut-out in the rock exposed to the rush of the falls, the curtain of water so heavy it gave complete privacy from the court beyond. The room was beautiful despite the stone. The floor was covered with soft rugs in shades of green, mimicking moss, the walls decorated with plants and mirrors, giving the illusion that they were outside. Beyond the court.

"Goodnight," Holt said quietly, pulling Zylah from her inspection of the room.

"Oh. Thank you, Dalana. Goodnight," she said, forcing a smile.

The Fae waved, clicking the door shut behind her as she left, the sound of the waterfall filling the space. All of Zylah's energy had been used up on talking to people, and in the quiet of the room, she felt bone weak, drained, as if she hadn't slept for a hundred years.

"Mae wasn't very forthcoming when I pressed her about Marcus's old magic," Holt said, dragging a hand through his hair. "But playing with people is something she excels in."

Zylah thought of the way Mae had fawned over him earlier, the way she'd pressed herself against him. "I need my things," she murmured.

Holt flicked his wrist and their belongings appeared on the floor beside them. He took a step closer, and then waited.

Zylah swallowed. "Thank you. It's my turn to take the floor."

"No."

She looked up at him, at the way he'd squared his jaw, and wondered if he was preparing for a fight. Zylah was too tired to argue. "Then we'll share. It's big enough for five." She tore a shirt from her bag, fatigue tugging at every bone and muscle.

"You didn't eat anything," Holt said, facing away from her, inspecting the plants on the wall, arms folded across his chest.

Zylah shrugged out of her clothes and pulled her shirt over her head. Another of his. "I'm not hungry." She'd gone past hunger hours ago. Days, probably. She pulled back the covers, climbed into bed and lay on her side, watching the water as it fell past their window.

She heard the rustle of Holt getting undressed. Felt the movement of the bed as he climbed in on the other side. Now they were in it, Zylah was certain more than five could fit in the space between them.

Zylah rolled over, her head sinking into a ridiculously puffy pillow as she looked at him. He was lying on his back, his head resting on an arm.

There was so much space between them, but she could still feel the heat from him, could still smell the earthy acani berries and muskiness of his scent, the familiarity of him soothing her a little.

"Holt?"

"Yeah?"

"There's something strange about this place."

He moved onto his side to face her, his brows pinched together as he studied her face. "How so?"

"Something Ellisar said. About being free. They're trapped here. I don't know Lady Maelissa like you do, but... is there any chance...?"

Holt pressed a hand to his forehead, dragged it through his hair and rolled onto his back again. "Mae will use anything to get what she wants. Anyone."

A weight settled in the back of Zylah's throat. "She used *you*?"

"I was young. And naïve." He pushed out a breath, staring at the ceiling. "Too young."

Zylah didn't know how to respond to that. She picked at a piece of lint on the bedsheet, willing her cheeks not to burn as anger rose from her chest.

It turned her stomach to know he'd been taken advantage of by someone who knew better. And he'd shared so little of himself in the past. That he'd shared this piece of him... she tucked it away for another time.

He met her gaze again. "When I was old enough to realise, I called it off. But Mae doesn't like to be denied the things she wants."

Zylah thought of the clawed rings on Mae's fingers, of how tightly she'd keep hold of what she coveted, willing her anger to diminish. Though Mae seemed young and beautiful, something about the way she held herself, the way she moved, told Zylah she was older than Holt. Much older. Powerful, too.

Holt loosed a breath. "I think you might be right. I think at some point or another, she worked with Marcus. I shouldn't have brought you here."

Because she was a target. Because she was a danger to him, and to everyone in this court.

"I should have known better," Holt said when she didn't reply. "Mae used to conduct a lot of her business in her rooms when she thought I was sleeping. I heard a lot of things I wasn't supposed to."

Zylah looked up at him again. "Maybe she wanted you to hear those things. Maybe she let enough of the things you overheard be a lie, so you wouldn't know which was the truth."

Holt raised an eyebrow. "You're an expert at lying, are you?" The corner of his mouth tilted up. "I hadn't noticed."

Zylah didn't bite. She couldn't. "You knew Mae was here, back out in the forest. She was one of the allies you were seeking?

"I'd hoped she could tell me about the old magic Marcus has been using. But I need her archers, too. And I need her to send messages to the other courts that we're coming—that much I can count on without having to ask, she always loved to gossip."

Other courts. Something told her there would be time for that question later. "What's so special about her archers?"

"Their bows are forged from arrenium, each of her archers is worth five men in a fight. But it's been many years since I've seen Mae."

And Maelissa didn't strike Zylah as the kind of Fae to give things away for nothing. "What will you do?" Zylah asked.

"Remind her that she's not the rightful Lady of this court."

If Maelissa wasn't the rightful Lady, then who? And what had Maelissa done to secure the title? Zylah listened to the sound of the waterfall, the scent of wet rock and plants reminding her of the botanical gardens back in Virian, only now it was mingled with Holt's scent.

"Zylah?" He searched her eyes, strands of hair falling across his own.

"Yeah?"

"It was a long time ago."

Zylah frowned. "It was still wrong of her."

He loosed another sigh. "Mae has no concept of right and wrong. Only what needs to be done. For a long time, I thought I understood that. Even when my parents died. But when Adina…" His voice caught, and Zylah wanted to reach for him,

91

to offer him some comfort for the sister he'd lost because of Marcus. But she knew if she did, it'd put a crack in the wall she'd built around her own heart.

"Sometimes I think it was my punishment for what was to come," Holt said softly.

Zylah studied his face. The pinch of his eyebrows, the sharp angle of his jaw, and her eyes fell to his scar. "Your tithe?" she asked quietly.

"Yes." He held her gaze, his eyes full of the same hollow emptiness she felt inside of her.

He'd told her back in Virian that he had no regard for his own life. That was before Raif's death. This time, she did reach for him, rested her hand over his. "It isn't your fault. Their deaths," she said softly, his warmth seeping into her.

Holt's fingers flexed through hers. "It isn't yours, either." His eyes dipped to their joined hands, then slowly back up to her face until they met hers, but again she saw her broken reflection and pulled her hand away.

Zylah closed her eyes. She didn't want to see the way he must see her, didn't want him to see the truth of how she felt inside. She turned back to the waterfall, murmuring goodnight. There was no doubt in her mind that none of this would have happened if he'd just let Arnir's men find her that day in the springs. That so many would still be alive if it weren't for her.

There was no denying it.

She was a curse.

8

Zylah had dreamt of her father. They were walking the forest path together to Dalstead, the one that cut through the stream. He'd been talking about legacy again. About how our actions matter. But when she'd reached out to him, he'd turned to ash before her, carried away with the wind.

She opened her eyes. Holt was still asleep, and she studied his face. His head rested on his arm, and she followed the line of his scar to where it settled across his neck. He'd pulled his sheet away, and where the skin around the scar was puckered and ruined, the rest of him was perfect. Her eyes trailed down his chest, across the hard muscles of his stomach to where his trousers hung low on his hips.

Zylah's cheeks flushed, and she padded to the bathroom, clicking the door shut quietly behind her.

She bathed quickly, scrubbing her arms a little too vigorously as guilt crept in. She'd never told Raif she loved him.

But she had.

Hadn't she?

He'd been what she needed after Jesper. Patient, kind. And yet… She couldn't let herself finish the thought.

Zylah rinsed her hair and stepped out of the tub. The pain in her back was gone, and she felt better than she had in a long time.

She frowned, looking at the wall to where Holt lay in bed on the other side, wondering if he'd healed her whilst she was sleeping.

He'd have to approach Lady Maelissa before they left, and that only darkened Zylah's mood, layering it in with the guilt that already coated her tongue. She dried her hair, wrapped herself in a towel and stepped out of the bathroom to search for her things.

Holt was awake, one arm propped behind his head, sleepy eyes following her as she walked over to her saddlebag.

"Don't look at me like that," she murmured, heat creeping into her cheeks again, warmth flaring through her.

"Like what?"

Zylah knelt beside her belongings, her back to him.

Like you're hungry.

The scent of freshly baked bread carried through the gaps in the rock, accompanied by the sound of children laughing. She felt Holt move from the bed, heard him pause in the bathroom doorway, but she didn't meet his gaze.

"I'll meet you down there," he said quietly, and shut the door behind him.

Zylah let out a breath through pursed lips and ran her hands over her hair, shoving the feelings down. All of them, until there was only the sound of the waterfall remaining.

She dressed quickly, following the smell of the bread and the sound of the children's laughter to a breakfast room, a table piled with food and two boys chasing each other around it.

Dalana lit up as soon as she saw Zylah approach, rubbing her hands on an apron. The Fae waved with a bright smile, moving her finger and thumb together to form an O, one eyebrow raised in waiting.

"Oh, yes, I'm fine. Thank you. Good morning," Zylah blurted.

Dalana smiled, then clapped her hands.

The children stopped, and she threw another handful of gestures their way.

"Mamma says to help yourself to anything you'd like," the taller boy said.

Their mother's hands moved again, and the boy sighed. "I'm Vor and this is Bayde. Nice to meet you."

Zylah laughed. "It's lovely to meet you, too. I'm Zylah." Kopi called out from somewhere out in the court, before settling onto the window ledge. The children gasped. "And this is Kopi."

"Can we pet him?" Bayde asked.

Both boys untangled themselves from each other, tentatively stepping closer to Kopi, who sat preening his feathers, oblivious.

"He likes it when you scratch his head," Zylah offered.

Dalana pulled out a chair, and Zylah took a seat as the boys doted on the little owl. She rolled her eyes as he cooed and trilled in appreciation, hoping to disguise the feeling that had settled in her chest.

Being in someone else's home, the food cooking on the stove, the laughter. Her father's home, *her* home, had been burnt to ash, and no matter how much she tried to place the blame on Marcus, it was all her own doing.

Voices carried from out in the passageway, and Ellisar entered, followed by the two males Zylah had seen him and Lana with the day before.

Ellisar didn't hesitate to make the introductions. "Okwata, Ahrek. This is Zylah. She's a new friend."

Okwata's chair moved by itself to the table, two large wheels rolling either side of the seat by themselves. But it wasn't the chair that snagged Zylah's attention.

For a moment she thought she saw a tail swish out from behind Ahrek, but then she blinked, and it was gone.

Perhaps the hunger was starting to get to her.

She reached for a brin fruit from the bowl Lana passed her, taking a knife to slice it into thin pieces as the children ran out of the room.

"Will you be resting here for the winter?" Okwata asked, laying a napkin neatly across his lap. "Lady Maelissa was very gracious to open her court to us during the colder months, and Ellisar and Dalana even more so for offering us a room in their home. My chair is not well suited to the snow."

"We're hoping to… help some friends," Zylah said, uncertain how much information she should supply them with.

Marcus could have eyes and ears anywhere, for all she knew.

"A risk to travel now under Marcus's rule." Okwata held her gaze. The hints of amber in his brown eyes caught the light as he looked at her, but she felt no threat from him.

"Oh?"

Ellisar scoffed.

"Fear not. You'll find no love for Marcus here." He laid plates before Okwata and Ahrek, placed a basket of pastries in the centre of the table before throwing on an apron and taking a pan to the stove.

Zylah eyed a canna cake, considering her words. Revealing that she knew about the vampires would mean answering questions, and she wasn't ready for that. Instead, she settled on, "Marcus is using old magic. We hope to find his source, to counter him with a stronger footing."

Ellisar nodded, a bowl of eggs in one hand. "A wise move. As is gathering your allies." His gaze slid to Okwata and Ahrek, and he gave them an almost imperceptible nod.

Ahrek pulled a book from his coat and slid it across the table to Zylah just as Lana took a seat beside her once more.

The book was bound in leather cord, a violet stone set into the thick leather cover, just like the stone set into the hilt of Zylah's sword.

She couldn't read the words on the cover, although that didn't surprise her, but the images were familiar as she leafed through the pages, strange creatures looming over slaughtered animals— "I've seen these before. In Kerthen."

"You've been to the Kerthen forest?" Ellisar asked.

"I lived there for a few months."

"In Pallia's name. That's a story I'd like to hear." He cracked eggs into his pan, tossing the shells into a bucket on the floor beside him.

Zylah ignored his request.

It wasn't a story she wanted to tell. Three months in Kerthen had damn near broken her, scraping by on whatever food she could hunt and forage for, constantly evading the creatures that lurked there.

She pushed the memories down. "Can you read this?" she asked Ahrek.

"Only the title. It's called A Whisper of Light."

Zylah frowned.

"You recognise it?" Okwata asked.

"I… no. Just something about the name seems familiar." She turned through more pages, her fingers tracing across the strange markings on the page, tapping her finger against a familiar one. "These symbols. I've seen them before." In Raif's library, a book on his shelf.

"This book cannot be read without a key to the symbols within it," Okwata told her.

"The one I saw was full of symbols too. I didn't understand any of it." Zylah didn't need to look up to know that Okwata was watching her carefully, but she hadn't decided whether she trusted him or his companion yet.

"Can you retrieve this book?"

"I can't, but Holt might be able to."

"Describe it to me," Holt said from the doorway, pulling out a seat opposite her. His gaze slid to the untouched brin fruit on her plate.

"It's called Song and Shadow. Dark red leather cover, half the thickness of this, gold lettering on the front. It's on…" Zylah swallowed. "On the shelf in Raif's library. Third shelf from the bottom, closest to the bed."

Holt nodded and rested his hand on the table, palm up. "Either it's warded, or it isn't there."

"Both are likely. Marcus is searching for that book," Ellisar explained.

Zylah didn't need another reason to want Marcus dead, but the fact that he sought a book that Raif merely could have handed over to him sent a slice of white-hot rage through her. She resisted the urge to stab at the pieces of fruit on her plate, wishing she could take her sword and drive it through his heart instead.

Holt reached for a brin fruit, rolling it in his palm as his gaze flicked to Zylah's plate again. "And where did you come across it?"

Okwata smiled and clasped his hands in front of him. "A tale for another time, perhaps. Zylah, Ahrek and I are going into the forest today for the nastura, I'd be most grateful if you joined us."

Kopi flew up to Zylah's shoulder. She almost looked at Holt for permission, despite how out of place she felt amongst them all. He had to speak with Maelissa, and she had no desire to be part of that discussion.

"You seem familiar, little one. Have we met before?" Okwata asked Kopi.

Kopi hooed in response, and it was enough to quell Zylah's apprehension. "We'd be happy to go with you. Kopi needs to stretch his wings."

A feeble excuse, but Zylah needed to get away from the suffocating air of Maelissa's court. And sitting around all day waiting appealed to her about as much as driving her knife through her hand. Better to be useful, and to find out whatever she could about Okwata and Ahrek at the same time.

Ahrek had barely said a word, but Zylah didn't miss the way he watched everyone's movements, the way he sat like a cat ready to pounce.

"Take some of our water too," Ellisar said. "It will save you having to spell yourselves regularly. It conceals sound and scent, lesser acts of magic. It keeps us hidden here, anyway."

Zylah tried to disguise her sharp inhale. "Are you telling me we could have just had the water when we arrived?"

"Maelissa is fond of tradition," Holt murmured.

Ellisar laughed. "Come now. You and I both know she just enjoys making people feel vulnerable before they enter her court. It was the Hall of Hallows before, now it's that blasted pool."

Zylah stared at her brin fruit. She'd already seen and heard enough of Maelissa to know precisely what kind of Fae she was. She excused herself from the table, the memory of Raif's bedroom still occupying her thoughts, wishing the emptiness inside her would swallow her whole.

She barely heard Ellisar's instructions, only offered a blank smile and let her feet carry her back to her room. Her reflection stared back at her from every mirror, a monster lurking within the glass.

The first snow was yet to fall as Zylah followed Ahrek's and Okwata's horses back to Maelissa's court. She focused on preparing the moss she'd collected for Ellisar and Lana, as a thank you for offering up their home. This particular moss was excellent for thickening stews and covering grazed knees and scrapes for the children—abundant, but entirely useful. She'd located the nastura for Lana's sister and gathered a few mushrooms and herbs to gift to the family, too. Anything to keep her mind off Holt's meeting with Maelissa, of whether he'd secured her help or not.

"Who taught you about plants?" Ahrek asked as they approached the waterfall.

He'd been quiet throughout the day, silently observing as she and Okwata discussed plants and their remedies.

"My father. Me." More than one pair of eyes watched them from amongst the trees. Sprites.

Ahrek followed her gaze. "They've been following you all day."

Zylah said nothing, only watched the eyes staring back at them. Kopi was ahead somewhere, undisturbed by the sprites' presence. If they truly were forest spirits, she wished she knew what compelled them to act, and what held them at bay. Why they hadn't helped when—

"They pay no heed to us," Okwata added, as if he'd sensed her darkening thoughts. He'd remained on his horse throughout the day, carefully packaging the nastura Zylah had handed to him, offering up his own understanding of certain plants she pointed out as they made their way through the forest, and just like with Ahrek, every now and then she caught a shimmer of something else when she looked at him.

But unlike Ahrek, what lay beneath seemed human in appearance. Rounded ears, softer features.

"Perhaps they see the shadow over you, the way you wear deceits so differently to the rest of the Fae that pass through this forest."

She never had learnt to hold her tongue, and her curiosity always got the better of her.

Ahrek flashed Okwata a look, but Okwata merely smiled.

"You're the first to notice," he said softly. Curious. Zylah made a mental note to ask Holt about it later.

She dismounted, hiding the shake in her legs as her feet hit the ground. She hadn't eaten lunch when they'd offered, content to continue gathering her plants, to lose herself in the familiarity of it. "We may have only just met, but I've seen enough to know whatever reasons you may have for hiding who you are, are not meant with ill intent. And I... I know what it's like to have to conceal yourself from people who are kind to you. It's no easy thing."

Ahrek offered her a tight smile as he handed her the reins to his horse, perhaps as much acknowledgement as he was willing to show. Whatever they were concealing, whatever lay beneath those deceits, that smile told Zylah that the truth of who they were was too great to share even with Ellisar and Lana.

"I won't say anything to the others," she added.

Okwata's horse knelt on its forelegs, head low to the ground as he unbuckled the straps at his legs. Ahrek wheeled the chair closer, but Zylah looked away to offer them privacy as he helped Okwata off his horse. She'd lied about who she was for so long back in Virian. To everyone but Holt. And in the end... when Raif, at last, knew her name...

"There's a shadow over you, too," Okwata said gently from his chair.

Zylah couldn't bring herself to meet his eyes.

Not a shadow.

Something heavier. Darker. Something that snuffed out all light and air and sound, leaving nothing but an empty husk in its wake.

9

Faerie food turned Zylah's stomach. She surveyed the table before her, the murmur of chatter around her fading into one. With a wince, she forced herself to eat a mouthful of the grains she'd piled onto her plate. Resting beneath one of the great trees, a fiddle player began a lively tune, far too jovial for her mood.

Okwata and Ahrek were talking with some faeries, and Zylah silently counted the minutes until she could slip from the table and return to the quiet of her room. Ellisar barked a laugh nearby, and her attention fell on him and Lana, looking at each other as though everyone and everything else around them ceased to exist. Ellisar sliced some fruit, placing it on his mate's plate and watching her intently as she took a bite. They laughed again at whatever silent words might have passed between them, and all Zylah could see was the love that shone in their eyes, that radiated from them both.

Guilt churned the grains in her stomach again, and she laid down her fork as a shadow passed over her plate. Cloud violas and plumeria. Forcing a smile, Zylah looked up to meet Maelissa's gaze as the Fae took a seat beside her.

"This is the longest he's stayed away," Mae said, throwing a fat berry into her mouth. A sigh. "You're young. I'm sure—"

"I'm twenty-four," Zylah said flatly, uninterested in whatever Mae had to say, or where this conversation was leading. *Who you take to your bed is no concern of mine,* Holt had told her once. His history with Maelissa was none of her business. And yet…

"Precisely the number of years since the last uprising. Curious. Where did you say you were from?"

Zylah's gaze fell to the Fae's wrist, to the coils of gold wrapped around them that cobwebbed across her hands and connected with the clawed rings at her fingers.

Kopi landed on Zylah's shoulder, ruffling his wings, and she finally shifted her attention back to Mae's face. "I didn't."

The Fae pierced another berry with a claw and waved her hand. "Don't be too disheartened. He always comes back to me eventually. It was only a matter of time. This afternoon was inevitable." Her full lips closed around the berry, dragging it from the razor-sharp claw, and she scrunched her nose with a smile Zylah suspected might have usually been reserved for children.

Zylah ignored it, along with Mae's implication. "Holt and I are friends. Nothing more." She kept the words flat, emotionless, unwilling to give Mae anything to twist and pull apart.

"Good. I hope *we* can be friends, too." Mae brushed a clawed hand to Zylah's cheek, pressing a swift kiss to the other before she pulled away. The scent of the berries mingled with the cloud violas and plumeria, and it took every inch of Zylah's resolve not to push off from the table right away.

And Zylah knew, as she watched Maelissa stride away, that the Fae said and did nothing without intention. Sure enough, she could feel the eyes of other faeries watching her as she lifted her fork and scooped up her grains. Mae had seen her discomfort and had wanted to have her fleeing from their encounter like some frightened doe. Zylah forced down a mouthful of food. She wouldn't bend. Not to Mae. Not to anyone. No matter how—

Kopi's wings fluttered once before he flew off into the trees.

"Mae's just jealous because you reek of Holt," Thallan said with a grin, sliding into place beside Zylah in the seat Maelissa had left unoccupied. Here was the rejected mate gone mad. His words slurred ever so slightly, and he rested his glass on the table with a touch too much force. The other faeries had lost interest as Thallan threw an arm over Zylah's shoulders, and she thought of Arnir's vanquicite throne, of the cuffs she'd worn for three days, polished and gleaming as if she were staring at them in her hands.

She could have sworn she felt something in her mind, like a cat brushing up against her legs. He was trying to find a way in. "The last male who tried to touch me without permission," Zylah said quietly, shrugging Thallan's arm from her shoulder and angling herself to look him square in the face, "ended up dead."

The Fae laughed. Cocked his head to one side. "You don't eat. I'm fairly certain you don't sleep. I might not be able to get past that rather impressive shield of yours, but anyone need only take one look at you to know you're damaged goods." He clicked his tongue. "You walk around like you're broken."

Thallan's green jacket was dishevelled, his blond hair a little ruffled, and he ran a thumb over the rim of his glass as he waited, watching her through his eyelashes. Zylah knew it was the wine. Knew it was probably the news of Raif's death, of hearing updates about his rejected mate that fuelled his words. But looking at him, slumped over his glass, at the way more venomous words were waiting to spill over, she couldn't blame Rose for rejecting him. Not one bit.

"Naughty," Thallan said, waggling a finger. "*That*, I heard."

"Heard what?" Holt took a seat opposite, the gods knew where he'd just emerged from, and Zylah took it as her cue to leave.

She felt his attention on her as she looked at Thallan and said, "It's been a long day." Zylah didn't wait for a response as she rose from the table. From either of them. Didn't let herself think about the two awful conversations she'd just had as she made her way to her room and slid between the sheets... that seemed to be infused with the aroma of cloud violas and plumeria.

Music and laughter carried over the sound of the waterfall, the fiddle growing to a crescendo and faeries cheering. Zylah felt none of their joy, none of their elation. She felt nothing at all.

You walk around like you're broken. Thallan's words snaked their way into her thoughts as she focused on the sound of the waterfall rushing past the cut-out in the rock.

What if I am, she'd wanted to ask him.

Because she knew the truth. Felt certain he knew it, too, had seen it in that moment he'd heard her thoughts. She was broken and hollow, and she let the emptiness swallow her up as sleep claimed her.

107

The other half of the bed was still empty when Zylah awoke, and she brushed aside any thoughts on the matter before they had a chance to fully form. She skipped breakfast, opting instead to sit beside one of the pools at the base of the largest of the falls, the only place in the court that didn't feel too stifling.

The water was cool and clear, and some faeries bathed in one of the smaller pools, giggling as they washed each other's hair. Zylah wasn't sure how there were waterfalls on both sides of the rock, whether one was some piece of faerie magic, or perhaps several.

The court felt like it was neither inside nor outside… simply contained in whatever strange magic stasis Mae had concocted. Zylah couldn't wait to leave. Two nights in that strange court and she already felt trapped, she didn't know how the others could stand it.

Okwata and Ahrek approached, and Zylah attempted to conceal her frown.

"I can see your tail again," she murmured to Ahrek as his deceit seemed to shift and bend for a moment before it was gone. "You're not from here, are you?" The first Fae were not from this world, but not too long ago, Zylah hadn't even known the Fae still existed. Ahrek and Okwata could be from anywhere in the world, for all she knew.

Ahrek looked to Okwata as he said, "We fulfilled a promise, and our… reward to ourselves was to travel. But being simple observers is not really in our nature."

A deflection.

Fine, her question had been rather pressing given how little they knew each other. "And what is *in your nature*?"

Okwata took Ahrek's hand and squeezed lightly. "Fighting for something better. Whatever that may be. Wherever we may be. Marcus is not the first king we've helped to topple."

An offer. What assistance they could provide, Zylah wasn't certain yet. But they'd had that strange book and seemed to know far more than they'd let on. Marcus was looking for the book that was missing from Raif's library, the twin to the one Okwata possessed. A story for another time, he'd said.

"Where are you from?" Zylah asked, opting to be more direct this time. If they could truly help, now was the time to ask for it, before she and Holt were to leave and move on to whatever lead Maelissa had given him.

But before Okwata could answer, something cracked. Followed by a snap. A faerie cried out, and the air in Zylah's lungs turned frigid as the sound registered. A whip. She didn't wait for Okwata's response, didn't wait to hear the whip crack again, didn't consider the consequences as she felt herself slip through the aether, moving through the court to the source of the sound.

And reappeared between Maelissa and a lesser faerie.

Zylah's chest heaved as she took in Mae's raised hand, whip ready to strike, the faerie prone before her, back already split open from the metal claws in Mae's whip. *Shit.* She'd evanesced in front of the entire court—had been taught not to expose to anyone that she could do that, not even Fae.

She crouched low and touched a hand to the faerie's shoulder, letting her healing magic pour into him as his breath caught.

"How dare you," Mae seethed. Her lip curled into a snarl and her arm reached higher to wield her whip again, but Zylah didn't flinch, didn't move from the faerie whimpering beside her.

She opened her mouth to speak, just as vines erupted around Mae, wrapping around her body, twisting over her arm and around her wrist, shattering the rings at her fingertips and pinning her into place like some grotesquely violent statue. Mae swore viciously under her breath, but the colour had drained from her face.

"Lay a hand on her, and you'll lose it, along with your arm, and maybe even your head." Holt took his time striding through the court, power rolling from him as it had a few days before when they'd met the faeries in the forest. Lest anyone consider challenging him. "Lashes are to be saved for our enemies. Don't you agree?" he said, his voice loud enough for every faerie watching to hear him.

Zylah moved a hand to the faerie's back to check the severity of his wounds, unwilling to waste any more time on risking him bleeding out beside her.

Mae was silent, seething, completely restrained by Holt's vines, but Zylah knew without looking up, the Fae's attention was fixed on her.

The faerie's wounds healed, mercifully, beneath her touch. Nothing remained but the slashed fabric of his tunic, the adrenaline that likely still coursed through him. She'd known faeries could be cruel, but the sound of the whip, the sight of the faerie's wounds so similar to her own, to the ones caused by Arnir's bounty hunter… It sent a chill down her spine that Mae would do that to one of her own. And it reminded her of Marcus.

Zylah, at last, looked up, but not at Mae. Holt's gaze slid to her as he made his way over, eyes scanning her, and only when he seemed satisfied she was fine did he turn to Mae.

He flicked his wrist and the whip disappeared from Mae's grasp, reappearing between his fingertips. Mae's face paled as a thought seemed to linger there, faeries edging closer to watch whatever was unfurling between Holt and their High Lady. Holt glanced at the end of the whip, then let it fall to the ground where vines burst through the moss to encase it, pulling it under until it disappeared. His vines receded from Mae's arms, just enough to release them. She smoothed a hand over her hair, then over the folds of her lilac gown, the jagged ends of her broken claws catching in the silk.

Holt walked around her, pausing at her side once he was again facing Zylah, only to murmur, "Spread lies about me again and I'll have you removed from this court faster than you can fucking blink. Understood?"

The court watched in silence. None stepped in for their High Lady, no one spoke, and at last, Mae nodded almost imperceptibly.

"If I hear so much as a whisper of this kind of punishment from this court again, you will be stripped of your title, and I'll appoint someone else to rule in your stead," Holt said. He'd raised his voice again, loud enough for the entire court to hear him. Mae flinched beside him but held her head high. Vines still wrapped around her body, around her breasts, up to her neck, but to her credit, she stood there as if they were part of her gown.

Holt knelt beside the faerie Mae had beaten, hooked an arm around him and helped him to his feet. And only when he'd turned away, did he release his hold on Maelissa.

Zylah took one last look at the female, jewellery and hair all displaced from Holt's vines, her dress torn where she'd attempted to smooth it, half her claws broken, and followed Holt through the court.

Faeries stepped aside for them as they made their way to one of the pools, watching silently, and all Zylah could think of was that she'd evanesced in front of them, all of them. Pain sang down her back from the strain of using her powers, but Raif's words danced around her skull. *Don't let anyone see you do that. Ever.*

Even when she'd tried to help, she'd got it wrong. Exposed herself to the whole court. Holt would do better to leave her behind, to continue what he'd started without her. He'd be faster without her, and she couldn't help, only hinder. Only slow him down.

She slipped away between two rocks as Ellisar and Lana rushed to Holt's side, helping the faerie to rest beside the pool. Her fingers grazed the vial of tonic she had in her apron, and she twisted the glass between her fingers. But she didn't pull out the cork. She gritted her teeth against the pain and closed her eyes as the thought of Oz's whip against her flesh shook through her. As the scars on her back seemed to burn with the memory of it.

If she hadn't killed him, if she'd just let him keep lashing her, everything would be different. Raif wouldn't be dead. Her father might still be alive, too. And no punishment, no amount of pain would ever be enough for her to atone for their deaths.

10

Holt had been quiet since they'd left Maelissa's court. The air was crisp and still, as if the forest was waiting for winter's icy grip. Zylah knew snow would come soon.

"Thank you for helping back there," she said when she could no longer stand the silence that had stretched out between them.

Holt merely nodded.

Heat crept into Zylah's cheeks, and she angled her horse away from him as they walked through the trees. "I evanesced in front of the whole court. Don't you have anything to say about that?" It was a rare ability, she'd been told, one she should be careful about even amongst Fae.

"You've done enough hiding in your life already. I don't ever want you to have to hide who you are again."

Oh. That was not the answer she'd expected. But given what he'd been through, what he was fighting for, it made sense. And yet… "Then why do you sound angry? Because the magic can be traced? Because I've just sent the Fae equivalent of a beacon?" She twisted the reins in her fingers, studying the green embroidery at the edge of the gloves Lana had given her. Little leaves ran along the cuffs, curling into a circle along the back of her palm.

"The court is heavily warded. Your evanescing won't be traceable beyond its perimeter."

"Then what?"

"Mae could have ripped you to shreds," Holt said quietly, anger still coating every word.

She studied his face, the way he pressed his lips together, the shades of the forest in his eyes. "But she didn't."

His eyes slid to hers. "I heard what Thallan said to you last night."

"That I walk around like I'm broken?" She didn't know what answer she wanted from him, whether he would agree or challenge her. It didn't matter. Thallan was right.

"If you fought for yourself the way you fight for others—"

"What do you think I was doing in Kerthen, day after day, night after night?" She pushed herself up in her stirrups, fingers squeezing into the front of her saddle as her temper sparked. It was her turn to be angry. She'd almost died alone in that forest, on more than one occasion.

"It should have taken a month at most to get through Kerthen," Holt said so quietly Zylah barely heard him.

She'd been waiting for him to mention it, had hoped he wouldn't piece together how long she'd been lost in that dark forest. She slumped back down in her saddle.

Not lost, exactly.

Vapour clouded in front of Holt, as if he'd sighed heavily. As if she'd pissed him off, again. "You've been through a lot, Zylah. Your father. The bounty hunter. Raif. Kerthen alone. The last

114

six months can't have been easy. Don't let this… this guilt over Raif's death be the thing that breaks you."

There was something in his tone that made her chest ache, but she said nothing. Because there was no point trying to argue with him. Her life before she'd fled Dalstead had been a lie, and her life since had been nothing but running. From Marcus, from herself.

The forest was quiet; nothing but the crunch of twigs and leaves beneath the horses' hooves, and the strange grey light that seemed to cling to everything in winter.

Zylah looked up to find Holt frowning at her, still waiting for a response. She swallowed down the guilt, too proud to admit to him that he was right. The guilt was going to eat her whole; not just because Raif had died… but because… Zylah couldn't finish the thought.

Kopi landed on her mare's head, and she watched him settle for a nap. She wished she could look inside herself and find even a fragment of the person she used to be before Raif and her father had died. The person that had run from Arnir's men with only one thought on repeat: *Live. Live. Live.*

But no matter how hard she looked, that person was gone. "Did you get what you needed from Mae?" she forced herself to ask.

"She's promised her archers."

"Do you trust her?" *After everything*, she wanted to say.

Holt handed her the canister of Ellisar's spelled water. "No. I didn't want to risk asking her about a healer."

A healer for her, he meant. She didn't tell him how deep the pain ran. How it simmered beneath her skin day and night.

Though she'd woken up again feeling better than usual, and she suspected he'd had something to do with that.

"Lana and Ellisar think highly of you," Zylah said, flicking her chin towards the canister before taking a swig. The forest had thickened, with no sign of any road or trail, the horses taking a steady pace between the creaking boughs.

"I won't pull them away from their family."

Because he had lost his own. She didn't need him to say it to know it was what he meant. How he wouldn't let anyone fight on his behalf. For him. "How do you know how to speak with Lana?"

"My sister couldn't use her voice. Lana taught her, taught my whole family how to speak with our hands so Adina never felt alone." His gaze was ahead, deep into the forest, and Zylah was certain it was his sister he saw and not the empty forest that sprawled before them.

Her back ached but she let the feeling pass through her in waves, let it anchor her to her saddle. She thought of Holt with his family, of what their meal times might look like, laughing and signing to each other, Adina beaming back at them all. Happy. Whole. And Marcus had taken it all away, taken everything from Holt, even his freedom.

She thought about the debt he owed Marcus. If there was any way out of it. Okwata's words replayed in her thoughts, and she realised a shadow hung over Holt, too. "Ahrek and Okwata didn't seem like old friends," she said at last. "Do you trust them?"

"They gave you the book, didn't they?" His voice was distant, as if he were still lost in the memory of his family.

She thought back on the conversations she'd had with Ok-wata, the knowledge he'd shared. He wasn't familiar with the plants, but he had a wisdom to him, a kind of deeper, ancient knowledge Zylah couldn't place. "You know they were wearing deceits?"

Holt raised an eyebrow as he glanced at her, and she knew he was waiting for more.

"I don't know where they're from, but Ahrek... he wasn't like any other faerie I've seen before." And why disguise themselves in a court full of faeries? It didn't make any sense.

"A risk for them to be around Thallan." Holt held out a hand and a brin fruit appeared in it. He offered it to her, but she shook her head. "You did well with him, he had a lot of questions about you."

About Rose, most likely. Zylah pushed out a breath. "It wasn't enough. Is it possible to keep him out?"

Holt studied the brin fruit in his palm with a frown. "I had no idea he'd be there; I would have helped you prepare." He met her gaze. "I'm sorry for putting you in that situation." He pock-eted the fruit, untouched, but before Zylah had the chance to protest, he said, "Mae appointed him a general after the last up-rising. If I'd known, I wouldn't have taken you there."

"A good choice for a general. Someone who can slip inside people's minds without warning." A strange match for a seer, though. Zylah couldn't help but wonder if it was part of the rea-son why Rose had rejected him.

"That particular skillset takes its toll," Holt said quietly. "Thallan's brother was driven mad by it."

"His brother?"

Holt nodded.

"Raif told me once that Rose's mate had been driven mad from the rejection."

Holt pushed out a breath. "Raif was always very protective over Rose, even though she's the older of the two. Both Thallan and Rogan loved her, but the bond is only easy to disguise for so long. Thallan caught Rose and Rogan together one day, and it didn't end well."

Zylah didn't want to think about what damage a fight between two minds could do, how it could likely rob someone of any semblance of self. "Did Rose know that Thallan was her mate?"

"I don't know. But even if she hadn't felt it…" A frown creased his features for a moment, but then it was gone. "There is very little Rose doesn't see."

So she must have known, then. Rose was… *difficult*, but not cruel. She cared for Saphi, that much was certain. And for Raif. Rose struck Zylah as someone who cared very deeply. "Maybe she loved them both."

"Maybe."

But it wasn't Rose or Thallan that occupied Zylah's thoughts… it was that Raif had lied to her about Thallan. And it wasn't the first lie, the first piece of information he'd withheld. Every time she'd pressed him about her powers, about learning more, he'd found a way to deflect, to distract her or change the subject. Had he been worried about how it might affect her? Holt had explained that Raif's magic haunted him. Did Raif think the same would happen to her? Zylah hated that she already knew the answer. It wasn't his decision to make.

The horses found a trail, barely more than a thin line of dirt that cut through the springy moss.

"How did you do it?" Holt asked. "How did you stop Thallan?"

"I thought of the vanquicite." Zylah looked at her hands and flexed her fingers where the reins threaded through them. "Of how it felt to wear the cuffs for three days. I stared at them for hours up in the mountains." Hours to think of how she might kill Oz, the bounty hunter who'd taken her and lashed her in the snow like she was cattle.

"Then you've already had more practice than most," Holt said quietly, and Zylah could have sworn that trace of anger was back in his voice, that a small flare of his power rippled the air for a moment. "There are different techniques. But few have had first-hand experience with the very thing that can nullify our powers."

He was one of those few, but it *had* affected him. "Do you think it might also be the… the piece in my back?" She'd thought of taking a tonic, but there was no way of doing that without him noticing, so instead, she focused on the weight of the vial in her apron.

"Perhaps," Holt said. "But thinking of the vanquicite as a shield, wrapping it around your mind and then releasing it, up and down like a wall. That is precisely how I was taught to practice."

"And was it enough?"

A moment of silence. "No."

Another time, that word seemed to say. As if what had happened in Mae's court still followed him. Zylah couldn't blame

119

him. The sound of the whip, the sight of that faerie's back, it had turned her stomach, and she'd been glad that there was nothing inside her to bring up, nothing to force her to her knees at the spectacle of the faerie's mangled flesh.

Even now she could feel the white-hot sting of a whip in her own skin, against her spine, the searing pain where it had ripped her flesh apart. She'd wanted to snatch Mae's whip and hurl it away, but then Holt had ensnared the Fae in his vines. From the look on Mae's face and the silence of her court, no one had ever dared intervene before.

And yet no one questioned Holt. Not even Mae. Prince of the Forest, she'd called him. Zylah watched him murmur to his horse, encouraging it up a difficult slope and wondered when he had been given the name. Why. "Prince of the Forest. That's quite the title."

"Mae and her traditions," Holt said, though there was no trace of fondness in his tone, and as quickly as it had come, Zylah's curiosity dwindled. Thinking of Mae only further darkened her thoughts.

They said nothing more until the sun reached its peak, and Zylah was forced to dismount with the need to stretch her aching muscles. That was what she told Holt, anyway, and hoped he didn't notice when she finally took a swig of her tonic.

She bit into a brin fruit, chewing slowly, quietly aware of a pair of sprites watching her from amongst the trees. She thought of the stories her father used to tell her; wondered which of them were lies, half-truths to cover up the world outside Dalstead.

"You used to eat enough for three people," Holt said, sitting opposite, a brin fruit of his own in his hand.

Zylah shrugged. "I got used to not having much to eat."

"Looks like you had more than enough back in Varda, but you gave it all away." There was a challenge in his tone, as if he wanted her to fight.

Zylah finished her fruit in silence, refusing to meet his gaze, searching for the sprites instead. They were the living embodiment of nature, her father had told her. The spirit of everything. Holt had told her once that they were drawn to his magic. Maybe they were just drawn to *him*? Prince of the Forest. Zylah wondered if the sprites knew that title, too. But she was in no mood to ask questions. She took a swig of the spelled water and snatched up her sword to practice. Zylah hadn't practised once since Holt's arrival.

"Raise your elbow," Holt said after her third strike at nothing.

She huffed, slicing at the air again. "Show me."

From the corner of her eye, she saw him brush off his hands and rise to his feet. He held out a hand and a sword appeared in it.

"Show me how to do that, too."

"So demanding today." A smile tugged at the corner of his mouth. "We need a map. Get the one from our... my room at the tavern."

"How?"

"Close your eyes." She did as he asked. "Think of how it feels when you evanesce. Picture the map. And call out to it. Here." His fingers brushed her cloak just above her heart.

Zylah held out her hand, palm upturned, and concentrated. She felt the same rushing sensation as when she evanesced, but then it ceased. Something appeared between her fingertips, but when she opened her eyes, it was barely a scrap of paper. A corner of the map, to be precise.

Holt laughed quietly. "Not bad for a first attempt." The rest of the map appeared in his hand, and Zylah resisted the urge to punch him in the arm.

He set it on a rock beside them. "What remains of the Aquaris Court is here," he said, pointing to the Delmara Peninsula.

"How long on horseback?"

"A while. But Mae wasn't convinced the spell would cover evanescing outside her court, so we can't risk it."

Zylah agreed. She'd been too afraid to evanesce in the months since she'd left Virian, for fear it would get her noticed, and Holt had confirmed the magic was too strong to risk it. "Can Marcus evanesce?"

He surveyed the forest, and she wondered if he'd heard something. "Aurelia can."

Marcus had said as much back in Virian, but now Zylah questioned everything she'd ever heard him utter. Everything was a game to him, a play, a prospect waiting to be pounced upon.

Holt folded up the map, slipped it into his pocket. "Marcus uses whatever he can to his advantage, anyone that might be an asset to him."

Even if it meant having his son killed. Rage sparked in Zylah's chest. "If I ever see him…"

"Then we better make sure you're prepared. Sword."

Holt swung at her before she'd barely got a decent grip on her blade, but she parried the blow regardless. Zylah let herself get lost in the movements, let herself forget about why she was there and what they had set out to do.

He smirked. "Good."

"Who taught you to use a sword?" Zylah asked as they moved.

"My parents," he said, and she didn't miss the hint of pride in his tone.

"Both of them?"

"My father was an excellent swordsman, and my mother was the only Fae who could best him. You're using her sword."

Zylah stilled. "Why didn't you tell me?"

"I didn't think you'd take it if I did." Another challenge in his expression.

She examined the blade anew, the twist of the vines around the hilt, the stone in the centre. "The purple stone?"

"She said it was in honour of an old friend." He raised his sword again, encouraging Zylah to continue.

They repeated the action: strike, block, strike, block, until Zylah had removed her cloak and their breath was clouding in the cold air in front of them.

It felt just like it had back when he'd been training her in Virian. It was so easy not to think, to just get lost in the movements. Easy. Effortless.

He raised his sword to strike again but Zylah pivoted away from his blow, using her short height to duck low behind him as he righted himself. The moment of surprise was all she'd needed to touch the tip of her sword to his chest as he turned to face her, a wide grin on her face to celebrate her victory. So easy to get lost like this.

Holt laughed, swatting the sword away with a bracer. "Don't get cocky."

"Afraid I might surprise you?" Zylah asked, a breath of laughter escaping her as she ducked again, pivoting away from him. But this time she let him catch her, let him slide his arm around her waist and pull her back to him as she dropped her sword and reached for her dagger instead.

She felt his puff of laughter in her hair as her dagger pressed into his ribs. "You always surprise me," he said, his other hand closing around hers over the hilt of her blade.

Zylah looked up at him, their laughter replaced with something else, her heart beating hard in her chest. She let him take the dagger, let him toss it away from them, just as a roar tore through the forest and Kopi cried out from amongst the trees.

Zylah sucked in a breath. "That sounded like—"

"Asters. Get the horses. Ride east, and don't stop, I'll catch up to you." Holt looked in the direction of the roar, but Zylah didn't move away as she gathered up her weapons.

"I faced worse in the Kerthen forest than a couple of Asters, Holt." Far worse.

He tilted his head as if he were listening, but he didn't take his eyes off her, all trace of the lightness from moments before gone. Whatever words he seemed to be warring with, he instead settled on, "Over there, we'll secure the horses."

Kopi cried out again as Zylah attempted to soothe her horse. "How many?"

"Three, I think." He led his horse deeper amongst the trees, and Zylah followed. A bank provided a small amount of shelter, disguising the horses amongst thick bushes.

Zylah *had* faced far worse than Asters in Kerthen. But as more of the creatures called out to each other—strange cries that sounded as if they were injured—she knew there were more than three headed their way.

She followed Holt through the trees away from the horses, a rush of adrenaline spiking through her. Without her evanescing, she was at a disadvantage. A big one.

"Stay together," Holt murmured, as if he'd had the same thought.

She looked up at him, hoping her expression was more convincing to him than she felt. "Just like old times, right?"

He huffed a breath in response, vapour clouding in front of him, and paused. They crouched side by side, and again Zylah had the strangest sensation that the sprites were watching them.

The first Aster appeared through the trees, rising from all fours onto its hind legs. It had the head of a wolf, thick horns and fangs and blood-red eyes, exactly as Zylah remembered. Wiry black hair covered its enormous body, its ghastly lips pulling back in a sneer as it sniffed at the air. Only it was wounded, just as Zylah suspected. Which didn't make any sense, because nothing would be foolish enough to attack an Aster... would it?

Holt charged for it before Zylah could voice her concerns. He was at a disadvantage without his evanescing, but Zylah didn't stop to dwell on that fact. As Holt occupied the Aster's attention, she circled it from behind, swiping her sword at those strange hind legs that ended in hooves. The creature screamed as her blade hit bone, the force of her swing shaking through her. The beast twisted, but Holt was faster, his sword piercing through the Aster's chest as it reached for her.

Blood sprayed from the wound as the creature howled, falling to the ground with a heavy thud. Echoing howls called out around them, branches snapping and breaths puffing.

Five Asters surrounded them, all wounded like the first, claw marks gouged into their flesh; one even had a splinter of bone glimmering white against its black fur. One sniffed at the air, huffing and chittering as if it were communicating with its two companions. It was afraid. And angry. And the only thing worse than a wild beast was a frightened, wounded one.

"Fuck," Zylah breathed, her back pressed to Holt's.

This was definitely worse than Kerthen.

11

Three Asters broke off towards Holt, but Zylah didn't have time to watch what happened next. The remaining two swung for her, all fangs and claws and snarls. She rolled between the feet of the first, bringing her sword up to slash against its legs.

Only a flesh wound.

The beast roared and swiped for her, and she pulled herself to her feet, blade swinging.

The second Aster was distracted, and as Kopi's cry tore through the forest, Zylah sucked in a breath. He was drawing the other Aster away from her.

The one she'd wounded growled as it faced her, blood dripping into wiry black hair. It towered over her on its hind legs, clawed hands swiping wildly at its face. Zylah stared into the creature's hideous red eyes, wet and glistening with blood. It couldn't see clearly, which meant that whatever had wounded it had been intelligent enough to go for its eyes.

A chilling scream sounded in the distance, and the Aster jerked its head in the direction of the cry, a small whimper escaping from its ghastly lips.

Zylah tightened her grip on her sword, pushing her fear down into that hollowed-out place inside her. She backed up a step towards a low-hanging branch, and before the Aster could reach for her, swung up onto the branch and shimmied up as high as she could get. Teeth snapped at her cloak, but Zylah didn't falter.

She paused on the branch, heart racing in her chest, watching the Aster as it flinched at another cry from wherever they were coming from within the forest, its enormous head swinging left and right, hot breaths puffing from its snout in clouds. It was right beneath her, its horns dangerously close to her soft flesh as she slammed her sword into the creature's neck, shoving the blade down until she felt it connect with bone.

The beast shrieked, clawed hands reaching for her sword and ripping her from the tree. Zylah's breath left her in a broken gasp as she hit the ground, her sword narrowly missing her face. The Aster staggered forwards a step before it let out a wet sigh, collapsing to the earth and trapping her legs beneath it.

The moment Zylah wasted looking at it was a moment too long, and this time fear flared within her, sharp and sudden. The second Aster howled and charged her. Zylah pulled one foot free, and the Aster roared. She heaved at her other leg with frantic movements, the Aster closing the space between them, claws shredding through flesh just as she pulled her foot from its hold. Adrenaline numbed the pain, and Zylah didn't dare look down. Her sword was in her hands and she struck and slashed and sliced, blood spraying across her face as the Aster did the same, nothing but sheer desperation urging her to keep going until her final blow struck the Aster's head and it stilled.

Zylah didn't see it fall. She fell back in the dirt, clutching her sword to her chest and watching the first few flakes of snow fall. Tiny wings fluttered at the corner of her vision, the sound of the strange scream-turned-roar getting closer, leaves and vines creaking and cracking.

And then darkness.

Zylah blinked.

Looked down at herself, which was the first thing that told her something was wrong. She was looking *at* her body, lying still in the dark. She crawled over to herself and pressed a hand to her wrist to check her pulse, but her fingers were nothing but a shimmer of blue.

"Am I dead?" she whispered, inspecting her ethereal hand and arm as she knelt before her physical body.

"Do you want to be?"

Zylah whirled at the voice.

A woman.

Braided hair and violet eyes like her own, a shimmer of blue edging her silhouette in the dark.

Zylah looked at her body again. Swallowed. She had wanted to live. To see the world. To be free. And yet… She had nothing to lose now, *no one*. "Sometimes," she whispered. Because sometimes she wished it had been her instead of her father. Instead of Mala and Asha. Instead of Raif.

She heard her name as if it were being called from somewhere far away and looked over her shoulder into nothing but darkness.

"Do you know who I am?" the woman asked. She held herself like the statues Zylah had seen so many times beside doors and in streets and outside temples.

"Pallia," she murmured.

"Blood of my blood. You have been through so much. But so much more awaits you yet."

"Zylah!" the voice from before called, and this time Pallia looked in the direction the sound came from.

Zylah frowned, her gaze travelling down her body, her real one. One of her legs was covered in blood, a wound so deep she could see bone in several places. The other didn't look much better. Her face was ashen, her chest barely rising and falling. Kopi sat on her chest, tiny eyes quietly watching.

"You sent him to me?" Zylah asked.

"I did."

"Is he yours?"

"Very few things in this life belong to us, Zylah."

Something thumped, like a fist on a wooden door, and Zylah looked over her shoulder again into nothing. She looked back at her body, bleeding out in the dirt. *I thought you wanted to live*, Holt had asked her once. *I do*, she'd told him. And no matter how much she hated herself for what had happened to Raif, to her father, to Mala and Asha, a tiny spark of that version of herself still remained.

"Can you help me?" Her voice broke on the words, like something inside her had been cracked open.

Pallia smiled. It was full of warmth, familiarity. She reached out a hand and brushed a strand of hair from Zylah's eyes. "What is it that you want, Zylah?"

"Second chances are for people who deserve it," Zylah murmured, reaching out a hand to Kopi. He inclined his head towards her fingertips, but they passed right through him. She didn't deserve to go back. And yet… she felt a tug… the pull of her physical body, a feeling in her chest screaming at her to stay.

"Zylah!"

Pallia took her hand. Squeezed it, and Zylah felt the warmth as if she were real. As if they both were. "There are people waiting for you," Pallia said. "People who need you."

Wood snapped and cracked; the thumping increased.

"Marcus is doing dark things with old magic." Pallia's voice became rushed, eyes darting in the direction of the sound. "You must stop him. Get the stone removed. It was put there to keep you safe."

"I don't understand."

Pallia smiled, ran a thumb over Zylah's cheek. "I'm so glad I got to see you."

"Zylah!"

Light broke through the darkness, and Zylah sucked in a breath so deep she started coughing. She closed her eyes, pressed a hand to her throat, and when she opened them again, she was back in her body, the pain in her legs like a fire had been lit across her skin.

Something cracked and creaked again, and Pallia was gone. Kopi fluttered around Zylah's chest, making tiny, distressed noises.

"Zylah!" It was Holt, and he'd broken into… whatever it was she was inside. "Don't you fucking die on me." He was breathless, his movements frantic as pieces of wood splintered and sprayed beside Zylah. "We had a bargain," he said, his hands trembling as they rested on her face, eyes wild and full of concern as he looked down at her. She'd never seen him like that, never seen such desperation in his eyes.

Zylah reached a hand up to his cheek, ran her thumb along the blood that had smeared across it. "You always find me," she murmured, her eyes closing, her hand falling from his face.

She heard his intake of breath, felt the warmth of his hands near her wounds, his magic pouring from him. "You agreed to live, and I agreed to help you find your family, remember?" he said roughly.

The pain cut so deep, in every nerve, every vein, she could barely breathe through it. "What happens if I don't? Will it hurt you?" Her fingers curled around the hilt of her sword, squeezing against the pain. "The bargain?"

"Just stay with me," he pleaded.

She tried to hold on. Tried to focus on the sound of Holt's breathing, of his comforting scent filling the tiny space between them. But darkness slipped in, unbidden.

>»»» «««<

Zylah's eyes fluttered open, her fingers brushing against the hand at her waist. Holt's hand. She ran her fingers over the bracelet she'd given him, the bell tucked between the leather. She flexed her toes to test her legs, covered by a rough blanket that Holt had no doubt summoned from somewhere. They ached, but she was certain the bone was no longer exposed.

Holt stirred behind her, his arm tightening at her waist as she moved.

"Sorry," he said, loosening his grip. His voice was hoarse with sleep, and he began to pull his arm away. "The snow. It's cold. I couldn't risk moving you." He slid away, the cold rushing in at once in the space he'd occupied.

"Where are we?" Her eyes adapted to the darkness, to the tangle of vines and leaves that arched over them.

Holt must have been sleeping with his back against the wall of the structure when she awoke, with her body propped up against his.

"The sprites made you a shelter. I… adapted it."

Zylah shivered, shuffling back over to him.

He laughed softly and draped an arm around her shoulders. "How are you feeling?"

"Like an Aster just clawed half my leg off." Zylah lifted the blanket, looked down at the scraps of fabric from the thigh down where her trousers had been and ran a hand over the smooth skin. No trace of the wounds remained, not even a hint of a scar.

"That about sums up everything you missed." His voice was still rough, and back when she'd only just met him, she'd have thought it was with irritation, but she knew better now. Knew *him* better. He was worried.

Zylah was too cold to dwell on that, her mind still reeling from—*Pallia*. Gods above. Had she dreamt it? She closed her eyes, leaning into Holt's warmth as she tried to separate dream from reality. "Where's Kopi?"

"He's fine. He's outside keeping watch."

Very few things in this life belong to us, Zylah. Pallia's words echoed on repeat. *Get the stone removed. It was put there to keep you safe.* Surely it had just all been in her mind, nothing but a fever dream brought on by the pain, the loss of blood. "Do you think the dead look over us?" she asked quietly.

"Why do you ask?"

Zylah pulled at a thread on the blanket, deciding on how much to tell him. "My father told me that once. That we are their legacy."

"I used to think my family looked over me. Hoped it, really. But after a while I realised…"

"Realised what?" She twisted around to look up at him, her face close to his.

Holt's gaze dipped for a moment, but then his eyes met hers, pain flickering there for a heartbeat before he shut it down. "That it wasn't right to tether them to me. That they weren't mine to keep."

That was the hardest part about letting go, Zylah had learnt. She'd thought about that on so many nights in Kerthen. How to hold onto the people she'd lost and yet be at peace with the thought that they'd moved on to whatever came next. She searched Holt's eyes, and though she hated that he understood what that felt like, it made her feel less alone. He had always made her feel like she wasn't.

Zylah cleared her throat, forcing her attention back to the blanket.

"I don't know what my legacy will be," Holt said. "But it will be something of my own making. Nobody else's." He pulled away to rummage through a bag, pulling out a bundle of cloth and handing it to Zylah. "We lost a horse. Can you stand?"

She nodded, unravelling the fabric he'd handed to her. Another pair of trousers. The attack came back to her in fractured pieces: the Aster's fear, the pain in her leg. That strange sound in the forest.

"I'll give you some privacy," Holt added, raising a hand to the wall of twisted roots and vines before them. She watched in fascination as the roots untangled themselves, spiralling around each other to make an opening in their little shelter.

It was his voice she'd heard, calling her name. Snow blew in, and Zylah pulled the blanket tighter around herself. *Just stay with me*, she'd heard him say.

"Holt?" she asked as he stood outside, his back to the opening of the little shelter. "You told me once you have nothing to lose. Do you still feel that way?" She shrugged into the trousers, pulling her boots back on and fastening the laces. *She'd* had nothing to lose, she'd told Raif when she wanted to join the uprising. And then she'd lost him. Her father. Had left her friends behind.

Holt's attention was on the forest as she stepped out into the snow, snowflakes peppering his hair and falling onto his eyelashes as he turned to look at her. "No." There was a weight to the word. A finality. But then he said, "There's a town just east of here. We can make it by nightfall."

Zylah surveyed the structure he'd made, *adapted*, already covered in a thick layer of snow. She wanted to ask him what had made him change his mind—who.

He could have met someone in the six months she'd been away, deserved to be happy with someone.

But she said nothing, just shoved aside the feeling that crawled along her skin, made her feel as if her bones were hollow and empty.

135

Holt held her sword, a bag slung over his shoulder, following her gaze, his brow pinched. "I'd prefer to dismantle it, but more magic is a risk."

"Leave it. Let the sprites decide." *Get the stone removed.* It was a dream, surely. But she'd heard Holt. Heard his voice so clearly, calling to her. The wildness in his tone.

She focused on keeping her breaths steady; closed her eyes and searched for the tiny ember she'd seen inside herself when Pallia had come to her, the spark of the person she'd been before her life had turned to shit. She didn't want to die, but she didn't know how to exist like this, either, and she'd fought not to let that feeling consume her in Kerthen.

Zylah was certain, if she truly could look inside herself, that there would be nothing left now but ash. Kopi landed on her shoulder, and with a heaviness she hadn't realised had settled over her before, followed Holt across the snow.

12

Snow blanketed the forest as their remaining horse cut through the trees. One of their mares had been taken down by an Aster, and Zylah had kept her distance as Holt had gathered their things.

Pallia was a dream. She had to have been. Zylah shivered at the memory of it, of how real Pallia's hand had felt against her cheek.

"We'll be there soon," Holt said quietly, easing her back to him, just a fraction, in the saddle to keep warm. He'd been quiet since they'd left the shelter. Distant. He'd lost a lot of friends, Zylah knew that. Her thoughts drifted to the way he'd carried her back to his cabin after she'd escaped from Arnir's bounty hunter, of how he'd found her, stumbling through the snow.

"You broke rule number two," he said over her shoulder.

This close, she could feel his deep voice rumble through her. *No hurting each other.*

He'd said it the first day they'd met. And she'd known he'd meant it, could sense that he would never do anything to hurt her. It was those words that had helped to chip away a little of the lingering hold the prince still had on her, had made her feel safe in Virian. She'd never once doubted him.

"I didn't know bargains could hurt if one party died." Zylah still knew so little about her heritage, and the first opportunity she got she intended to rectify that.

Holt was quiet for a moment, the mare's steady breaths clouding against the flutter of snow. "I'll honour our bargain as soon as I can."

"I know." Zylah hadn't put much thought into meeting her real family. Part of her didn't want to know the truth. If they were gone, like her father, it would just be another loss she didn't know how to find her way through. And if they weren't, would they tell her the truth? Or would they hide it—lie to her as everyone else had? *Hypocrite.* She'd done nothing but lie since fleeing Arnir's gallows.

The forest thinned out and they joined a dirt road, with only a few tracks visible through the fresh snow. The road was empty at this hour. No guard torches lined the way, but whether that was unusual for this part of Astaria, Zylah couldn't say. A sharp wind blew from the Depths to the north, that much she knew from what she'd taught herself over the past few months, the frigid air biting at her cheeks.

"I've been trying to find a pattern in your abilities," Holt said as Kopi landed on the mare's head.

"Oh?"

"You've passed through wards; you can see through deceits. You blocked Thallan out."

Zylah was grateful Holt couldn't see her face twist in frustration. "None of those were very successful. The wards at the safe house… fine. But the deceits? I couldn't see through them entirely, only a peek. As if someone had pulled back a layer for a moment, but only a small corner." Kopi preened his feathers in front of her as she thought about it. "And Thallan… I didn't keep him out at all. The second I let my attention slip from the vanquicite, he was in."

She'd felt his presence in her mind as if he'd dragged his fingers across it. To some, Zylah supposed, it might have felt like a caress. But to her, it just felt like a violation. She shifted in the saddle at the memory of it, wanting nothing more than to shake off the feeling of him brushing against her thoughts. He'd been like a loose thread at the hem of a tunic; one tug and the whole thing would come undone. Zylah gritted her teeth at the thought, at the stark similarity between them.

"Did you notice anything in Kerthen?" Holt asked, as if he knew she wanted to change the subject.

It was inevitable, Zylah supposed, that she would become what she loathed the most. But she had no choice. "No. I only used magic once." Through the light snow, Zylah surveyed the cluster of buildings up ahead, so few it could barely be called a village. The day had slipped away from them, and though she was hungry, the bitterness of her lie coated her tongue. She was just as bad as the rest of them.

Holt stabled their horse and led the way to the brightest of the buildings, a small tavern, the air thick and stuffy after they'd been so long out in the cold. Zylah took a seat in a dark corner, angling herself so she could keep an eye on the occupants as Holt spoke to the bartender about a room. She could imagine the discussion she'd have with him; she'd protest about taking the bed, and he'd tell her there was no way he'd let her sleep on the floor after she almost died.

For a moment she considered telling him how close she'd been. So close she'd hallucinated talking to a *god*—no, not a god, an original Fae. *Blood of my blood*, Pallia had called her, as all Fae were. Descendants of the original nine.

A lute player strummed his instrument beside the bar, one elbow dangerously close to a tankard of ale that would no doubt be topped up by another patron in thanks for a fine tune. Given the size of the village, Zylah wondered if every single one of its occupants was inside the tavern, laughter and chatter filling the air.

The lump in her back ached again, but rummaging through her bags for a vial might draw attention from those around her. Her eyeglasses had been lost during the Aster attack, so she kept her head down, her face angled away from the light as she watched the lute player, wondering if Kopi would be comfortable out in the snow and if Pallia had sent him, whether he even felt the cold at all. She shook her head at such a ridiculous thought just as a drunk patron knocked over a stool at the bar.

Normally a drunk would have been berated for such behaviour, but the barman didn't pay him any heed. Zylah frowned, her gaze roving over everyone in the tavern.

Holt returned with a tray of steaming food and took the seat beside her so that he too could keep a close eye on the room, Zylah presumed.

A handful of the drunk's companions helped him off the floor, laughing with the barman and downing another round of drinks, but something about it seemed off. Zylah's fingers grazed the dagger in her bracer as she kept a close eye on the group.

"I didn't handle things very well with Mae," Holt said, passing her a plate of meat and potatoes.

"It looked like you had everything under control to me." The way he'd spoken to Mae, the way he'd bound her with his vines. The way every faerie in the court had stopped at his words. He knew exactly what he was doing.

Holt frowned as he poured water from a pitcher and handed Zylah a cup. "I want you with me next time. At the next court."

"With you?"

"In any of the meetings. Some are friends, like Mae. Some aren't. But I'd like you to be present for all of them."

Zylah arched a brow as she stabbed her fork into a potato. "Friends like Mae?"

"Just friends." He held her gaze as he said it, and Zylah didn't question him. "The next court is still a few days' ride from here."

"My knowledge of the courts is still limited." She'd read all the books in Raif's library, but none covered the faerie courts or their locations, or what was left of them. They were mostly story books, save for a few, and now she thought of it, it seemed a strange collection given Raif's character. No history books, nothing of the world. Perhaps he coveted an escape from the realities of Virian more than she'd realised. She pushed her potato around her plate, swallowing down the lump that had formed in her throat.

Holt leaned back against the bench, his attention solely on her, his plate of food untouched. "There was a time when the courts overlapped with human lands, when they were vast sprawling territories. Those that remain now are small. Not quite as small as Mae's but closed off from humans. Sheltered. Protected."

Trapped.

Mae's court had been trapped, whether they admitted it or not. Even just a few days had been stifling.

Zylah took a bite of her food, and at last, Holt seemed content to start on his meal.

Of all the books she'd read, none explained the workings of the downfall of the Fae, only that humans had driven them all to this *sheltered* life they now lived. Not that that privilege extended to all of them. She'd taught herself about the human lands in her time away from Virian. The history she should have learnt as a child in Dalstead, the history her father and brother should have told her, but instead, they chose to follow Arnir's rules.

Stupidity meant compliant citizens; knowledge meant questions. Gatherings. But why had her father and brother hidden those things from her, too? "It seems strange that humans could overthrow the Fae," she said at last between mouthfuls of food.

A group entered the tavern, a priestess and her acolytes, easily identifiable by their fine cloaks. Zylah knew Holt tracked their movements just as she did.

"Not all faeries have powers like yours," he said. "They have strength, yes, speed that humans don't possess, but they have families too, weaknesses to be exploited. For every faerie that walks these lands, ten humans walk alongside them. It's why most conceal themselves now. Safer to go unnoticed, to remain in hiding, rather than face being used by the humans, or worse."

Zylah glanced around the room. She'd already surveyed the space, the patrons, where the doors and windows were. None of the occupants seemed as if they were Fae wearing deceits. It was just a room full of ordinary humans, none of them so unusual that they would turn a head. With the exception of the priestess, perhaps. "How many courts remain?"

Holt ran a thumb around the rim of his cup. "The last I knew, there were still twelve courts. All part of the four kingdoms."

Saphi had told her there were four kingdoms. Holt's and Raif's families were from two of those, but the other two... Raif's library had held a book on Holt's line, but no others. The books had been mostly human story books, some in languages Zylah couldn't read, like the twin to the book Okwata had given her. Nothing of the courts and who ruled over them. "Are there any courts that don't sit within a kingdom?"

A nervous chatter seemed to settle across the tavern. Zylah tried to hear snippets of conversations, but perhaps it was the effect of the day catching up with her because she couldn't quite focus on their words.

"Good question," Holt said, following her gaze across the crowd with a frown. "And one that, before the last uprising, could have got you killed."

"I thought Marcus was the only unfair ruler."

"The Fae haven't got things right for many years." He sighed, one arm tucked under the other as he held his cup. "My parents were good people. But they weren't always fair. They had to make decisions that ultimately favoured Fae over humans. And it cost them."

"Cost them what?"

Holt's frown deepened, and she hated that she knew what his answer would be. "Everything."

Living in a cage was no life if that was what the other courts were doing. And there was something else he wasn't saying. Zylah chewed her lip, wondering if he was ever going to trust her enough to tell her whatever it was he was keeping from her. Maybe that was why her father and brother had never told her the truth… maybe they thought she'd cause too much trouble for them, risking Zack's position with Arnir.

She'd finished every last mouthful of her food, the first full meal she'd eaten in… too long. The drunks at the bar cheered as the lute player started another tune, revellers raising tankards, words slurring, or maybe it was just her exhaustion. The hours on the horse, the food, the Aster attack, it had depleted her, but she didn't want to sleep, not yet.

"Tell me about Kerthen," Holt said, as if he'd sensed her restlessness, as if he too wanted to shake away whatever shadow had fallen over him since the attack.

Zylah looked up to meet his gaze, silently questioning how much she should tell him. *I'll find you*, he'd promised her when they'd said goodbye outside of Virian. And he had.

A commotion at the bar pulled her attention away from him, but still, she couldn't hear what words were being exchanged, could only observe the hands that rested on shoulders, the weary faces that knocked back their ale. She knew the look in their eyes, recognised their nervous glances at the door. They were afraid of something.

"On that first night I remembered my father's words," she said quietly. "He'd told me once that if you can light a fire your morale will be raised; if you fail it will plummet like a stone. But I was too afraid to light a fire, so I wandered in the dark until dawn."

Holt was utterly still beside her, the air between them seeming to hum for a moment and though it barely lasted the span of a breath, she knew it was his magic.

"I ate plants to begin with," Zylah continued, wiping at the crumbs on the table. "I figured out how to track, but I had no bow. Hunting and tracking felt familiar to me, seeing without being seen, since I'd already spent enough of my life doing that. And tracking was just about observing. About watching and listening. Looking for the scuffs and disturbances of other animals. But I soon learnt that few animals were safe to eat."

"How?" She knew he was watching her. But she didn't want him to see the truth—how her time in Kerthen had broken her. Didn't think she could stomach his disappointment.

Zylah shrugged. "By examining what was left behind." It was her turn to frown. "One day I came across a corpse, not my first, but I took the bow and quiver that lay beside it. And I used it to hunt swamp crabs. My training with Zack was basic, you saw that for yourself, but I had plenty of time to practise."

Holt's mouth twitched. "Crabs?"

She felt her face involuntarily grimace at the thought, but a small laugh escaped her despite herself. "If I never have to see another crab again, I'll die happy. I could make one last a week, but they're fast and if you don't hit them right, they scuttle away with your arrow."

Holt chuckled softly, some of the tension seeming to ease out of him.

She told him about the creatures she'd seen, some that he had names for, others he didn't. About the nights she didn't dare go to sleep because they were close by. She told him everything, and it felt good to share it with someone, to hear it spoken out loud and know that it hadn't all been in her head.

Well, almost everything.

There had been difficult decisions—mistakes. A bargain that should never have happened, should never have been possible when Zylah let herself dwell on it, but telling him now wouldn't change that it had.

"But then I ran out of arrows," she said at last, "and I was forced to leave Kerthen for good." The group at the bar had grown bigger, but Zylah was far too tired now to make out what they were saying. She waved a hand over her shoulder. "The pain was too much to keep digging for plant roots to grind down into food, and I knew I couldn't stay."

Holt's hand slid across the table, but the lute player abruptly stopped, and all heads turned towards one of the patrons.

The priestess.

"A great darkness is coming to Astaria," she said, walking amongst the crowd. The patrons mumbled to each other in hushed voices, some pulling their partners close. "And we must protect ourselves." The priestess took the hand of one of the barmaids, the prettiest one, the one most eyes would pay attention to, and looked at her with equally beautiful eyes.

"We must join together and spread light across our lands, to chase these shadows away as we have done before, time and time again. We cannot falter. For the sake of our children, and their children. Join us."

She cupped her free hand under the barmaid's chin the way one might hold the face of their child, a look of unrelenting love written across her face.

So polished. So practised. Zylah resisted the urge to roll her eyes. She knew a lie when she heard one. The priestesses were merely preying on humans to use them. And yet… "A great darkness. Does she mean what I think she does?" she asked Holt so quietly only his Fae ears would hear.

He leaned closer, angling his head to hers as they watched the priestess move through the crowd, her acolytes close behind her. "Marcus has done little to keep the vampires a secret. They suffer from bloodlust when they're first created and can take time to settle. But an army requires substantial numbers—one that is made, relying on creating soldiers; it's taking him much longer to grow his force. But this could be a problem."

"The priestesses?"

"You said it yourself. They're recruiting a human army. If they have their own cause, they're less likely to fight with us." Against Marcus. He didn't need to say it. "I'll need to send word to Zack; he isn't just our liaison, he's coordinating the Black Veil back in Virian."

It was no surprise Zack was coordinating them too, despite the risk to his life. Despite the fact that Marcus would have had eyes and ears across the city.

Zylah hadn't truly stopped to think about the magnitude of what was coming, but now she understood Holt's eagerness to recruit allies.

The Fae were truly at risk of being wiped out for good. She watched the acolytes pulling aside the members of the crowd the priestess had spoken to, murmuring into drunk and eager ears as the realisation settled.

War was coming to Astaria, and its people were more divided than ever.

13

It took more than a few hard days of riding through snowstorms to cover any noticeable distance. The flurry had become so thick that on a few occasions, they'd almost turned back. Holt had purchased another horse for them back at the village, and they'd since been heading east, towards the Delmara Peninsula, towards the next court Holt hoped would offer aid.

If Aurelia and Marcus were slowly making an army, if the priestesses were recruiting humans to their cause, Astaria was on the brink of an all-out war. Whether it was months away or a year from now, it was coming, and though Maelissa had made no promises about her archers, Holt hadn't let that deter him. If anything, it had only seemed to urge him on.

Travelling together had been as easy as it had been to live together in Virian. Uncomplicated, Zylah thought as she dismounted and discreetly knocked back the contents of a vial. She'd need to make more of her tonic soon. There were plenty of ingredients to be found in the forest—but making it without Holt noticing would be an issue. This pain was her tithe, and she would pay it. She ran a hand through her mare's mane as she made a mental list of everything she would need, which plants would be accessible in the forest and which she might need to buy.

Holt had dismounted the moment the snow had thinned, surveying the forest as his horse rested. Zylah followed his lead, looking for any signs in the snow. Nothing but animal prints dotted the white powder, their hot breath clouding in front of them the only motion breaking the stillness. They moved in comfortable silence until something snagged Zylah's attention.

"What is it?" Holt asked. He was a short distance away, seeing to the horses, but still on alert.

"Tracks," Zylah said, crouching to take a closer look. "Something big. Two somethings." As large as a wolf, but no claw marks.

Holt moved closer as the snow fell again. "Identical?"

"Yeah," Zylah said with a frown, her attention on the snowflakes that had fallen onto his eyelashes.

Holt offered a rare smile, glancing at the forest about them. "Didn't Jora ever teach you not to taunt your prey?" he called out into the snow.

Zylah arched a brow, just as a grey wildcat approached them, fangs bared as it growled. But Kopi didn't cry out, didn't even budge from his position in one of the nearby trees.

"Suggestions?" Zylah murmured, glancing sideways at Holt. He folded his arms across his chest, waiting. For a moment Zylah wondered if he could talk to animals, whether he'd been silently communicating with Kopi this entire time. Prince of the Forest.

It wouldn't be the strangest thing she'd seen, by far.

The trees around them rustled, snow-laden branches creaking in the breeze. Light flashed, and Zylah raised a hand to shield her eyes.

"Imala's tits, Kej. I thought we said I was the evil twin today?" A young woman dropped down from a tree, landing lightly and barely making a dent in the snow. Silver-grey eyes met Zylah's, but they were soft, unthreatening. Her black hair was short, exposing her pointed ears. She was High Fae.

"Two big identical somethings," Holt said with a smirk.

Another flash. The wildcat turned into a young man, dressed in similar cobalt attire to the female, his black hair braided close to his head, the same silvery eyes, the same pointed ears. Their clothes were fine, with silver details at their cuffs and hems. A uniform, perhaps, Zylah thought.

"Holt. It's been too long." A wide grin stretched across the male's face as he reached out a hand.

Holt threw an arm around the Fae, pulling him close. "You're looking rather dressed up for a trek through the snow."

"It's for Jora's funeral."

Holt frowned. "When?"

"You'll make it if we leave now," the female said, shoving the male aside to give Holt a hug. "Come on."

"They won't let him in, Rin," the male added.

"Of course they fucking will."

Holt cleared his throat as the two continued to bicker. "Kejin, Aerin, this is Zylah."

"Rin," the female said, a wide grin on her face. "Kej for my halfwit brother. Sorry if we startled you." She held out a hand in greeting.

"No… not at all. Kopi would have warned me if there was trouble."

Kej scoffed, a hand pressed against his chest. "Oh, Zylah. How you wound us. Two fierce wild cats, prowling through the snow."

"I… Sorry?" Zylah glanced between the two of them. "Can you change into anything else?" She couldn't resist asking. Zylah had never met a Fae that could change their form.

"Anything *else*? Where did you find this one, Holt?" Snow-flakes settled in Kej's hair, peppering it with white. His grey eyes sparkled with mischief as he folded his arms in mock offence, and Zylah held back a smile.

Holt led the horses from where he'd left them nibbling at some exposed grass. "Kejin and Aerin can only shift into one form. Multiple forms are incredibly rare."

"They're a fucking children's tale, is what they are," Rin added.

"What happened to Jora?" Holt asked.

"That bastard held on for as long he could. Kept saying he wanted to live to see *it*, whatever the fuck *it* was." Rin watched as Kopi flew down to Zylah's shoulder. "He never made much sense a hundred years ago when you were around this way more, so you can imagine what we all made of him lately. Everyone thought he was a mad old goat. But seeing you turn up, today of all days, maybe he wasn't as mad as we all thought." Rin nudged Holt's elbow with her own.

"Or he just let you think he was mad," Zylah said quietly, following Rin and Kej beyond the thickness of the trees to the snow-covered rocks beyond them.

She'd taken the horses from Holt to let him walk ahead with his friends.

"Fuck me, she's sharp, this one. I like you." Rin glanced over her shoulder and flashed a grin.

"Thanks. I'm sorry about your friend." Zylah didn't meet Rin's eyes as she said it, coward that she was. But a funeral… she tried to keep her breaths even and steady, to focus on putting one foot ahead of the other.

"Grandfather." Rin sighed. "He was a good man. Holt can attest to that."

Holt nodded. A moment of silence settled over them, and Zylah wasn't about to try and fill it. She knew where their thoughts would have taken them all. Where hers had taken her. She pressed her fingernails into her palms, letting the pain ground her.

"Is it true what they're saying about the vanquicite, Holt?" Kej asked after their path cut deeper into the rocks and angled up a slope.

In the snow, it had been difficult to see much ahead of them, but now Zylah could make out the rock face looming above, the way the path inclined alongside it. They were heading up, and she hoped her huff of breath would pass for physical exertion rather than surprise at Kej's words. Any talk of vanquicite could only mean trouble.

Holt said nothing at Kej's question, pausing only to help Zylah ease the horses up the rocky slope. Zylah held her breath, wondering if she should press him.

"We heard they're mining it," the male added. "But for what?"

"An army." Holt rubbed a hand against the end of the scar on his neck. He hadn't told her about the vanquicite mining. *He still doesn't trust you.* An army of vampires was terrifying enough. But armed with vanquicite? No wonder he'd wanted to find Marcus's source of old magic. The scales were severely off balance.

They stopped ascending, the path levelling out to a platform, rock curving around it until they reached a heavy wooden door, so discreet Zylah would have missed it had she not stopped before it.

Rin swiped a hand across the dusting of snow and tapped her knuckles on the old wood. "Open the door, Nye. You know it's us."

"You have visitors," a female voice called out.

Kej rolled his eyes. "You know who he is, too."

"And the girl?" Nye asked.

"My name is Zylah, and this is Kopi. The horses don't have names, but you can name them, if you'd like."

Rin and Kej flashed their identical grins.

"Did my cousins tell you to say that?" Nye's voice was flat, stern.

"No." Zylah stroked the horses' noses one by one, waiting for a response.

A sigh. "Fine. Come in, we're going to be late if we don't hurry."

The door creaked open, snow blowing into the darkness beyond. Nye had been standing in the dark, Nye who… stepped out of the shadows as if she hadn't been whole moments before. As if she'd been part of the shadows beyond her. Zylah thought of the cheating Fae she'd fought back in Varda as wisps of shadow receded *into* Nye's body.

She had the same rich brown skin as her cousins, but where their eyes were silver-grey, hers were a deep amber, almost golden. Her black hair reached to her shoulders in tight spirals, sectioned with gold rings, and like her cousins, she wore fine clothes; funeral attire, Zylah now realised, but hers were a deep red. A sheath sat snug across her chest, laden with knives, completely at odds with the rest of her outfit. She looked Zylah up and down as if she were sizing her up. She likely was, given her position at the door and the blades on display.

Nye reached up to the wall beside her and pulled an unlit torch from its sconce. "I always said you were useful for something," she muttered, handing the torch to Holt with a half grin.

"Good to see you again too, Nye." There was no embrace this time as Holt took the torch, the tip sparking to life almost immediately.

Nye stepped to one side to let them in, shadows flickering against the walls in the torchlight. "Jora will be grateful you're here to see him into the afterlife."

"I'd have preferred to have seen him before," Holt said flatly, leading the way into the darkness.

Afterlife. Zylah had never believed in it. Had never let herself hope it might be real. As a child, she'd been taught the gods welcomed those who were good into the afterlife with open arms, but even then, she'd seen it for the lie it was. No one was good in Dalstead. Only her family, all of whom had turned out to be liars.

And Kara.

Had Kara known the truth? Sweet, naïve little Kara, who would never hurt anyone. Or had that all been a façade too?

She felt the wards as soon as she stepped through them, the caress of magic as it rolled over her skin. Holt's deceits had been lifted, the points of his ears poking through his hair. But even with her keen eyesight, she could make out little of the tunnel ahead, could tell nothing of what lay beyond the darkness, but Kopi gave no warning, no sign of unease.

"Humans cannot pass through our wards," Nye said, her eyes flicking to Zylah's ears. "Nice to meet you, Zylah. Don't listen to anything these two tell you, they're full of horseshit."

"Cat shit," Kej corrected with a grin.

"Asshole," Nye muttered.

Zylah nodded in greeting as she guided the horses in, the door just wide enough to accommodate one at a time. "You're cousins. Can you turn into a cat?"

Nye arched an eyebrow. "A fox, of sorts, so I tend to keep away from these two when they're out on patrol." She took one of the horse's reins and followed Holt down the passageway, nothing more than a hollowed-out tunnel through the rock.

"Afraid of a little rough and tumble?" Rin asked as Zylah tried to unpick what a *fox of sorts* might mean. She could almost feel Nye's eyes rolling, and she wondered if they were always like this, or if it was their attempt to stave away the heaviness of what they were walking towards. Focusing on the flicker of the torch-light was the only thing keeping the ache in her chest from splitting her in two. She wasn't ready for a funeral.

"The army is why you're here, isn't it?" Nye asked Holt, ignoring her cousin.

"If Malok will see me," Holt said quietly.

An unfamiliar smell permeated the air, and although it wasn't unpleasant, it reminded Zylah of the fish cart back in Varda. The passageway twisted to their left, widening out on every side until they reached an area where the torchlight no longer bounced off the ceiling.

Nye hummed. "Malok will be glad you're here today. Jora's death has hit him hardest."

"Our people are afraid, Holt," Kej added.

Holt glanced over a shoulder, shadows flickering across his face. "With good reason."

"What are we going to do?" Rin asked.

Holt sighed. "Everything we can." He turned away from them, darkness seeming to swallow the torchlight.

They left the expanse of the room, cave—whatever it was, heading up another unlit passageway. A breeze hit them as they ascended, and a constant, unrelenting roar seemed to reverberate through everything. They passed no one, and Zylah wondered if the last uprising had anything to do with that fact. Holt had told her when they first met that few Fae remained outside of Dalstead, and now she finally understood what kind of numbers *few* actually meant.

That the few who were left here were afraid told Zylah all she needed to know.

Nye followed her wondering gaze as daylight seeped into the passageway, revealing carved pillars and arches in the rock. "It's said that Imala's lover built this for her." She ran a hand down a carving of waves, and they seemed to move beneath her finger-tips. "A safe haven. Magic flows freely here."

Imala. Another of the original nine Fae.

It was strange to think of them as anything but gods—but it made sense to Zylah that the humans would have seen them with their powers and their beauty and assumed that they were.

They turned another corner, where two guards greeted Nye and took the horses from them. The roar was louder here, the breeze now a bitter wind as the passageway opened up into a large courtyard of white stone, high above a stretch of blue.

The ocean.

Zylah sucked in a breath as she made her way to the wall on the far side of the courtyard. She'd read about it in books, seen the great expanses at the edges of maps, but she'd never truly appreciated the enormity of it, the power, as waves slammed against the rocks far below, the rhythmic crashing as they ebbed and flowed, crested and broke. It was mesmerising to watch.

"Holt," a female voice said, but Zylah didn't look away from the water, not yet. "Good to see your reins have been loosened enough for you to join us today."

That was enough to turn Zylah's attention to the High Fae who stood before them.

Long braids coiled with silver and gold rings swept over one shoulder, a silver gown the same colour as her eyes fell snugly over her curves and pooled to the floor. A delicate diadem sat across her forehead, fine strands of silver and gold twisted together, small sapphires dusted amongst the strands. The female's face remained impassive despite her comment, her attention falling on Rin and Kej.

Holt didn't move to greet her, merely gave a polite incline of his head, barely a bow, as he said, "Cirelle."

"He's in there if you want a moment." The Fae gestured to a blue door off to her right, torches set into sconces on either side. *He.* The body of Holt's friend, Zylah presumed, as if he weren't dead. As if a funeral wasn't about to take place.

Zylah pressed a hand to her stomach, dragging Cirelle's attention to her at last. The Fae frowned, and Zylah silently prayed she wouldn't throw up all over the white stone at her feet. She couldn't go to a funeral, considered evanescing anywhere but there, but there were too many eyes on her, too many pairs of ears listening.

Holt made the introductions. "Zylah, this is Cirelle, High Lady of the Aquaris Court."

Zylah introduced herself, offering a polite dip of her chin, unsure what to make of this High Lady after her last experience. Holt glanced at the blue door, and Zylah knew he was hesitating for her benefit. "Go," she murmured.

He shot her a grateful look before excusing himself to pay his respects, and Zylah watched him leave, fingers twitching at her sides with the urge to do something for him, anything to ease the pain of what lay on the other side of that door as Rin and Kej spoke quietly with Cirelle behind her.

The High Lady circled her slowly, her gaze resting on Kopi at her shoulder. "I suspect you have quite the story to tell." A faint smile danced across her face before she turned and left through a doorway on the opposite side of the courtyard.

Zylah barely registered the words. Barely registered Rin and the others leaving after Cirelle. She was too busy focusing on the crashing waves. Too busy telling her feet to comply, to turn back to the wall and to breathe slowly. She took in the cliff edge as it fell away beneath them, the way windows and platforms cut into the white rock as far as she could see. The passages they had walked through must have been carved through the cliffs as if this were a small city set amongst them.

The vanquicite sent a splinter of pain searing through her, and she welcomed it. Her tithe. And it wasn't enough. Would never be enough for what she'd done. For six months, since Raif's death, time had stopped. Had they held a funeral for him, without his body? Had they spoken words of remembrance? She wasn't sure she wanted to know the answer.

As a child, Zylah had watched funerals in Dalstead with Kara, hiding out of sight. Once, after an old woman's burial, Kara had scratched their names into the trunk of an old tree. *So that everyone will know we were here,* she'd said, breathlessly. *That we existed.*

Zylah gazed across the water, to where the sky seemed to melt into the sea. Bhuja was out there, a continent twice the size of Astaria. A bird cried out, its call not unlike the pained sound she'd heard back in the forest before the Aster had attacked her. She frowned at the memory. Had Holt seen what the creatures were running from? Now was not the time to press him on the matter.

An army of vampires, armed with vanquicite. Neither humans nor Fae would stand a chance against Marcus, and perhaps that had been his goal all along. Holt had said he coveted Fae with powers… to turn them? To make them into creatures loyal only to him?

Astaria was on the precipice of change, and for the first time since his death, Zylah was glad her father wasn't alive to see it.

He was too old, too frail to endure a war. But Raif... he would have wanted to fight. To make a difference.

Her attention drifted to the room Holt had entered, where he no doubt sat beside the body of his old friend. How many more friends would he lose before this was over? *Don't you fucking die on me.* Did his guilt swallow him whole every night, too?

The waves crashed beneath her, spray misting her face and prompting Kopi to ruffle his feathers at her shoulder. Running from Arnir had been about her freedom, no one else's. Running from Marcus had initially been about that, too. But she couldn't ignore what she knew now. This was so much bigger than her, and her freedom, her fate, was now tied with the rest of Astaria's.

And for as long as she could, Zylah was willing to fight.

14

"Your first time seeing the ocean?" Cirelle asked, stepping into place beside Zylah.

Jora's body had just been committed to the water, swirling waves swallowing the bundle of cloth in seconds, and already a celebration of his life had begun around them. High Fae filled the terrace, drinks in hand, music matching the chatter of voices.

"I was raised in Dalstead under Arnir's rule. As a human." Zylah didn't know why she offered up the information, why she felt a little lighter in Cirelle's presence, but the words fell freely from her lips. "My schooling was limited to the very basics: letters, numbers, the gods." Her attention shifted to Kopi in a small alcove, nestled from the wind, and Cirelle followed her gaze. "My father taught me his love of plants, and I believed the books I shared with my friend were just that, stories. Believed the storybooks I read back in Virian, too. Up until a year ago, I didn't know what I was, didn't know the gods were Fae."

It was a risk, to be so honest.

But lying had got her nowhere, had done nothing but complicate things, and Zylah was done with it.

Cirelle's expression remained impassive, as if she were used to people confessing their histories to her in a single breath. "You're offering up a lot of information about yourself."

For a moment back in Varda, it had humiliated her. The sum of all the lies stacked up on top of each other; that no one had supplied the information to her freely when she was in Virian. She'd felt a fool. But how could they tell her, if they didn't know? If they assumed it was common knowledge? She sifted through her recollections of Raif's books, trying to pick out what was history and what was fable. All of them were written as a story, perhaps because Raif considered it too great a risk to keep any evidence of the Fae in his home. She pushed out a breath, choosing her words carefully. "Secrets and lies only ever seem to cause pain."

"And you're tired of hurting?"

"Something like that."

Zylah's attention snagged on three males, their gazes lingering on her for longer than they should, their lips upturned in an unmistakable sneer as they sipped their drinks and spoke amongst themselves.

"Half Fae are rare these days," Cirelle offered, her eyes roving over Zylah's ears, across her face. "Mortals, *humans*, are too afraid of us to invite us into their beds, so to meet someone like you…"

Zylah waited.

She knew Holt was seeking allies who were tired of the division, not in favour of it. Perhaps that was why he'd brought her along; because she represented both sides of this war. But this court had wards to keep humans out, for safety, or because the

Fae here detested them, perhaps the latter given the response of the males opposite.

Cirelle reached out, a quick squeeze of Zylah's hand, but there was nothing spiteful about the gesture—it was soft, gentle. Reassuring. "I was in love with a human once. Long before I met my husband," the Fae said.

An offering. In return for the truths Zylah had imparted.

"We've not always been fair to humans. We haven't always handled things the right way. But so many of us are tired of this strange existence we find ourselves in now. Living in seclusion. We want nothing but peace."

Zylah studied the Fae's face, her silver eyes and the way her lips pressed together. "Freedom."

Cirelle nodded, turning her attention to Holt and a male that Zylah had realised soon into the funeral service was Malok. "My husband has had a very different experience. It will take a lot to win him over."

"But you think we can?"

Malok rested a hand on Holt's shoulder, but it seemed like an apologetic gesture more than anything. Holt looked up to meet her gaze, his eyes flicking between her and Cirelle.

"Time will tell." The Fae dipped her chin, her brows pinching together as she watched Rin and Kej approach. Though they looked a lot like their father, it was their mother's eyes that gleamed at Zylah as they approached, both with a glass in each hand.

Cirelle raised an eyebrow and took the fullest glass from Kej's hands, before shooting a swift look at them both and wandering into the crowd.

Zylah hid her smile at the silent scolding Cirelle had given her children.

"So half Fae, huh? What's that like?" Rin asked as she passed a glass to Zylah. Fae ears missed nothing.

"You can shift into a wildcat, and you expect me to believe you're interested in my half humanness?"

Kej scoffed before knocking back his wine. "Father always taught us it was good manners to ask our guests about themselves."

Zylah resisted the urge to comment on Cirelle confiscating one of his glasses. "You have your mother's eyes, both of you."

"The shifting ability comes from our father. And it's fucking great, to answer your question," Rin said with a dazzling grin.

"So how did you and Holt meet?" Kej asked, discarding his glass on a tray and reaching for another as a redheaded Fae ambled through the crowd. Zylah didn't miss the heat in Kej's gaze as he stared after her, or the knowing smile the Fae flashed back at him as she looked over her shoulder.

In the past, she might have blurted out a lie. Some kind of cover-up that most people might have bought. But these were Fae. And Zylah was tired of lying. "I was running for my life from Arnir after killing his son. Holt found me running."

"Only you didn't kill him, did you?" Nye asked, snatching the glass from Kej's hand before he could down it.

Zylah had no idea where she'd come from, but then she hadn't really been paying attention to the bustle of the crowd, had been too busy trying to keep herself together throughout the funeral service, soul-deep exhaustion weighing her bones, making her feel brittle.

Zylah looked up into Nye's eyes, intent on focusing on the Fae before her and not the memory of Jesper killing Raif. "No."

"We've been keeping tabs on Jesper since word of Arnir's death reached us," Nye said as she rested against the wall beside her cousins.

So they had numbers then. Eyes across Astaria perhaps, where Holt did not. Holt seemed to have a history with these people, was familiar with many of them. He'd chosen their route carefully—this part of Astaria was nothing but the peninsula curling into the ocean, and Zylah doubted there were any humans living beyond the boundary of the court, cut off from the mainland. Which meant the help he sought was here, with the Fae they stood amongst now. How long did they have to secure aid before Aurelia and Marcus succeeded in building their army, and how many would help? She studied the contents of her glass, letting the lull of conversation and laughter around her drown into the waves below.

Rin elbowed Zylah gently. "None of us have seen a vampire up close. What was he like?"

"The same disgusting lowlife he was when I tried to kill him. Only worse."

Rin was quiet at that. Neither Kej nor Nye spoke, but not out of fear, Zylah thought, some silent promise seemingly passing between the three of them. Her attention fell upon Holt and Malok again, at the way Holt nodded at Malok's words.

"We want the same thing he does," Nye said quietly, following Zylah's gaze. "Holt has done a lot for our family over the years, things not easily forgotten."

"Does everyone here share the sentiment?" Zylah asked.

"Father has a difficult history with humans," Rin murmured, snatching another glass from her brother.

Zylah waited as the three Fae shared another look. "So I hear. But?"

"Our existence here is simply that—existing. There are those who live beyond what's left of the courts in secrecy, but that's not the life we want. The life we deserve," Rin said as Kopi flew down to Zylah's shoulder. "A half Fae with Pallia's owl."

Zylah rolled her eyes. "Not you as well."

"This is where Zylah tells you how many coppers she'd have if she received one for every time someone mentioned Pallia and Kopi." Holt had joined them, but Zylah hadn't needed to look up to know that. She caught his eye as she finished her wine, her gaze falling to the way he'd opened the top buttons of the fine jacket he'd changed into for the service, to the way he took up space in the court the same way he had in Mae's. Those around them seemed to regard him with the same respect the Fae had back in Virian, though here he was not their leader. Here he stood alone, asking for their help, and still they treated him as if he were royalty. Which, Zylah supposed, he was, yet he never used the title, never needed its weight.

Kej rested an arm on his sister's shoulder and leaned in, eyes glassy from the wine. "How many coppers?" he asked, and Zylah remembered herself, remembered that the others were still standing there beside them.

"Three," she said at the same time as Holt, one side of his mouth lifting.

Nye shot them a smile before she slipped away into the crowd, a blond-haired male hot on her heels. The redhead

167

beckoned to Kej, and Rin quickly dispersed into the celebration behind them, leaving Holt and Zylah alone.

"I'm formally meeting with Malok tomorrow; I'd like you to join me," Holt said, offering Kopi a light scratch on his head. The little owl hopped off Zylah's shoulder into Holt's palm, puffing out his chest in satisfaction.

"Am I here as your friend or as your example?"

"Example of what?" Holt reached over Zylah's head to deposit Kopi safely back into his alcove, and she ignored the warmth of him, averting her gaze to avoid meeting his.

"Of humans and Fae coexisting," she said at last, taking a step away so she didn't have to tilt her head back to speak to him.

"You're here because I need your help. I can't do this without you."

Zylah had to turn away from the look in his eyes. "I'm sorry about your friend."

"We parted on good terms. I have no regrets when it comes to Jora."

"And Raif?"

"Raif was… complicated." He shifted beside her, and Zylah knew the expression that would have fallen across his face, the pinch of his brow, the tightness in his mouth, but she kept her attention on the party instead of meeting his eyes. The three males from earlier had disappeared, mercifully.

Before, the music had been slow, quiet. Sorrowful and sweet. Now the tempo was faster, a musician beating their instrument like a drum between plucking the strings. Couples danced together, lost to the music, bodies moving as if they were aching to be anywhere else. Or maybe they enjoyed an audience—the people of this court were certainly not shy of showing affection. Then again, Raif had never shied from it, either.

A stab of guilt pressed at her chest, and she rested her empty glass on the table beside her, loosing a breath between tight lips. If she let the guilt surface… if she gave it space to breathe— "What I hate the most is that I can't go back and change it. That I can't take back the things I said. The things I didn't say."

"Zylah."

"Did you have a funeral for him?" She looked up to find Holt watching her, his hair a little more ruffled than it had been a few moments before.

"A small service, yes."

"Good."

A line appeared between his eyebrows. "He loved you."

"Then why did he lie to me about so much? So many seemingly little things that keep stacking on top of each other, things he hid from me, and I can't…"

"Zylah."

"He even lied about knowing you were training me. Why would he do that, Holt?"

Holt's frown smoothed out, and in its place was the same blank expression she could never quite decipher in the past. "We grew up together. He was…" A quick pinch of his brow, and then it was gone. "Like a brother. But Raif was competitive, particularly when it came to me."

"There are the helpers, and then there are the tricksters, the deceivers," Zylah murmured, lost in a memory.

Holt studied her, waiting for an explanation.

"Raif told me that once. Maybe it was a warning." She couldn't meet his gaze again, so she watched the Fae dancing before them, willing herself not to think back to the festival of Imala and the time she'd spent with Raif.

"He loved you. From the moment he laid eyes on you."

"For six months I've torn myself apart over that. He told me he loved me, and I never said it back."

"You cared for him deeply, everyone knew that."

The music stopped, dancers broke away from their partners or walked off together into the crowd, and Zylah's heartbeat was so loud in her skull she'd have given anything to silence it along with the music. "Not the way he loved me."

"Maybe it wasn't the kind of love you wanted it to be. But it was enough. Take it from someone who knew him his entire life."

The truth—the ugly truth she'd been fighting with for months and couldn't hold onto any longer, sat on the tip of her tongue. *No more lies.* "I used him," she said so quietly it was barely a whisper. Zylah turned to her friend. "I hate myself for it. But I think I… *I know* I used him to get over what happened with Jesper. I just needed…" To feel in control, for one decision to be hers. And it had been that way with Raif, in the beginning. He'd made her feel comfortable, at ease. Made her feel like she could move past what happened with Jesper and move on from it.

"He wanted to help you. Whatever you felt for him was strong enough to cause you this much pain." Zylah was only half listening to Holt's words. "Raif was happy. So were you. Everyone could see it. I'm sorry—"

"Don't finish that sentence. You don't owe me an apology for anything, Holt. You lost him, too."

He lowered his gaze, emptied the contents of his glass. "What else do you think he lied to you about?"

Zylah had known for a while Raif hid things from her. She was new to their world, to what was happening with the uprising, so she wasn't sure she could fault him for that.

Not entirely.

"I think his reluctance to teach me anything about magic was what stung the most. You said he had a complicated relationship with his own abilities. But it felt like something else. It felt… stifling. Why would he lie to me about knowing you were training me?"

"Like I said, he was complicated. Competitive. When I asked him to meet you at the gardens, all I told him was that you could help, that you were capable. But I didn't think…" He swallowed, but he still kept his expression blank, a look of indifference she'd come to recognise now as anything but. "My scent all over you, from the tavern, it would have been like a challenge to him at first."

Zylah shook her head. "Deceivers."

"He didn't use you. And no matter what you've told yourself, you didn't use him, either. Raif was flawed but, he was doing the best he could. And so were you."

Zylah let the words sink in. She wanted to believe them. Truly. She did care for Raif deeply, but—*Maybe it wasn't the kind of love you wanted it to be*. It wasn't. Zylah had known that for a long while back in Virian. And they had been happy together, for the short time they had. It wasn't perfect.

Raif wasn't perfect, but neither was she.

And maybe it was enough, that fleeting happiness.

That it existed.

"Did you know?" she asked at last. "Did Rose tell you she'd seen Raif's death?"

"No," Holt said quietly beside her.

She searched his face for any hint of a lie, but all she saw was his raw honesty, and she had to look away from it.

"I know I haven't exactly done a lot to earn your trust. But can we make a deal? No more lies from here on in." She looked up to find him watching her still. "Only truths. I can't live that way anymore."

"Everyone has secrets to keep," Holt said, and Zylah could have sworn there was an edge of sadness to his voice. But then the corner of his mouth lifted. "Truth number one—"

"You both look like you could do with a top-up." It was Rin. Followed by her brother and his redhead, and Nye.

"Rin's hiding," Kej said with a gentle elbow to his sister's ribs, his other arm hooked around the female at his side.

Zylah raised an eyebrow.

"Father's been trying to pair me off for ages with a male from another court, but he has about as much charisma as my top button," Rin added, knocking back the contents of her glass.

"And he's a bit too proper for Rin, isn't he?" the redhead beside Kej added with a giggle before pulling him away to dance.

"Proper?" Zylah asked.

"Old fashioned. Thinks touching hands in public is far too outrageous and a chaste kiss to the back of the hand is absolutely obscene," Nye explained.

Rin rolled her eyes dramatically. "Can you imagine what he'd be like in bed? I don't have time for all that. I can lie still on my back when I'm dead."

"I think we can all drink to that," Zylah said with a smile, clinking her glass against Rin's. Her eyes met Holt's, but before he had a chance to speak, a chilling scream tore through the celebration.

15

The music stopped; dancers scattered. The whine of metal against metal told Zylah more than just a handful of swords had been drawn by the guards, and instinctively she reached for the dagger she kept tucked into her wrist bracer.

A charred hand fell upon the white stone that was the only barrier between the court and the water far below, and then another, and with a chillingly animated swing a creature hauled itself over the wall.

Not a creature.

A male Fae.

Or it had been, once. Zylah sucked in a breath as she realised its skin was not charred, but decayed, pieces of flesh missing entirely and exposing a mass of sinew and bone beneath. It smoothed a shaky hand over its skull as if it were used to there being hair there, as if it were a gesture it might have once made, and then it paused, frowned in confusion. As if it wasn't sure how it had got there.

And then Zylah noticed the thing's eyes. They were wholly black, like Jesper's.

"Stand down!" Cirelle commanded as the guards took a step closer.

The creature's head jerked towards the sound of Cirelle's voice, the movement unnatural, head tilted to one side as if it were assessing prey.

"You will not harm me, will you, my friend?" She reached out a hand as Rin and Kej flanked her sides in their wildcat forms.

Zylah hadn't even noticed them shift. Nye was gone too, but Holt remained beside her, arms folded, and this close she could feel the tension coiling in him.

"Come inside, Nevan, let us see to your wounds," Cirelle said with a slight tremor in her voice. She took one more step, and the thing screamed. It was the same sound Zylah had heard back in the forest, the sound that had the Asters on edge. *The Asters.* A chill danced its way down her spine, and for the first time, Cirelle's cool composure faltered. The Fae took a stumbling step back, hands smoothing the fabric of her dress to try and disguise the tremor in them.

The guards waited for a command, positioning themselves before Cirelle and Malok. Malok's eyes were fixed on his wife, and Zylah wondered if something had transpired between her and the creature before it had become the thing it was before them. If Cirelle felt his attention on her, she didn't meet her husband's gaze.

Kopi called out a warning from his little alcove just as more decayed hands landed on the wall, and more of the strange creatures hauled themselves up over it. Guards sprang into action, swords swinging. The creatures were unnervingly fast, but Zylah needed a moment to observe, to look for any weaknesses she could exploit and a way to ensure she was a help rather than a hindrance. Rin and Kej dived into the mix, snapping and tearing at the creatures with teeth and claws and snarls, and a shard of fear wedged its way under Zylah's ribs. The Asters were frightened of these creatures, and there was no time to warn anyone.

Holt evanesced into the fray, a sword appearing in his hand and driving through the chest of the thing before him. Only seconds had passed since Cirelle had beckoned to—*what had she called him?*—Nevan, yet the entire balcony was littered with entangled bodies and the clash of weapons.

Cirelle. Zylah blinked, calculating the distance between Cirelle and Nevan, who hadn't taken his eyes off her. She evanesced just as Nevan charged, her wrist closing around Cirelle's and pulling her through the aether. They reappeared a few steps away and watched as Malok swung a sword across Nevan's middle.

Malok looked directly at his wife as he drove his blade through Nevan's heart.

"Can I take you somewhere safe?" Zylah asked, her fingers still wrapped around Cirelle's wrist, the Fae's other hand pressed flat against her chest.

"I will not leave my children." Cirelle snatched her wrist from Zylah's grasp; surveyed the brawl as if she were about to throw herself into it.

"Can you fight?" Zylah flipped her dagger to the hilt and waited for Cirelle to make a decision.

The Fae nodded, fingers closing around the weapon and Zylah took that as her cue to leave her unattended. She unsheathed another dagger from her boot, evanescing behind one of the creatures as it clawed at a guard, and slammed her blade into its calf. The thing shrieked as she dragged the hilt down, black liquid oozing from the rotting flesh before she snatched her dagger and evanesced away.

All she could do was make use of what she had: her dagger and her evanescing, and that meant small, quick cuts, in and out, moving between the aether, between bodies, between the Fae and strange creatures, helping whoever she could with fast, precise blows of her blade. Buying them precious seconds in the hope it was enough to help tip the balance against the strange beasts.

She moved until sweat dampened her tunic, until her breathing became heavy and her chest tight and her back burned with the effort.

One of the wildcats cried out, and Zylah didn't have time to think, just evanesced to the creature clawing at it, her hand reaching for the ghastly thing even as she reappeared. Her fingers closed around the rotting flesh at its wrist, and before it could even turn to face her, she evanesced them both across the wall, over the churning ocean below to release it before evanescing back to the wounded Fae. The manoeuvre hadn't even covered the span of a blink, and just as well, or she'd have followed the creature tumbling to its death in the roiling water below.

"Aerin," Cirelle called out, rushing to her daughter's side. The Fae pressed a hand to Rin's flank, blood seeping too quickly through her fingers.

Zylah was already lightheaded from the evanescing, had already succumbed to the throbbing pain in her back, but there was too much blood, Aerin's breaths coming out heavy and wet.

So Zylah sucked in a shaky breath and pressed her hand over Cirelle's. "Here."

Pain bloomed through her shoulder blades, through her chest and into her heart as she summoned her power, willing the healing magic to flow from her to Rin. The grey fur was almost entirely crimson beyond Cirelle's hand, the jagged edges of a wound visible beyond the Fae's fingertips. Even as tears ran down her cheeks, she kept one hand pressed over the wound, one hand gently stroking the soft fur.

Zylah sighed as the magic poured from her, as the flow of blood ceased. She was vaguely aware of things slowing around them, of Malok barking commands at his guards. Kopi landed on her shoulder, burbling his comforting noises, and it was enough of a reminder to Zylah to stay present, to not let herself sway and sink into the stone beneath her, no matter how much she wanted to. The wound had been deep; her magic still pulled from her to fix it.

Kej rushed to his sister's side, fingers stroking through her fur, eyes darting from Zylah's hands over his mother's fingers to Zylah's face. "Thank you," he said breathlessly, blood splattered across his cheek.

She nodded, too exhausted to speak. Only when she was certain the last of the damage had been repaired did she remove her hands, pressing them to the stone beside her to keep herself upright.

Rin made a sound somewhere between a purr and a rumble in the back of her throat, her nose nudging against Zylah's knee.

"Don't shift yet," Kej said quietly, scratching a finger behind his sister's ear. "Give yourself a minute."

Sound advice, Zylah thought, or perhaps she mumbled it as she pushed to her feet, because Cirelle looked at her strangely. She hadn't removed her hands from her daughter's flank, just sunk her fingers into the fur as Rin's ribcage expanded and contracted with each laboured breath.

Zylah staggered over to a bench against a nearby wall, fingertips reaching for the vial in her pocket, willing herself to stay upright. She pushed off the cork with her thumb and brought the glass to her lips with shaky fingers, taking the contents in one as she closed her eyes.

"Don't waste your tonics." The bench dipped, and Holt's scent wrapped around her.

Zylah smiled weakly but didn't open her eyes. The tonic was already doing its job; the pain in her back had eased a little, just enough to take the worst of the pain away. "You were occupied," she said, hoping the shake in her voice didn't show. "Otherwise I'd have tapped on your shoulder."

"We both know you can't reach."

She laughed quietly but kept her eyes closed as the tonic continued to work its way through her system. "What were those things?"

"We call them thralls."

Zylah opened her eyes at the sound of Kej's voice. He had an arm wrapped around his sister, who held a hand to her side in her Fae form. Cirelle's cerulean shawl covered her, and Rin dug her fingers into the fabric where she held the two halves together.

The wound had healed, but the pain would still linger. Zylah knew that all too well from experience.

"They're vampires that haven't properly turned—half-dead Fae," Rin explained as their mother helped Kej lower Rin to the adjacent bench. "And they do whatever their master bids them."

"The Asters were afraid of them," Zylah said quietly, willing her face to remain impassive against the lingering feeling that still held onto her. The healing had almost depleted her, and she wanted desperately to lie down. But not here. Not yet.

"They're rather difficult to kill." Nye had joined them, kneeling beside her cousin to rest a hand against her cheek.

Zylah surveyed the terrace. Pieces of thrall were scattered everywhere: limbs, torsos, heads. Guards had already begun a gruesome clean-up.

"I dropped one," she muttered, trying to stand and failing.

Holt steadied her, his hand resting on her back as he eased her onto the bench beside him. He was quiet as she sagged against him, but she felt his flow of magic, ground her teeth together as he eased more of her pain.

"You dropped—" Cirelle began.

Kej shot his mother a look, before patting Zylah on the arm. "It'll be in several pieces on the rocks below, Zylah, I wouldn't worry about that. Nicely done, though."

Zylah didn't return his smile. *Half-dead Fae.* Only Marcus would be sick enough to attempt to turn the Fae into vampires, knowing that many of them wouldn't survive. Perhaps he didn't care whether any of them did, and they were all simply soldiers to him. Slaves to do his bidding.

Holt was silent beside her, and Zylah was grateful for it. She didn't want to explain the vanquicite to the others, not yet, and thankfully he hadn't mentioned it in front of their audience.

180

"We anticipated Nevan's return," Rin said as her mother sat beside her. "It's why we were patrolling the forest earlier."

"We hadn't expected there to be so many of them, though," Kej added.

Zylah gave a weak laugh, watching a pair of guards haul the remains of another thrall over the wall. "Seems like you were well prepared to me." Her attention shifted to Malok, barking instructions at his guards. A splatter of black—thrall blood, Zylah realised—dotted half his face, and for a moment she thought she saw something strange beneath it. But then he turned to the light, and whatever she'd seen was gone. Her attention fell to the sword at his hip, stained black along with his clothes.

Malok dismissed the guard beside him as he made his way over. "We lost two guards, but no guests were harmed." He looked between Holt and Zylah as he spoke, and again she thought she saw something ripple beneath his skin, but the intensity of his stare forced her to look away as she watched the other guards carrying out the two who had fallen. The numbers hadn't seemed that badly stacked, to begin with, but having seen just how fast the thralls were, Zylah couldn't say she was surprised.

Malok rested a hand on Rin's shoulder as he kept his attention on Zylah. "Thank you for healing my daughter." A nod in Holt's direction was all the acknowledgement offered for his help. "Get some rest, all of you." The High Lord held out a hand for his wife and led her away. Whatever Nevan had been to Cirelle, something told Zylah a difficult conversation was about to follow.

"You said their bloodlust takes a while to settle." She turned to face Holt. "But this is…" Her brow scrunched. "Do you think this is Aurelia's doing?"

Holt at last removed his hand. His jacket sleeve was torn in several places, dried blood crusting the fabric. Zylah's frown deepened. He'd been quietly healing himself too, and she suspected from Malok's behaviour the High Lord had witnessed whatever injuries he'd received.

Holt watched Malok and Cirelle walk away, but as usual, his expression gave nothing away. "Marcus is proud. An army of strong, obedient vampires with a multitude of skills is far more his style. These…" He gestured to what remained. "They're strong but wild. Good front-line fodder, but a mistake in Aurelia's experiments." He turned back to Zylah, and she saw the flicker of worry in his expression before it was gone. "Perhaps this was a test, to see how they fare. I'll need to get a message to Rose and Saphi, they were heading to the Northern Territories."

Not for the first time since leaving her old life, before she'd thought she'd killed Jesper, before she'd evanesced from the gallows, Zylah realised how little she knew of this world. How sheltered her life had been, how growing up under Arnir's rule had left her uneducated and unprepared for life outside of Dalstead.

She had no idea what kind of numbers of Fae remained in Astaria, or if Fae lived across the oceans, too. Thanks to one of Sasha's books, she knew the Northern Territories were once overflowing with Fae, and that they had slowly made their way south across Astaria.

How many there once were, or where, or how many remained were facts she still didn't know.

But if Marcus unleashed his army of vampires and thralls across Astaria, neither humans nor Fae would be safe, and all that would remain would be those loyal to him, the creatures Aurelia had created in his name.

"Let me walk you to your room," Nye offered, at last leaving her cousin's side and motioning for Zylah to join her.

Zylah quietly murmured a goodnight to Holt and the others, casting a glance over her shoulder to wait for Kopi before she followed the Fae out of the night air. Nye led them through the corridors Zylah had familiarised herself with briefly earlier, after a quick moment to change into the clothes Rin had let her borrow. Tall, arched windows cast strange shadows on the stone at their feet, moonlight rippling over them as they walked.

"My uncle will not help willingly, no matter what transpired here tonight," Nye finally said, perhaps when she deemed them far enough away from any of Malok's guards who might be listening. Orblights flickered in their sconces, illuminating arched doors leading off to various bedrooms.

"Why? Is it that he won't help Holt, or is it about protecting what's his?" Zylah willed her voice not to sound too thin, but she had little left in her to amplify it.

"Holt trained here; I think in many ways Malok used to think of Holt as a son. But my uncle is a soldier. The loss of his guards is nothing but a consequence of war to him. He will defend his own, but this is the first time he has seen the thralls up close. Persuading him to allow his army to leave the court will be difficult."

Zylah paused beside the door to the room they had offered her, adjacent to the one they'd offered Holt, and waited.

Nye's amber eyes searched Zylah's. "Be careful. Whatever he asks of you, it will benefit him far more than whatever you stand to gain from this. Even if it means Holt secures the army. Malok will ensure the payment far exceeds the debt."

"Why are you telling me this?"

"Because you saved Rin's life." Nye rested a hand on Zylah's shoulder, her touch warm and gentle. "Thank you." She held Zylah's gaze for a moment. "Good night, Zylah."

Zylah didn't get a chance to reply. Nye's form seemed to shimmer, her body disappearing into the shadows, leaving Zylah alone in her doorway. Kopi chirped once on her shoulder, and Zylah let out a shaky sigh, fingers twisting over the door knob.

"You're right, buddy, time to sleep." She watched the little owl fly to the window, before kicking off her boots and falling onto the bed.

She didn't trust Cirelle or Malok, but she trusted Holt. And Holt was going into this likely already knowing that Malok would take more than he could give. But what choice did they have? For so long all Zylah had wanted was her freedom. But tonight had shown her there would be no freedom for anyone if they let Marcus win.

16

Black, empty eyes. Rotting flesh that exposed bone. A hand, outstretched. And a face Zylah recognised.

Raif stood amongst the creatures on the terrace, one hand in his pocket, the other reaching for her, a half grin tugging at what remained of his lips.

His skin was ashen and rotten, just like the other thralls, but his long black hair remained intact. He took a step closer, and Zylah whispered his name.

"Zylah."

Zylah's eyes flicked open, sweat-soaked sheets clinging to her skin.

She dragged a shaky hand through her hair, chest heaving with erratic breaths and pushed off the bed. Shoved open the door to the balcony, swallowing down the frigid night air.

"Couldn't sleep?" Holt asked quietly from his side of their shared balcony.

Zylah's eyes found his in the darkness and fell to the sheet around his shoulders. "You're sleeping out here?"

"Strange dreams."

Zylah wasn't sure if it was a question or a statement, but he eyed the glass in his hands and frowned at the amber liquid inside.

"Strange day," she offered, though she didn't move from where she stood. She closed her eyes and turned her head to face the ocean, letting the breeze wash over her until her skin chilled and the memory of her dream faded. When she opened her eyes, Holt was beside her, eyes dipping to her loose hair and her bare shoulders. She'd slept in her underclothes, but it was nothing he hadn't seen before.

Holt held her gaze as he took the sheet from his shoulders and wrapped it around hers, his warmth enveloping her. This close, she was at eye level with his chest, the scent of earthy acani berries clinging to his bare skin. She shifted her attention to the angular lines of his face as he took a step back.

"No robe to call to you?" Zylah asked with a half-smile.

He rested his arms on the wall, facing out to the inky depths of the ocean beyond them. Her gaze fell across the thick muscles on his back, and for a moment she found herself wondering what they would feel like if she traced them with the pads of her fingers. Then she noticed a new scar he hadn't had back in Virian, just above the waistline of his trousers, and the thought was snuffed out.

"Does the vanquicite hurt?" he asked, his attention still fixed ahead, his voice distant.

"No." She wondered if he knew. If he could see the weight of it consuming her.

"Then summon anything you like."

Zylah dug her fingers into the sheet and frowned. "I can't."

"Try." He turned back to face her and rested against the wall, arms folded across his chest, head ever so slightly angled to one side, challenging her.

A smile tugged at the corner of Zylah's mouth, and she held out her hand, *reached* for the item she wanted and her dagger appeared in her palm, fingers instinctively curling around it.

"Any pain?" Holt asked as he carefully prised the dagger from her fingers, and it disappeared to the gods knew where.

Zylah shook her head, too surprised that she'd actually done it to chide him for asking.

Holt raised an eyebrow. "Try again. Something else."

Asshole. Either he didn't think she could, or he wanted to test her abilities. Zylah held out both hands, one for the bottle of amber liquid that had been left on the dresser in her room, the other for the matching glass to the one he'd been drinking from moments before.

"Smart ass." His lips twitched. "Another." His skin was warm against hers as he took the bottle and glass and placed them on the wall beside them.

Zylah thought of her bracers on her bedside table, reached for them with her mind's eye and watched with satisfaction as they appeared in her hands, black blood smeared across the leather. There had been losses earlier. Rin had almost died. "Why do I get the feeling that no matter how many Fae step up to help us in this, it's not going to be enough?"

"Because it isn't," Holt said quietly, taking the bracers and sending them to wherever he'd sent her dagger. "Not against an army of vampires, thralls—whatever the priestesses are amassing. Our world is going to look very different when this is over."

"Why is Marcus doing any of this?"

Another flick of his chin, urging her to summon something else. "He and Aurelia had a vision of how this world should be a long time ago, and everyone dismissed their ideas. Their greed was partly what led to many of the High Fae being murdered in their sleep."

"And what was that vision?" Zylah asked as Holt's shirt appeared over her arm, the shirt she usually slept in.

She'd managed to ignore it, but now a sharp stab of pain settled between her shoulder blades, a fire lighting up beneath her skin.

She'd suspected as much during her time in Kerthen; using her magic made the effects of the vanquicite much, much worse.

"To take us back to our roots. To what the original nine had intended. Lines of pure power. No humans, no lesser fae."

"And how do vampires and thralls bring them closer to that?" She handed him the sheet as she shrugged into his shirt, hoping to disguise her wince of pain. The sheet disappeared the second it left her hand and his fingers closed around it.

"Because they're far easier to control."

Zylah held out her hand for her last vial of tonic as his words sank in.

"I told you not to waste those," he said, his voice a little rougher than it had been moments before, but his expression gave away his concern. His fingers brushed hers again as he touched the vial and it disappeared. "Turn around."

She did as he asked, partly because she was too tired to argue with him, but partly because not even ten of her tonics would provide as much relief as his healing—the only reason she'd been relying on her tonics so easily since he'd found her. "That was a thrall chasing after the Asters back in the forest, wasn't it?"

He hummed his agreement as his fingers pressed against her shirt, warmth pouring from him.

"Did you see it?" Zylah asked over her shoulder.

His attention was fixed on his hand, his jaw tight. "No. I saw you fight the Aster. Saw it claw at your leg, but I was dealing with two more." He paused, his eyes flicking up to hers for a second. "And then the sprites covered you, and the distraction nearly cost me an eye." His throat bobbed. "Then something screamed—a thrall—the remaining Asters fled, and I couldn't get you out."

Zylah pivoted to face him, but he kept his hand pressed to her back, still healing her, his hold firm but gentle. "I'm sorry. It must have reminded you of Raif." The sprites had covered his body, too. Protecting him from Jesper. But it was too late.

She thought of her dream. Of Raif's empty eyes. But the memory faded as she met Holt's stare, his eyes every shade of a spring forest, his dishevelled hair falling in waves over the tips of his ears. "What were you dreaming of?" she asked softly.

His thumb brushed her back for a moment. "That I couldn't get you out of the sprites' cage."

Like he couldn't get Raif out. Zylah frowned, and Holt re-adjusted his hand.

He'd lost so many people. And yet he still kept going, fighting for the freedom of the Fae. "I saw Pallia that day," she said so quietly it was almost a whisper. "She told me few things in this life belong to us."

"A difficult truth to swallow."

Zylah looked up to meet his eyes again. "What was truth number one?"

A rare smile. A real one, and it squeezed at something deep within her chest.

"I missed Kopi when you were gone," he said.

"Don't let him hear you say that. He'll puff up bigger than a pigeon."

"Don't let him hear you liken him to a pigeon."

It was Zylah's turn to smile. "Kopi missed you, too."

Holt's hand fell from her back, his smile fading. He slid the same hand into his pocket but didn't take a step back. "Practise summoning items to you and sending them away. Start with something in the next room. Something you can see. Then start increasing the distances."

Zylah nodded. "That's what I did with the evanescing. Back in the tunnels in Virian, after you left."

Holt's expression darkened. "I had to go. Marcus…" He looked away.

The urge to reach out to him tugged at her fingers, but instead, she fisted them into the hem of her shirt. "What does he have on you, Holt? It's more than a life debt, isn't it?" She took half a step closer, so close she could feel the heat from his skin.

Holt's eyes snapped to hers, dipping lower for a moment. Zylah willed herself to remain still, to not take the final half step to him, no matter how much her bones screamed at her to do it. It had always been the same with him. It was why she'd felt so safe back in Virian. He'd somehow known to be a constant, steady presence in her life but had given her the space she needed, too.

"Truth number two?" he said quietly.

Zylah nodded.

"I had nothing to lose until I met you." He removed his hand from his pocket and tucked a wayward strand of hair behind her ear, his fingers stilling near her cheek for a moment.

She brushed her fingers against his. And frowned.

It didn't matter what he'd said. She'd used Raif. She wouldn't use him, too. If she lost this, *him*, she would have nothing left.

Whatever he'd read in her expression made him drop his hand, and she fought for an explanation, of how to tell him everything that slithered its way through her thoughts, but the words seemed to knot in her throat.

Holt took half a step back, his eyes searching hers as if he'd find the answer to a question there. Sadness seemed to settle over him, his voice a little rougher than it had been a moment before when he spoke. "Get some rest, Zylah."

The knot lodged deeper as she left him alone on the balcony and returned to her room.

17

A snowstorm had moved in overnight, Zylah had been informed. A note written in fine, slanted writing had notified her at breakfast, signed with an *N*. Nye. That meant no tracking, no leaving the walls of the court to search for signs of which direction the thralls came from.

She picked at her breakfast, if only so that she wouldn't have to lie to Holt about eating it. A little bowl of seeds sat beside her plate, and she carried it over to Kopi, nothing more than a tiny ball of feathers on his perch above the wardrobe, still fast asleep. There was no sound from Holt's room, but that didn't surprise Zylah.

She'd barely slept, lying awake with only her poisonous thoughts to keep her company. Holt was right. She *had* loved Raif. But not the way Raif had loved her. And she hated that she'd strung him along. That she'd used him to get herself through… everything. It was wretched. *She* was wretched, and the thoughts cycled on repeat until morning, the weight of them pushing and pressing at her chest, threatening to pull her back to the dark oblivion she'd found herself in during her time in

Kerthen, the hollow pool of black she only just managed to keep herself out of every day. At some point in the night, she'd taken the necklace Raif had given her and stuffed it under a spare blanket inside her wardrobe.

As the golden light of dawn filtered in through the balcony doors, she realised Holt had never answered her question about Marcus. He owed Marcus a life debt for his sister, but there was more, Zylah was certain of it. A bargain; some reason that Marcus continued to let him wander freely around Astaria, something he sought, perhaps.

She laughed dryly to herself as she dressed. If it were true, maybe she'd feel better about her own reckless choices. Zylah knew the kind of desperation that drove a Fae to make a bargain like that. The memory of it danced along her skin every morning.

Still half asleep, Kopi had flown to her shoulder before she left her room to explore the court. She wasn't about to sit around all day waiting to be summoned to a meeting, and something told her Malok had every intention of making them wait. No, if she had time to spare, she needed to fill it wisely. And first on her agenda was looking for supplies to replenish her tonics.

With sleep evading her she'd practised summoning items— the book Okwata had given her, a besa leaf from her apron thrown over a chair—until the pain had forced her to take her last vial of tonic. She'd pictured the amantias back in the forest beside Virian, had pulled and pulled on the feeling inside herself, but nothing had appeared in her upturned palm.

So she'd need to seek out the ingredients just like she was used to.

193

The corridors were empty as she made her way silently through the court, arched windows revealing flashes of blue beyond, the inky ocean blending seamlessly into the horizon. Plant displays were dotted throughout, wall-mounted planters of species Zylah recognised from one of the domes back at the botanical gardens in Virian, with no medicinal properties whatsoever.

She wove through empty hallways until the smooth white rock became jagged, untouched by skilled Fae hands. This far along the clifftop, the corridors were nothing but passageways gouged from the rock by simple hand tools, the arched openings replaced by basic holes through which to let in the light.

And where the daylight fell, plants grew. Baylock. Zylah ran her hands along the strings of tiny, round leaves, sifting through her recollection of its properties. *Mild pain relief.* If she could source some nastura, it could be worked into something a little more potent. Not quite what her tonics provided, but better than nothing. She prised off a few leaves, moving slowly from plant to plant to make sure she didn't harvest too much, working her way deeper into the jagged rooms, the scent of the ocean permeating everything.

If there was any chance of getting close to Marcus and Jesper, Zylah knew she would need to get the pain under control until the vanquicite could be removed. Holt hadn't trusted Maelissa enough to ask for her healer, and Zylah was glad of it. Something told her he wanted the decision to be hers here in the Aquaris Court.

The thought of thralls wielding weapons made from vanquicite had Zylah's steps quickening. She followed the plants until the corridor danced with shadows, filling her pockets until the light thinned and the passageway turned a corner in the rock. Kopi darted off her shoulder into the darkness, and Zylah took it as a sign to follow him.

It opened up to a large cave, light pouring in from one end, but most of the chamber remained in darkness. With her keen eyesight, Zylah could make out the ash root spilling out of the rock, its unmistakable arrow-headed leaves pointing to the dirt. Ash root was excellent for wounds, and although it wouldn't help with the pain from her vanquicite, she'd be remiss not to dry some for future use. It was also susceptible to damage, so she took her time searching for a large enough plant that would survive her harvest, shoving the pointed leaves into the front of her apron.

Holt had managed to slow the spread of whatever poison the vanquicite was leaking into her, but Zylah knew it wasn't enough. The feeling still lingered, like liquid fire was coursing through every vein in her body, slowly burning her alive from the inside out.

A few small rocks fell at the entrance to the cave, but Kopi's silence told her it was safe to continue, packing the leaves down tight. If Holt hadn't come to Varda when he had, there were no doubts in Zylah's mind that she wouldn't still be walking. She had Rose's vision to thank for that, wherever the Fae and Saphi were right now.

More rocks ricocheted and Zylah's eyes flicked to the direction of the sound, only to find Kopi before an enormous bird, eyeing Kopi like he was his next meal.

The little owl sat tall, as though he wasn't the size of one of the great bird's claws.

"Don't eat him!" Zylah whispered, evanescing to scoop Kopi off the dirt and coming eye to eye with the giant creature. Kopi remained docile in her palms, and he made no sound as the bird's head twitched to the side, eyeing them both. Its black beak edged closer, tugging at the front of Zylah's apron. Instinctively she took a step back, and the bird reared up, stretching to its full height, towering above her and Kopi. And it was only then that Zylah noticed the ash root it had taken from her apron and released a breath.

"Vegetarian. Good. That's good." She remained still, taking in the bird's glassy black eyes and its slick black feathers, not a speck of colour among them. It had the shape of the eagles she'd seen in the Rinian mountain range, only much, much larger.

"Rava eats meat."

Zylah whirled at the voice.

"Cirelle." The Fae stood in the narrow entranceway Zylah had used, one hand resting lightly across the other in front of her, barely an indent from her touch in her lilac gown.

There were few Fae that made Zylah acutely aware of how very different they were to humans; the way Cirelle stood perfectly still, her face impassive, marked her as one of the rare exceptions.

"But she has always had a taste for the ash." Cirelle walked right up to the bird, pressed a hand to its neck, and Zylah watched in awe as the creature nuzzled its head against Cirelle's with care.

The Fae ran a hand along the bird's beak. "Rava always knows when I'm in distress."

"How?"

"Where I come from, we are paired with the Iyofari when we hit puberty, and they stay with us for life."

Zylah gave a small smile but didn't move, not with Kopi still in her hands. "A beautiful tradition."

"Rava acts as an intermediary for me between this court and the one back in Bhuja. We don't see each other often."

"I'm sorry." Zylah couldn't imagine life without Kopi after such a short time together. But he wasn't hers, Pallia had reminded her of that. Not in the way Rava was Cirelle's. *Very few things in this life belong to us.*

Cirelle shook her head. "It matters not."

"And I'm sorry about your friend," Zylah offered, stroking a thumb against Kopi's head.

The Fae smiled weakly. "The pain I caused my husband is greater than the pain of losing Nevan. He was a childhood friend. From Bhuja. But his presence here always upset Malok."

Zylah held her tongue, too aware of how easy it would be to say the wrong thing with Rava still looming over them. Kopi hopped onto her shoulder, as if he too was silently waiting for Cirelle to continue.

Grief did strange things to you, Zylah had learnt. Sent the strangest thoughts into your head, the most peculiar memories when you least expected them. She knew the glazed look in Cirelle's eyes all too well, recognised the way she moved automatically around Rava, and understood that it was no doubt why she'd sought out her companion in the first place.

Cirelle frowned. "My mother died when I was seven, and my father felt her loss so very deeply." She ran a hand down the silken feathers at Rava's neck, each one as large as her hand. "For months I would wake in the night to check on him because I was so afraid he'd take his life just to be with her."

Zylah silently sucked in a breath at the admission.

"Then one day, he met a beautiful faerie at court, and they fell in love. Father would come to me every day, reassuring me he still loved my mother just as much as he always had." Cirelle's attention was fixed on Rava, but Zylah knew it wasn't the bird before her she saw, but whatever memory she'd lost herself in. "I realised how hard he'd been fighting the whole time, struggling not to lose himself to his despair over my mother."

The Fae took the ash root that Rava had dropped, picking at a leaf. "I couldn't be angry with him. I was relieved. So relieved it was like a weight had been lifted from my chest."

Zylah willed her expression to remain neutral, to not let sympathy shine through her features. Something told her it would not sit well with Cirelle.

But the Fae didn't seem to notice. She was too busy handing the remainder of the ash root to Rava.

"Nevan was there, for all of that," Cirelle said softly. "He made sure I was never alone, even when I understood that my father still loved my mother, even when he was with Namira."

Zylah knew all too intimately the desire to talk about the people she'd lost, to share their stories with others. Sasha had been kind enough to listen to her speak about her father on several afternoons back in Varda, and it had offered Zylah some small moments of peace to know that now someone else might remember him, too. That if the vanquicite took her life, there was someone else who could recall stories of him long after she was gone.

Cirelle took Zylah's hand in her own, holding her gaze. "I think we all like to think we can fix ourselves. That our pain and loneliness won't swallow us whole." Her eyes searched Zylah's, and there was kindness there, as if she were speaking to one of her children. "The truth is there's nothing to fix. We're just lost in our despair, just like my father was. And I am forever grateful to Namira for pulling him out of it. Even if she had no idea what she was doing. What her loving him meant."

Despite Cirelle's kindness, a wall of vanquicite soared in Zylah's thoughts, for fear that the High Lady was like Thallan.

But the Fae smiled gently. "Love and death are the only two things that truly change us, Zylah."

Zylah's thoughts scattered, and she willed her breathing to remain steady. A seer, perhaps, like Rose.

"I can sense emotions, can help ease them, too. And you." She searched Zylah's face as if she could see every feeling written across it. "You wear your guilt like a shroud. But in my experience, the actions rarely justify the guilt." Cirelle angled her head, gave Zylah's fingers a gentle squeeze. "The burden is often… misplaced."

Malok. Cirelle's father. Everything they felt, she could feel, too.

How could she bear it? The otherworldly stillness made sense now. As if she used it to anchor her, to take control of the maelstrom of emotions that must pass through her every day. Zylah willed herself to feel nothing. To dive into the empty hollow within herself and let it surround her, so the Fae could feel nothing, too. "We are responsible for our own actions," Zylah said, her voice sounding weaker than she'd have liked.

Cirelle gave a knowing look, as if she knew what Zylah had tried to attempt. "We are. But often things happen that are outside our control."

If you fought for yourself the way you fight for others, Holt had said to her back in the forest. She wasn't worth fighting for, she'd wanted to tell him. Wasn't worth the trouble she had caused him again and again. Wasn't worth saving when so many had died instead of her. Because of her.

Kopi found himself a small alcove to settle into just as another burst of pain pulsed through Zylah. She pushed a baylock leaf into her mouth out of habit, her attention fixed on Kopi.

"Why do you eat that?" Cirelle asked, pulling Zylah from her thoughts.

Shit. "Pain relief." Not a lie. Not entirely.

The Fae tilted her head to one side, and for a moment Zylah could imagine Cirelle giving that same silent treatment to her children to get whatever answer she wanted from them. "Your injuries from last night? We could use someone with your knowledge here."

Zylah didn't correct her. The trouble was, the truth was complicated. But she didn't give herself time to dwell on that. "Until Holt is ready to move on, I'll be here. If there's any poultices I can make, small remedies, just let me know."

Cirelle bowed her head in thanks, and Zylah turned to leave. *Tell her.* It was Holt's voice she imagined in her thoughts.

No more lies.

Zylah bit her lip. Sucked in a breath. "I have a piece of vanquicite in my back. Since I learnt I could evanesce it started to hurt, but it was dislodged when…" Zylah cleared her throat.

"One of Arnir's men whipped me. The pain has been…" Like a fire inside her. "Much worse since then, and I've yet to find a healer that can remove it." She didn't add that she hadn't tried. Or that she wouldn't have had the coin to pay for one, anyway.

"Holt's been trying to heal it for you," Cirelle said, no trace of emotion on her face.

It's my tithe, Zylah wanted to say, but she snuffed out any feelings Cirelle might latch onto. "Using my magic makes the pain worse."

"That doesn't surprise me. Your body is fighting the very thing the vanquicite does. That's precisely why Marcus is having it mined. I can send word across the water to Bhuja. There's an excellent healer there who I trust with my life, and they can be here within a few weeks."

Zylah swallowed. Forced herself to smile politely. To stamp out any feeling Cirelle could pick up on. She wouldn't give the Fae any more cause for sadness today, only offered her thanks and a quiet goodbye, leaving Cirelle alone in privacy with her friend.

She didn't let herself think about Cirelle's offer until she was clear of the cave; didn't allow herself to dwell on the fact that she might not live to see the healer.

Because Zylah knew, deep in her bones, that the vanquicite was slowly killing her.

18

There were still more ingredients Zylah needed to source if she was going to be able to make something half decent for her pain. But with the storm, there would be no returning to the forest just yet. Winters in Astaria were never easy, but if it meant slowing any progress Marcus had been making, Zylah would endure the cold forever if she had to.

It was barely noon and already she felt drained, emptied out. Her lack of sleep hadn't helped, and she shifted her thoughts from Cirelle's lingering words to the nightmare that had first woken her. To the way Raif's skin had been rotten and decayed like the other thralls', how she'd awoken to someone calling her name.

It had been the same back in Kerthen, night after night. The nightmares had been different, but, then it had happened again, with Pallia.

Only she hadn't been dreaming then, had she?

A tongue clicking was the only warning she had before a male voice behind her said, "Half Fae scum. We've been looking everywhere for you."

Zylah froze for a heartbeat, fear stealing her breath. But she snuffed it out. Turned to face the male, head held high, one hand on the hilt of the blade tucked into her bracer. She silently scolded herself for how much she'd come to rely on Kopi keeping watch, that she'd let herself walk around in a strange place with her guard down as not one, but three Fae males blocked the corridor from the way she'd just entered just a few strides away from her.

"You look familiar." Zylah recognised the three of them from the funeral, how they'd smirked at her the night before. A tall, stocky blond; an older Fae, with a lean build and peppered black hair fastened above his head in a knot. And the one who had spoken, cropped brown hair and a wide grin across his face like he was the biggest asshole she'd ever have the pleasure of meeting.

She took a moment to assess their clothes, the way they held themselves, what weapons they might have had concealed on them. She hadn't seen them fighting during the thrall attack, but that could have been equally as advantageous for her as otherwise. And though she'd had a few months of training from both Raif and Holt, Zylah wasn't a fool. Three against one was something, but if they were highly trained? That was another.

"Take a good look. Ours will be the last faces you see." The asshole nodded once to his companions, and they both drew pencil-thin daggers from their sleeves, the same ugly sneers from the night before plastered across their faces.

Zylah sucked in a breath. Once she would have frozen. Would have succumbed to the fear as it rooted her to the spot. But where there was once fear, now there was only an icy rage, sharper than the tips of the blades the Fae held before her. She'd fought so hard to claw back the piece of herself Jesper had taken from her, and she would not let go of it without a fight. She would not be a victim again.

Zylah didn't wait for the males to make the first move. She evanesced to the blond, slashed her dagger across the back of his hand and moved away before his blade clattered to the stone floor. She'd already moved behind the older Fae, pressing her dagger to his ribs.

"Drop it," she hissed, as Blondie swore and clutched his hand to his chest.

The male didn't move. Zylah pressed harder.

"Do as she asks, Daven," the asshole Fae commanded.

Zylah shot a glance at Blondie as he swore again, inspecting his wounded hand, and the moment cost her. Daven whirled away from the tip of her blade, swiping at her face with his dagger.

She reacted just a fraction of a second too slowly, the bite of metal so sharp she could feel the warm trickle of blood on her cheek before the burning pain from the wound. But Zylah didn't stop to think about it. She evanesced back to Blondie, reaching for his knife only to slash it across his thigh. The Fae cried out as Zylah reappeared beside Daven, slamming the blade into his knee so hard it pierced right through the other side.

Daven screamed as she evanesced away, chest heaving, back to where she'd been before they'd crept up on her. She held out a hand to summon Daven's blade and didn't let her flicker of surprise show across her face as she held it ready to throw at Asshole.

"I've had plenty of target practice," she said quietly, with as much of a bite to her words as she could manage through her pain. She didn't need to tell him the target had been a poster of her own face, on countless nights alone in Kerthen and Varda.

Asshole looked between his two companions, grinding his teeth together as if he was thinking. Slowly.

But he didn't have the chance to speak; Holt and Malok evanesced between them, and the Fae stumbled back a step.

"What is the meaning of this, Selas?" Malok demanded.

A ripple of power filled the space between them all, and Zylah knew the three males had felt it from the way the colour leeched from their faces.

She recognised Holt's magic at once, didn't need to look up to know he'd done it as a silent warning, didn't need to move her gaze just a fraction to know he was watching her, his attention fixed on the wound on her cheek.

Zylah loosed a breath, but she didn't lower the blade. Not yet.

Blondie had fallen to his knees, clutching his good hand to his thigh and his injured hand to his chest, blood smeared across his tan skin.

"Which one of them did this to you?" Holt asked, taking a tentative step towards her. Another wave of his magic thickened the air around them, his eyes darkening. The three males yielded a step, backing away from the threat of that power. Lethal. Deadly.

With a flick of her wrist, Zylah released Blondie's blade. "I'm fine." It hit her target in the dirt, right beside his feet. She looked Selas in the eye as she said, "It's nothing."

Malok glanced between them, and again Zylah saw something pass over his features, as if he wore a deceit to disguise his true face. "Go to my chambers. I'll deal with this."

Holt evanesced them before Zylah had the chance to object. When he released her elbow, she brought a hand to her cheek, knowing he'd healed her wound as they'd travelled. *Smart.* Because he'd known she'd have protested if he'd asked.

"We heard Daven's cries," Holt said, as if he knew precisely what she was about to ask. He remained close, and Zylah knew without looking up he was scanning her for any signs of additional injuries.

She didn't need to look up to feel his anger, either, despite how hard he was trying to hide it.

Zylah folded her arms, willing herself not to shake with the adrenaline. She should have just evanesced away the moment she'd seen them. But that wasn't who she was anymore. Whatever she deserved, she didn't want to be the person she was. Someone who ran from their problems. She wanted to be someone who faced them, no matter how much it frightened her.

"I came to your room right after training this morning, but you'd already left. I thought you might want to rest after so long on the road," Holt said when she didn't reply.

"Training?" she asked, looking up at him, at the apology in his eyes, even though she didn't need it.

He nodded.

"Ah, so you do have to train like the rest of us?" She willed some lightness into her voice, to offer him some reassurance that she was fine, that she didn't need an apology from him, and raised an eyebrow at him playfully.

He relaxed a fraction, but she knew he was still on alert, could almost feel the storm of emotions warring inside him, an echo of everything she felt.

Zylah observed their surroundings as she steadied her breaths, wishing she had another vial of tonic in her pocket. A large table cut from the white rock sat in the centre of the room, with carved seats of white wood dotted around it. A map of Astaria had once been painted onto the table's surface, its colours long since faded, details chipped away.

"They're not fond of a half Fae in their court," she murmured at last, fingers tracing across the map. A collection of black pebbles sat over Virian, and around it, a few brown pebbles were dotted here and there; a much larger number of white ones scattered across the continent.

"These represent humans," Zylah said quietly, fingertips brushing against the nearest white pebbles. "And these are Fae," she added, touching the brown pebbles that rested over their location at the Aquaris Court.

She felt Holt step into place beside her. "The black is—"

"His army." Zylah swallowed. If the ratios were accurate, Marcus was building himself a sizeable force. "I think my presence here might hinder your request for aid. But perhaps we shouldn't care for his help, after all."

"I can assure you, they were acting of their own accord." Malok had evanesced into the room, standing at the head of the table.

Zylah said nothing, just held his stare, waiting for him to speak. She knew how ruffled she likely looked; how her hair would have been falling out of her braid, blood staining her clothes, her cheek. But she wanted him to see it. To know that it had happened in his court, because of *his* people. High Lord or not, she was not one of them, and she didn't wish to be.

"Mining has halted since the weather front moved in," Malok said, waving a hand at the map markers. A large black rock sat on the outskirts of Virian, and Zylah knew without explanation that it was the vanquicite mine. "They will have to down tools or risk being snowed in. We're approaching a very harsh winter, I've been informed."

Zylah fixed her attention on the magic that seemed to ripple over Malok's face like water on the surface of a pond. "Tell me, why does a High Lord hide behind a deceit in his own court?"

A look of surprise lit up his eyes for a moment before he shut it down. "No one has seen my true face in centuries."

Zylah took a step closer but left enough of a respectful distance between them that she wouldn't have to tilt her head back to look up at him. This close, she could see through pieces of the magic in parts; could see the thick burn scars marring most of his face. Despite the pity she felt for the pain he'd suffered, she let no emotion show on her face as she asked, "Humans did this to you?"

Malok's brown eyes narrowed a fraction, lips pressed tightly together, but he merely nodded.

"And this is where you wait for me to what? Defend humans? Chastise the Fae?" Zylah asked, stepping away from him. Holt had said nothing about the altercation back out in the court, and though his anger still dripped from him he remained silent. Perhaps he didn't want to risk any favour with Malok. Zylah silently scolded herself for not thinking of that sooner.

The High Lord unstrapped his weapon, laying it on a stone mantle before fixing his attention on Holt. "This is where he convinces me why I need to leave my court vulnerable, part with what remains of my army, and send my children off to certain death."

"Because the alternative is that they come for all of you, like they did last night. And they *will* keep coming, Malok," Holt said with lethal calm.

Malok moved to the window, looking out at the ocean, arms clasped behind him. "You're asking us to follow you."

"Don't tell me this is about pride," Zylah cut in. Cirelle didn't seem like the type to suffer fools, but at that moment, Zylah couldn't see Malok as anything but.

"Marcus always had a fondness for puppets." A quiet challenge flashed in Malok's gaze as he watched Holt.

But Holt gave nothing away as he said, "And yet Jora didn't share your reservations."

It was the second time since their arrival that someone had made a comment about the hold Marcus had over Holt.

Did they know what Marcus had done? Whatever bargain might have been struck between them?

Malok poured them a drink from a glazed blue pitcher, handing them each a glass of amber liquid. Holt placed his on the map table.

Zylah eyed hers silently, a familiar scent drifting from the glass she couldn't quite recall or put a name to.

"We'll have Maelissa's archers when the time comes," Holt offered. "War *is* coming, Malok, you cannot hide here at the edge of the continent and deny it."

The High Lord looked as if he might interject, but Holt cut him off. "I have always respected you, Malok, but do not stand by and let the world burn. Your children will leave whether you permit it or not. Let them leave with pride in their hearts. With the reassurance and backing of their father."

Malok held his glass, swirling his drink as if lost in thought. "We've no evidence arrenium will work against the vampires or their thralls," he said, all but dismissing Holt's words. "My spies are looking for an item that once belonged to this court. A key to a device built by Imala herself, a shield to protect the people within the court should they need it. I believe it will be all the defence we'll need against these abominations."

And there it was. He would defend his own, but he would not venture out into the rest of the continent. Would not offer aid to others who were not so fortunate as to live in a fortress like he did. Zylah didn't miss the flicker of disappointment that passed across Holt's face before he shut it down. But it had been enough, and no matter what she thought of Malok, she couldn't bear Holt's disappointment.

"My father often spoke to me about legacy," Zylah said to Malok. "About what will be left of us long after we are gone from this world. You said you will not send your children off to certain death, but if you think that they are safe here, or that they will stay and do nothing simply because you are too afraid to, I can see my father had more in common with Jora than with you."

If he was a male who cared about pride, his father's opinion should've meant something to him. At least, Zylah was counting on it.

Malok held her gaze for a moment. "You may stay here until the storm shifts, but when it does, you'd do well to move north in your search for aid." He raised his glass, and the movement sent another surge of the familiar scent into the air.

Zylah lunged forwards, smacking the glass from his hand and letting it smash to the floor. Holt picked up his glass and took a sniff, an eyebrow raised as he waited for an explanation.

"Agera," Zylah said, tipping the contents of her own glass to the floor. "It causes rapid heart failure."

Malok was silent, but this time he made no effort to disguise the surprise that danced across his face.

"It's gracious of you to offer up your court to us," Zylah said, placing her glass on the table. "But it looks like you have plenty to resolve here." She made to leave, but Malok stopped her.

"Wait. Your mix of abilities makes you uniquely positioned to retrieve the key. When my people locate it, if you bring it to me, I'll hand over my army. Holt will have whatever resources he needs at his disposal. This at least guarantees the safety of those that wish to remain in my court."

Zylah didn't let her satisfaction show. "And Selas and his companions? Will I be looking over my shoulder every time I walk through the court?"

"Niossa will be your personal guard." Nye, Zylah presumed.

"I appreciate the sentiment, Malok. But I don't need minding like some helpless child. I could have quite easily killed Selas and his friends, but I chose not to."

She let the words settle.

She wasn't certain she could have killed all three of them, but he didn't need to know that. "I'll stay. But only so that you give him what he deserves," she added, flicking her chin at Holt. "Not for your key."

Kopi landed on the window, and Zylah resisted the urge to ask him where he'd been. She held her arm out for him instead, and he flew over to assume his position on her wrist as she again turned to leave. Malok said nothing to her offer, but Zylah knew it was pride holding his tongue.

Holt broke the silence. "If anyone else touches her in this court I'll kill them myself." A vicious calm seemed to settle over him as he looked at Malok. Too still.

Zylah willed herself not to smile at the moment of fear that passed over Malok's face. Instead, she excused herself, Holt's words echoing in her head as she made her way back to her room.

19

Nye had agreed to training as a compromise when Zylah refused Malok's offer of a personal guard.

"If it keeps him off your back," Zylah said as they made their way through the court together the next morning, "And Pallia knows I need it."

She could hold her own. Would have been able to hold her own back in Varda had it not been for that cheating Fae. Even before Raif and Holt had trained her for those few months back in Virian, her brother had given her enough of the basics to get herself out of trouble.

But Zylah knew it would take many more months of dedicated practice to develop the kind of skill, the precision with which they moved. Years, even.

Nye nodded, leading the way through the court. Zylah had left Kopi asleep in her room, determined not to rely on him as her personal alarm. He wasn't hers, and he could choose to leave at any moment, just as easily as he had chosen to stay.

This early in the morning, thin shafts of golden sunlight sliced across the corridors, dust motes dancing in the air.

The ocean sparkled beyond the arched windows, bright and dazzling beyond the white stone, and Zylah thought of Cirelle's court across the sea, of the story she'd told of her father.

The half a brin fruit she'd managed to eat for breakfast threatened to force its way up from her stomach as a wave of pain rolled through her, but she gritted her teeth together and inhaled through her nose until it passed, hoping Nye wouldn't notice. She had some baylock in her pocket but didn't want to risk slipping any into her mouth just yet. Not under Nye's watchful gaze.

The Fae had given her another bundle of clothes the night before, attire more suited to training, she'd explained. Zylah dragged a hand across her exposed stomach, brushing the hem of the lilac top that wrapped across her breasts and over her shoulders.

Close-fitting and supportive, it was perfect for training. And like the trousers Nye had provided, left very little to the imagination.

"They're made from a blend of cotton and rubber, woven here by skilled hands who love to rise to every challenge I set them," Nye had told her when she'd first pulled on the form-fitting trousers.

"You gave them this idea?" Zylah had asked, running a hand over the charcoal fabric, fingertips tracing the silver stitching at the cuffs.

Nye had merely shrugged. "I put in the request. They delivered."

But now multiple voices echoed down the final corridor, and for a moment Zylah wished for something less revealing.

"I hope you don't mind," Nye offered, "We share our training spaces with the rest of the court." She pushed aside a large door and waved a hand for Zylah to go first.

Zylah's apprehension from moments before dissipated the moment she stepped out onto the balcony, the frigid air wrapping around her.

Pairs and small groups of Fae were dotted around the space, talking and training, weapons clashing, and none wore more than a few scraps of clothing not too dissimilar to those Nye had given her. Some were guards Zylah recognised from the attack at Jora's funeral, others were new.

She felt some of the soldiers' attention shift to her, no doubt taking in her rounded ears—evidence of her half human side. She'd seen only High Fae since arriving and realised now that perhaps Malok's distaste for humans spread deeper than she first thought. It seemed it wasn't just humans he disapproved of if only High Fae inhabited his court.

"It's fine," she said absentmindedly, turning to take in the scene. "I've fought in front of an audience before."

"Now there's a story I'd love to hear."

Zylah turned to the sound of Kej's voice, only to find him tugging off snow-dusted layers of clothes beside his sister, who had her own pile beside her.

"Where have you been?" Zylah asked, holding Kej's gaze as his eyes roved slowly from her feet up to her face.

The skin on her arms prickled from the cold, but she refused to fold them across herself, unwilling to show any weakness in front of what she was now certain were members of Malok's army training around her.

Kej winked. "Out all night. We like to let off some steam and there are only so many places here that are big enough to accommodate us in our wildcat form." His firm muscles flexed as he peeled off his shirt, and Zylah wondered if the pair of them ate in their wildcat forms or if he'd just delivered an outright lie, judging by the way Rin shifted uncomfortably beside him.

"You're lucky you can sneak out," Zylah said, rolling her neck and following Nye's series of warm-up stretches, willing her hands not to shake from the chill air. "I'll be glad to get rid of some of this pent-up energy."

Kej took a step closer, eyes blazing with heat. "I can think of plenty of other ways to attend to that."

Zylah huffed a laugh.

"Kej." Rin rolled her eyes, tugging at her brother's elbow, but he merely offered a wide grin in response.

If things were different, she might have risen to his challenge. Followed through on his invitation. He was handsome in the way all High Fae were, kind, but his cocky lines reminded her too much of Raif, and that only twisted the knife in her chest deeper.

"What's the deal with you and Holt, anyway?" Kej asked, snapping Zylah from her thoughts.

Rin elbowed him. "You can't ask that."

"Why not? I want to know whether my efforts will be worthwhile. Even in Nye's old clothes, she stinks of Holt, and they both look at each other like they're starved for air."

Zylah sniffed at her shoulder and blinked.

"Excellent work, Kej, she'll definitely want to train with you now." Rin sighed, offering Zylah an apologetic glance.

He shrugged off his sister's hold, his attention fixed on Zylah. "Who says I wanted to train?"

"Pent-up energy indeed," Zylah murmured, following Nye's lead. "We're just friends. I was… with someone, and…" She'd never said it out loud before, but the three of them were watching her, waiting for an answer. She looked away, watching a nearby pair in the middle of a sparring match. "He died." Her voice felt distant, like she was losing herself, floating away from her body. She dug her nails into her arm to keep herself present, focusing on the sting instead. "He was a good friend of Holt's."

"Ah. So you feel guilty." Kej's words still held the cocky tone, but he took a step back. Fell into a starting position opposite his sister, his gaze snagging on something at the corner of the room. "Pity. My friend over there was looking for a third."

Zylah mirrored Nye's pose, her eyes following Kej's to a guard watching from a level above. He waved two fingers in a half salute, a wide grin brightening his face as his gaze remained fixed on Kej.

"Your redhead friend seemed rather lovely," Zylah said with a huff, dodging an attack from Nye who had started without warning.

Kej laughed. It was light and joyful, as if he didn't have a care in the world. "She is, but she likes to have my full attention."

"Her loss," Zylah murmured, her own attention darting back from the guard to Nye just in time to block another attack.

"You see, Rin," Kej said. "She's not offended. She's—"

"Kej. You're letting Lirian get away." Rin gave him a firm shove, but he offered nothing more than a wink and a slight dip of his chin before taking off after the guard.

Zylah concentrated on Nye's attack as Rin scooped up the bundle of clothes Kej had left behind.

"My brother will fuck anyone with a pulse. No offence," the Fae said, shaking her head in her brother's direction.

"None taken." From someone else, it might have been an insult. But from Rin, it was simply an observation. Zylah knew enough about her and her brother already to understand that. Nye merely smirked, continuing her pattern of blows. The movements were fast, but there was a sequence to them Zylah was quickly picking up, and the blocking became a more natural rhythm, the movements almost meditative.

Rin mumbled a goodbye, something about someone she was trying to avoid, but Zylah's attention remained focused on Nye's attack. Despite the company, despite some of the unsettling looks, the court gave her the same feeling Maelissa's had; its occupants were trapped here, and this was the first opportunity since her arrival to shake the overwhelming feeling.

The world beyond this court was not safe for the Fae that resided in it, and to Zylah, their sanctuary felt more like a prison. Surely Malok understood. That was why it was so important Holt secured his support—so that all Fae could be free to live amongst the humans. And yet he wanted to go one step further in keeping his people here by raising a shield around the entire court.

The moment Malok's spies sent word, she'd be leaving with Holt to find his key, and Zylah couldn't wait to leave. She concentrated on blocking Nye's strikes, losing herself in the steady rhythm, as they moved around each other slowly until Zylah could meet Nye's blows without thinking.

"I met Raif once," the Fae said after they'd built up a sweat. "Don't look surprised. I read all of Malok's reports before he gets them and it's not difficult to string it all together. It was well known Raif was helping Holt in Virian."

Zylah schooled her expression. Heat prickled her skin, and something else, but she willed it away. "Raif was… good to me." She swallowed the lump in her throat. "But I couldn't give him what he wanted."

They switched positions; it was Zylah's turn to strike and Nye's to block, and already Zylah's arms and legs were aching.

Holt's words cycled on repeat in her head. *Maybe it wasn't the kind of love you wanted it to be. But it was enough.*

"I can see he meant a lot to you," Nye said, her voice a little gentler than it had been a moment before. "But there's a reason why you held back. Maybe even more than one." She pivoted, swinging a leg behind Zylah's knee and knocking her to the floor.

"That doesn't make it right." Zylah wiped the back of her hand against her brow. "Show me again."

Nye offered a hand, pulling Zylah to her feet, but didn't release her grip. She held Zylah's gaze as she said, "Grief is messy. It's such a tangle of feelings all knotted into one, like a net of spider silk has been thrown over you. Whatever you had, it was real, but now he's gone. So you have two choices: stay here. Stuck under the net. Or push through it and take whatever you need with you. He died. Not you. Don't forget to live." A light squeeze of her hand, and then she pulled away, already back to training.

It was a choice, Zylah realised.

The way she had chosen to keep going when Pallia visited her. The same way she had chosen to get up every morning in Kerthen, putting one foot in front of the other.

But it didn't change anything. She was still a monster for all that she'd done.

"Do you know why Holt covets these soldiers?" Nye asked, as if she'd sensed the previous conversation was over. She'd moved on to alternating blocking and striking now, using the moves she'd gone through in sequence so that Zylah could keep up.

Zylah remained silent, waiting for Nye's answer.

"Our scouts can evanesce."

Zylah had been told it was a rare ability, had been warned back in Virian not to do it in front of other Fae. But Holt had never discouraged it, had never asked her to conceal who she was.

"A male who once belonged to this court, a cousin of Malok's, had the ability," Nye continued, "and he wanted to pass it on to as many as he could, with the intention of using them for his own gain."

Zylah halted halfway through the strike she was about to deliver. "Please tell me this isn't going where I think it is."

"He wanted to sire an army." Nye nudged Zylah's fist with her own to encourage her to keep going. "Malok was hunting in the woods one day when he heard the male conspiring against him."

It was Zylah's turn to block. "What did Malok do?"

"Ate his heart."

Zylah's hands faltered at the admission. "He can shift?"

"Rin and Kej inherit their ability from him. He ate the male's heart and raised the children in a sectioned-off part of the barracks."

"He made them his spies instead."

Nye dipped her chin. "They are loyal to Malok. But it is true loyalty, I think, from what I have observed. He has given them a good life."

Zylah let out a breath through pursed lips. What constituted a good life? A roof over your head? Food on the table? What about everything else that they missed without their mothers or their father? Nye had shown her kindness, seemed to care greatly for her cousins and her aunt and uncle; Zylah didn't take it lightly if the Fae considered Malok's spies to have had a good life. But what kind of life was it if they had no choice in how it was lived?

"Malok will be holding meetings with the other courts whilst you're gone," Nye said a short while later.

So he was following through on his promises. That was something, at least. Zylah did her best to focus on Nye's movements, anticipating when she'd switch up the blocks for attacks. "Why not just have one meeting and be done with it?"

"After the attack at Jora's funeral? It's too great a risk. Court rulers will be spoken with on an individual basis."

Court rulers. Zylah stifled a sigh. She'd thought there was nothing left of the courts until they'd arrived in Maelissa's. "I know so little about Fae society. I didn't even think there were any courts left."

"Two more rounds, some stretches, and then I'll show you." Nye took her through every movement, and Zylah was glad for the stretches that finished off their session, following Nye back inside just as the cool air started to chill the sweat that slicked her skin.

A group of soldiers were heading out to the balcony, and as Nye turned away, one of them stepped into Zylah, shoving her back a step. The group laughed, the doors already swinging shut behind them as Nye threw her a fresh towel from a bin beside the door, unaware of what had just transpired.

"Who would want to poison Malok?" Zylah asked, her gaze darting back to the door for a second. She saw no use in telling Nye.

"Those who believe his position was not earned."

"And was it?"

Nye was quiet as another group of soldiers walked past them, all nodding at her as they passed, and Zylah suspected she held rank amongst them. She was far more serious than her cousins, her expression often giving little away, like she'd been schooled in court politics her whole life. "My parents ruled this court," she said, at last, confirming Zylah's suspicions. "They were murdered in their sleep, and I was too young to take their place."

She might have offered a quiet *I'm sorry* before her father and Raif had died. But she somehow knew the words would be meaningless to Nye. "You're not too young anymore."

"I don't want it," the Fae said firmly.

"Because of the responsibility?"

"Because my uncle manages things… efficiently." She pushed aside another door, and for the first time all morning, a small smile tugged at the corner of her mouth. "And because I've got too much living to do."

Zylah followed her into the room. Books lined every wall from floor to ceiling. Light from a small window illuminated the entrance, and an old Fae sat beneath it at a narrow desk. The air was thick and heavy, as if no one had moved through the space in some time, as if it stretched far beyond the shadows clinging to the nearest bookcases.

"Greetings, Serrula," Nye offered with a dip of her chin. The old Fae nodded her head, hands still busy scribbling notes into her book.

"Welcome to Imala's library," she said without looking up.

Zylah resisted the urge to take a deep inhale of the scent of old paper permeating the air as she watched Nye make her way to a shelf opposite the door, the last place the light fell before the library beyond slipped into darkness.

A thick book sat open on a stand, and Nye flipped through it quickly. An index. The Fae tapped a finger, muttering something that sounded a lot like *thought so*, to Zylah. Nye's smile had faded, but Zylah didn't miss the shine of delight in her eyes as she said, "This is my favourite place in the entire court. You'll have to forgive me if I slip into the shadows more than once."

Zylah wasn't entirely sure what she meant by that, but she followed her regardless, orblights flickering to life as they stepped into the dark.

20

"There were no kingdoms across our world, to begin with, and little record of what life was like here for the humans before the nine original Fae arrived from their world," Nye explained as she searched a shelf deep within the library. Her finger traced along dusty spines until she stopped, tugging a large book off the shelf with both hands.

"Thousands of years ago, war had torn apart their home. Each arrived with a vision of how they wanted this world to be." She placed the book on a small table, gently resting the crumbling cover to one side and stepping back for Zylah to look.

"We think they led groups of refugees here to safety. So they could start over, away from the bloodshed that had taken over their world." Nye pointed to the faded ink drawings; groups of Fae filling the double-page spread, some clutching children, all following a group of nine that led the way to a swirling patch in the sky that looked like the surface of a pond tipped on its side.

"What is that?" Zylah asked, squinting under the dim glow of the orblight and pointing at the strange blotch of ink.

"A window from their world to ours."

For some reason, it made Zylah think of Okwata and Ahrek, but she couldn't pinpoint why. "Why do I get the feeling very few Fae know this story?"

Nye turned a page. "Pallia. Imala. Altais. Gentris. Diotin. Acrona. Farian." She pointed to each of the seven faces Zylah knew of once as her gods. Had been raised to believe it, anyway. "Ranon. Sira." A child sat in Sira's arms, Ranon's arms around her, looking down at their baby.

"They were together? Ranon and Sira?"

"They were. Ranon and Sira lost their child either in the war or in the process of coming to our world, we aren't certain which. But it was the loss of their child that set them on their path."

All Zylah saw in the pages were grieving parents, desperate to fill the void their child had left behind.

"Their vision didn't quite align with the others, so Ranon and Sira took matters into their own hands, creating new life as they thought it should be. And they almost succeeded in reshaping this world in their vision. They started a war that lasted four hundred years. What were once called Lesser Fae are all descended from the creatures Ranon and Sira created."

Zylah leafed through the pages, each image becoming worse than the last. Asters and all kinds of creatures filled the pages, the ink thicker and more menacing in all the spaces they occupied.

As the pages went on, the creatures became slighter, some with wings, some scaly. More recognisable as the Lesser Fae she'd seen since fleeing Dalstead.

Lesser Fae. An old term, Zylah had been told. And now it made sense. It truly marked them as less than their High Fae equivalents. She thought of Mala and Asha. Of their fierceness and strength. Their loyalty and love. They hadn't been her friends. But they were not monsters, far from it. Marcus, on the other hand. She bit down on her lip, silently repeating her promise to herself. She would end him and Jesper before the vanquicite took her life.

"The others?" she asked, meeting Nye's gaze. "They drove Ranon and Sira away?"

Shadows seemed to leech back into Nye as she pushed off the table. "Not exactly. That's the version our children are taught. That Ranon and Sira realised the severity of their mistake. The truth is they kept going, and the remaining seven had to stop them. Ranon was put to sleep. Entombed. No one knows where he is. But it's said he let it happen to allow Sira time to flee to safety." She flipped the book a few pages ahead, an illustration of Ranon's tomb spread across two pages, crosshatched sections of faded ink eating up all the parchment. A mask lay over a shrouded body, vines wrapping over it.

"And did Sira succeed?"

"All we know is that the remaining seven tried to remove whatever remnants they could of Ranon and Sira. They established the four kingdoms, divided them into twelve courts, appointed High Lords and Ladies." Nye pointed at two kingdoms splitting Astaria, one in Bhuja and one in Ilrith.

I am still the King of Feoldran, Marcus had said once back in Virian.

"Each kingdom was ruled by two monarchs, with courts managing most of the responsibilities of the land."

"That makes eight."

Nye raised an eyebrow. "Imala's lover was not Fae. But he was not from here." She pointed to a man with feathered wings that arched above his shoulders and almost reached the ground. Not a Lesser Fae, but not a High Fae, either. Something else entirely.

Zylah pieced everything together, connecting the dots between what she'd been told and what she'd taught herself in the last few months. Nye slipped in and out of the shadows almost as if she didn't realise she was doing it, her face impassive. She was far more guarded than her cousins, but given the life she'd likely led, it made sense. To anyone else, she might have seemed cold and unfeeling. But Zylah saw it for what it was: armour. The Fae said nothing as she played with the shadows, letting Zylah flick through the remainder of the book, including the pages she'd skipped through to show Ranon's tomb.

Zylah couldn't understand what was left of the faded ink, the language so old she wondered if anyone could speak it. But the images were clear. War. Death. Suffering. The four hundred years Nye had spoken of, condensed into a handful of pages of scratched ink. She flipped past Ranon's tomb again, the page too dark to linger on, as if the drawing held some of his presence within it. Her fingers slowed at more images of war, and without asking, Zylah knew. It was the beginning of the rivalry between humans and Fae.

"Virian was the old Fae capital," Zylah murmured after a stretch of silence. "When?"

"After the first uprising, when many of the ruling Fae were murdered." Nye had disappeared into the shadows entirely, although Zylah could somehow still feel her nearby.

"Marcus wanted to become High King," she said quietly. And now he was king there once more. How long had he planned this, how many centuries?

Everything Ranon and Sira had created were Lesser Fae. Even the Asters and the vampires. And vampires hadn't been seen since Holt was a child. Over three hundred years, and he'd said he remembered the first uprising.

It didn't strike Zylah as a coincidence that the two might be connected.

"What happened just over twenty years ago, during the last uprising?"

Nye stepped out of the shadows. "Marcus was moving his pieces around the board. And Holt got tired of waiting. He's built up a network of people over the years since his parents' deaths, but Marcus was one step ahead of him. I guess he was whispering in Arnir's ear all along." She shook her head. "We heard Arnir ruled Dalstead as if Fae never existed."

Zylah willed herself not to frown. "He did. I thought they were all gone. Speaking of them was forbidden."

She'd been nothing but a puppet in Dalstead. As if it wasn't enough to be a woman in a man's world, King Arnir had stripped away all access to the truth. But Kara had always managed to get her hands on the Fae storybooks, so there *was* a source, a way. Zylah had just never opened her eyes enough to see it, to find it for herself.

She flipped back to the map showing the four kingdoms, her attention snagging on Feoldran, Marcus's kingdom, and Lanaros, Holt's. "Holt told me once he didn't believe the gods were Fae," she murmured to herself.

Nye laughed under her breath. "Knowing something and accepting it are two very different things. But I couldn't tell you any more of Holt's story even if I wanted to."

There was so much weight to her words, but Zylah didn't press her for more. It wasn't her story to tell, and Zylah respected that. She tapped a finger to the map, tracing the journey she and Holt had made together. Maelissa's court didn't exist, but that didn't surprise Zylah. It had belonged to someone else, been located somewhere else, once. "Why did Imala have a court here?"

"This was her second home, but after the first uprising, the members of the court fled here for their safety." Her head tipped to one side, steady eyes assessing. "I know Holt's reason for fighting this cause. Why he won't stand back and let this be someone else's problem. So tell me. What's your reason for being here?" She flared in and out of the shadows as she spoke, as if staying in the light was beginning to grate on her, even if the glimpses of her face gave nothing away.

Zylah swallowed. "Marcus needs to be stopped. No matter what it takes. This affects everyone now: humans, Fae. All of us. There are no sides anymore."

Shadows consumed the Fae, and Zylah could have sworn she heard a soft sigh. As if Nye was replenished by them. At the corner of her vision, a shadow of a bushy tail swept across the stone floor. *A fox of sorts*, Nye had said when Zylah had asked her if she could shift. One that didn't seem to be entirely whole.

Zylah turned another page, and a sketch made her pause, a quiet breath of surprise leaving her.

"What is it?" Nye asked, appearing right beside her, fully corporeal.

"These symbols." They were the same as the ones in the book Okwata had given her. The same as the ones in the book he had asked of, the one that had been in Raif's library. *Marcus is looking for that book.*

Zylah bit her lip, hesitating. Nye stared back at her, searching her face. Malok might not be trustworthy, but something told Zylah the Fae before her was.

She explained about the books, that Marcus was looking for them. If there was anything that could help them stop him, or anything they could do to stop him from causing more chaos, they had to take every opportunity.

"You have one of them here with you?" Nye asked.

Zylah held out a hand, sucked in a breath as she thought of the book in her room. It appeared in her palm a heartbeat later, and the corner of Nye's mouth twisted up in another of her almost smiles. Zylah handed her the book, watching Nye's eyes flick back and forth over the pages.

"This is an old dialect," Nye murmured.

"Can you read it?"

"I can read the words. But without the key, it's nonsense. Can't you do your thing and bring it here?"

"I'm…" Zylah cleared her throat, turning her hand over and examining it. "…new to this. Holt has been helping me. I know he doesn't necessarily need to know where an item is to summon it, but I do. I've only been successful with a handful of items so far."

"And Holt has tried, I take it?"

"He thinks it's warded. When I described it to him, he couldn't retrieve it."

"Cocky bastard, isn't he?"

Zylah grinned. "I can ask him to try again."

"I'd like to study this, if you'll permit me. We have texts here that might help us at least figure out why Marcus covets it so badly." As if she sensed Zylah's hesitation, she added, "I'll keep it locked in the restricted section. No one will be able to access it but me and Serrula, who I'm fairly certain lives between the rows of books somewhere."

"You have a restricted section?"

"It wouldn't be a very impressive library without one, would it?" Nye's half-smile became a grin, and Zylah couldn't help but match it. For the first time since learning vampires existed, she allowed herself a moment to believe there might be an end to all of this mess.

Hope bloomed in Zylah's chest as they left the library, Nye's promises lodging themselves firmly beneath her ribs.

21

Zylah's steps would have felt a little lighter the next morning as she accompanied Nye to training, had it not been for the pain simmering beneath her skin. She'd avoided Holt the day before because she knew he'd have taken one look at her and known. Instead, she'd added some of the baylock leaves to her morning tea, but alone, the relief it provided was minimal. Enough that she could move without stumbling, but inside, *gods*. She was on fire. And she welcomed it.

She'd had plenty of time to think, the pain keeping her awake throughout the night. Just taking out Marcus was no longer an option, not with everything he'd created. Whatever vampires and thralls remained needed to be stopped, along with the vanquicite mine. At least he was posing as a human, ruling as one of them. Zylah didn't dwell on how badly things would go for the future of both humans and Fae if Marcus revealed he was one of them. *When* he revealed it.

Nye was halfway through inviting Zylah to dinner that evening as they reached the doors to the training balcony, the sound of whoops and cheers carrying through them. The Fae rolled her eyes. "Kej," she muttered, but not unkindly, pushing open the doors to the frigid air.

A large group of soldiers had gathered in a circle, blocking whoever was fighting from view.

But Zylah knew.

Could feel the way the air changed, *thickened* wherever he went, as if his magic fed on the atmosphere around him. *Holt.* She hadn't properly caught up with him since he and Malok had intervened with the three Fae. Since Zylah had stopped Malok from being poisoned. She hadn't filled him in about Nye researching the book, either.

"Is that all you've got?" Kej's voice carried over the cheering, and Zylah followed Nye as the crowd stepped aside for her.

Her cousin rolled to his feet, one eye purple and swollen, his bare chest slick with sweat.

A quiet laugh rumbled somewhere in front of him, but Zylah and Nye still hadn't quite made it through the throng. Zylah felt certain some of the soldiers whispered to each other as she passed, could have sworn one of them hissed *half Fae* under their breath, but she kept her head forward, didn't give them the satisfaction of seeing a response.

"Always with the dick-swinging contests," Rin muttered beside them as they reached her at the front of the crowd.

"It's his coping mechanism. Let him have it," Nye said with an almost shrug.

Zylah's gaze fell on Holt as he ran a hand through his hair, dragging it out of his eyes. The movement flexed every muscle in his arm and down his sculpted torso, his shirt discarded somewhere at the edge of their makeshift ring.

Like Kej, he had strips of cloth wrapped around his knuckles, the fabric of his right hand stained rusty from Kej's blood.

Her attention slowly lifted to Holt's split lip and then higher, his eyes meeting hers as if he'd caught her watching.

The first time they'd met she'd thought him a god, and watching him now, his chest rising and falling, the way he relaxed into each movement as if it centred him, the way his eyes had brightened so that they seemed more gold than green, the way his rumbling laughter only delighted the crowd even more, it was easy to see why.

The corner of his mouth twitched, and he turned his attention back to Kej. *Shit.* She hadn't said that out loud, had she? He'd looked at her like she had.

Zylah cleared her throat, willing the heat warming her cheeks to diminish, and reminding herself she had been part of a conversation moments before, instead of gawking at the two beautiful males before her. "His coping mechanism for Jora?" she asked, angling her head to Nye.

"For tonight," Nye replied, her attention moving around the soldiers watching, some of them stepping away from the fight as they caught her scowl.

"Last time I checked, he's not the one being sold off like cattle," Rin said flatly as Kej swung for Holt and missed.

Zylah turned to say something, but Rin had already slipped through the crowd.

The soldiers roared, and Zylah spun back around to see Holt rubbing his jaw, Kej walking around him in a slow circle with his arms held high as if he'd won the entire fight.

Zylah smirked.

She knew Holt was holding back, for Kej's sake. Knew he could have the whole balcony recoiling the moment he peeled back the layer he kept over his power.

As if he'd again heard her every thought, a small burst of his power rippled from him, sending Kej staggering back a few steps.

"Oh, two can play at that game, my friend," Kej said, gritting his teeth against the magic. He rolled his neck before ushering the crowd to step away, and something told Zylah he intended to shift right in front of them. To meet magic with magic.

"That's enough for today," Nye said firmly, stepping between them. Shadows slipped around her in warning, and she shot a look at the crowd, soldiers already dispersing before she'd even turned full circle.

She stopped when she at last faced Holt, dismissing her cousin entirely. "You're always welcome to train with any of my soldiers, but next time you might like to pick a more worthwhile opponent."

"You still won't be able to take him, Nye," Kej said, unfazed by the fact that she'd just put a stop to all his fun.

Nye's attention slid to him, her face impassive. "Now would be a good time for you to slink away with your latest fad." Zylah knew she was referring to the guard from the day before but hadn't spotted him in the crowd.

Kej's grin widened as he clasped Holt's forearm in a swift goodbye. "I guess I've got to let off that steam somehow. Right, Zy?"

With a quiet chuckle, he took off for where his *fad* had appeared at the guard post beside the stairs.

Bastard. Zylah watched him go, wondering whether it would be appropriate to throttle him in front of Malok later.

"Malok told me you wouldn't join us this evening unless Zylah was present," Nye said, shifting Zylah's attention back to her and Holt.

He unwound the cotton strips from his knuckles, flexing his large hands one after the other. "I'm surprised he didn't request her presence himself after she prevented him from being poisoned."

Nye flinched ever so slightly, but just enough that Zylah caught it.

"You're his general, Nye. Not his assistant. That comment wasn't directed at you." Holt's expression was earnest as he said it, his eyes never breaking away from the Fae so that she could see the truth in them.

General. Zylah had been right to suspect her position.

Nye merely dipped her chin in acknowledgement. "I've been trying to convince him since you first sent word from Virian. I'm not confident he's going to help you once he has the key."

"Neither am I," Holt admitted. "But we need to try. We have to."

Because it was their only option, Zylah gathered from what he didn't say. There was no one else to turn to. No one else willing to stand up against Marcus and his plans for Astaria.

Perhaps this was her tithe.

The last thing she could do for her friends before the vanquicite took her.

"If the shield works and this court is protected, at least it might soften the blow when Rin and Kej inevitably sneak off in the middle of the night without uttering a goodbye," Holt added.

"It's why you haven't pressed him," Nye said, an eyebrow raised at Holt.

He nodded. "I came here out of respect to Malok, to Jora, not to cause a rift amongst this family."

Nye seemed satisfied with that. "I'll be researching the book whilst you're gone," she explained, and Holt's attention flicked to Zylah.

She'd been avoiding him because of the pain, and now, in such form-fitting clothing, she felt he could see every spot where the pain licked beneath her skin. "I recognised some symbols in one of the books Nye showed me yesterday."

"Symbols like the ones in the book Okwata gave you?" he asked, sliding the neatly folded cotton into his pocket.

Zylah nodded.

He squared his jaw. "The one that was in Raif's room must be warded, wherever it is. I've tried several times to retrieve it. I can't feel it anywhere."

"Warded, spelled, protected. A book like that is not meant to be found so easily," Nye said, one hand rubbing at her chin in thought.

For a heartbeat, Zylah wondered if Raif had known the book was warded, poisonous thoughts whispering to her that it was another lie, another thing he'd kept from her.

"Do you have anything in your library about nullifying van-quicite?" Holt asked Nye, pulling Zylah from her thoughts.

She stilled at his words. He wouldn't tell Nye about the piece in her back, not without asking for her consent, Zylah was certain of it. But she wasn't ready to tell Nye and the others, not yet.

"I can look," Nye said confidently. She clicked her tongue as two soldiers barrelled past them, grappling each other into a roll. Another soldier caught her attention, and she excused herself from the conversation, leaving Holt and Zylah alone to watch the soldiers.

"Not what you expected?" Holt asked.

"The court? Or this?" Zylah waved a hand at the sparring.

He studied her face for a moment. "All of it."

Zylah hadn't known what to expect after Mae's court. She didn't trust Malok. Or Cirelle, if she was being entirely honest with herself, but she'd shared her circumstance about the vanquicite out of desperation. "Nye seems duty bound, but she's been kind to me. Rin and Kej have too. They think a lot of you, even when you're giving one of them a beating."

A quiet puff of air escaped Holt in amusement. "He likes to provoke me."

"And you gave in so easily?"

He cocked his head, lips pressing together before asking, "What makes you think I gave in?"

"Hmm, I think Kej's black eye gave it away," she said, fighting the smile threatening to burst from her. Truthfully, she knew he'd done it as much for himself as for Kej. That it helped lessen some of the burden he seemed to carry. For the first time since he'd shown up outside her cabin in Varda, a little bit of the tension seemed to have eased from his shoulders.

"Kej is persistent," Holt said, one eyebrow raised. Zylah couldn't help but smile at the thought of Kej making *that* kind of move on Holt. The smile tugging at his mouth told her she'd guessed right. *My brother will fuck anyone with a pulse*, Rin had warned her.

Holt added, "If he thinks I gave him what he wanted, then he'll back off and give me space."

Zylah elbowed him playfully. "You're an expert at coercion now, are you?"

But Holt's expression darkened for a moment at her words, just as Nye returned from her conversation with the solider.

"Plans of the mine are on their way to us," Nye told Holt.

Whatever Zylah had seen in his face before was gone as Holt said, "Even if we can destroy the mine, we need to be prepared for whatever Marcus is forging into weapons."

Weapons like the one Jesper had taken from Arnir. The sword he'd wielded to keep Raif and Holt's powers diminished when he took Raif's life. Zylah shifted on her feet, hoping it might be mistaken for discomfort watching the two soldiers who were still sparring. One of them was the soldier who'd almost knocked her off her feet the day before, strands of hair falling across his face that he slicked back with a swipe of his hand.

"My uncle believes he has a lead on that," Nye said, just as Slick ducked from the other soldier's grasp in an impressive evasive move.

"Another advantage he hopes to hold over me?" Holt asked quietly.

"Give him time, Holt."

"We don't have time, Nye. The moment the scouts locate the key, we'll be leaving to retrieve it. And I hope it's enough to convince Malok."

"He knows he cannot run from this. None of us can," Nye said with finality.

No one could argue with that.

"I'll leave you to your training. I promised Rin and Kej my help with something today." Holt made for the door, his eyes meeting Zylah's for a moment. "Zylah," he said quietly. As if it were an apology rather than a farewell.

We don't have time. Zylah had never been so acutely aware of the minutes and hours ticking by whilst they were trapped in the court, all too mindful that her ability to find the key might be the difference between them succeeding and failing in securing Malok's soldiers.

If she found it, she would still be a murderer. It wouldn't make her any less of a monster, either. It wouldn't help chase away the feeling that wrapped itself around her heart and left her feeling empty. But it could be her legacy. The one thing she could do to make a difference before she left this world.

"I need more time to look at the book," Nye murmured absentmindedly, as if she'd felt the shadows snaking their way into Zylah's thoughts.

Out of the corner of her eye, Zylah knew Slick and the other soldier had finished their sparring session, but she made sure he didn't know she was paying attention. If he had any connection to Selas and the others, she knew she needed to tread carefully.

"I love my uncle, but I don't trust him," Nye added.

"What's happening tonight?" Zylah asked. "Who else will be present at this meal?"

"There are representatives here from the Lychnus Court. They remained after Jora's funeral. They'll be in attendance."

240

Discomfort slid along Zylah's bare arms, and she wrapped them around herself to hide her shiver.

"Come on." Nye gave Zylah's shoulder a nudge. "We've got our own shit to work through here first."

The Fae stepped into a starting position, and Zylah didn't have a moment longer to dwell on her unsettling thoughts.

22

Trepidation turned to ire the moment Zylah stepped into the dining room. Daven, one of the three Fae who had attacked her a few days before, sat at a large table beside Malok, swirling a glass of amber liquid.

Nye bristled beside her. "I wasn't aware he'd be here; I wouldn't have asked—"

"It's fine," Zylah murmured, flashing a small smile to her friend. The effects of the baylock tea she'd sipped at whilst getting ready had already begun to fade, and she smoothed her hands down the dress Rin had let her borrow in an effort to still the tremor threatening to roll through her.

Floor length and figure-hugging, the dress had a slit up to one thigh, the navy silk concealing a dagger disguised with a deceit. She wasn't taking any chances, and now she was glad she hadn't.

She took in the dimly lit room, tiny orblights crisscrossing over the ceiling to the arched windows, leading to the glittering stars beyond. Zylah had expected a hall, had anticipated more members of the court to be present, but from the size of the table almost filling the space entirely, it was clear that this was to be a more intimate affair.

Kej and Rin cut them off on their approach to the table, passing a full glass to each of them.

"Squeezing them in before Cirelle arrives?" Nye asked with a raised eyebrow, accepting her glass from Kej.

"We're going to need it tonight," Rin murmured. She wore a similar dress to the one she had loaned Zylah, the silver shimmering beneath the orblights. Though hers was less revealing, and Zylah wondered if it was merely because of the nature of the meal or because of the company.

"Who's flavour of the night then, Kej?" Zylah asked, hoping to ease the discomfort that had seemed to settle across his sister's shoulders.

He knocked back the contents of his glass before asking, "Are you offering?" He might have winked, but his eye was still too swollen from earlier to close fully.

Rin elbowed him. Kej was dressed in fine attire too, a notched, silver-grey shirt tucked into charcoal trousers, silver detailing running down the side panels. Nye wore a slightly smarter version of the uniform she wore throughout the day; fitted trousers and a long-sleeved, form-fitting shirt, her weapons still firmly in place.

It had only made Zylah question the nature of their evening even further when Nye had arrived at her room to collect her earlier, her teacup long emptied, Kopi huddled up against it for warmth.

"Looks like your flavour just arrived," Kej murmured, another half-empty glass already in his hand.

Zylah didn't take the bait. She let Rin tug her towards the table, taking a seat beside her. Kej slipped into the seat beside his sister, Nye took a seat one along from Malok, leaving another empty space between her and Zylah, and one between Kej and Daven.

Zylah looked up just as Daven's attention shifted to her, his features pinching for a moment.

"Are your companions not joining us?" she asked politely, the sweet smile painted on her face she might have once used for customers in her father's apothecary.

Daven schooled his face to neutrality, but Zylah didn't miss the way he straightened a piece of cutlery in an attempt to hide his discomfort. "They left."

"A wise decision." She didn't move her attention away from him, let him feel the weight of her stare until he found the balls to look her in the eye. A chair scraped gently beside her.

"My suggestion to leave extended to you as well, Daven," Holt said quietly as he seated himself beside Zylah. She didn't let her surprise show at his words, didn't take her eyes off of Daven, certain that Holt's face echoed the threat in his words.

Cirelle was next to join them, breaking the tension that had fallen over the table as every male's chair scraped back and they stood, waiting for the High Lady to take her seat. Daven's knee seemed to give him trouble as he moved, the knee Zylah had put a dagger through a few days before, and she bit down on her smile as she caught the movement.

"What happened to your leg?" Rin asked him, as if she didn't already know in precise detail exactly what had transpired between them.

"Lots of sharp things to bump into in this court. Spears. Swords. Daggers," Zylah said coolly, toying with her knife on the table.

Daven cleared his throat. "I apologise for our misunderstanding."

Zylah cocked her head to the side, making sure not to let any trace of emotion flicker across her face as she let silence settle for a little longer than was comfortable. "It didn't feel like a misunderstanding when your blade sliced my cheek."

Holt stilled beside her, a small pulse of his power rippling at the bare skin of her arms before he reeled it back in again.

"Arlan, good of you to join us," Daven said, just as a finely dressed male took a seat beside him, his amber eyes assessing the table.

"Rin," he said quietly, as if there were no one there but the two of them. Rin shifted uncomfortably in her seat, her chin dipping in acknowledgement, and suddenly the pieces clicked into place for Zylah. *Father's been trying to pair me off for ages with a male from another court,* she'd said at Jora's funeral. And just that morning she'd mentioned being sold off like cattle. To the male sat opposite, Zylah realised.

Malok made the introductions. "Zylah, may I introduce you to Arlan, next in line to the Lychnus Court? I believe you've already met Daven, Arlan's personal guard."

A faint smile twisted Arlan's mouth. Polite. Polished. Practised. As if there was absolutely nothing underneath it, or he was so well trained in hiding everything else. A bit of both, Zylah presumed. Here was the male *lacking in charisma*, as Rin had put it. The one she'd been hiding from at Jora's funeral. From the little Zylah knew of her, she didn't seem the type to baulk from anyone.

Malok launched into a lengthy speech about trade between their two courts, the strength of a union between Arlan and Rin, the merits of its success, and Rin only sank further into her seat beside Zylah.

Kej knocked back another glass, and Zylah realised he'd chosen his seat purposefully, to act as a buffer between his sister and Arlan. Had Rin requested it, or was Kej merely protective of his twin?

Arlan pressed his fingers together, elbows on the armrests of his chair, listening in silence. When Malok paused to let the staff fill his plate with food, Arlan took his opportunity to speak. "You're wasting time on court politics when a war is being waged out there. Don't you think we should be out there doing something about it?"

Daven shifted beside him. "You are young, Arlan, I think Lord Malok—"

"Daven. You insulted me already by attacking someone in this court. Once was enough, thank you. Your presence is no longer required for the rest of the evening, and I believe you've already been asked to leave. I'll expect you ready to depart first thing." Arlan didn't even look at his guard as he spoke, only turned to the male who had filled his plate and offered a quiet thank you.

Daven blanched. Placed his glass soundlessly on the table and inclined his head. "As you wish, my Lord." With a scrape of his chair and a not-so-graceful rise to his feet, Daven excused himself from the table. His wounded knee undermined any dignity he might have held onto for his exit, and Zylah bit back her smile of satisfaction.

Arlan smoothly offered his apologies to the table, continuing the conversation without hesitation. From the corner of her eye, Zylah noticed Rin's brow pinched together in a slight frown, and at that moment, she knew the Fae's words about him lacking charisma had been an excuse.

As a member of staff filled her plate with food, she couldn't help but inhale deeply, sifting through the scents for any hint of poison.

Nothing.

She took a bite, happy with her assessment, and looked up to find Malok watching her. Only when she'd swallowed her first mouthful of food did he start eating. *Asshole.*

The rest of the meal became an argument between Arlan and Malok over the distribution of his army, of Marcus's presence in Virian, his mining, and his plans for the army he'd been creating, Holt interjecting now and then to try and offer some semblance of peace. Discomfort formed a knot in Zylah's stomach the more she heard, lacing itself with the pain that had been gradually getting worse throughout the meal, her plate barely touched.

They were wasting time sitting here, pretending nothing was happening beyond the walls of the court. Time Astaria didn't have.

Time she didn't have.

And yet, she took in every word, every detail for anything that might help her get closer to Marcus.

Arlan made his stance on Malok's withdrawal clear; he too wanted to act now against Marcus after the thrall attack, before

Marcus had time to form a full army, to forge enough weapons to arm them all.

"My general has her orders," Malok said with a hint of finality.

"I'd like to hear Niossa's ideas," Arlan countered, ignoring the warning in Malok's tone and turning his attention to Nye.

"If you'll excuse me," Cirelle said as the staff cleared away their meal. "All this talk of war."

Seats dragged back as Cirelle departed, and Zylah silently scolded herself for realising too late: the emotion in the room was too much for the Fae to take on top of her grief. For a moment she wondered if there was some reason she could offer to excuse herself too, to get a moment of air just to steady herself against the pain.

Nye spoke of the Fae uprising, of all Holt had tried to achieve back in Virian. "Marcus is posing as a human, making a Fae alliance with the humans more unlikely by the minute."

"I think the priestesses have their own plans for the humans too," Zylah said, hands folded in her lap.

"Explain," Malok commanded.

Zylah offered up her observations of the priestesses since leaving Virian, of their strange recruitment drive.

The lord's features darkened. "Power is like a drug, even to those who claim a life of virtue. Niossa." His gaze pinned Nye. His general.

"I'll look into it first thing." She held her head high, nothing in her stance holding anything but pride.

She may have said she believed Malok managed court matters efficiently, but she wasn't afraid of her uncle.

Zylah wondered if Nye was afraid of anything.

Arlan tapped a finger against his glass, a muscle feathering in his jaw. "This is why a united front is more important than ever, without any…" His attention flicked to Rin for a moment. "…unnecessary delays."

Rin said nothing, but Zylah didn't miss Kej's scowl at Arlan's dismissal. Her hand moved to the arm of her chair as a burst of pain rolled down her spine, and she willed herself not to dig her fingers into the wood.

Holt broke the silence, relief washing over Zylah that she wouldn't have to speak. "It doesn't matter what lies Marcus spreads about his circumstances. Soon enough he will have no choice but to reveal who he truly is. We need to ensure by then that the strength of our actions will have convinced the humans to work with us. That we are no threat to them."

"And how do you propose we do that?" Malok asked.

"Simple. Let them see the vampires, the thralls. Fight for them. Let them share stories of the atrocities Marcus has created. They wish for the same as us—to live freely, without fear." His attention slid to Zylah's fingers, now curled over the edge of the armrest closest to him, fingernails grazing the wood.

What Holt suggested was no easy feat. Humans were the very reason the Fae lived the way they did.

The reason they hid themselves and banded together out of sight of the humans.

The reason Malok weaved a heavy deceit over his appearance, hiding the scar the humans had given him.

Malok's eyes narrowed. "Marcus will no doubt call you back to him soon."

"Perhaps." Holt was already on his feet, dismissing Malok entirely. "We should take a break, come back to this after we've all had some air. Zylah?"

Zylah looked up at him in surprise as he held out a hand for her, and she bit her tongue as realisation sliced through her. He knew.

She didn't take his hand. The rest of the guests were already moving, their attention no longer on her.

Zylah stepped into place beside Holt, following him through a doorway into another room, furnished with a few chairs arranged around a low table and a bench beside the arched window.

Holt said nothing, and neither did she. He led her out onto the balcony, and she knew as the silence stretched, he was pissed.

"Are you this fucking stubborn you'd rather sit through an entire meal suffering in silence than ask me for help?" he said at last when they were far enough away from the others. He kept his voice lowered, but there was no doubting how angry he was, the restraint he always held in place slipping away. "Turn around," he added roughly.

"No." The word came out small, breathy from the pain. It was too risky. If he knew the truth, there would be no going with him. No getting close to Marcus or Jesper.

"Don't argue with me, Zylah, turn around." His eyes flashed, challenging her, but Zylah didn't fight him. He knew she didn't have it in her.

She rested her hands on the balcony wall, looking out towards the ocean, and he stepped into place beside her, one hand on her lower back. Zylah felt herself sag with relief as magic poured from him, and Holt shifted closer, his arm wrapping around her waist, taking her weight as she leaned into his side.

Slowly, the fire in her veins receded, a quiet sigh escaping her. She felt Holt relax too, taking more of her weight like it was nothing, tucking her into him a little tighter.

His familiar scent wrapped around her, soothing her, and she could feel his heartbeat gradually slowing where her head rested against his chest.

"This place is stifling," he said at last, his voice quiet and rough.

"You feel it too?" Zylah asked without looking up at him, not yet ready to move away even though the pain had dimmed to a hum. The best she knew it was going to get.

"I was sent here every winter as a boy to train with Jora. I couldn't wait to leave. But now…"

She looked up at him then, at the way his gaze fixed on the dark horizon. "I wish I'd appreciated those moments a little more."

Zylah knew all too well what that felt like. "I always wanted to see the world. But I never stopped to think that one day my father wouldn't be in it. For all his talk of legacy, I don't think I ever really thought about death. And now…" It felt as if her days were made up of the what-ifs and the whys. What if she'd never stayed in Virian? Why did her father have to suffer for her actions? What if she hadn't poisoned her captor's tea, and instead succumbed to the lashing he'd given her?

Holt's fingers flexed across the fabric of her dress, his touch like a brand where his power still flowed from him. "What else did Pallia tell you?"

"What?" Zylah asked, twisting away to look up at him better. He pulled his arm away slowly, as if he knew she didn't need any more magic from him, but he was worried about doing it too quickly.

His attention fell to her shoulder, to the loose strands of hair that had fallen across it before his eyes met hers. The gold from earlier had dimmed, but the green was as bright as the forest leaves in spring. "You said she came to you when the Asters attacked, but you didn't say what happened."

"You believe me?"

"Why wouldn't I?"

"She told me to get the vanquicite removed." Zylah chewed her lip. "I told Cirelle. Not about Pallia, I mean. Just about the vanquicite. She's sent word for a healer from her court to help me." She didn't tell him that it was too late. That it didn't matter who Cirelle had sent for.

"You healed her daughter. She owes you a debt."

Zylah said nothing. No Fae healer would be able to use their healing abilities and touch the vanquicite without it nullifying their powers, she felt certain of it. The thought urged her to look away, to not let her eyes reveal the truth to him.

"I won't let anything happen to you, Zylah. We'll get the vanquicite removed." Holt gently eased the hair off her shoulder, his skin warm and rough where his fingers swept across hers. His brow pinched together for a moment as he pulled his hand away, as if a little more of the restraint he always showed had slipped unintentionally.

She hated that she would be another friend he had to lose. Another person in his life he'd feel responsible for. Her attention

252

fell to his wrist, her fingers brushing against the leather bracelet she'd given him before she even realised she was doing it. The silver bell sat nestled between the leather strands, still shiny, as if he touched it often. "Do you always wear this?"

"I never take it off." His eyes searched hers, and Zylah felt herself lean into him. Felt the pull that always drew her to him, wherever he was in a room. She hadn't allowed herself to dwell on it, had always made herself stay away, afraid of that same pull she'd felt the first day they'd met when she was running from Arnir's men. Holt had made it clear that day too; he wouldn't touch her. But she knew, now. He'd said it for her.

It isn't right to want them both, Rose had told her once. And even then, the guilt of being with Raif and feeling this… whatever this was between her and Holt, had kept her awake on countless nights back in Virian. *Monster*, a small voice whispered to her.

Holt's gaze dipped, but he remained so still she wasn't sure he was breathing, as if he was waiting for her to decide what she wanted, as if he knew the war raging in her thoughts.

"Imala's tits, this evening is dragging!" Rin's voice carried from the door, and Zylah took a step back, her eyes darting to the Fae and her brother. "At least dessert is worth waiting for."

Kej's attention flitted between Holt and Zylah, a wide grin across his face. "I think these two might be skipping dessert."

Holt's hands slid into his pockets, his impassive expression back in place as he acknowledged their arrival, but he didn't take a step away, as if he couldn't bring himself to do it just yet.

Zylah broke away first, cold air rushing into the small space between them. She took the glass Rin handed her, eyeing the fizzing liquid inside. "So how do you pass the time here in winter? Is it just endless days of training and evenings of food and wine?"

Malok called out to his children from the dining room, and Kej rolled his eyes, looping his arm through his sister's. He glanced back over his shoulder with a wink as he left the balcony. "You two have interconnecting rooms, I'm sure you'll figure it out."

In Pallia's name, he was relentless.

Rin pulled her with them, and Holt followed them all back to the dining room, the mood sobering the moment Arlan's attention settled on Rin.

"Your father and I have reached a stalemate over the… agreement between our two courts." His eyes remained on Rin as he spoke, his expression giving nothing away despite the bite in his tone. It seemed like the idea repulsed him, not Rin, Zylah suspected. But the idea of an arranged marriage. "Zylah, I wish you well in retrieving the key. Perhaps Malok will be more forthcoming knowing this court is protected. A luxury the rest of Astaria do not have." His gaze slid back to Rin for a heartbeat. "Goodnight."

Malok scowled at the dismissal, but he said nothing, taking his glass from the table and heading for the small adjoining room.

"Why do I get the feeling that if you don't find the key, we're all completely fucked?" Kej said quietly.

"Because our father likes to play god," Rin muttered, shrugging out of her brother's reach and heading for the door after Arlan.

"I'm happy to swap this one in as our third," Kej said with a wink at Zylah, flicking his chin in Holt's direction.

She knew he was trying to lighten the mood, but he couldn't have known he'd hit a nerve. "Goodnight," she murmured, exhaustion wrapping around her.

Zylah left her friends without waiting for a response, her thoughts darkening with every step closer to her room.

23

Rin and Kej were hiding something.

A few days had passed since the dinner with Malok and the others when Zylah realised the twins were only turning up to training every morning for people to notice their presence. To make it known.

Kej would leave first, usually under the pretence of running after his guard, Rin shortly after. And though Zylah knew it was none of her business, on the third morning she'd caught them arguing, catching a few words that had her silently following them deep into the court, further than she'd yet ventured. Kopi joined her soon after her pursuit began, finding her from the gods knew where since she'd left him in her room that morning.

She kept her distance from the twins, hanging back as far as she could, occasionally losing them through a doorway or another corridor. An ocean breeze teased wisps of hair around her face, and Zylah marvelled at the magic of this place. Nye had explained during training how it was spelled to keep out the worst of the cold, how the wards on the boundaries also meant any magic within couldn't be detected from the outside, but

Zylah still couldn't quite adjust to feeling the wind against her skin but not the bite of the cold air.

A wrong turn had her pausing, holding her breath to listen for any sign of the twins. This end of the court was deserted, and at first, Zylah had wondered if she was merely following them to their chambers. She tracked their hushed conversation, gaining sight of them again at the end of a long passage lined with columns, more of those glassless windows facing out to the sea. She paused in the shadows, watching them as they slipped through a doorway halfway down, voices sounding from within.

Movement at the other end of the corridor caught her attention, and instinctively she hid behind a column, but then a flare of power pressed at her skin as if alerting her to his presence. Holt evanesced beside her, pressing a finger to his lips.

Zylah tracked the movement, her eyes lingering for a moment before darting up to meet his. He tilted his head to one side, and Zylah followed his silent instruction to listen.

Children laughed beyond the door Rin and Kej had disappeared through. Then a rumble of amusement from Kej, followed by something that sounded an awful lot like a scolding from Rin.

Zylah looked at Holt, one eyebrow raised.

"I think they're human," he murmured.

Humans couldn't pass through the wards, Nye had said when they'd first arrived. And Malok loathed humans. Which meant...

"They're hiding them," Zylah said quietly, making no attempt to hide her surprise. Not just hiding... Rin and Kej had somehow ferried the children inside the court, undetected.

Holt nodded, leading the way to the door, and then paused. Kopi rustled his feathers at Zylah's shoulders, ocean waves breaking on the cliffs beyond the court, and still, Holt waited.

Zylah rested a hand on his arm. "Malok will never give you his army if he finds out."

"Then he won't," he said, his attention shifting to where her fingertips touched his scar. "But that's not why I hesitated." More laughter rang out. The children were young, if Zylah had to guess, no more than five. "I don't want to frighten them."

Zylah couldn't help her small smile. She slipped past him, easing the door open a crack to slip through. A cluster of children climbed over Kej, laughing as he tried to gently wrestle them off him. Rin rose to her feet as soon as she saw Zylah, and at once a hush fell over the children.

"She's like us," a boy whispered, pointing from his place on Kej's shoulders.

Zylah knew from their worried glances that the twins had no idea which way this was going to go. Could imagine what they must be thinking—anyone would—that she might use this to gain favour with Malok. To help Holt secure the army.

"Sort of," Zylah said, turning her attention to the little boy with a small smile. "But my friend is like them," she added, waving a hand between the door and Rin and Kej. "Can he come in?"

Rin and Kej shared another look, Kej's shoulders sinking as he released a breath, before Rin said, "Of course."

She knew what they were risking. They hadn't known her for very long. Would see her exactly as she was, half Fae, having spent most of her life amongst humans. Half Fae, with

258

something to gain from her time in the court. And though Zylah wanted to earn their trust, glancing around the room full of small grubby faces staring back at her, more than that was the desire to help.

One of the children hid behind Kej's back as Holt entered the room, fingers curled into the Fae's shirt.

Zylah lifted Kopi from her shoulder, reached for Holt's hand and deposited the tiny owl in his palm. Kopi didn't even open an eye, just sank his head further into his feathers and nuzzled into Holt's warmth.

"See?" Zylah said brightly. "A friend."

Holt raised an eyebrow at Kej. "Looks like we have a spell to teach you," he said quietly, lowering to a crouch as Rin led a little girl over to examine Kopi more closely. The spell that concealed sound and scent, the spell they'd been using since leaving Varda.

The spell that Marcus had discovered, and they were still no closer to finding out how.

Zylah sat on the floor beside Holt, answering the children's questions as they crowded around Kopi. Most of them weren't old enough to string a proper sentence together, and there were far more than Zylah had first realised.

Blankets and pillows were strewn across the room, toys and drawing materials scattered here and there.

"Where are their parents?" Zylah asked.

Rin jerked her chin to another door on the far side of the room. "Through there with the older children. They're sick and they don't want to pass it to the little ones, so we've been helping out."

Now that Zylah paused to listen over the noise of the children, she could hear coughs and splutters from the next room. Disappointment and anger flared in her chest, all of it directed at Malok. That not only would he let the world beyond this court suffer, that he would deny Holt his army, but that his own children would have to conceal *this* from him. That helping humans had to be such a secret, they were hidden here, in a forgotten part of the court that looked as if it had been abandoned years ago.

She didn't need to glance at Holt for his confirmation before she spoke. "We can help. If they can't be healed with magic, I've worked in apothecary most of my life."

Rin shot her brother a look. Kej had been quiet, watching the situation unfurl, children still dangling from him as he sat amongst them.

He heaved a sigh. Peeled another child from his shoulders and deposited her beside him, passing her a doll made of brightly covered fabric. "This will jeopardise your position with our father. But I can't deny we need the help. We're sort of drowning here." As if on cue, the little girl ascended his shoulders again, resuming her previous position, hands holding firmly to the Fae's forehead.

Zylah hid her smile in her shoulder, eyebrows raised at Holt, willing him to answer for her.

"We'd be glad to," Holt said to Kej, but his eyes remained fixed on Zylah's, and she knew he was holding back a smile of his own.

They left Kopi with Kej and the children, following Rin to see to the adults and older children in the adjacent room. The space was much larger than the first, thirty or so bedrolls laid out across the floor with humans either curled up asleep or huddled up beside each other.

Zylah quickly established that they all had a mild flu she'd seen countless times over winters past, listing off items for Rin to retrieve from the kitchen and for Holt to summon from around the court as she set up a space to work. It hadn't quite been a week since Rin and Kej had brought the humans into the court, and Zylah advised them that they would likely still be contagious to the smaller children for a few more days, that keeping them separate had been the right decision.

By late afternoon, with Holt's help, she'd made tonics for everyone, and a balm for them to rub onto their chests and ease their breathing. It had been slow, steady work, that she'd fallen into with a familiar rhythm, her hands methodically working with barely any thought. She couldn't count how many times she'd made these exact items alongside her father, night after night in his little shop. For the first time, when she thought of him, there was no stab of guilt over his death. Only the quiet desire to talk to him, to argue with him about what ingredients made the best salve, to hear him complain about the customers who never listened to his recommendations.

"What were you thinking about just now?" Holt moved quietly beside her, helping her tidy away her temporary workstation.

She considered an excuse. But then she remembered her promise to him. "My father. Why'd you ask?"

"You looked… peaceful." He held the door open for her as they made their way back into Rin and Kej's makeshift nursery.

The pair had left for a meeting—*damage control*—as Rin had referred to it and asked if they could watch over the children until their return.

"So this is what they do every night? Go searching for humans in need of help?" Zylah asked, picking up empty bowls that had been filled with soft fruits only moments before, half the contents smeared across tiny hands and faces.

Holt took a seat on the floor beside a little girl who played alone. "Their village was destroyed by thralls," he said softly, watching the girl closely. He clicked his fingers. One of the other children began to cry, and Zylah scooped him up to soothe him, wiping fruit off his face with her thumb. Some of the others started crying, but the little girl didn't look up from her wooden blocks.

Zylah wasn't a natural with children. But enough had come into the apothecary with their parents for her to know how to calm them, to tease a laugh from them when she needed to administer a drop of tonic under the tongue or a balm to a scraped knee.

Holt tapped the little girl on the arm and waved his hand. She put down her blocks and waved back. "Hi," he said, waving again. She rubbed at her eyes and tried to fight a yawn.

"Tired?" Holt asked, pressing his hands to the side of his face, palms together, head tilted as he looked down at her.

The girl curled into the nearest cushion, and Holt carefully pulled a blanket over her.

"Sleep," he said softly, moving his right hand over his face, eyes and fingers closing as he reached his chin, sighing like he was tired too.

"She can't hear?" Zylah asked, realising he'd been signing like he had with Delana back in Mae's court.

"I'm not sure. But I don't think she speaks."

She didn't need to ask to know he was thinking of his sister. And as she sat beside him with the little boy still in her arms, she couldn't help but think about what he'd told her before she'd left Virian. That the female he'd been with had left him because she wanted children and he didn't.

Zylah hadn't pieced the two together before, but now she wondered if it had been because the loss of his sister had still been too raw.

"Adina used to play alone," he said, his voice still quiet as more of the children started to settle.

"She'd be proud of you. Of what you're trying to do." Zylah didn't doubt it for a moment. Hoped he could hear the truth of it in her words.

Holt tucked the blanket around the little girl, moving the blocks a safe distance away, but he didn't reply. Whatever memory he was lost in, the grief that it had awoken, silently took over him for a moment.

Rin and Kej returned, arms full of supplies, and the moment to ask Holt about Adina was lost. She hadn't wanted to pry, only for him to know that she understood the desire to talk about the people she'd lost.

To keep their memory alive.

Rin took the little boy from Zylah's arms, handing over a small basket. "You haven't eaten all day; it was the least we could do."

"We'll be back tomorrow," Zylah said with a smile.

She was hungry, but she was used to the gnawing in her stomach. Preferred it to the ache of her emotions that she fought so hard to block out.

Holt held his hand out for the basket, but when she handed it to him, he'd evanesced them to another part of the court. "I used to come and hide here as a boy," he said, by way of explanation, releasing Zylah's hand. A blanket appeared in it a moment later, and Zylah gratefully shrugged it over her shoulders. She'd worked all day in her training clothes as Rin had been wearing hers too, but here, in the open cave Holt had brought them to, the breeze was cool against her skin.

"Rava comes here too?" Zylah asked, waving a hand at what looked like a large nest in the shadows behind them.

"Sometimes." Holt handed her a roll of bread, still warm from the kitchens.

Kitchens that were overflowing, food no doubt wasted each day, when the humans they'd been treating looked half starved. As had most of the humans in every village and town she'd seen since leaving Virian.

Zylah turned the roll over in her hands. "Why is Malok so dismissive of you, if he let you come to his court to train year after year?"

"An agreement with my parents. But there were decisions they made that he didn't approve of."

"I thought you said they ultimately favoured Fae over humans?"

He looked out over the water, the wind blowing hair across his eyes. "They did, in the end. But it was already too late. Marcus had already intervened."

"He killed them," Zylah said quietly. "Your parents. Your sister. Even his own son. He's taken so much from so many." She frowned, picking at the bread as she thought about the humans, homeless now thanks to the thralls and in no less danger should Malok discover them.

Holt watched, arms folded, waiting for her to eat. Only when Zylah had finished the roll and he'd passed her a brin fruit did he say, "He'll take much more before this is all over."

For the first time, she wondered if there was a way to pull apart a bargain the same way she could lift the edges of a deceit. If there was a way to release Holt from whatever tied him to Marcus. She'd filled him in on everything Nye had shown her in the library whilst they'd made the tonics, and he'd listened quietly. And though she wanted to ask him now if he thought there was a connection between Marcus's source of old magic and what Nye had explained, she decided against it. Whenever she brought up Marcus, he seemed to shut down, and that dark voice returned in her thoughts, whispering and taunting her.

"Truth number three," she said, discarding the brin core over the drop before them. "My greatest fear is that you're right."

24

Two weeks passed, and the snowstorm had still not relented. Two weeks for Zylah to pick through her thoughts, to train, to help Rin and Kej with the humans, to bury every feeling that tried to push its way to the surface. Two weeks of baylock tea and a mild tonic she'd managed to make from a few other ingredients sourced within the court, which had meant she hadn't had to ask Holt for help again with her healing.

He was right, she'd realised, about Raif. She had loved him, even if it wasn't the kind of love she'd wanted it to be, knew it could be. She didn't think she'd ever forgive herself for that. But she'd accepted it. He was gone, and with whatever little time she had left in her life, she was prepared to pay for the lives that had been lost because of her. If retrieving Malok's key took her closer to Marcus, she would find it, find *him*, and make him pay for everything he'd done. For every life he'd taken, every life he'd destroyed.

Zylah sipped at her tea as she picked at the canna cake on her breakfast tray. One had appeared every morning since the meal with Arlan and Daven, and though Zylah suspected Holt had somehow got her favourite snack added to the court's breakfast menu, neither of them brought it up during their time spent with the humans.

Kopi made a quiet murmur of satisfaction on the table before her, nuzzling up to her warm teapot. She'd made sure to leave him behind each day, intent on teaching herself not to rely on him but she suspected he sometimes followed her from a distance. Whatever Pallia had intended by sending him to her, something told Zylah it wouldn't be long now before they were separated, and a quiet part of her knew that this time apart was as much for him as it had been for her.

With the bitter tea finished, Zylah ate the last of the canna cake as her reward and gave Kopi a gentle scratch on the head before leaving. She made her way to training, easing herself into her stretches as she waited for Nye to join her. A group of soldiers were practising in pairs, their blows staggering each other back across the balcony.

They were using magic. She focused on her stretches, trying not to openly stare at their display of power. Zylah had been careful not to use any of her own magic over the last two weeks—it was the sole reason her tonics and baylock tea had almost been enough to keep the pain at bay.

A cool breeze carried the scents of the ocean with it, and again Zylah marvelled at how the magic around the court kept the worst of the frigid air away. The sound of the waves crashing against the cliffs below pulled her into a steady rhythm, each movement easing a little more tension from another night of broken sleep.

"Care to spar?" A male voice asked her.

Zylah looked up to find Slick striding over. The soldier who had almost knocked her off her feet, and who Zylah was certain had just been waiting for an opportunity to find her alone.

She didn't have the energy to deal with him. Barely had the energy to get out of bed. The training grounded her, helped her feel alive even when she knew the vanquicite was slowly chipping away at her, and though most days she had the pain locked down, the feeling buried somewhere deep inside her, today she felt like it leaked from her every pore.

"Not today," she said, dismissing him and returning to her stretches.

"Afraid?" he asked, taking a step closer.

More like bored. Zylah moved just as he did, ducking away from his grapple and swinging behind him to land a blow to his ribs. She swiped him off his feet with a single kick, one foot pressing into his chest as he looked up at her. "I said. Not. Today."

"Zylah," a voice said behind her.

She released Slick, waiting for him to try again, but he didn't move, and Zylah knew why.

Holt had moved in beside her so quietly that she had no idea where he came from. He wasn't dressed for training, she noticed, the cut of his shirt revealing a glimpse of the scar on his neck. His gaze slid to the soldier on the ground, and back to Zylah. "I'm starting to think you like picking fights." The corner of his mouth quirked, but then it was gone. Power flared from him for a moment, and the soldier stumbled as he tried to push himself to his feet.

Coward.

Zylah smirked, eyes darting to Slick. "Only when I'm bored and I know I can take them out with a single kick." One of his friends was already pulling him away, his face paling as he took in Holt beside her.

"Malok asked to see you," Holt said, pulling her attention back to him.

"Now?"

"Nye came to your room, but she'd just missed you." He held out his hand for hers.

Zylah hesitated for a moment before taking it, willing herself to get a hold on the agony burning beneath her skin. And as if the pain in her veins responded to her even acknowledging it, the familiar sharp sting rolled its way down her spine.

She snatched her hand away the moment their journey was over. But they weren't inside Malok's rooms. They were in the corridor, outside.

"I thought you might like a moment," Holt said, his voice sounding clipped and distant.

He knew. The asshole knew she was in pain, just like he had at the meal with Arlan and Daven. Zylah raised an eyebrow and flicked her chin at Malok's door. "Why aren't his rooms warded?"

"Just tell me what to do, Zylah."

"About what?"

"Don't." He closed his eyes for a moment, rubbing a finger and thumb across his brow as if he were trying to will away his anger. "I won't stop wanting to help you, and I can't stand back and watch you punish yourself over something that wasn't your fault. So can we just call a truce?" Zylah's mouth opened to protest, but he cut her off, taking a step closer. "It doesn't drain me in the slightest to heal you."

She looked up at him, remembering how he'd been at the meal with Arlan, of how his restraint had seemed to slip then, too. Something between fury and longing danced in his eyes, his words from that night echoing on repeat. *I won't let anything happen to you, Zylah.*

It cracked something inside her to see that look on his face. A fissure in the wall she'd so carefully constructed around her emotions. She took half a step towards him. *Just let me help you. Please,* his expression seemed to say. Or maybe he'd said it out loud, and she was too busy trying to come up with a reason to object that wasn't completely pathetic to notice. She wanted to tell him. Wanted to tell him it wouldn't matter if he tried to heal her. Wanted to tell him she was afraid.

The door to Malok's rooms opened, Nye appearing in the doorway. "He's ready for you."

Kej and Rin sat around the table with their father, their faces grim. More black pebbles were piled up on the table. Marcus's army had grown, and they were simply letting it continue to do so. The humans might have wanted her dead that day she was marched to the gallows, but they were just as much at risk against Marcus as the Fae were. And from the large mass of pebbles covering Virian, Zylah knew they would be the first to suffer, along with the Fae that secretly resided there, her friends included.

Holt had been filling her in on the reports of attacks and had explained how the attempts to make more vampires had been failing, producing more thralls instead. An army took time to grow, but one made of dark creatures? Zylah wasn't sure she wanted to know the answer.

The air was thick with whatever discussion Rin and Kej had been having with their father before her and Holt's arrival, the emotion so palpable Zylah could almost taste it. She didn't address Malok. He had asked to see her, so she wasn't about to make this easy for him, and as if the High Lord sensed this, he said, "You have another skillset which I find myself in need of."

"I don't think you're in much of a position to barter with me, Malok," Zylah murmured, eyes still fixed on the table, taking in all the changes and updates scattered across it. Rin and Kej shifted uncomfortably in their seats, and it was their unease that made her at last meet Malok's stare.

"Cirelle takes a tonic to help with the side effects of her gift… but our healer has been delayed by the storm," the High Lord said, his pause betraying the emotionless expression he held.

Zylah hadn't seen the High Lady since the dinner with Arlan and Daven. Since Cirelle had excused herself. She'd assumed it was from the heat of the moment, but Cirelle was a High Lady, and far stronger than Zylah had perhaps given her credit for. She felt Rin and Kej's gazes burning into her, breaths held as they waited for her response. Zylah told herself to ignore them, to not let her emotions get in the way.

If Marcus wasn't stopped, his army would only continue to grow, and whatever chance they might stand at stopping him dwindled further with each passing day. They'd wasted enough time already. "I've no knowing whether you'll deliver on your last promise," she said, at last turning her attention to Malok.

"Promises can be broken. Bargains cannot."

Zylah was well versed in bargains from the two she'd made. Her first, with Holt, when he was saving her life. Again. The second… when she'd been desperate. Foolish. Holt shifted in his spot by the door, and she met his gaze, caught the way his brow furrowed together for a moment. *A bargain with a faerie is never pleasant*, Raif had said to her, almost a lifetime ago back in Virian. And for months during her time in Kerthen, he'd been right.

She'd promised Holt she would live in return for him helping find her family. And living hadn't just been unpleasant… it had been torture. And her other bargain… nothing about it had been pleasant.

"The key has been located. See that both the key and the ingredients for my wife's tonic are delivered to me directly, and I'll hand over my army," Malok said, a hint of desperation tinging his voice.

She took in the High Lord, the way he sat, the way his deceits flickered over his scars. The perfectly pressed charcoal tunic he wore, the sapphire ring that gleamed on the hand he'd rested on an arm of his chair. He'd had no intention of helping them before, he'd just as good as admitted it. And he'd been careful with his words too. Typical faerie behaviour. But his hopelessness leaked through—his concern for his wife.

And though Zylah hated herself for it, she had to use it. "To Holt. You'll hand full control of your army to Holt?"

Malok swiped a hand across his knee, as if he were carelessly dusting away a crumb. "Niossa will remain in her position as general."

A nod from Holt was the only agreement Zylah needed.

She tried not to think of the fate of the humans hidden within the court should Malok discover them, instead reminding herself of the thousands they could save if they had an army on their side. She waited for Malok to speak, Rin and Kej practically buzzing with anticipation beside her, as if their thoughts were divided between their mother and the humans.

Malok didn't hide his glare. "I will hand over my army to Holt in exchange for the key and the ingredients."

But still, Zylah didn't move.

"Do you trust your spies?" Holt asked Malok.

The High Lord merely nodded.

"Fae raised here?"

"Two others."

"We don't have time for games, Malok."

"I trust them."

Holt levelled him with a heavy stare. "I don't need to remind you what the consequences will be if Marcus continues down this path."

Malok spared a glance at his children, as if they were all the reminder he needed.

"Then we have a bargain," Zylah said, offering her hand. She didn't move. Wanted the High Lord to come to her. Wanted to know he truly would do anything for his wife, that he deserved the protection that they were about to offer him. And for a heartbeat, she thought the bastard might refuse.

He was on his feet with the grace of a wildcat, and for the first time Zylah considered whether it wasn't just the ability to shift the twins had inherited from him, but his form too. He clasped her forearm, and Zylah willed herself not to let anything show on her face as the magic rattled through her, scraping against the vanquicite lodged in her spine.

"It's the dead of winter. No one is to follow them, Niossa. See to it that my children do not attempt to leave."

"My Lord."

Malok left without another word, without even a glance in his children's direction. But Zylah didn't miss the way they'd sagged with relief once the bargain had been made.

"This room is warded now," she said, glancing at the door. Zylah had felt something in the air, but when Malok had moved through it, she'd been certain.

"After the attempted poisoning, I managed to convince him," Nye admitted.

Rin swirled whatever liquid was concealed in her cup. "Everything's gone to shit since Jora's death, and he's trapping us in here like wild beasts."

"We kind of are, sis," Kej said with a grin, elbowing his sister gently.

Though she'd pushed Malok, Zylah wouldn't fail them in this. Finding the ingredients for Cirelle would be a priority, and she knew Holt would agree with her even without asking. "We'll send the ingredients as soon as we have them," she offered as reassuringly as she could.

Rin pushed herself from her seat, throwing her arms around Zylah's neck and pulling her in for a crushing hug. "If you find anything in the snow, it'll be a miracle. Stay safe, both of you."

"Body heat is the best way to stay warm out there," Kej said with a wink, already on his feet too, one arm draping over Zylah's shoulder in his best attempt at casual indifference. But

Zylah knew he was deflecting, covering up his concern for his mother the only way he knew how.

"We're researching all we can about the thralls, and I'll continue looking into your book during your absence," Nye said.

Zylah heard the silent plea in Nye's words, though she knew the Fae would never ask. Cirelle was her aunt, and Zylah knew she cared for her deeply. After almost a month in this court, Zylah knew the three Fae before her would do anything for each other, for their family.

And though Malok had made a bargain with her, one that couldn't be broken, dread still sang through her bones. Because something told her if there was a way out of their agreement, he would find it.

25

"This would be a whole lot quicker if we could evanesce." Zylah patted her horse's neck reassuringly as it made its way along a narrow path. These weren't the horses they'd arrived at the Aquaris Court with; Nye had told them they'd never survive the journey if they took them. In their place she'd given them two of Malok's finest draft mares; all thick muscle and twice the size of a regular horse, their limbs and bodies better suited for trekking through the snow.

"I'm not testing the limits of the spell until we have to," Holt said from his spot behind her. They'd managed to leave during a break in the storm, but judging by the thick clouds moving closer, they didn't have long before it started again.

Zylah shrank deeper into the fur-lined coat Nye had given her, the hood concealing her hair and sheltering her from the worst of the wind. They'd barely been travelling for half a day, and already she'd had half a flask of her baylock tea. She'd forgotten how painful riding had been before, the vanquicite scraping against her spine with each step her horse took. But Zylah was better prepared this time.

They were heading west along the south coast; the slower route, but the one least likely to bring them face-to-face with any thralls. Or so they hoped. She thought about the spell they were using, the one that concealed them, sight and scent. The snow would cover their tracks, but it hadn't snowed since they'd left the court, and although they'd covered more ground because of it, it left them vulnerable. Zylah had remained on alert since the moment they'd left the safety of the court.

A thought had been nagging at her, about Marcus using old magic. Of Aurelia's creation of the vampires. Of why she'd let her children believe she was dead. What was it they were all missing?

Her stomach grumbled unceremoniously as they paused to let the horses rest for a moment. They didn't dismount; the rocky path was too narrow. One misstep and the drop would lose them a horse. The route was an old one used by traders, Nye had told her, and though Zylah knew it was the safest option to avoid the thralls, every stumble of her horse made her wish for the safety of the forest far below them. She'd studied enough maps in the last few months to know that this edge of the coast was mostly crag, the ocean somewhere beyond the rocky bluff above them.

Holt tossed her a canna cake, pulling her from her thoughts.

"Don't tell me you baked it?" she asked, watching Kopi fly off into the grey.

"I asked in the kitchens if they could make us a few."

It was one of the only things she could keep down lately, and she had a feeling he knew that, from the way he was always bringing her things to eat, as if he were exploring what she could stomach. The horses stood side by side on the narrow path, Holt's mare leaning across to nibble at the mountain grass peeking through the snow, hers tucked up against the rock.

The last two weeks looking after the humans had given her a sense of purpose she hadn't had in a while. She still felt the bone-deep tiredness, but some of the dark thoughts had grown quiet throughout the days that had passed, hands taking over and pulling her into the familiar rhythm of work. She took a swig of her tea, wishing she'd brewed a second canister.

"Why do you drink that?" Holt asked beside her.

"I love the taste," she said, flashing him a grin.

"Liar." The corner of his mouth twitched as he held out a hand for the canister, waiting.

Zylah took a deep breath and handed it to him. Waited as he took a swig.

To his credit, he didn't react to the awful taste, other than to raise an eyebrow in question.

"It dulls the pain," she admitted, because she wouldn't keep lying by omission.

"We've been over this." There was no trace of anger in his tone this time, nothing but patience in his eyes.

"I know." Wind blew wisps of hair across his eyes and he swiped it away, waiting for her to continue. She offered a small smile. "But it's not going to happen all at once. Not everyone has as much discipline and self-control as you."

One eyebrow raised, and she could have sworn he was fighting a smile. "Is that what you think? That there's no limit to my self-restraint?"

"Is there?"

That earned her a half smile. "Keep fighting me on this and you'll find out."

Zylah held out a hand, stealing back her tea canister with a small tug on her magic.

"You're getting better at that."

"I've been practising." She cleared her throat. Scrunched her face in frustration. "Had been. Not for the last two weeks... because I'm too stubborn to ask you for help."

"You *are* stubborn," he said softly. He pulled his gloves back on, fingers flexing as he fastened the fur-lined leather at the cuffs. He was waiting for her to keep talking.

Patient. Always patient, and it urged her to say, "Thank you for not giving up on me, for sticking with me all this time."

That look shone in his eyes again, the way his face seemed to soften only when he looked at her. "Time is the only thing I could give you, Zylah."

That wasn't true. He'd given her so much more. His friendship. His trust. But something about the way he'd said it, the sadness in his tone, cracked her open a little bit more.

"Truth number four," he said, his throat bobbing. "After Adina died, I couldn't let myself feel anything. And for a while, it worked. To just be hollow, empty."

Zylah's breath caught. Despite the hooded coat, she felt bare, exposed, like he could see right through it to the hollowness inside her, like he knew just how empty she'd become.

"But then I realised I was just delaying the inevitable." He was frowning, fingers buried into his mare's mane. "The moment when everything would rush back in. And I think the point isn't to just leap past it, anyway, but to figure out how to make room for it all. The grief, the sadness. The instants of happiness, however fleeting."

"Like it took more energy to keep it all shut out than it did to let it in," Zylah whispered.

He nodded, just as a loud crack split the air. Just as Holt's horse fell off the side of the path, pulling him with it.

"Holt!" Zylah screamed, her mount lurching forward past the crumbling path.

Snow and rocks kept falling, the horse whinnying in disapproval, but to the mare's credit, it didn't bolt. She slid off the moment it steadied, throwing herself flat against the snow to peer over the rocky ledge, panic bubbling up her throat. "Holt!"

Nothing but endless grey stared back at her, not even a hint of the canopy she knew was below them. She swallowed down a panicked sob, searching for a way to climb down, a foothold that could withstand her weight. More rocks fell, and Zylah held her breath, straining to listen, just as a gloved hand reached up from the grey. *Holt.* She didn't dare reach for the horse to help them. She grabbed hold of Holt, pressing her body into the snow to anchor them both as she held on. *An anchor.* That was what he needed.

Zylah grabbed the thickest dagger she had, the one she kept tucked into her left boot and slammed it into the ground beside Holt's hand. "Here," she called out, wrapping his fingers around the hilt so he could use it to secure his grip. Snow began to fall, a gust of strong wind burning at Zylah's cheeks and obscuring her vision, but she ignored it. She heaved at his coat as he crested the ledge, her fingers fisting into the fabric as he hauled himself up to solid ground inch by inch.

Another piece of rock gave way, and Zylah was pulled down with him for a heartbeat. Her dagger disappeared into the grey right before roots and vines erupted around her, weaving through the rock and snow, anchoring her to the path. She knew without asking that Holt had made them.

They pulled themselves back up to solid ground, Holt huffing a laugh as he rolled onto his back like he hadn't just fallen off a cliff, and Zylah collapsed into the snow beside him.

"You're really sticking to this whole *no evanescing* thing," she rasped, somewhere between laughing and crying.

For a few seconds, she truly thought he'd fallen. That she'd have climbed down and found him bloodied and broken on the rocks below.

Her heart was beating so loud in her ribcage, she was certain he could hear it.

"I saw movement in the canopy, I couldn't," Holt said, pulling himself up to look down at her. What he'd shared, in those moments before his horse had fallen. Zylah swallowed. She didn't know how to tell him what it meant that he knew. That he understood.

His hand reached up to her face, fingers gently brushing the snow from her hair where it had escaped her hood, his eyes searching hers. "We need to get out of here."

"The horse?"

He shook his head. "I don't want to risk recovering anything with magic, either—better for it to look like a trader accident. We'll have to make do with what we have." He uncoiled to his feet, pulling her with him before she had the chance to protest their lost belongings.

Kopi landed on her mare's head, a quiet *hoo* announcing his arrival. "Good of you to return," Zylah murmured, stepping away from Holt and brushing more snow from her clothes.

A shrill cry rent the air.

Zylah's attention snapped to Holt, a chill dancing down her spine at the sound. Where there was one, there were undoubtedly more of them, and there would be no chance of fighting them up here, not when the path was so narrow, so vulnerable to breaking away beneath them.

Holt didn't wait to listen for more of them, murmuring instead to their mare and urging her to follow, his fingers tugging loosely at her reins. It moved tentatively at first, as if it were testing the stability of the earth beneath its hooves, but then another chilling scream carried to them on the wind, and it was all the encouragement it needed to pick up its pace.

With the snow falling harder and the wind slamming them into the rocky rise beside them, Kopi tucked deep into her hood, Zylah led the way along the path.

※⇝⇝⇝ ⇜⇜⇜※

They'd walked for hours before making it out of the pass. The thralls had long since gone quiet, and the snow had stopped shortly after it started, just enough to cover up their tracks, as if Pallia herself had sent them a momentary blizzard. Some quiet part of Zylah wondered if she had.

But her feet had barely hit solid ground when a distant cry halted her steps. A thrall. Holt mounted their horse without a word passing between them, pulling her up into the saddle before him and urging their mare through the forest. They ran until the light began to fade, until the shadows between trees became a dense grey, until the pain from riding had Zylah sagging forward in the saddle.

Holt's arm slid around her waist, pressing her tightly against him, and again she thought of how he'd refused to evanesce.

All magic left a trace.

Marcus was likely tracking his movements if Malok's and Cirelle's comments were to be believed. But if that were true, what reason had he given Marcus to leave him in the first place? Her thoughts were sluggish, the words slipping away from her. Their mare jumped a small log and the impact had Zylah gritting her teeth together, fingers reaching for Holt's hand and squeezing tight.

Within moments she felt the familiar prickling of his magic, his power sliding into her bones, easing her aching body. But something about it felt different this time. As if he didn't even realise he was doing it. Or maybe he did, and he was just too focused to notice.

The horse slowed as Holt tugged gently at the reins, its hot breath clouding the air.

"Back in Virian," Zylah asked, her voice barely a whisper over the horse's snorting. "When Marcus made you wear the vanquicite cuffs. Did he touch them?" Her thoughts were still a little muddied, but the question had been nagging at her for a while now.

Holt was quiet, listening for any sign of the thralls, Zylah assumed, his arm still bracketing her close to him.

"Did he touch them?" she asked again.

His voice was clipped, pained, almost. "Why do you ask?"

"Because they didn't affect his abilities." She scanned the forest for any movement, Kopi wriggling his way out of her hood and jumping down onto the mare's head. "He still used his magic on you. How?"

Holt shifted behind her. "He must have built up a tolerance to it."

Zylah frowned. She supposed it was possible. But... "What is it that he holds over you? It's more than a debt, isn't it?" Not just the life debt for his sister, there was more, she was certain. Malok's and Cirelle's comments back in the Aquaris Court had confirmed her suspicions.

Holt was quiet for a while, so quiet she thought he might not answer her. Until at last, he said, "It *is* more, Zylah. More than a debt, a bargain. He owns me."

"Hearts cannot be owned," she said, twisting round to look up at him.

His gaze dipped for a moment before his eyes lifted to meet hers. "No, they can't."

She tried not to think about the solidness of him, or the way their bodies were pressed together. Tried to not to let her attention drift to his mouth and failed.

Kopi hooed and Zylah turned to see him fly off between the trees.

Marcus had taken so much from them. But from Holt, he'd taken everything. His family. His friends. His freedom. "I know you think you're protecting me," she said, once darkness had long since covered everything. "But I want to help you. With Marcus."

Holt remained silent.

"And I know I've made some stupid decisions—what happened with Asha back in Virian—but you can trust me, Holt."

"I do," was all he said behind her.

Zylah's stomach twisted. She didn't want to press him if he didn't want to discuss it, so she said, "I think I might be able to offer some help with the mine."

"What did you have in mind?"

"I have a theory that needs testing. But first, we'll need an accelerant."

He huffed a quiet laugh. "Always full of surprises. Did you share your idea with Nye? She's likely to have some knowledge in that area."

"No, but she's taught me a few good tricks over the last couple of weeks. I think I could bring even you to your knees." Gods, she hadn't intended that to sound so—but Holt chuckled quietly behind her.

"You'd enjoy that, wouldn't you?" His low laugh rumbled through every inch of her, heat pooling low in her belly. She couldn't shake the thought of him on his knees before her. Not with his warmth enveloping her, his arm wrapped around her, holding her steady. She was too tired to feel guilty. Too exhausted to lock her feelings away in that part of her that she tried to ignore. Had tried to overlook for so long.

The forest was quiet, only the crunch of their horse's hooves in the snow and its breathing breaking the silence, the occasional sprite darting out ahead of them. With her heightened half Fae sight she could make out the tops of barrows beyond the trees, fresh flowers scattered around their entrances. She wondered if her father had a space in his barrow beside his wife. If her birth parents lay side by side in a barrow together somewhere in the dark, or just the human one of the pair.

She'd long since known they were likely both dead, given that Zack had found her during the last uprising, in the midst of the fighting. That, or they simply hadn't wanted to keep her, the risk of a half Fae child disrupting their peaceful lives being too great. *Live,* Holt had said to her. *Live, and I'll help you find your real family.*

Soon enough she would have to tell him that she couldn't uphold her end of their bargain.

26

The sound of cart wheels and chatter pulled Zylah from her sleep. She tried to ignore it, wriggling deeper into the warmth wrapped around her. That shifted in the saddle. Zylah's eyes shot open.

"Sorry," she murmured, grateful her hood was still up to hide her blush as she eased forward. Holt unhooked his arm from around her waist, and she wondered if he'd held onto her the entire night. "Where are we?"

"Morren."

"You rode all night?"

Holt hummed his response as they approached one of the many stables outside the gates. With the threat of a thrall tailing them, Zylah couldn't say she was surprised.

"Give her an extra bag of feed," he said, tossing a coin to the stable boy before helping Zylah off their horse. Every part of her ached, but Holt moved just as smoothly as he always did, unbuckling their saddlebags and patting their mare on her neck in thanks. Holt's ears appeared rounded, human, his deceits firmly in place for their time in the town.

Two days. That was how long they'd agreed to wait for Malok's spy. How many thrall attacks would there be in that time? There was no evidence of any incidents here, no extra guards on duty, nothing more than two sentries stationed on either side of the gates, one of them occasionally demanding papers from traders. Zylah glanced over her shoulder to convince herself they hadn't led the thralls to the town.

"We'll warn the guards," Holt said beside her, as if he'd had the same thought about the thralls following them.

He stood close as they made their way through the town gates, the streets bustling with people. All human. All free, unlike the two Fae courts they'd visited. Zylah tried to picture the streets with Fae walking amongst them, humans and Fae living alongside each other. Even in her imagination, it felt like a fool's dream. A thing of stories. Still, she would do whatever she could to make it a reality.

Morren was far busier than Varda, and much louder because of it. The snow had been shovelled away, pushed aside into dirty mounds beside shops and houses. A trade caravan came to a stop just ahead of them, chicken feathers billowing out around the last cart.

"Just like old times," Holt said quietly as she stepped closer to him to avoid a food vendor. She shot him a small smile as she looked up at him, just in time to notice him hide the quirk of his mouth. He must have thought of their first day in Virian together too, using the words she'd said to him when they'd left Mae's court.

Zylah tugged off her hood, Kopi making a small noise in protest. Morren felt stifling with so many bodies around, and she quietly wished she had her old cloak on instead. The fashion here was different; her and Holt's attire made them stand out, earning a few looks from strangers as they passed through the crowds.

"I need to get us some supplies," Holt said beside her.

She needed more of her tonic, but she wasn't about to admit that to him. "I'll go look for the ingredients I need for Cirelle."

Something undecipherable flickered across Holt's face before he said, "We're staying at the Bridge Tavern."

"Let me guess, it's by the bridge."

One side of his mouth lifted. He'd been rifling around in one of their bags, pulling out her cloak and swapping it with her coat. It was a little closer to some of the clothes the women wore, enough to help her blend in if she didn't wear the hood up.

"Stay out of trouble," he said as he draped the cloak over her shoulders, his long fingers easing her braid out from underneath the fabric.

"Don't fall off any cliffs."

His quiet laugh danced down her spine as she walked away without looking back, but she could feel his attention on her until she slipped into the crowd. Kopi had flown off when she'd swapped out her coat for her cloak, and just as well because there was already too much about her appearance that made her stand out here. She unwound her braid as she walked, hoping to hide her face a little with her hair. She'd long since lost her eyeglasses, and she couldn't maintain the deceit of changing her eye colour in her current state. Holt kept his ears hidden at all times outside the courts, but she'd been able to see through his deceits for some time now.

She thought about his confession back on the pass, of Cirelle's and Nye's words to her back in the Aquaris Court. It had been a small change, barely a change at all if she was honest with herself, but it felt like something had shifted inside her. She had been cruel to herself since leaving Virian, she'd realised, at a time when what she'd really needed was kindness.

A group had gathered in the centre of the market as Zylah made her way through the crowds, but she didn't need to look closely to know it would be priestesses and their acolytes. She followed the scent of herbs and incense, turning down an alleyway with a large bookshop on the corner. A familiar tale sat on display in the window, one she'd read many times. She'd have loved nothing more than to duck inside and explore the shelves, but the sway of wood strings two shops down snagged her attention. Her gaze drifted to the sign the wood strings twisted around. An apothecary.

Zylah pushed the door open, the aroma of herbs and incense wrapping around her. This wasn't an ordinary apothecary. There were jars filled with ingredients on almost every surface, but it was bursting with other objects: books, plants, bottles and vials, bunches of dried herbs, candles, and crystals in every colour. *Skulls.* Apprehension had her stomach flip-flopping, but Cirelle was relying on these herbs, and Zylah cast aside her worries to continue her search.

Dozens of shelves reached high above her head, blocking out the light and sound from the town beyond, the incense thick and heavy in the air. Some held bundles of cloth, and once Zylah thought she recognised the familiar fabric of the priestesses' robes. The deeper into the shop she walked, the more the contents of the jars changed. Eggs. Beaks. Claws. Things in liquid Zylah didn't want to look too closely at. Something told her most customers didn't venture this far in, and with good reason. She felt like a fly trapped in a spider's web, sweat beading on her brow, but she couldn't bring herself to leave, her feet carrying her further into the shop against her volition.

Her fingers traced the label on a jar. The plant she needed for Cirelle. Zylah had no doubt she'd find almost everything else she needed here too, despite every bone in her body screaming at her to leave. Her thoughts were stuck under a layer of oil, her feelings secondary to her body, pulled by whatever force was at the heart of the shop.

Magic flowed through every shelf, every plant that snaked and wound around jars and bottles as if they imbued life into every item they touched.

She swallowed down her hesitation and followed the only path through the shelves that didn't have a dead end until she reached a small sitting area, tendrils of power urging her towards the only empty chair.

An old woman sat opposite, thick grey curls falling over her shoulders, her dark green dress hugging her petite frame in mismatched pieces of knitted fabric. Crystal-adorned jewels sat heavily around her neck and on each finger, and every hair on Zylah's arms stood on end as ancient, primal power bled from the woman, wrapping around the space, pushing and poking at Zylah as if it were a living, breathing thing.

She schooled her expression to remain blank, silently scolding herself for not turning back and leaving the shop the moment she'd set foot in it.

"Just in time," the woman said, her voice far lighter than Zylah had expected. *Deceiving.* "The tea's just finished steeping."

Zylah had no control over her legs as she sat in the empty chair, but she didn't reach for the tea. Even without her knowledge of plants, she'd had too much first-hand experience with poisoned drinks to take something from a stranger, let alone someone who seemed older and more dangerous than anyone she'd ever met. Her throat felt like sandpaper, her fingers twitching to move against her will as she said, "I'm not much of a tea drinker. But thank you for the gracious offer."

The woman's lips turned up into something resembling a smile, but it was cold, empty. "You're the first customer to step into my shop with half a brain for some time." She assessed Zylah with cool grey eyes. "But it will help your ailment. It certainly soothes mine." She took a sip from her cup, but Zylah still wasn't convinced. The old woman could have built up a tolerance to whatever was in the tea and used this as part of her ploy to make others drink without hesitation.

But... *Your ailment.* If alarm bells hadn't already been sending Zylah's heart pounding in her chest, those two words had her casting a glance over the woman's shoulder again for any sign of a hidden exit, despite having already looked twice. She resisted the urge to reach for a dagger—for all the good it would do—twisting her sweaty palms in her cloak instead.

This close, she could make out the flicker of a deceit that settled over the woman from head to toe, only there was no trace of what it hid beneath. She let her magic tug at the invisible veil, only to feel unseen claws rake at her attempt.

Zylah pictured a wall of vanquicite, imagined herself holding it in place before whatever this woman was.

She was no human, that much Zylah knew.

The old woman smirked, but no trace of humour shone in her eyes. "I saw your soul the moment you stepped into my shop, little fly," she said, as if she knew precisely what Zylah had attempted.

Zylah said nothing.

Willed the colour not to drain from her cheeks as she held the woman's gaze. There would be no running; her feet still weren't responding, her thoughts swirling into each other as if they were under that layer of oil.

"You have your mother's eyes," the old woman said. "Your grandmother's, too." There was a trace of emotion in her voice, but Zylah couldn't pinpoint what.

And no matter how much her heart soared at the words, the mention of her family, she didn't take the bait.

If the woman was trying to catch her in her web, what better way than to reel her in with lies about those she'd lost?

"Oh, I know more about you than just your family, Zylah. I know everything about you. I know you're searching for Malok's key in the hopes of securing his army. I know you're slowly dying from the vanquicite lodged in your spine. I know all about your little bargain back in Kerthen. I even know who your m—"

"That's enough." Zylah levelled her with a stare, willing herself to think of nothing else the old woman could latch on to, to find a way out of this that didn't end up with parts of her in jars along the shelves. She didn't want to remind herself about the bargain she'd made in Kerthen when she was desperate, how she'd so recklessly agreed to the terms laid out for her. "What do you want?"

"Don't you want to know who I am?"

Something about her seemed familiar, but Zylah couldn't pinpoint what.

For a heartbeat, she saw a hint of pointed ears beneath the deceit, but they were gone as quickly as Zylah had seen them. "If you were going to tell me, you would have already." The words were difficult, and she clenched her jaw around the magic's hold. "What is it that you want from me?"

The woman drained the last of her tea, settled her cup on the small table between them and gave the slightest of shrugs. It was a strange movement. As if it came from whatever, or *whoever* sat beneath the deceit, as if it were not a gesture belonging to the woman speaking. "I want what you want. To find Malok's key."

"Then you know why I seek it."

"Yes." The woman sighed, spinning an emerald ring on her finger. "Marcus has become a bit of a thorn, hasn't he? Men usually overstay their welcome, and he is no exception. His time of playing king is over."

"And I suppose you've a replacement in mind?" Zylah tried again to tug at the deceit, more carefully this time, feeling for snags as if it were a fine fabric.

The woman was quiet. "You won't be able to pull back my deceit, little fly. Though I must say, it irks me that I cannot pull back yours."

"I don't—"

"Not intentionally, no. But one exists, nonetheless." She rose from her chair, crystals swaying across her chest. "As for the key.

I wanted to know whether you were truly capable of retrieving it."

Because of the vanquicite. Because Zylah didn't know how much time she had left, and somehow, something told Zylah, this woman did.

You told me once you have nothing to lose. Do you still feel that way?

No.

For the first time in months, Zylah wanted to live. To fight the vanquicite coursing through her. To see what her days might look like if she silenced the guilt and the self-loathing.

A grin broke across the old woman's face as she retrieved jars from the shelves nearest to her. "I know a little about dying. I've done it many times. But creatures like you and I, we defy the odds. Over and over. And we suffer for it."

The suffering was just; it was no less than Zylah deserved. The price she would pay until she took her last breath. And yet she knew in her bones that she was nothing like whoever sat opposite her.

The woman laughed. "*Tricksters and deceivers.*" She placed two jars on the small table before Zylah. Ingredients for Cirelle. "Be careful of your friends, little fly. Everyone has secrets to keep."

Zylah froze at Holt's words. *No more lies*, she'd told him. But he'd made no such promises in return.

That old voice that belonged to a past version of herself whispered in her ear, *Why would he tell you the truth, anyway? He doesn't owe you anything. You're nothing but a murderer. A monster. A curse. And everyone knows it.*

The old woman smiled, as if she knew the seed of doubt she'd planted.

"Two things I've always had a knack for sniffing out: poison and lies. Often they are one and the same."

Almost every ingredient Zylah needed for Cirelle sat before her on the small table. Nothing for her tonic, but a bundle of baylock leaves had been secured with a piece of waxed thread. It was then that something occurred to her, and she forced herself to look the old woman in the eyes as she said, "You can't retrieve the key. You need me to get it."

"More than half a brain, perhaps." She rested a hand against Zylah's cheek, though Zylah couldn't say when the woman had got so close, cold grey eyes staring into her own. "I had a daughter once. But she was taken from me. And with my… ailment… my movements are restricted. In my old age, I rarely leave the shop." Her expression darkened, and she pulled her hand away as if burned. "It's serendipity that we finally got to meet, Zylah. I was good friends with your grandmother."

Zylah didn't fall into her trap. She couldn't be certain anything the woman had told her was the truth. She reached into her cloak for the coin Malok had given her, depositing a pouch on the table.

"She was smart, too," the old woman said. She waved a hand and the ingredients disappeared, replaced with a worn leather satchel, the baylock leaves poking out from the flap.

Zylah snatched up the bag, her feet at last responding to her thoughts as she pushed to her feet, just as the old woman grabbed her wrist. "All things in this world have a price, little fly. In order to receive something, you may have to give up something else." Zylah had no doubt that was the case. "Be certain you're prepared to defy the odds."

And to suffer for it. Zylah heard the woman's words in her head, even though her feet were already carrying her back out of the shop, fingers reaching for the doorknob. She didn't dare look back as she stumbled out into the street, the scent of incense burning her nostrils and the old woman's strange words following her all the way back out into the safety of the market.

.

27

It was late afternoon by the time Zylah found her way to the Bridge Tavern. She'd needed to search the fields bordering Morren for the remainder of the ingredients, using the time to clear her head, to replace the incense clinging to her clothes with the aromas of the town around her.

She was passing a food cart selling sweet biscuits when a grubby bruiser took a step around the side of the cart to get closer to the vendor, the younger man's face paling as he twisted the top of a paper bag around his product.

"No." The vendor's voice was loud and clear as he handed over the paper bag to his customer.

Bruiser closed the space between them, pushing the bag into the vendor's chest and grabbing his chin, their faces close together. "Well, what do you say?"

"No. Thank you." The vendor clutched the paper bag against his heaving chest, eyes wild with panic as he looked up at his customer.

Bruiser smiled, and it was all the invitation Zylah needed to close the last few steps between them.

"He said no. Twice, I believe." She stood half a head shorter than the vendor, but she stopped beside him nonetheless, tucking her body as close to his without touching him as she could. From the corner of her vision, she spotted two guards on patrol heading towards them.

"And who the fuck are you?" Bruiser asked, his hand falling from the vendor's chin as his attention flicked down to her face.

"No one of note." Zylah looked up at him through her eyelashes, her expression playful, daring him to take a step closer. He did.

"This blade, however," she said so quietly only he and the vendor would hear it, pressing the dagger she kept in her left bracer against his groin. "Is considerably more noteworthy, for a multitude of reasons."

Bruiser stilled, his skin leeching of colour. All bark and no bite, just as she'd expected.

"Leave," Zylah bit out, loud enough that it earned a few gazes from passers-by, the heads of the two guards snapping in their direction.

Bruiser caught the movement, just as she'd hoped. He narrowed his eyes at her, his pallid expression now flushed pink, snatched his paper bag from the vendor and disappeared into the crowd.

Zylah had already slipped her dagger away as the vendor cleared his throat beside her.

"Thank you," he said brightly, scooping some biscuits into another bag. "That's the third day in a row. I should have known better than to set up here again."

Zylah finally took in his features.

Tousled blond hair that swept across hazel eyes, a small bump in his nose and a gentle smile. Human, as far as Zylah could tell. No deceits settled over him, no hint of magic. He took her hand and placed the paper bag in it with a grin. The biscuits were still warm, cinnamon infusing the air, and it was the most interest she'd had in eating something that wasn't a canna cake in months. "The debt is paid," she said, returning his grin and raising the bag to him in thanks before making her way into the tavern.

It never ceased to surprise her how packed these types of establishments were even at this time in the afternoon. The familiar tang of ale and sweat filled the air as she eased past the patrons, making her way towards the bar.

She hadn't spotted him yet, but she could already feel Holt's presence, his magic pressing against her own the moment she set foot inside. She slid onto an empty stool, hooking the satchel around one leg and placing a coin on the bar to catch the barkeep's attention.

A moment later, a tankard of ale sloshed down in front of her, the barkeep swiping up her coin. Not what she wanted, but she twisted the tankard around and eased it towards her nonetheless.

"Bad day?" a voice asked beside her, his presence so familiar Zylah hadn't needed to look up.

She huffed a laugh, twisting to face him. He wore the same style of jacket as the locals, and Zylah bit back her smile. "Nice jacket."

"Don't." Humour danced in his eyes, and something else, something she knew he tried to hide just as much as she did.

"I wouldn't dare." Zylah couldn't fight her smile as he took a step closer. Her skin bristled at his proximity, her blood roaring in her ears.

"It was the only thing they had that fit, and we're trying to look like locals, remember?"

"Of course. It suits you. You look like a woodcutter." She tugged playfully at one of the laces crisscrossing his chest.

"A woodcutter?"

"Yeah. It's what I overheard one of the women over there saying, anyway." She flicked her chin in the direction of three humans. Three very beautiful humans, heated gazes lingering on Holt. "The three of them look like they'd do just about anything for you to notice them." They probably would.

His gaze didn't so much as shift in their direction. He took another step closer, one hand resting on her ribs, his thumb brushing the fabric of her tunic just beneath her breast. His touch was like a brand, sending white-hot heat through every inch of her. The buzzing in her veins increased, the constant thrum of need she tried to snuff out whenever she was near him.

"Three?" His voice was light and teasing, his head tipping to the side slightly as he tried to fight a smile. Even on her stool, Zylah had to tilt her head back to look up at him as he leaned in closer, his voice quiet enough for only her to hear. "Good thing I have all that self-restraint to keep me in line."

"Pig," she said, shoving at his chest, but there was no bite to it. He didn't yield a step, and she didn't remove her hand, her thoughts instead drifting to what his bare chest would feel like beneath her fingertips, to where his hands would slide over her skin if there wasn't a scrap of clothing between them.

Holt's eyes darkened, his attention falling to her mouth. "Zylah."

Two tankards slammed down on the bar beside them, and Zylah remembered they were sitting in the middle of a tavern, surrounded by half-drunk humans.

"From your friend. In the corner." The barkeep flicked his chin over Zylah's shoulder, but she resisted the urge to turn and look. She watched Holt's eyes darken in an altogether different way for a moment before it was gone.

"What's wrong?" she asked, trying not to think about the absence of his hand at her side or how much she'd wished they were anywhere but in the middle of this tavern.

"The Wolf," Holt said quietly, power flaring from him for a heartbeat as he unhooked her satchel and slung it over his shoulder.

The Wolf. The cheating Fae who had beaten her back in Varda and had used his shadow magic to win the fight after leaving her broken and bloodied. Zylah still didn't turn to look, Holt's shift in demeanour had already earned them a few looks from strangers. She snatched up the two tankards and followed him across the tavern.

He wore his hair in a high knot, exposing the lines of tattoos running from his scalp down one side of his face, his dark eyes tracking them as they approached.

"Do we get to learn your real name?" Zylah asked casually, sliding onto the bench beside him and placing the tankards down in front of her.

Holt's expression gave nothing away, but she could feel his anger dripping from him. He took the stool on the other side of the Wolf, angling it so that he could watch the tavern and the Fae at the same time. He'd let a small drop of his power fall over their table, the male at his side trying to hide his flinch as it passed over him and brushed against Zylah.

The Wolf disguised his discomfort with a casual laugh. "That depends, Little Bird. Do I get to learn yours?"

"Zylah. But I'm sure Malok already told you our names." She didn't dwell on the fact that Malok had barely given them any information about the situation they were walking into, other than that his contact would make themselves known once they arrived in Morren.

The Wolf's eyes flicked to Holt, but he said nothing.

"Daizin." The Fae's eyes narrowed. "How did you slip through my shadows that day?"

"Luck," Zylah said with a shrug of her shoulders, taking a bite of one of the street vendor's biscuits. Daizin eyed the paper bag, eyes flicking to the door as if he knew the biscuits had come from the cart out front. "So you're going to lead us to Malok's key?"

"My partner will take us. He's the one who knows where it is."

Malok hadn't said anything about his contacts, other than that there were two of them. And there was the question of why Daizin couldn't lead them to the key, instead of his partner, but instead, Zylah asked, "And why should we trust you? You've cheated me once, how do I know you won't do it again?"

"You don't. We leave at dusk. We'll meet you by the stables, but we're travelling on foot, so travel light." Daizin was already on his feet by the time he'd finished speaking, and Zylah barely had a moment's warning to slide out of his way. He didn't so much as turn to acknowledge them before he left, easing his way through the busy tavern and heading for the door.

Holt slid onto the bench beside Zylah, placing the satchel between them in the shadows. "Tell me what needs to go to Cirelle."

"All of it except the baylock."

Holt raised an eyebrow.

"The bits poking out of the top," Zylah said with a lazy smile, holding out a hand for the bundle of dried leaves.

Holt handed them over, the satchel disappearing a moment later. No one would have noticed its absence in their dark corner, and he understood the urgency to get them to Cirelle. "I've some messages to send. Things are changing in Virian. The Black Veil numbers were growing, but they're a last resort. I need to make sure Zack has everything he needs."

The familiar temptation to shove every thought and feeling into that empty hollow inside her rose to the surface, but instead, she let herself think of her brother, of the good he was doing back in Virian. Let herself feel nothing but pride at what he was trying to achieve for the Fae.

A drummer began a steady beat on the far side of the fire, revellers clapping in time to his rhythm before a woman began singing.

It was a farmers' song, one Zylah had heard many times back in her village, but only now did she appreciate the words as the woman turned and smiled, urging the patrons to join in with her. It was a song about freedom, and it had half the tavern on their feet, clapping and dancing, cheering and whooping, and it reminded her of the Festival of Imala, watching the faeries celebrating in the botanical gardens, hidden from the humans.

Was it fear that made the humans hate them? Or was it because they had been taught to do so, by their parents and their parents before them? *They wish for the same as us—to live freely, without fear*, Holt had said back in the Aquaris Court. Such a simple wish, a right that should be granted to humans and Fae alike, without limitations, and for the first time, Zylah felt a flicker of sadness that she wouldn't be alive to witness it.

They had no idea their new king was Fae, that he was plotting to wipe the board clean and start over, no idea that the Fae were on their side, and Zylah wished she could stand on the table and scream it, beg them all to realise what was coming.

But instead, she kept her attention fixed on the minstrel as she weaved through the crowd, her fingers wrapped tightly around her mug though she had no intention of drinking it. "I hope you have another ally with an army if this doesn't go to plan."

"Rose and Saphi haven't had much luck in the Northern Territories, and there isn't time to travel to Bhuja and Ilrith." There was a tired edge to Holt's voice, but not from lack of sleep, Zylah thought, though he'd ridden throughout the previous night to get them away from the thralls.

"We'll stop him, Holt. We'll put an end to all of this." *I am his*, Holt had said when she'd pressed him about Marcus. It was his freedom he was fighting for, too.

I won't let anything happen to you. She couldn't bring herself to tell him that his magic wasn't healing her like it had before. It numbed the pain, but it didn't stop the spread, and for the first time she allowed herself to be afraid. Not for herself, but for him. That she might die and never see him secure his freedom.

She studied his face, but he'd shut down whatever she'd heard in his voice, his throat bobbing as he stepped away from the table. He tapped his knuckles against the wood. "The stables. Dusk."

Zylah watched him leave, wondering if he knew he might not secure his freedom *and* his life, too.

28

Kopi had joined her as soon as Zylah left the town gates. And as the last of the daylight began to fade, she made her way to the stables with a freshly brewed canister of baylock tea secured to her belt.

The paths were still busy, people weaving in and out between stables, traders easing their horses back to their carts before readying their harnesses. Zylah focused on the simplicity of it all, rather than letting herself think about what lay ahead. If she couldn't find Malok's key, they'd have wasted weeks at the Aquaris Court. Worse than that, there was the risk that if the healer arrived, Malok might deny her any contact with them.

She didn't let herself dwell on either thought as she came upon the stable she was looking for. Daizin had said to travel light, but Zylah wasn't foolish enough to go anywhere without her sword, largely concealed by the drape of her cloak. She'd picked up a heavier one in the market, along with a thick, wine-coloured sweater secured by her belt. As she rounded the entrance to search for any sign of Daizin and Holt, her hand instinctively reached for her weapon.

"What a handsome little fellow," a familiar voice said. The biscuit vendor from outside the tavern stepped out from behind her and Holt's mare, awe lighting up his face as he took in Kopi at Zylah's shoulder.

Zylah chewed her lip. "You're Daizin's partner?"

The vendor smiled and held out a hand in greeting. "Laydan. I told Daze we'd catch up." His grip was firm and gentle, and he slid another bag of biscuits into her hand. "I never go on a night hunt without snacks, and you're looking a little peaky, if you don't mind my saying."

Zylah couldn't help but smile at him. "Zylah. This is Kopi." She followed Laydan out into the half-light but paused at the entrance to the stables. "We need to wait for—"

"Holt? I told him to go on ahead with Daze. He didn't seem to like the idea of leaving you to catch up, but I filled him in on your rather terrifying performance earlier, and he seemed satisfied with the reminder of your capabilities. Is he always so brooding?"

Another smile broke across her face. "You get used to it."

"Careful, this is meant to be a serious mission," he said conspiratorially, his hazel eyes lighting up with mischief as he glanced at another vendor readying his horse.

They followed the path out of town in companionable silence, and Zylah realised she'd been wrong earlier. There *was* an air of magic about him, but it wasn't Fae.

It wasn't human, either. Something else, but she had no idea what.

He led her off the main path and into the forest, a pair of sprites darting out ahead of them as if they were leading the way.

"He's like a beacon for them. For you too, it would seem." Laydan glanced at her with a smile, head tilting ever so slightly. "Or maybe it's the other way around; you're the beacon."

"They're drawn to him," Zylah said, watching the furry heads bob and tiny wings flutter in the last of the light, Kopi flying off to join them.

Laydan merely hummed his agreement. "So you can see through deceits. A useful skill to possess."

"And you? Part-time biscuit vendor, full-time tracker?" She didn't want to think about what was ahead. Why someone like Daizin, with his affinity for shadows, or Laydan, a tracker if that was indeed what he was, needed her to get to Malok's key.

But any reply he might have offered was cut off by Daizin's scowl as he stepped out from behind a tree.

"There's the light of my life," Laydan whispered energetically, throwing his arms around Daizin's neck.

To Zylah's surprise, Daizin softened, rested his forehead against Laydan's and murmured something too quiet for Zylah to hear.

"Hmm. So broody," Laydan said, turning to wink at Zylah. "Maybe they think it's charming?"

Zylah bit back her smile. She had no way of knowing if Laydan was always this way, bright and playful, or whether it was just to ease themselves into finding the key. Malok had said his spies were locating it, but it was clear now there were no guards, just Daizin and Laydan.

Kopi hooted softly as Holt approached from the gods knew where, his eyes roving slowly over her, and Zylah felt her skin burn beneath the thick sweater from his heated gaze. She'd had all afternoon to think about their almost kiss, about the way he'd held her, the way she'd leaned into his touch for more.

And when the corner of his mouth twisted into a half smile, she knew he scented the change in her. Could likely see it written all over her face.

She turned away, taking a swig of her baylock tea in an effort to hide the tremor that coursed through every tightly wound muscle.

"It's going to be a long night," Daizin said, breaking away from Laydan.

Wasn't it just.

"Let's get moving," the Fae added.

⟫⟫⟫ ⟪⟪⟪

"What have you got in there?" Laydan asked. "Is it strong enough to turn the pain in my feet into blissful numbness?"

Zylah laughed quietly, her breath clouding in front of her in the darkness. They'd been walking for hours, and Zylah wished she'd brought three canisters with her.

Twice she'd felt the press of Holt's hand at her lower back, and each time she'd let him try to heal her because she knew she wouldn't have made it through the night without it.

"It won't numb them, but it will help the pain. Here." Zylah handed Laydan the canister, watching the twist of his features as he took a hearty swig.

"Goddess, what are you trying to do to me." He took another swig. And another. "Actually, it's not bad once you get used to it, and very effective." He bounced his weight from one foot to the other and beamed. "Not bad. Thank you."

The forest had thinned, and mercifully, there had been no fresh snow. Rows of barrows bordered the edge of the trees, sprites' wings shimmering around them in the moonlight. They'd always been drawn to the ones back in her village, too. Drawn to the spirits, her father had told her.

They'd paused to listen for any sign of movement amongst the barrows, Daizin's shadows swallowing him and Laydan almost entirely. Zylah and Holt had a little protection from their spell, but their tracks, that was where Laydan came in.

She'd been right, about him having magic.

A witch, on his mother's side, he'd said simply when she'd questioned him earlier in the night, long before the day had turned into another.

Holt had given her a cautionary glance, as if he were urging her not to mention the vanquicite lodged in her back. Not here, not yet, that look had seemed to say. And Zylah shared the sentiment.

Laydan seemed trustworthy enough, but Daizin? Who knew who he might sell the information to, given the chance?

They slipped one by one through the barrows, darting for the safety of the forest on the other side of the field, and not for the first time since finding Daizin back in the tavern, Zylah wondered if they were walking right into a trap.

The forest on the far side of the barrows dropped down into a maze of passageways of moss-coated rock, forcing them to either press ahead or turn back the way they'd come, and Zylah didn't like it one bit.

"We'll rest here until just before sunrise," Laydan said, turning a corner in the rock into a section that opened out into a cave, roots twisting through every crack and moss covering every surface.

"Why?" Zylah asked as Kopi swooped up to a perch above the entrance. Any notion of manners had left her hours ago, nerves and pain eating away at her, shredding her patience.

Laydan tilted his head to one side, a lazy smile tugging at his mouth despite how tired he must have been. "Because I can only open the tomb at first light."

"If you could find it yourself, and you can open the tomb yourself, why are we here?"

Daizin's shadows pulsed around him for a moment, but Laydan rested a hand on his arm.

"Items like this were never hidden by one person, always by a collective," Laydan added. "So that no one individual could break in and retrieve it. It would have taken several witches and Fae working together to conceal it. Which is why I know the key is there, but I can't see it."

"And now?"

"Now we wait. There's a network of caves here to rest in, and this is the only exit. Take your pick." He winked and slid his hand into Daizin's, the Fae's shadows sliding around them both.

By the time the shadows cleared, Daizin and Laydan were gone.

Zylah released a heavy breath. "I wonder if all witches are like that."

"I'm sure he'll insist there's no one like him," Holt said dryly. "I'll check the rest of the caves if you want to rest. Kopi's watching out front."

"I couldn't, even if I wanted to. I'll come with you."

She unbuckled her sword belt, and Holt took it from her silently, sending it to the tavern in Virian, she presumed.

She followed him into one of the passageways that connected the caves, the air still and quiet. It was cool inside the caves, but there was no bite to the air, as if a layer of magic coated everything. Knowing Laydan for the short time that she had, it probably did.

The passageway opened out into another space, grooves in the walls holding rows and rows of smooth rocks, some lighter than others. Zylah followed the rows, her eyes tracing the patterns created by the contrast of dark and light stones. The lighter ones looked like star constellations, a map of the sky wrapping around the room. The rest of the cavern—room, Zylah supposed, held nothing but a moss-covered table and bench, so they pressed on to the next passage.

Pain swelled through Zylah's body as she followed Holt, but she bit down on her lip, willing it to pass. She didn't make a sound, careful not to—

Holt paused, and Zylah almost crashed into him. He turned to face her, a wild look in his eyes as they searched hers. "The healing isn't working anymore."

Zylah stilled as he took a step closer, her attention falling to the scar at his neck, to how close he was, to how little space there was in the passage. "What makes you say that?"

"I can feel it."

Zylah didn't dare look up at him, wasn't ready for him to see the truth of his words. "Key first. Then the vanquicite. I trust Cirelle." *If* the healer was there by the time they made it back to the Aquaris Court.

She didn't know how long she had left, but she would do this one thing for him, even though it didn't come close to repaying him for all that he'd done for her. If it got him one step closer to his freedom.

She only wished she'd live to see it.

"What happened to no more lies?" Holt asked, his fingers closing around her wrist. His thumb brushed over her skin and sparks danced in its wake, a heady need unfurling within her.

"Everyone has secrets to keep," she murmured, her gaze lifting to his mouth before she met his eyes. "But I don't regret coming here. Do you?"

"I only have three regrets when it comes to you, Zylah," he said, closing the last of the space between them, his fingers flexing through hers. "That I didn't go with you into Kerthen. That it took me six months until I could come after you. That when I finally found you, I couldn't—"

His voice broke on the last word, and Zylah thought she might have stopped breathing.

"Couldn't what?"

Holt dragged a hand through his hair. "I can't look at you…"

Without being reminded of what they'd lost, of what they were up against. Zylah began to turn away, but his fingers closed around her chin, urging her to look up at him. She met his gaze, bracing herself for whatever he was going to say.

"I can't look at you like I don't want to do anything but fuck you, taste you, worship you every damned day of my life. I can't look at you like I'm just a friend and fine with that, no matter how hard I try to conceal this thing so that every person we meet, Fae or human doesn't see it. It's why I left Virian, before I even knew the truth of it. I can't look at you like I'm not…" He released her chin, ran a hand through his hair again.

Zylah braced herself against the side of the passageway, her back pressing against the rock as that need turned into an ache, his words settling over her. She'd fought against the pull to him for so long, too afraid to voice whatever it was between them, as if speaking it out loud would breathe life into it.

"I'm tired," she began, and Holt shook his head, schooling his features back to neutral as he waited for whatever she was going to say. She tugged at one of the laces on his jacket, urging him not to move away from her. "I'm tired of shutting it all out," she whispered, looking up at him through her lashes.

Holt took a step towards her, one arm above her head on the rock, bracketing her against him. "Tell me what you want, Zylah." His eyes searched hers. "Say it." His other hand found her face, fingers threading into her hair, the warm pad of his thumb tracing her face.

Zylah looked up at him, his mouth so close to hers she'd only have to angle her head to get what she wanted. She didn't fight the feeling. Didn't try to conceal the shift she knew he could sense in her. His eyes darkened with the same need she felt coursing through every inch of her body, and her voice was breathless as at last she said, "Kiss me."

29

Holt closed the last of the space between them, his lips crashing against hers, his tongue sweeping in to demand all of her at once, and Zylah kissed him back just as fiercely. His hand remained threaded in her hair, the other fell to her waist, his grip firm and solid like he had no intention of letting her go.

Zylah arched into his touch with a breathy moan, the swell of his muscles flush against her body as her fingers curled into the ends of his hair.

There was no room for thought, only the feel of him pressed against her and her frantic need for more. As Zylah angled her hips for the friction she so desperately craved, Holt pinned her in place with his own, the thick length of his arousal pressing against her stomach and an ache settling between her thighs. She tore at the laces of his jacket without breaking their kiss, demanding to feel more of him, to touch him before she burned away into nothing with the need coursing through her.

Holt's hands swept down her body, fingers pressing into her thighs as he eased her up to wrap them around his waist, pinning her to him with one arm. Zylah locked her legs behind him, her back scraping against tree roots as she arched into him further and he growled a low sound of approval.

He lifted the hem of her sweater, his rough skin tracing against the softness of her stomach and running along the waistline of her trousers. This. Him. She had wanted it for so long. Fought it. Shoved it down in that empty pit inside herself. She shivered as his fingers swept up and down as if he needed to touch her everywhere all at once.

Holt pulled back just enough to look at her, enough for her to still feel the way his heart beat just as furiously as her own, chests heaving as they held each other's heated gazes.

She drew him back to her, and it was all the invitation he needed to dip his fingers beneath her trousers, another low growl sounding from deep in his chest as his fingers found the wetness pooling between her thighs. He claimed her mouth again as he eased her underwear aside, his thumb finding the exact spot she wanted him to as two fingers slid inside her. Zylah cried out against his mouth, but he captured the sound with a kiss, his fingers and thumb building a steady rhythm, her legs clamping around him as every muscle in her body tightened.

"Zylah," Holt said roughly against her lips, his fingers moving faster as he kissed her again. Zylah couldn't speak, the delicious tension coiling tighter until every inch of her skin was on fire and she gave herself over to it, to him, to the way she felt in his arms.

Her fingers fisted into his shirt, his warmth and his scent enveloping her, his powerful body flush against hers as Zylah whimpered into his mouth, her release stealing the breath from her lungs and leaving her shaking in his arms.

"Fuck," Holt groaned, fingers and thumb slowing as he trailed kisses along her jaw and down the sensitive flesh of her throat, gripping her tightly as ripples of pleasure echoed through her.

He pulled back again to look down at her, eyes hooded with desire and his ragged breathing matching her own. Zylah held his gaze, biting down on her swollen lip as he eased his fingers out of her, his thumb still tracing its idle circles. She mourned the loss of him instantly, his hand tracing up her side to rock her against him, her hands tugging at his belt to return the favour. Holt's mouth collided with hers a heartbeat later, her fingers grappling with the top of his trousers as he strained against them. But as she dipped her hand to reach for him, a cry echoed through the caves.

They both stilled, their frantic breaths the only sound for a moment just as a thrall shrieked in the distance. Holt released her gently, taking half a step back as his heated gaze swept over her. His thumb traced across her swollen mouth before he stole another kiss, grabbing her hand to lead her through the caves without saying a word, both of them straining to listen for how close the thralls might be.

Anticipation snaked its way up Zylah's spine as she fought to calm her racing heart. The thralls had been tracking them, but why follow them here? She focused on steadying her breathing as Daizin and Laydan met them in one of the passageways, smoothing a hand over her sweater.

"Only one exit?" Holt asked Daizin in a way that said they all knew it was a lie.

The Fae ground his jaw together for a moment. "This way."

"What about your little friend?" Laydan glanced over his shoulder to Zylah, one eyebrow raised.

"Kopi will find us."

Holt released Zylah's hand only to summon her sword and hand it over to her. Her fingers grazed his as she took it from him, trying not to think about everywhere his hands had been a few moments before. The corner of his mouth tilted up for a moment as if he'd known exactly where her thoughts had taken her.

"There's been a group of thralls outside of Morren since we arrived," Daizin said quietly as they followed him through more passageways. He came to a stop, pressing a hand to a rock with vines crisscrossing the surface before raising an eyebrow at Holt expectantly.

"You can get us into an ancient tomb, but you can't get us out of here?" Holt asked, one eyebrow raised at Laydan. But he didn't wait for a response, he raised his palm to the surface, the vines receding, rock shaking as his power bled into it. Small pieces of rock and dirt cascaded down on either side of it as fresh air hit them, the darkness just beginning to peel away and giving way to the dull grey of dawn.

"What other tricks can you perform?" Laydan asked, clapping his hands together silently, ignoring Holt's question entirely.

Holt frowned for a moment but didn't rise to the bait, just as Kopi hooed softly and flew down from outside to land on Zylah's shoulder.

"Can he tell us how many there are?" Laydan asked with an amused smile.

Thralls screamed in reply, closer than before, and Zylah's grip on her sword tightened. They still couldn't evanesce, and with the effects of the vanquicite searing in her veins, she knew she wasn't likely to last long in a fight. Still, she would make it count, no matter what.

"I count four," Holt said under his breath. "How much farther?"

Laydan waited behind Daizin as the Fae peered out into the grey. "We're almost there, but we're a little pressed for time. Keep up."

"If we're pressed for time, why did we stop?" Zylah asked.

The witch scoffed, eyebrows flicking up as his eyes darted between her and Holt. "You can thank me later."

Asshole.

Zylah chewed the inside of her mouth to keep herself from saying anything as they followed him outside. Daizin's shadows flickered out from him for a moment before folding back in, his frame concealed entirely in darkness for barely the span of a breath. When the shadows dispersed, Daizin was gone, the swipe of a black tail disappearing around a bend in the rock.

"This way," Laydan hissed as a thrall shrieked in the direction Daizin had disappeared. The witch led them left and right through the maze of rock, climbing up to bring them out of the shelter of the stone.

Kopi flew on ahead, a wild cry escaping him as a thrall hauled itself up and over the crest of the rock they'd been ascending. Holt launched himself at the creature, a sword appearing in his hand as he willed the rock to crumble and shake beneath the thrall's feet.

Laydan's eyes widened just in time for Zylah to spin around and swipe at the chest of another, its eyes bulging from their sockets like some nightmarish beast as its lips peeled back on a scream.

Zylah swung at it with her sword, her feet finding purchase on the crumbling rock as her blade sliced through the mottled flesh on the creature's arm. The thrall wailed, head tilting to one side as it assessed her, and for a heartbeat, Zylah wondered if, despite what they'd witnessed back in the Aquaris Court, part of the Fae these creatures had once been remained beneath the monsters they'd become.

But whatever she thought she'd seen, it disappeared the moment the thrall lunged for her, bony fingers clawing at her clothes as it pushed her back into rock. It snapped and thrashed at her face as she fought to butt it away with the hilt of her sword, the sinews of its jaw muscle peeking through its decayed flesh. Zylah fisted a hand into what remained of its blond curls, swinging her short sword in her hand to slam the blade into the thrall's ribs, where a chain with a familiar sigil rested.

It staggered back with a pained cry, and Laydan took a step towards it, hands raised as he murmured words Zylah couldn't make out. The thrall threw its head back in a breathless scream as tar-like liquid oozed from its nose and mouth. Zylah slashed her sword across its ribs, and with one firm kick to its chest sent it flying off the ledge back into the maze below.

Laydan swayed on his feet as she turned back to him.

"What was that?" she asked.

"A handy little spell. But I need to keep my reserves topped up for opening the tomb."

Zylah frowned, thinking of the sigil the thrall had been wearing; it was the one all priestesses usually wore. A quiet sense of foreboding took root in the pit of her stomach, but she willed herself to ignore it as the witch grabbed hold of her wrist. She looked up to find Holt wiping his blade clean over a thrall corpse. Two, Zylah realised as a howl sounded nearby.

"All clear," Laydan said with a grin. "Let's go."

Holt's eyes slid over her before she followed Laydan's route up the rocks, her thoughts scrambling to keep up with her body. The thralls operated under the command of a vampire, and Zylah wondered if she might at least fulfil her wish of driving her sword through Jesper's black heart before the vanquicite took her. She kept her thoughts to herself, feeling Holt's presence close behind her as they climbed.

A black wolf leapt onto the rise at the same moment Zylah hauled herself up over the ridge, smoke curling around it as it transformed before her eyes into Daizin. *The Wolf.* Only the Fae was just like Nye, not his shadow beast, but in the way he wielded the shadows and the way he could shift into a shadow form. Whatever they were, Daizin and Niossa, they were the same.

Laydan waved them over to the centre of the peak, a large slab of rock jutting up behind him. Only it wasn't a slab, Zylah realised as she stepped closer. It was a door, deep swirls and marks gouged out of its surface, flowers and burnt-down candles and little offerings crowding the entrance.

"A witch, a Fae, a deceit breaker and a dazzling bae walk into an abandoned tomb… it sounds like either the start of a joke or a cautionary tale," Laydan mused, cracking his knuckles in front of him as he eyed the door. "Don't worry, Daze, you're the dazzling bae, obviously."

Daizin raised an eyebrow but said nothing, his gaze sweeping over the rocks and trees falling away from them on either side of the ridge. Another thrall screamed in the distance, and Laydan took that as his cue to get to work.

"You want to trap us in there with them?" Zylah asked.

The witch merely grinned at her, his fingertips pressing against the stone. "Don't worry, they won't be able to follow us in."

And what would be waiting for them when they came back out? Zylah didn't voice her question, for fear that uttering the words out loud might bleed some morsel of truth into them.

The witch muttered a spell under his breath, the stone slab splitting with a loud crack between some of the patterns etched into it as it opened, stale air greeting them mingled with the unmistakable stench of death. Kopi darted in first, undisturbed by the darkness of the tomb, and Holt followed him.

Zylah suppressed a shiver as she stepped inside after them, whispers sounding in the darkness as if from some long-dead spirits. Not just old. Ancient. Holt took a torch off the wall sconce, and it flared to life in his hand, shadows flickering on a stone staircase that spiralled down into the dark.

All they had to do was find the key and get themselves out of there. But as Laydan sealed the door to the tomb shut behind them, something told Zylah this wasn't going to be that easy.

30

Wards bent and flexed against Zylah's skin as they made their way down the staircase, so many she had to grit her teeth against the sensation curling over her.

Holt had gone first with the torch, Laydan and Daizin close behind. Though Zylah had seen Holt light fires with nothing but a flick of his wrist, she knew he held the torch to preserve his pool of magic. She'd seen first-hand how deep his well of power was, and though she was certain it had a bottom to it, she'd yet to see it.

Her thoughts drifted to sitting with him in their room at the tavern back in Virian after they'd fled from Marcus, of how he'd moved and fought against Jesper the day Raif died. Holt had fought and fought with a savagery that some part of her knew should have been frightening, but she had never been afraid of him. Not even on that first day when he'd found her in the springs.

The staircase twisted on, the air growing colder the further they descended, magic pressing at her skin. If it hadn't been for the vanquicite already draining her, she'd have felt nauseous, weak, at the way it seemed to cling to her. She pressed a hand to her chest as they seemed to step through yet another ward.

Daizin cleared his throat behind her. "There are spells in place to weaken any who enter. A constant drain on your life force to encourage you to turn around and leave."

To prevent raiders, Zylah presumed. "How many are buried here?"

Laydan chuckled quietly. "To begin with? No one. It's a decoy tomb. But now it's the resting place for the countless foolish creatures that came to pillage it."

"A decoy for what?" Zylah asked, uncertain if she truly wanted the answer.

"*Who*," Laydan said as the staircase ended, and they stepped out into a space so large the torchlight disappeared into the darkness.

Ranon. Zylah didn't want to say his name out loud. Not in this place. But somehow, she knew that would be Laydan's answer.

He gestured to Holt for the torch. "There are fake tombs dotted all over Astaria, warded and spelled not only to prevent anyone from entering but to keep them trapped inside should they succeed in getting past them. So although the tombs were once empty, that is no longer the case." The witch seemed almost happy as he spoke, the torchlight casting flickering shadows across his features, and Zylah hoped it was just his cheerful nature as she stayed alert, her eyes taking in small details in the darkness.

It wasn't as large a space as she had first thought; the walls looked as if they had been gouged by claws in some spaces; in others, there were stacks of rock, great columns stretching above their heads. And every now and then, scattered across the stone beneath their feet, were large bones, picked clean by whatever had discarded them.

There were remnants of the lives that had managed to breach the wards at the perimeter: a scrap of fabric that might have once been a cloak, a rusted sword, a few scattered arrows. It felt more like a prison than a tomb, but Laydan had been inside before and made his way out, so it eased some of Zylah's discomfort to hold onto that thought.

Holt was quiet beside her as they followed Laydan and Daizin, but as if he'd felt her watching, his attention slid to her, a smile lifting the corner of his mouth as his eyes met hers. For a moment that familiar voice whispered in her ear all her faults and failings, telling her she shouldn't have kissed him, shouldn't have given him the hope of something that was doomed before it had even begun. That she would be nothing but a curse to him, and how could he care for her like this, when she was nothing but a broken shadow of herself? But this time when the thoughts came, she let them go.

He slid a hand to her lower back, healing magic pouring into her and pulling her from her thoughts. "Just in case," he said quietly, as she raised an eyebrow at him in question.

She didn't regret kissing him. She just wished they'd had more time. And as she offered him a smile in thanks, she realised she owed it to him to tell him the truth about the vanquicite. She was nothing but a hypocrite if she didn't.

The moment they were back at the Aquaris Court, Zylah vowed to offer him the truth.

Laydan led them through passageways and down stone stair-cases that crossed others, darkness yawning open beneath them as if it had no end to it.

Every now and then there were signs of people who had come before them, and the treasure they had tried to pillage.

"Why would an item, an actual key to protecting an entire court, be concealed in a decoy tomb, and how did it end up here?" Zylah asked.

Laydan shrugged. "We're just here to retrieve it."

Zylah wanted to press him further but felt it unwise given they might need him to get them out of the tomb.

He stopped at a wall, pressing a hand against the stone, and as Zylah stepped closer, she realised it was another door. This one was circular, more swirls and lines gouged into it, and as Laydan murmured, two halves split away from each other with a grinding sound, opening just enough for them to pass through.

Zylah sucked in a breath at the sight that unravelled before them.

The torchlight glinted off more glittering gold than she could ever have imagined, and as Laydan grinned at her, a loud boom echoed through the tomb, his smile fading at once.

"I'll go check it out," Daizin said quietly. "Get the key. Stay together." He shot a look at Laydan before his shadows con-cealed him, and he was gone.

"I thought you said they couldn't get in?" Zylah asked Laydan as he paled.

He tipped the torch to a channel etched into the wall above them, and the room lit up with firelight. "Let's just find this thing," he said, waving his free hand at the room before them, piles of gold and stacks of items on every surface: chalices, crowns, swords, statues and thrones.

Zylah tried to shake off her unease. "Why do I get the feeling that if I take the wrong thing this entire tomb is going to swallow us whole?" It occurred to her then, that the boom might not have been from someone entering the tomb, but from something that was already within it.

What better way to protect a hoard of gold than with a creature to guard it?

She silenced the thought. Focused on the task at hand, her attention sweeping across the room. It could take her days to search the space, and she had no idea what she was looking for. *Find the key, find the key, find the key*, she repeated to herself, as if thinking of it might make it appear before her. Wishful thinking. Every item glittered back at her, winking as if to mock her in the firelight.

And that was when a thought occurred to her. The key might be veiled in a deceit to look like it was made of gold, but the key itself would not be.

She assessed the room again, her gaze taking in as many items as she could, concentrating to see if there was anything concealed beyond the lustre of the bright metal, something dull, rusty even. Something that would be out of place amongst so much treasure.

Another boom sounded, rattling the gold before them and this time Laydan winced. "Daze is alone out there, please hurry."

Zylah swallowed, ignoring the burn of the vanquicite as she looked harder, her attention snagging on a statue of a woman, arms reaching above her head as if in offering, an object in her palms. It reminded Zylah of Imala, and she frowned as she made her way closer to look at what she held.

A golden brin fruit.

No, not golden. She looked again, the deceit rippling, falling away like water.

Arrenium.

Zylah took a step towards it, just as Daizin cried out from beyond the room full of gold.

"Go. Help him. I think I've found the key," she said to Holt, flicking her chin at the statue.

He looked between her and Laydan. "Stay together." He didn't wait for a response, just made for the door, out into the darkness beyond.

Zylah didn't hesitate. She closed the last of the distance between her and the statue, searching for a foothold to pull herself up.

"I'm sorry," she murmured as she grabbed onto the statue, hauling herself up golden robes, a thigh, a hip, a breast.

With her legs on either side of an arm, she shuffled forwards to reach for the brin fruit, the clash of weapons echoing from the space beyond as her hand closed around the metal.

"Hurry!" Laydan called out from the door.

But something made Zylah pause.

She inspected the brin fruit, the seam running around it and the gnarly twist of the stalk as her eyebrows pinched together.

She placed her hands on either side of the seam and twisted, the pieces falling apart to reveal the twisted core that was one solid piece from the tip of the stalk all the way through the centre of the fruit.

The key to protect Imala's court, hidden within the hands of a statue of her likeness.

She snatched it up, shoved it into her pocket, twisted the piece back together and placed it back into Imala's hands, just in case.

Voices cried out from the room beyond, followed by the shrill cry of a thrall. Zylah shuffled back down the statue's arm, almost losing her footing as she scrambled back down to the ground, just as Laydan grabbed her wrist and yanked her towards the door. "You're sure you have it? It wouldn't surprise me if there were a handful of decoy items in here, just to throw us off track."

Zylah reached into her cloak and handed him the key to inspect, and at the same moment, two men burst through the gap in the rock, trapping them inside the room full of glittering treasure.

She couldn't evanesce. Not yet, not if she was going to fight. Laydan pocketed the key and held his palms forward, but the two men were already closing on them, swords drawn. Zylah pulled her own, swiping at the first just as Kopi burst through the rock and clawed at the head of the second.

Laydan swiped a hand and the two men fell to their feet, their eyes turning milky white as they punched and swatted at an invisible foe above them, frantic whimpers erupting from their lips. Zylah noticed they both carried the sigils the priestesses wore, and with a start, she realised where she'd seen them before. In Nye's book about the original nine.

She grabbed Laydan's arm, pulling him out of the door to the space beyond, stopping short when Daizin's wolf ran past them, his shadows brushing against Laydan.

"Here, take this." Zylah shoved a dagger into the witch's hand, pulling him with her deeper into the space. Someone had rolled orblights across the floor, but beyond them, in the darkness, Zylah's heightened eyesight allowed her to focus on Holt, fighting with four aggressors. Human, as far as Zylah could tell.

Which meant—

Laydan was shoved to the ground beside her, a thrall crying out as it dug its nails into his ribs, pinning the witch beneath it. As she moved to pull it away, a hand fisted into her cloak and yanked her back, a human squeezing his other hand to her throat. Zylah elbowed him in the ribs, swinging around to drive her sword beneath his ribs and twisting up. His sigil glinted in the orblight as he fell into her, pressing a hand to his wound and wheezing as blood trickled from his mouth. Zylah pulled her sword free, pushing her assailant away and turning back to Laydan.

The witch screamed as the thrall sank its teeth into his abdomen, and a heartbeat later, the creature shrieked in agony and flung him aside. But Zylah couldn't help Laydan, not yet. Two more humans were upon her, a man and a woman, both swiping blades at her. She drew them away from Laydan, just as Daizin's shadow wolf emerged beside him, tearing into the thrall.

The humans were skilled with a sword, but with the training she'd had from her friends, it wasn't difficult for Zylah to spot the weaknesses in their movements and expose them. She disarmed the woman, knocking her off balance to throw her into the man, his blade driving through the woman's stomach. He barked in alarm, yanking the weapon back and turning it on Zylah, a wild gleam in his eyes as the woman fell beside him.

Beyond him, Daizin had forsaken his shadows for his Fae form, kneeling beside Laydan where he lay bleeding. She spared a glance at Holt, dead bodies scattered around him as he fought back more humans, and Zylah's blood ran cold as another group entered the chamber, led by a man with eyes that were wholly black. A vampire.

Her assailant swiped at her with his blade, and Zylah only just managed to call out a warning for Holt as the vampire rushed towards him. She pivoted away from the sword strike, the man's sigil swinging wildly at his chest with the force of his movements, the tip of his blade nicking her elbow as she moved.

Holt was moving faster and faster, rocks smashing and exploding into humans as he moved around the vampire, the entire tomb shaking beneath the force of his magic, despite the spells that would be preventing him from reaching his full potential.

Zylah swung around, driving her sword across the man's abdomen, and didn't spare him a glance as she ran towards the other humans surrounding Holt. She'd seen how this played out; the vampire would toy with him until he'd spent every last drop of his power, and then use his moment of weakness to strike. But then Holt surprised her; a ripple of power erupted from him, stone and rocks shaking to swallow up the vampire, pinning him beneath the stone.

"He's losing too much blood, help him!" Daizin pleaded, shadows wrapping around Laydan's wound. Kopi had landed on the witch's hand, a few stray feathers falling as if he'd been fighting.

"Holt. Laydan's hurt," Zylah managed to call out, swinging away from another swipe of a sword as three humans came for her. Holt took out the first and began moving towards the second. "I've got this," Zylah assured him.

He hesitated for only a moment before running over to Daizin, the Fae's shadows lifting to let him in.

Zylah fought off the two humans, her limbs burning with the effort, her arms beginning to tremble. She sheathed her sword to pull for another dagger, just as the makeshift tomb around the vampire cracked and he shot out.

Empty, black eyes stared down at her, short chestnut hair ruffled from his fight with Holt. "He wasn't lying when he said you were beautiful."

"Tell Jesper he can go fuck himself." Zylah gripped her dagger, but the vampire darted forwards, sinking its teeth into the soft flesh of her throat before Zylah even realised what was happening. It recoiled immediately, eyes flashing wild and mouth stained crimson with her blood as it hissed, but before Zylah even had the chance to register what had happened, Holt barrelled into its side and knocked it clean off its feet.

She pressed a hand to her neck; the vampire hadn't bitten deep, whatever had made it recoil had stopped it, but already she was weak, light-headed, as Holt grappled with the vampire in the dirt. An orblight had smashed beside them and he was wielding the fire, bursts of flame shooting at the remaining humans, their screams filling the space as they dropped to the ground to try and extinguish the inferno threatening to consume them whole.

Zylah kept pressure on her wound, fighting back her drowsiness as she scrambled over to where Daizin still held Laydan. Holt was using more and more magic, and she searched the space around them for a way to lure the vampire away from him before he burnt out, her hope plummeting when she saw none. She couldn't breathe watching him, couldn't look away, her heart in her mouth at the sight. He landed a blow to the vampire's jaw, his flames spiralling around the creature like rope, and it roared against the constraints.

Just as Zylah thought it might yield it lurched forwards and sank its fangs into Holt's throat, pushing him back towards where she sat beside Daizin. She reached for him with a strangled sob, but Daizin hooked an arm around her waist, pulling her back. Holt's name was a scream on her lips as his flames burnt hotter, squeezed tighter, Daizin's shadows pulling everything into darkness, protecting them from the blaze, his arm still tight around her waist.

"No!" Zylah swiped frantically at the shadows, a sickening fear twisting her stomach at the thought of the vampire draining Holt, but the darkness cleared just in time for her to see it go rigid against him. He dug his hands into the creature's arms, pressing tight, a roar erupting from him and his body convulsing as his flames consumed it, burning so bright Zylah had to shield her eyes.

She fought against Daizin's grip, her hands trembling from her rising panic. Zylah called Holt's name again, the light almost blinding as she fought to see him protected from his own inferno, the vampire burning until all that remained was ash. Holt staggered against the absence of the vampire's weight, pressing a hand to his throat, his eyes lifting to meet hers.

"Let go of me!" she seethed against Daizin's touch, her panic all-consuming, just as two more groups of humans burst into the chamber surrounding them, and Holt fell to his knees. "Holt!" Power flared from her, and Daizin recoiled, freeing her from his grasp. Zylah didn't waste time weighing up her options. If she tried to heal Holt, they'd still be surrounded. There was only one way out of this. She lunged for his hand, reached out for Daizin with the other, and evanesced them all back to the safety of the Aquaris Court.

But it was too far, and with three others, four, if she included Kopi, they were too many, the burn of the vanquicite searing through every inch of her. Zylah screamed as the pain set her nerves alight and willed herself to travel just a little bit farther until she could smell the scent of the ocean and hear the crashing of the waves.

A choked sob escaped her as she took in the white balcony of the Aquaris Court, the feeling of Holt's hand tightening around hers and a flurry of relief in her heart at the sight of his eyes fluttering open.

And at last, she let the pain pull her into oblivion.

31

Just stay with me.

Zylah was dreaming. She was back in the tavern in Virian with Holt after she'd brought him back to their room and healed him. His hand was warm around hers, and something in his voice made her pause, the way he seemed as if he didn't want to let her go.

"Zylah." His voice cut through the haze of her dream, and she remembered he was injured.

She tried to say his name, but every breath felt like fire, her throat full of ash. Everything hurt. Burned white-hot like thousands of blades slicing through her blood, her nerves, her flesh. Tears pricked at the corners of her eyes as a strangled sound escaped her, and the arms around her tightened.

Holt. He was trying to heal her, and *he* was injured. She wanted to tell him to stop, to hold onto whatever he had left for himself, but she was shaking so badly she couldn't get the words out.

Voices talked over each other, people shouting. Kopi quietly hooed somewhere nearby.

"I can work here. Get the others away. Aerin, towels. Niossa, bring Cirelle." Zylah didn't recognise the voice that spoke. Female, raspy. Old.

Another burst of pain made her curl in on herself, and she realised Holt had pulled her into his lap, his comforting scent wrapping around her, his warmth leeching into her too-cold skin.

I won't let anything happen to you.

Zylah wasn't sure if he'd said it out loud or if she was just recalling his words from that night on the balcony, but her panic flared again as she remembered how badly he'd been hurt, how deeply he'd pulled on his power to kill the vampire.

She reached a hand to his neck where the creature had bitten him, the warm stickiness of his blood coating her fingertips and her heartbeat wild in her chest at the thought of losing him.

He caught her hand, his fingers twining through hers. "I'm fine, Zylah," he said roughly. "Look at me."

Her hand slipped from his, her palm falling to his chest as she pushed a kernel of her power into him. She gritted her teeth as he pushed back against it, his magic pressing against hers.

"Don't fight it," he said, his tone commanding. "You need it more than me."

For a moment, Zylah could feel her power twining with his, spiralling back and forth between them.

Her eyes flicked open, and she met his, focused on the way the green deepened at the magic weaving between them, the way his shoulders and chest heaved against the feeling of their power wrapping around each other.

She felt his groan deep within his chest.

"Zylah, stop," he breathed, his attention flicking down and then back up to her eyes, and all she saw in his was pain.

The last thing she wanted was to hurt him. She pulled back, his magic pouring into her again without resistance, his shoulders sagging a little as if in relief.

"It would save you both, Holt." Cirelle's voice carried over the hum of movement.

"Not like this," Holt barked, a broken edge to his voice halfway between rage and fear. "Not like this," he said again, his voice softer as another spasm of pain rattled through Zylah's body.

Cirelle murmured something else, but Zylah couldn't work out the words. There were hands on her back, carefully cutting open her clothes. "We're going to get this poison out of you, my child," the voice from before said over her shoulder. A Fae healer, she presumed. They were going to touch her. They were going to be affected by the vanquicite, and Zylah couldn't let that happen, wouldn't. "You can't," she rasped, her eyes fluttering shut. "It will kill you."

The healer clicked her tongue. "I have seen my death, and it is not today." Warm hands pressed into the bare skin on Zylah's back. "Don't let go of her. Keep healing her if you can," she said to Holt.

Zylah tried to make a noise in protest, but Holt's hand rested against the side of her face, and he tilted her head up to look at him again. "Don't think anything you can say would make me stop."

A retort formed in her thoughts, but it was sluggish, falling away to nothing on her lips. She was vaguely aware of someone gasping, of voices muttering. Rin and Nye, if she had to guess, but she focused on Holt, grinding her teeth against the pain as the healer started to work at the vanquicite, moving as if she were coaxing it from her body.

But it had already reached her heart. Like spears of lightning, the vanquicite seared through her veins with each stuttered heartbeat, the poison leeching into every part of her. No matter how hard Zylah tried, she couldn't hold on. Could do nothing but let herself slip away into the cocoon of pain that beckoned her.

Zylah. She wasn't sure if Holt had said her name out loud again, or if in her delirious state, she'd imagined it. But then his eyes narrowed, and he said, "We have a bargain, remember."

To live. That was the deal she'd made with him. She pressed her hand to his face, her fingers leaving a bloody print as she looked up into his eyes, to the way they frantically searched hers. A frown pulled his eyebrows together, his hair ruffled and wild from his fight. *Will it hurt?* she'd asked him once before. If she broke the bargain. She couldn't bear the thought of causing him pain.

"Don't think like that," he whispered, his eyes turning glassy, and she realised she must have said it out loud.

There was movement around them, but Zylah's vision had narrowed to him, to the way his eyes searched hers, to the feeling of his magic flowing through her, chasing the vanquicite in her veins.

Someone swore under their breath. Rin. "This is fucked up. He's going to—"

"Rin," Nye warned her cousin.

The healer hummed as she worked, *tugging* on the vanquicite, pulling on every spot it had taken root within Zylah, but she let the sight and the feel of Holt anchor her, focused on the warmth of the magic he poured into her instead of the way her body was shutting down. She tried to speak, but she couldn't summon the words. *It was never about living forever, Holt. Just living free,* she wanted to tell him, but she couldn't even manage a whisper.

"Stay with me," he murmured into her hair as he pulled her close, pressing a kiss against her head and rocking her against him.

Darkness crept in at the corner of Zylah's vision as the woman muttered words at her back, the pull against the vanquicite throbbing and pulsing and threatening to pull her under completely.

"Am I dead?" she'd asked Pallia.

"Do you want to be?" Pallia had asked in return.

Zylah's eyes fell shut again, thoughts swirling and looping over each other, memories blurring into one. And though she had accepted that the vanquicite was taking her life, she didn't want to give it up. Because she *did* have something to lose. Her friends. Her freedom. Holt.

A sharp tug against her spine had her crying out again, but she concentrated on the sound of Holt's breathing, the thread of magic that weaved between her and him where he was still trying to heal her, to keep her there. How he had anything left to give she didn't know. She'd seen how much he'd depleted himself against the vampire, watched him collapse after it sank its teeth into his neck. And she'd known then, known that she

340

would do anything, *anything* to keep him in this world, no matter the cost.

"I can't watch this," Rin said somewhere nearby, her voice wavering.

"Then leave," Cirelle snapped, "I'm trying to keep them calm, and you're not helping."

Another tug against Zylah's spine, her back arching against the jolt of pain, Holt's arms tightening again as if to remind her he was there.

The vanquicite was pulling her apart, piece by piece, and for a moment it was as if she was above her body, watching all the threads of vanquicite the woman was trying to shear away from her, and another that anchored her; the one between her and Holt.

"Just a little while longer, Zylah," Holt said as he brushed the hair from her eyes, his voice strained. She wished she could look at him, wished she could fight away the darkness that had taken hold of her, but her head was spinning, her body shaking, her heart like a trapped bird against her chest as she realised she could no longer feel her legs.

Zylah couldn't speak. A dull roar had started to accompany the pain, and she could do nothing to fight it.

"I've got you," Holt murmured, his thumb wiping gently at the tears that rolled down her face, his forehead pressed against hers.

Zylah couldn't open her eyes, could do nothing but hold on to that feeling between them, the power that spilled from him, seeking out all the places the vanquicite had occupied, replacing darkness with light.

Holt's breaths were shallow, each one more laboured than the last, and she knew he was reaching the end of what he had to give, the roaring in her ears growing louder.

Stop. The thought was sluggish. *Please,* she wanted to beg him.

His mouth pressed against hers, and she felt him tremble above her. It was a soft kiss. Tender. Slow. One that felt too much like a goodbye, his breath catching as if he knew it too.

Hot tears streaked down her cheeks, and he eased back to wipe them away. *Stop. Holt. Please. Let me go.*

But he didn't stop, because she no longer had the strength to say the words out loud.

Panicked voices moved around them, but all Zylah wanted to see was him. She willed her eyes to open as everything seemed to light up within her, her body rigid with the agony of the poison being pulled from her bones, the roar of it being torn from her blood.

She held his gaze as the light intensified, grateful that the last thing she would ever see would be him before the darkness pulled her under.

Only it wasn't darkness that finally tore her away from him, but a flame so blinding it felt as if it ripped from her chest and set light to everything she was from the inside out. A flame so bright it incinerated every thread that spilt from her.

Everyone except his, and her fear grew tenfold as she realised she was going to pull him under with her.

But the thought was cut off before she could act on it, because the light flared, and the vanquicite finally won.

32

Feathers stroked her face. Something hooed, and the sound was so loud it had Zylah's head pulsing. Kopi buried deeper into the crook of her neck, his feathers tickling her ear, and she groaned in protest.

"Zylah?"

Her eyes flicked open at the sound of Holt's voice, and she drew in a shaky breath. It felt like she was seeing him for the first time. The vibrancy of his emerald eyes, the angular lines of his jaw, the richness of his bronzed skin.

There was no wound on his neck, and he was wearing different clothes. Dark shadows swept beneath his eyes, stubble peppered his jaw, and his hair was mussed and ruffled like he'd been running his hands through it over and over.

He eased himself out of the chair he'd been sitting in, *sleeping* in, Zylah realised, and sat on the edge of her bed. He reached for Kopi, depositing the tiny owl on the bedside table, but his eyes never broke away from hers.

They hadn't properly spoken since before the tomb, since he'd asked her what she wanted, and it seemed now like so many words hung unspoken between them that Zylah didn't know where to start. Outside, the ocean crashed against the rocks below the court, so deafening Zylah wondered if it was the tail end of another storm. Inside, the sound of Holt's heart beating fast beneath his chest felt like a beating drum, and she reached up and pressed a hand to it, if only to reassure him that she was really there.

Maybe she still needed to convince herself, too.

"I didn't mean to fall asleep," he said softly, placing a hand over hers, his shoulders moving as if he were taking his first true breath since they'd returned from the tomb.

"You look like you haven't slept in days," she said, but her voice sounded strange to her ears.

"I haven't." His eyes moved over her, as if he were checking her for injuries. She ached as if she'd been in bed for too long, but otherwise, she felt good. Better than good. And she knew that in part, it was because of him. Knew that whatever the healer had been able to do, had only been made possible because he'd refused to let her go.

"Is it all gone?" she asked, though she wasn't sure she was ready for the answer, didn't think she could accept it now if it was still going to end her life. She brushed a hand to her shoulder as if she might feel some trace of the vanquicite lingering in her spine, her fingers catching on thin straps of silk. Someone had put her in a nightgown but given that the healer had cut open her clothes, Zylah couldn't say she was surprised.

She studied Holt's face as his heartbeat began to steady. As if he had finally accepted that she was fine. Watched the way his throat worked as he said, "All of it."

Zylah dipped her chin in acknowledgement, pressed her eyes shut.

The vanquicite wasn't the only thing that was gone. Somewhere between leaving the Aquaris Court and coming back to it, she'd let go of some of the hate she'd been holding onto. Some of the animosity towards herself that had consumed her, night and day, for months. She hadn't entirely forgiven herself, for the way she'd handled everything since fleeing the gallows in Dalstead. But she'd meant what she'd said to Holt. She was tired of shutting everything out. Everyone. And punishing herself, pushing everyone away, it had only been harming her more.

She eased her hand away from beneath Holt's, began to push herself upright against the headboard. He watched her closely, every muscle coiled with tension and restraint, his attention only shifting when he seemed satisfied that she was comfortable before he poured her a glass of water from the pitcher on her bedside table.

"I'll make you some tea as soon as Deyna has checked on you," he said as she took a sip, his voice still soft and quiet.

"The healer?"

He nodded.

There was so much she needed to say, but everything had happened so quickly. The last thing she remembered was him holding onto her, healing her as Deyna pulled the vanquicite from her body. How much pain he'd been in and how, for a moment, her magic had coiled around his before he'd told her to stop. Before he'd poured and poured so much of himself into her to keep her heart beating, she'd been afraid his was going to give out first. The air seemed to thicken around them, and she knew from the way he carefully assessed her that he was thinking of it too.

"You almost died," she whispered, her brow pinching as she tilted her head to look at him. She'd never seen him look so ruffled; the cool mask of indifference he normally wore eroded to the raw concern etched across his features.

"I'd die a hundred times for you."

Her heart beat faster at his admission, and without thought, she reached for him again, but he caught her hand. Swallowed.

"You need to see something," he said, his thumb brushing over her knuckles and sending a shiver through her body. "Can you stand?"

Zylah pulled the blanket aside, the silk night dress riding up her thighs as she lithely swung her feet to the floor. She felt weightless—hadn't realised how heavy a burden the vanquicite had become. The tiles were cool against her feet, the silk of her nightgown a soft rasp against her skin. Holt's fingers closed around hers as she looked up at him, and he gently urged her to follow him to the corner of the room, to the door that connected her room to his. But then he stopped. Angled her towards the mirror. She watched his reflection as he took a step back, looking at her over her shoulder in the glass.

And then her attention snagged on delicately pointed ears. *Her* pointed ears. Not his. Her heartbeat quickened as she reached a hand up to them to check they were real. Her eyes were brighter, too. Zylah glanced down at her hands, turning them over. Her eyesight had improved. How was this possible? She took a step closer to the mirror to examine her face. She had the same preternatural look about her as all the other High Fae she'd seen, a wild kind of otherworldliness that even without the pointed ears, would have marked them as different.

For a moment, she felt like a fraud. Let that familiar voice that used to whisper dark things in her thoughts tell her that she'd deceived so many people, made them believe she was half human. Tricked them. But then she pressed a hand to the mirror, her breath clouding on the glass, and willed the voice to be silent. To do nothing except take in the sight of herself, the flecks of blue in her eyes that were so bright they were almost aquamarine, the way her hair fell over her ears and spilt over her shoulders.

And with the silence came a sense of rightness. A settling in her bones she hadn't felt before. It didn't matter that all trace of human was gone. It had never been who she was, and hiding had almost killed her.

"Pallia said the vanquicite was put there to keep me safe. Is this what she meant—to hide me? From whom? Marcus?" She met Holt's eyes in the mirror. He hadn't moved since he'd stood behind her. Just watched her carefully, as he had since the moment she'd woken up, every inch of him still coiled tight.

"I—" A knock sounded at the door. Frustration flickered in his eyes, but he shut it down just as quickly as it had appeared. "Come in, Deyna," Holt called out.

An old woman slipped into the room, the door closing softly behind her. Not Fae, Zylah noted. "Aren't you magnificent?" she said with a bright smile, her face all soft creases and wrinkles. Her eyes were as blue as the ocean beyond the court, her white hair swept up into a messy top knot, ringlets escaping their binding and bouncing as she strode over to the mirror to stand beside

Zylah. "I believe the vanquicite was left in there far longer than it was intended to be, but you've built up an almighty resilience to it, haven't you?" She took Zylah's hand and led her back to the bed.

Zylah realised Deyna was speaking quietly, just as Holt had been, and why her own voice had sounded so wrong. Everything was louder. She sat on the edge of the bed, questions turning themselves over on the tip of her tongue as she took in the truth of what she was. Not half Fae. But High Fae, and already she could feel how her body had changed, become stronger, not just without the vanquicite, but because of the pure Fae blood that now ran unhindered through her veins.

Deyna sat beside her and pressed the back of her hand to Zylah's forehead. "In all my days I've never seen vanquicite used this way. It nullifies Fae abilities, but to hide it in you when you were just a babe." Her smile turned sympathetic, sorrowful as she checked Zylah's pulse at her wrist. "Someone must have been desperate to hide you. To keep your Fae identity hidden. I'm told you used your abilities for the first time only a year ago?"

Had it been a year? Zylah supposed it had. It felt like years had passed since she'd fled Dalstead. She nodded at the healer.

"Your body was fighting back, trying to expel it from your system. I don't think it was lodged in your spine to begin with. I think that happened as you grew up, grew around it, but in trying to dispel it, it was pulled into your bones. Your blood," Deyna added.

Zylah paled, and the healer patted her knee affectionately, as if she were speaking with a grandchild. "I'm sure you don't need me to tell you this. But I want you to know that whoever put it there meant you no such cruelty. It would have been done out of fear. Out of love." She pulled a vial from the folds of her brown dress. "Add this to your tea, it will help with any headaches as your senses adjust. Just a few flakes at a time though."

Zylah took it from her, uncorked the vial and winced. The smell was so potent, she had to cork it immediately. It reminded her of her own tonic, with a heavy undertone of baylock. The scent snapped her out of her daze, her eyes widening, and she turned her attention to Holt. "The baylock tea. Both the thrall and the vampire. Laydan. Is he alright? And Daizin?"

He eased the vial from her hand, a muscle feathering in his jaw. "Laydan stole the key."

Zylah felt the colour drain from her face. "Laydan?"

Holt nodded. "And the book."

Deyna murmured something and pressed a hand to Zylah's back. "Just checking, then I'll take my leave. You'll have some scarring, but—"

"Thank you," Zylah said, taking the woman's hand in her own. "I don't know how you did it, but you saved my life."

The old woman laughed, patted her hand. "He helped me." Her eyes flicked up to where Holt was making tea. "You both did. And I'm glad to have helped. You did Cirelle a great service, and Rin, from what I understand. This world needs to hold on to people like you."

Zylah squeezed her hand in thanks, and Deyna made for the door. "I've managed to secure a few more days for you to rest here, but after that Malok has requested that you leave. I'm sorry we won't get to spend more time together. But you're in good hands." Her attention flicked to Holt then back to Zylah. "Send for me if you need anything." She left as quietly as she'd come in, leaving only the sounds of Holt making tea and the ocean crashing on the rocks far below the court.

"Laydan stole the key," Zylah said to herself, pushing up onto the bed to rest against the pillows. He'd been attacked in the tomb and almost bled out in Daizin's arms. "Why?"

Holt placed the teacup on the bedside table, the bed dipping beneath him as he sat beside her, hands on his knees. "He was here when you brought us back from the tomb. Daizin asked him if he had the key. He said it was safe. And the next morning he was gone, the book too. He was a thief through and through."

Zylah shook her head in disbelief. He'd fooled them all. "And Daizin?"

Holt blew out an exasperated breath. "Daizin looks like a man who just had his heart broken."

Zylah thought of how they'd been together. Of Laydan taking Daizin's face in his hands and teasing him lovingly. She barely knew Daizin, but enough to know the look in his eyes as he'd wrapped his arms around the witch and pulled him close. It was love.

Deyna said she'd managed to secure them a few more days at Malok's court. Of course, he wouldn't hand his army over without the key; the court would not be protected as he'd wished, and he wouldn't part with the only thing he had left to defend it. Even if it meant sacrificing countless other Fae across Astaria.

It didn't matter that Zylah had sent every item Cirelle needed for her ailment, of course, it wouldn't matter to a male like Malok.

There was also the matter of Zylah's evanescing.

That there were multiple witnesses, and if none of them could trace her magic, they'd have sent for someone who could. Malok would know it, too.

She thought of the thrall attack at Jora's funeral, and the severity of her mistake hit her. But their spell could have covered it, couldn't it? She desperately hoped it was the case—the Fae that resided within the court stood a better chance of defending themselves than the humans Rin and Kej had been hiding there.

"What did you mean, about the baylock tea?" Holt asked, watching her closely.

"I think it hurt them. The vampire and the thrall. Laydan had been drinking it too, and when the thrall attacked him, it recoiled. The same thing happened when the vampire bit me. But not to you." Her attention fell to his neck, looking for any sign of the vampire's teeth. It had mentioned Jesper to her with those same dead eyes the prince had looked at her with, as if being turned into a vampire had devoured whatever had been left of the soul beneath.

She repressed a shudder. "If we could get enough of it, administer it to the soldiers, it might not be much of an advantage, but it's something."

Holt arched an eyebrow. "More surprises." His tone was teasing, but he didn't smile.

Perhaps it was his exhaustion, but there was something else, something he was holding back.

Something had changed between them. Like he was being careful not to touch her too much, and a small, vicious voice inside her tried to whisper reasons why, but she snuffed it out.

"The tomb. It was for Ranon. One of the decoys, wasn't it?"

There were fragments of thoughts, puzzle pieces Zylah knew fit together but hadn't quite figured out how.

Holt dipped his chin in acknowledgement.

"The sigil the humans were wearing. I've seen it before, in a book Nye showed me. It was on the page with a drawing of Ranon's tomb. Do you think… do you think Marcus's source of old magic, Aurelia and the vampires, that it's connected to Ranon, somehow?"

"I hope for all our sakes that isn't true. But you were right about one thing: the priestesses. They must have been working with Marcus this entire time."

Perhaps Marcus had promised them something; a place in his new version of Astaria, some position of power. Zylah shook her head. "And now Malok won't hand over his army, doesn't need to fulfil his end of the bargain, because we didn't get the key. So, was Laydan working for Marcus, too?" She ran a hand through her hair, her fingers catching against the point of an ear, unfamiliar with the shape of it. "I'm sorry, Holt. I really wanted to do this for you."

"For me?"

"Get you the key, before—"

"Before the vanquicite took your life?"

She searched his eyes, but there was no judgement there. "You knew?"

"I knew I was willing to do anything to not let it take you."

She pushed up onto her knees and pulled his hands from his lap. "Thank you," she said softly, willing her voice not to break. She thought of his admission back in the caves. Of how the words had spilt from him and felt her own admission bubbling up in her chest. Felt the air crackle between them as she remembered again what he'd done for her, her chest tightening at the thought. "I felt you. Even when I couldn't speak. You brought me back."

"Zylah." He breathed her name like it was a prayer. Spoke it with such reverence, just as he always had as he looked at their intertwined hands, his thumb running over hers as if he'd allow himself just that one slip in his restraint.

But she could still sense resistance from him, as if he were trying to close up the layers he'd peeled back for her.

"Look at me," she said softly.

His eyes lifted to meet hers.

"I'm okay, Holt. Truly." So many times she'd been given a second chance. And finally, it felt as if something had snapped inside her. Or smoothed over. Not because she was no longer half Fae, but because for the first time in months, she could think clearly.

"I thought I was a monster," she confessed as she held his gaze. "A murderer. That they died because of me. Mala, Asha. My father. Raif." She saw the way Holt's mouth moved, as if he were about to say something, to protest, but he pressed his lips together.

"I thought I had dragged Raif along and that he was gone because of me. And I hated myself for it. Every day I hated myself for not giving him something better before he died. I thought the guilt was going to eat me alive. Not just because I didn't love him enough but because I…" She bit down on her lip, fighting back the sudden twist of fear that squeezed tightly around her heart.

It was as if she were on the edge of a precipice, one that she'd been standing on for too long now, too afraid to let herself fall. But Holt's eyes shuttered at her admission, and she knew at once it had been the wrong thing to say. That the words had come out wrong.

His attention fell back to their hands. "You should get some more rest before we have to leave."

"Don't do that. Try to wrap me up like I'm some fragile thing that can be broken. I know I haven't been… okay for a while, but every day it gets a little bit better. Don't push me away when I'm just starting to figure things out."

His eyes shot up to meet hers, the shadows in them diminishing as one hand pressed lightly to the side of her face. "I don't think you're fragile. I think you're strong and brave, and even on your darkest days you never gave up. Never gave in." His thumb hooked under the strap of her nightgown where it had slipped off her shoulder, his touch sending shivers along her skin as he readjusted it.

"You've been a big part of that, Holt. More than you could ever know."

"I lied to you," he said quietly, his attention fixed on his fingers brushing her shoulder.

"When?" Her voice came out like a whisper, soft and breathy, and she caught the shift in his scent. Knew what it meant. Knew she couldn't keep her desire hidden from him any longer even if she wanted to.

"When I agreed with you. When you said hearts cannot be owned." He took her hand and placed it on his chest as she'd done. "It's always been yours." His eyes dipped to her mouth for a moment. Then he took in her face, her ears, and then the light in his eyes seemed to dim. "But you and Raif..."

Zylah shook her head. "I told you I felt guilty about my father's death. About Raif's. But I also felt that way because of this." She waved a hand between them. "Because of you." He rose from the bed as if the words had unsettled him. She hadn't meant for it to sound as if she were blaming him. "Is this because of—"

"It's because you're still healing, and I can't trust myself around you. And because—"

A knock sounded at the door. "Zylah?" Rin's voice carried through the wall.

"I'll give you some privacy," Holt said quietly, already halfway through the door between their two rooms.

Zylah looked away for a moment just as Rin stepped into her room, and when she looked back, Holt had already gone.

33

Zylah willed her heart to steady. Willed herself to wear a blank expression, to not let Rin see that inside she felt as if she were falling, tumbling in a free fall with no end.

"Deyna told me you were awake. Shit, did I just interrupt something?" the Fae asked, following Zylah's gaze to Holt's door and wrinkling her nose.

Zylah shook her head and put on a bright smile. "It's fine. It's good to see you."

She tried to hide her surprise at Rin's hug, keeping her smile plastered in place.

"I'm supposed to be mad at you," the Fae murmured into Zylah's hair.

"Mad?"

Rin pulled back to inspect Zylah, her eyes passing over the pointed ears. "You didn't tell us you were sick. We just thought you were unhappy, that you needed time." She looked as flustered as she had in Arlan's presence that evening at the dinner table.

"I'm sorry," Zylah said quietly.

"No, it's not…" Rin grabbed Zylah's hands. "*I'm* sorry. We should have been paying closer attention. I'm just glad you're okay. We thought you were…" Her voice caught for a moment. "Both of you." *Dead.* She didn't need to say the word. She glanced over her shoulder to Holt's door, a frown etched across her forehead. "Mother received everything you sent."

"I'm sure it wasn't much use if Deyna was here."

"The ingredients arrived before Deyna did." Rin squeezed her hand. "Thank you."

Zylah tried to focus on Rin. But her eyes kept falling on Holt's door over the Fae's shoulder. *I'd die a hundred times for you.* It was as if she could feel him moving around in the next room, feel his presence even with a wall between them.

"…let you get some more rest; Holt can fill you in on everything before you leave. Zylah?" Rin raised an eyebrow, head tilted to one side as she looked at her cautiously.

"Sorry," Zylah murmured. She hadn't heard half of what her friend had been saying. "Rest would be good." But rest wasn't what she needed. She needed to move. To burn off the energy of all that had happened, to move through it all, to not be still, not for a minute longer.

Rin gave her a warm smile as she paused beside the door. "It never mattered to us that you were half Fae."

"I know." And Zylah believed her.

She waited for the door to click shut, and then she was on her feet, moving, her hand resting on the door between her room and Holt's.

Time is the only thing I could give you, Zylah.
I can't look at you like I'm just a friend and fine with that.

Tell me what you want, Zylah.
I'd die a hundred times for you.
It's always been yours.

She took a deep breath. Tapped her knuckles against his door and waited. The doorknob twisted a few heartbeats later, and Zylah cleared her throat. "I didn't—"

She looked up from the knob as the door opened to Holt standing before her, hair dripping wet, a towel at his waist, the wildness she'd often glimpsed in him darkening his eyes as they swept over her body.

"I needed to cool off," he said by way of explanation.

She didn't need to look down to know it hadn't worked, the thick length of him tucked against his stomach beneath the towel. Zylah swallowed, a delicious heat dancing along her skin in anticipation, not caring what scent she was throwing off. She was bare beneath the nightdress, and she knew he knew it, too.

"Damn it, Zylah. We should talk first." There was a roughness to his voice as he pulled her into the room and pushed the door shut behind her, but his eyes were full of the same hunger and need she knew he could see in her own.

But she didn't move away from the door. Planted her feet firmly, grounded herself in the strength of her own body and let it fill her with confidence. "What's there to talk about? I want you." She tilted her chin up to him as he stepped closer, his half-lidded eyes taking her in. "You want me?"

Her gaze fell to his lips as her back pressed against the door, down to his heavily muscled chest where she could hear his heart racing in time with her own. His skin was still wet, his heat mixed with his intoxicating scent radiating from him as he ran his knuckles lightly down the bare skin of her arm and she waited for his answer. Waited as he lifted her with one hand, her nightdress riding up her thighs and she ran her fingers through his wet hair, their eyes locking for a moment as he held her close enough for them to share a breath.

"Yes, I want you, Zylah," Holt said, his lips brushing over hers.

She couldn't help but arch into his touch, her voice breathless as she said, "Then there's nothing left to say."

It was as if something inside him snapped. His mouth was on hers, his tongue parting her lips to taste her, one hand gripping her waist as he claimed her with his kiss. Zylah's fingers tightened in his hair, her tongue sweeping across his and matching him stroke for stroke.

She'd almost lost him. And the thought made her curl her fingers tighter, claim him in return.

Holt's hand slid under her nightdress as their kiss grew hungrier, needier, her skin sensitive and every muscle in her body tightening at his touch, but it wasn't enough. Heat curled through her as she pulled the straps off her shoulders, the silk falling over her breasts, and Holt's gaze turned predatory as he drew back to take her in. His fingers fisted in her hair, pulling her head back for him to trace kisses down her throat, over the swell of one breast, until he took her nipple into his mouth and Zylah let out a breathy moan, her hips moving against the hard length pressed between her thighs. He made an approving sound in the back of his throat, his teeth coming together over the soft flesh, his tongue quickly following to soothe over the hurt as she writhed beneath his touch, demanding more of him.

She'd been so afraid to give in to this feeling that she hadn't realised how long she'd been waiting, wanting him, and with the way he moved against her, she knew he'd been waiting, too. Knew he'd been trying just as hard to conceal it as she had, and that he'd done it for her, no matter how difficult it might have been for him. Zylah pushed the thought away, no longer willing to let the guilt get in the way of what she wanted. What she'd craved, for so long.

Her hips rocked faster against him where their bodies pressed together, his thin towel the last barrier between them, the scrap of fabric driving her crazy, the wild heat burning inside her threatening to burn it away to nothing. She ached to touch him, to feel him, reaching for the towel as he moved to her other breast. There would be no more hesitating. No more waiting. Only him.

But as her hands found the towel, he caught both her wrists, planting them above her with one hand and capturing her mouth again. He pinned her against the wall with only his hips, his free hand caressing every place his mouth had just been until it rested on her cheek, his thumb tracing her swollen lips like he couldn't get enough of them.

"Holt," Zylah whispered as she tried to move against him, desperate for more friction between her thighs, her ragged breathing matching his. She needed to touch him, to taste him, to explore him the way he had her, to map out every inch of him with her mouth and her tongue until they were both breathless and sated.

The corner of his mouth lifted into a knowing smile, eyes smouldering as he released her wrists to wrap both arms around her, kissing her fiercely as he moved them away from the door and across the room.

Zylah let herself get lost in the heat of his kiss, the feel of him against her, the strength of his arms wrapped around her as he set her down on his bed, his teeth biting into her lower lip before he pulled away.

"Do you have any idea how distracting this mouth of yours is?" he asked, his thumb rubbing over the sensitive skin.

Her attention was fixed on his mouth as she said, "I think I might, yes."

"Smart ass."

Zylah tugged off her nightdress, throwing the silk to the floor but he didn't remove his towel. He knelt before her, a ravenous look in his eyes as he drank her in, one hand sliding underneath a thigh, the other wrapping around the ends of her hair again, easing her head back until she was completely exposed before him, her skin pebbling with anticipation.

Zylah knew what she felt for him went beyond wanting to feel him, needing to touch him. Beyond raw desire. Had known it for a long time now, but instead of dwelling on it, she let herself get lost in the moment, in the feel of Holt's demanding and possessive touch.

He took his time trailing kisses from her mouth down every inch of her body, arching her back further and further until he reached her navel, releasing her hair only to hook his hand under her knee and yank her closer to him, his breath hot against the apex of her thighs where a liquid heat had settled.

"You're beautiful, Zylah. So damned perfect," he said as his eyes met hers.

Zylah sucked in a too-thin breath, her hips tilting towards him, but he placed a broad hand flat across her stomach to hold her steady. He hummed in satisfaction as he pressed his mouth to her sensitive flesh, every nerve in her body coming alive at the feel of him between her legs, and the last of her thoughts eddied away from her.

At the first stroke of his tongue, Zylah called out, her fingers knotting into his hair as his thumb moved in circles against her and he devoured her with his mouth. Zylah almost bucked off the bed, but Holt held her firm as he pushed two fingers inside her to move in time with his thumb, her body coiling tighter and tighter around him. Her hips arched against him as the tension built and built, her skin too tight against her bones and her limbs stiffening until she shattered against him, her vision hazing as his tongue and his fingers wrung out every last inch of her pleasure.

Holt didn't pull away until she stopped shaking, tracing kisses against her thighs before he stood before her, eyes roving over her reverently, drinking her in.

Zylah swallowed as she saw he'd at last removed his towel, her mouth going dry at the size of him as he fisted himself once, twice. He looked down at her on the bed, but she didn't back away from the intensity of his gaze. She let herself enjoy the sight of him standing over her, her eyes trailing over the cut of his stomach muscles to the thick vee between his hip bones, to the way his hand wrapped around his shaft as he watched her, her body aching to feel him. There were things that needed to be said, but this moment between them felt like a language all in itself. She needed it, but so did he.

Zylah reached for him, but he caught her wrists again, his mouth crashing against hers as he positioned himself over her, his other hand wrapped tightly around one of her thighs and the tip of him brushing against her entrance. Zylah moved her hips, a quiet whimper escaping her in a begging plea.

"So impatient," Holt murmured against her mouth, his lips twitching as he held back a smile.

He held her in place, his grip firm and his eyes fixed on hers as he eased into her slowly, a hiss of satisfaction leaving them both.

Nothing but raw desire and devotion etched his features as he filled her slowly, inch by inch, easing further until he was buried to the hilt, their bodies pressed flush against each other, and Zylah didn't think she could take any more of him.

"Fuck, Zylah," Holt breathed, a shudder of pleasure rippling through his body as she moaned, the way he filled her so entirely just dancing the line between pleasure and pain.

Her legs clamped around his waist and her fingernails dug into his shoulders as she bit down on her lip, adjusting to his size. His hand came down on the exposed skin of her throat, his hips moving slowly at first as he kissed the column of her neck just above where he held her possessively, as if he was claiming her, branding her.

Her body blazed with the heat of his skin, the feel of him moving inside her, sparks dancing along her flesh as he began to move faster, his hips building to a punishing rhythm, tension spiralling through her again, higher and higher, and Zylah lost herself to the feel of him.

At the first slip of her magic, the air stirred around them.

"Zylah." A quiet warning in his tone, as if she'd hurt him again.

She pulled back on her power, tugging it back inside herself, an apology spilling from her lips, but Holt cut her off with a kiss, his hips slowing.

"Don't," he murmured against her mouth.

Zylah pushed against his chest, and without breaking them apart, he adjusted them both, lifting her into his lap, his feet planted on the floor and his hands firm around her rear. Zylah's head fell back at the size of him, the way he filled her even more in this position. He stilled for a moment, but at the first rise of her hips, he lost himself to her again, his thrusts deep and fast and brutal.

He slid a hand between them, fingers working the knot of nerves at her core, her body throbbing with the feel of him, ecstasy taking over her body as he kissed her deeply. But Zylah's magic started to slip just as she did, just as her pleasure threatened to consume her once more. Too afraid of hurting him, she coaxed the power back, raw pleasure snuffing out her momentary panic. Holt slammed into her again and her climax tore through her, her body shattering against him as he followed her over the edge.

His arms came around her waist, holding her tight against him as her shudders eased and she focused on the sound of their racing heartbeats and ragged breaths, her cheek resting over his heart.

Words tripped over themselves inside her thoughts, a confession she'd been holding onto for too long, but then Holt said, "I'd have waited. If it was what you wanted."

"I know," she whispered, tilting her head up to look at him.

"And I know Pallia told you few things in this life belong to us. But I am yours. And you are mine. And nothing, no one will ever convince me otherwise."

"I know," she whispered again, her throat painfully tight as she fought back the sting of tears.

Holt rested a hand against her face, his thumb stroking her cheek. His voice was rough and raw as he searched her eyes. "I'm in love with you, Zylah. And I have loved you for far longer than I had any right to."

She answered him with a soft kiss, then pulled back to tug his hand over her heart. "It's always been yours." He rested his forehead against hers as if he were letting the words settle over him, but Zylah went on, "And I have been in love with you for far longer than I had any right to be, too. Since before you left Virian, and I…" She shook her head, a frown creasing her brow as she silently cursed herself for the mess she'd made of everything.

Holt grabbed her chin, tilted her head up to look at him. "The past doesn't matter, Zylah. What matters is this." He pressed a kiss to one corner of her mouth. "Here." And then the other corner. "Now." His lips were on hers, his tongue parting the seam of her lips and finding hers, hungry, demanding.

She answered by arching into his touch, and he hardened again inside her.

Zylah didn't try to apologise for the mess she'd made of everything. There would be time for that after. Instead, she kissed him back just as fiercely, grinding against him, already insisting on more.

365

Holt smiled against her mouth, pulling her back with him against the bed to give her everything she needed, and this time, Zylah let herself fall.

34

Holt had insisted Zylah rest, but there had been very little of that. They'd spent the day exploring each other's bodies and in each other's arms, and Zylah had managed to keep her magic reeled in tight. A thought had been tugging at the back of her mind, one that had been whispering to her for a while now, but she wasn't ready to face it just yet.

They'd managed to keep their hands off each other long enough for Holt to fill her in on the plan he'd made with Nye, Rin and Kej, and that they would be leaving after dark, Malok's army already en route to Virian without his knowledge. The vanquicite mine was their first stop, but it would take the soldiers a few days to arrive on foot. They weren't ready to take on Marcus's army yet, Holt had explained, but they were going to put a stop to as many of his plans as they could in the meantime. Starting with the mine.

"Malok's going to figure it out," Zylah said as she tugged on her trousers after the bath they'd shared together. Holt was still drying himself off, and she bit down on her lip as she watched him towel all the places her mouth had been.

His attention fixed on her hands as they fastened her trousers, and Zylah wondered if it was like this for all Fae. No matter how many times he'd taken her, she still wanted more. Wanted to lock themselves inside his room and never have to leave. She cleared her throat, held out a hand and tugged on her magic, his trousers appearing across her arm.

A huff of laughter escaped him as he grabbed the fabric, pulling them on without fastening them. He held out his hand and her tunic appeared in it, and she snatched it from him playfully.

"Cirelle has assured Nye she'll deal with Malok," Holt said, her cloak appearing in his hands next.

"And the humans? Malok will have them killed if he finds out."

"Cirelle won't let that happen. She has Rava protecting them."

Zylah slipped into her tunic, fighting back a laugh at the thought of the great bird facing off with Malok, some of her concern diminishing a little. But they'd failed in bringing back the key to activate the shield, and now the army had left, they'd taken away the Aquaris Court's only line of defence. Given that the thralls had likely followed them there in the first place, it was no wonder Holt was in such a hurry for them to leave, to draw any thralls after them instead, to minimise any repercussions of her evanescing them there after leaving the tomb.

For Rin and Kej to leave—even Nye—to *defy* Malok, a male like him would not take kindly to the abuse of his trust. Zylah only hoped that his love for his children and his niece was enough to smooth over the sting of their betrayal. She combed her fingers through her hair with a frown, separating strands to begin a braid as she contemplated whether Rin and Kej understood the weight of their decision.

Holt's fingers rested over hers, offering her a soft smile as he took over. "We're meeting Nye and the others at the mine. I told her you mentioned accelerants for the armouries, and she ran with the idea. She's tasked some of her troops with creating explosives. Daizin had some useful input that she's implemented."

"Daizin?"

"He wanted to help. He and Nye…"

"They're the same?"

Holt nodded, nimble fingers making light work of her braid. "He's been quite forthcoming about the work he'd been carrying out with Laydan. Described a book that Laydan asked him to find."

"Song and Shadow?"

Holt nodded again. "He said Laydan took it—that he and Laydan had met when the witch approached him to retrieve the book from the safe house back in Virian." His eyes met hers, a flicker of regret passing through them for a moment.

"From Raif's room?" Zylah asked. The thought didn't stir the same feelings it once had, nor did the sound of his name. But Marcus had been looking for that book, which meant Laydan had likely been working for Marcus all along.

Holt dipped his chin. He'd already packed their things, not that they were taking much. The plan was to put distance between them and the court on foot and then evanesce the rest of the way, taking it in turns to alternate in bursts, just in case someone could track them. There had been no sign of anyone following them back to the court, so the spell must have held, but Holt still wasn't willing to risk it, and Zylah couldn't fault him for that.

They made their way through the court, Kopi on her shoulder. There was no time for goodbyes with the humans or Cirelle, and though it felt wrong to be leaving like this, Zylah knew it was for the best. For their safety. She paused as she thought of the baylock, holding out her hand to summon a handful to her palm. "Eat this." She handed Holt a few of the leaves.

He raised an eyebrow at her in question.

"Just in case. It makes them recoil, the vampires and the thralls. It could buy us the few seconds we need if we're attacked." She watched as he slipped a piece into his mouth and chewed before doing the same.

Holt swallowed down the baylock, despite the bitter taste. "I knew it was only a matter of time before you had me stuffing my pockets with plants." His lips twitched as his attention dropped to her hands, where she shoved half the bundle of leaves into his trouser pocket.

Zylah resisted the urge to lean up and kiss him, knowing she'd want to take it further and wouldn't be able to stop herself. She took a step back, scratching Kopi's head as he ruffled his feathers. "So, Marcus has the book now. But why the key?"

Holt continued leading the way through the court, his footsteps quiet as the sounds of the ocean fell away from them. "Daizin said there was a key in the book, though he couldn't read it. He made sketches of everything he could remember, and Nye's been working on it with the notes she'd already made."

A chill danced down Zylah's spine. "This *is* about Ranon, isn't it?" More of the puzzle pieces seemed to fall into place.

Holt dipped his chin in acknowledgement, pulling open the door they'd first used to enter the court on the day of Jora's funeral.

Kopi darted out ahead of them into the fresh air, a light flurry of snow falling so lightly it seemed to hang suspended in the air.

"You said it before. Marcus has always craved power. If he's obsessed with finding out Ranon's secrets… his army will become more than just vampires and thralls." Zylah cast her attention out into the grey, searching for any movement, straining to hear anything that might be out of place in the forest below.

"He always gets what he wants. Always," Holt murmured to himself, stepping out into the snow.

Zylah followed him in silence, choosing her words carefully. He couldn't hear of any harm coming to Marcus, and she knew in the past that he'd used that as justification not to discuss Marcus at all.

Not to excuse, exactly, but to shield his friends from the reality of his situation. "Marcus can't keep this up forever, Holt. This is your life he's playing with. We'll figure this out."

He was quiet as they made their way down the winding path, for so long she thought perhaps he wouldn't answer. Or couldn't. But as they neared the bottom of the slope, he released a breath. "It's been almost a century of this. I've tried every loophole I can think of. Taken out every other player in his game. But now it's down to him."

He scanned the treeline as they neared the shadows of the forest, his attention fixed ahead, his voice strained, as if he felt the wariness of playing by Marcus's rules in the depths of his soul.

Zylah followed him into the thick forest, her heart twisting for him. "We'll find a way. Even if it takes us another hundred years."

"To living free," he said quietly.

Zylah stilled at the sound of her own words echoed back to her. Words she hadn't spoken out loud because she'd been in too much pain to speak. Words she'd wanted to say to him when he held onto her, pouring himself into her so entirely that she wasn't sure if he would slip away from this life before she did. Before the vanquicite took her.

"Holt," she whispered.

He turned to face her, the air humming between them.

She took a step closer, her breath clouding in the air as she tilted her head back to look up at him, just as Kopi called out a warning. A thrall cried out, and a scent carried on the breeze, one that Zylah recognised.

The colour drained from her face, her stomach twisting.

"Mint and lemongrass," she whispered, her heart hammering in her chest.

"Well don't look so surprised," a familiar voice said from somewhere nearby, both Holt and Zylah spinning around to find the source. "You didn't think a vampire could get rid of me so easily, did you?"

Zylah took a staggering step back, a hand pressed to her chest as what could only have been a ghost dropped down from the canopy above them. Her back collided with Holt's chest as she stared, mouth open, shock stealing her voice.

His hair was cut short, all trace of his once dazzling blue eyes now wholly black. One hand rested lazily in a pocket as he strode towards them, his attention fixed on Zylah and his lips twisting up into a sneer, revealing the tips of sharp, pointed fangs. She couldn't breathe, couldn't think.

Jesper hadn't killed him, and it hadn't been the sprites that had taken his body. Jesper, the man who had turned her whole life upside down. Jesper, the prince she thought she'd killed and who instead had tilted the axis of her world when he'd revealed himself to be very much alive.

A vampire, but alive.

He'd turned Raif into one of them.

Holt rested a hand on her shoulder, a quiet reassurance that he was there as she fought to keep herself upright, to keep her breathing steady.

Raif clicked his tongue as he pointedly wrinkled his nose. "I can't say *I'm* surprised."

"Surprised?" Zylah repeated, the only word she could coax from her lips. Surprise didn't even come close to what she was feeling, but she understood that the sight of her, her body now undoubtedly Fae, must have come as a shock to him, the sight of her standing so close to Holt.

Raif waved a hand at the two of them, a wisp of ash coiling around his wrist. "I can smell your scent all over him."

Zylah's cheeks burned. "We thought you were dead," she blurted, realising how stupid the words sounded the moment they left her lips. Like there was any excuse for what he was seeing.

She had no regrets when it came to the last twenty-four hours with Holt, to the confession she'd offered him. She'd meant every word of it. But this was not something she'd ever thought

Raif would have to bear witness to. The sight of him, standing before them, was not something she had considered possible.

"I mourned you." Her hand still pressed against her chest firmly, as if she could prevent herself from feeling everything she'd fought with since she'd watched him die. Or believed she had, anyway.

"Rose told me you'd figure it out sooner or later. She saw it," Raif said, dismissing her entirely and turning his attention to Holt, his expression blank. Raif's black, empty eyes fell to where Holt's hand rested on her shoulder, to the way his body pressed against hers.

"Figure what out?" Zylah asked, angling her head to catch Holt's eye, but he didn't break his attention away from Raif.

The wisp of ash snaked up Raif's arm, and a corner of his mouth turned up into a smile that was as cold and empty as his eyes. Soulless. That was how he seemed. As if the warm, kind Fae he had once been had been chipped away entirely. It made sense, Zylah supposed, that Marcus would subject his own son to this fate. To not have him killed, as she'd thought, but to use Raif's abilities to his advantage, to utilise his son as a weapon in his army of creatures against the humans.

Raif barked a bitter laugh. "He didn't tell you?" He shook his head. "Of course he didn't. Always so fucking noble."

Zylah didn't want to play whatever game he seemed to be delighting in, not as multiple thralls screamed in the forest around them.

Raif stalked closer, and it was all the invitation Holt needed to move in front of her, tucking her behind him, one hand falling to her wrist.

"What did Rose see?" Zylah asked, realisation slicing through her, her insides turning to liquid as she braced herself for whatever Raif was going to say. What he couldn't possibly have known, or else he wouldn't have—

"I always liked Thallan," Raif said thoughtfully, tucking a hand under his chin as he spoke of Rose's rejected mate, the ash spiralling around his arm as he moved. "But Rose never felt safe with him. And it made her wary of the mating bond, whenever she happened upon it in others. Something about you, Zylah, always set my sister's teeth on edge."

Holt had gone utterly still in front of her, his breathing shallow. The way Raif had said her name, like it was a bitter taste in his mouth, sent another flare of panic skittering along her flesh as his words sank in. She'd known for a while what she was to Holt, what they were to each other, knew he had been waiting for her to come to terms with it. But this truth Raif had offered, the implication of his words, turned her panic to icy rage. "You knew."

"Did I know that you were his mate when I fucked you every night for months?" He dipped his head to one side, smirking at Zylah with his fangs on full display, disdain dripping from his soulless eyes. "Yes."

Holt released her wrist, lunging for Raif with a vicious snarl. Jesper had kept them both at bay before because he held vanquicite, but Zylah could see none on her quick scan of Raif as Holt swung for him.

Raif darted away from the attack, so quickly that Zylah barely realised what had happened. He moved in that preternatural way Jesper had, as if he were death reanimated. Still, it did little to quell her fear as the ash that snaked from his fingertips extended towards Holt.

"Holt!" Zylah called out.

But she didn't have the chance to see if he'd heard her, because something barrelled into her side, shoving her into the snow.

35

The thrall knocked the air from Zylah's lungs, unrelenting in its grip as she grappled against its bony fingers. She braced herself for teeth to sink into her flesh, but it only persisted in trying to restrain her.

She didn't waste time dwelling on that, bringing her knee up to its groin and scrambling to her feet as the creature staggered back in the snow. This one was female, a half-head of ebony hair resting over one shoulder, the other half of her scalp exposed to the bone.

Holt and Raif fought without magic, but there was little time for Zylah to watch as another thrall stepped up beside the first. No time to think about everything Raif had said. With a dagger in her hand, she swiped for the female thrall, wishing she'd had time to coat all her blades with baylock. The thing hissed as the blade nicked rotting flesh, the second reaching for Zylah's cloak as she pivoted away.

She needed to put space between them, to not allow them to surround her, but she saw no easy route up the nearest tree. Instead, she tugged on her magic, evanescing behind them and thrusting her dagger into the second thrall's shoulder with all her strength. His scream was feral, the female spinning around to face Zylah, but she'd already evanesced back to her previous position, drawing another dagger and plunging it into the female's ribs.

Kopi flew down from the trees and clawed at what remained of the flesh on the male's face, tearing at rotting skin and clumps of hair.

Leave, Zylah. Take Kopi with you.

She froze at the sound of the voice in her head. The one she'd heard so many times before, the nights she'd been alone in Kerthen, all the times she'd questioned whether she'd been imagining things. It had always been him. He'd been with her, all this time.

"I won't leave you," she called out as she drew her sword, unsure if he could hear her thoughts just as she could hear him. She didn't dare look away from the thralls to search for him, but she could feel him near, could feel the frantic energy of his fight with Raif, and she didn't let herself think about the way she knew Raif could turn someone to ash at his touch.

I'll find you, Holt's voice said in her thoughts. The words he'd said to her when she'd fled Virian. A promise, even though she didn't realise it at the time.

The male thrall pulled the dagger from his back, his neck cracking and his head tilting to one side like it was barely held onto his body.

Zylah swiped her sword at his chest and it roared in pain, his rotting flesh sizzling where the blade had sliced it open, a frown drawing her eyebrows together at the sight.

She didn't doubt Holt, but there was no way she was walking away from him again. She thought of the way she'd seen him work with his surroundings, using his magic to pull from the earth and use it to his advantage. She evanesced behind the thralls again, ducking to slice her blade across sinew and bone and pulling on her power at the same time, trying to visualise the tree roots beneath the snow at her feet as the thralls screamed, their skin bubbling and blistering.

The ground shook, yet it wasn't roots that emerged, but a flash of eyes. And wings.

Sprites.

Hundreds of them fluttered down from the trees, pulling themselves up from the snow.

Kopi flew to her shoulder as Zylah staggered back a step. The sprites swarmed the thralls, teeth and claws slashing at the creatures. She didn't wait to watch what they would do next. She raced through the trees, darting between boughs to find Holt.

Her heart was in her throat by the time she came upon them, Raif moving unnaturally fast to dart away from Holt's sword. Everywhere Raif went, vines erupted from the snow and reached for him, but he cut them down with a sword of his own. Holt was attacking, but he was holding back, as if maybe he too wondered if part of who Raif had been remained somewhere within him.

It only seemed to encourage Raif. He noticed her approach, his face twisting into a grin. "Caleb didn't return from the tomb, but he was under strict instructions to announce I was coming for you. I can see Holt decided to keep that from you, too. I wonder, what other secrets does he keep from his mate?" He swung at Holt, the blade nicking skin enough to draw blood, but Holt pivoted away before it could sink deep.

Caleb, the vampire at the tomb, Zylah presumed. She didn't let any emotion show on her face at Raif's words. He was trying to get a rise out of them both, and she wouldn't, couldn't give in to him. All she had to do was reach Holt, and they could leave together. Could say everything that needed to be said once they were gone from here, safe.

She took a step closer, her sword gripped firmly in both hands.

Zylah. Holt's voice was a warning in her thoughts. But she didn't let herself look at him, not when she needed to keep Raif's attention on her, keep him distracted from Holt.

Raif barked a laugh as vines wrapped at his ankles and dragged him face-first into the snow. "I don't know how you fought the compulsion," he said, glaring at Holt. "But you won't be able to fight it forever. Not if your head is full of so many commands you don't know which to ignore first." He swiped his sword at the vines, darting towards Zylah where she held her weapon steady. If Holt had been compelled by Jesper…

She shoved the thought down, focused on the weight of her sword in her hands, the press of snow beneath her feet. "Why don't you just tell us what you want, Raif?" she asked as Holt appeared at her side.

Raif stopped a few feet away, one hand in his pocket, black eyes raking up her body and taking in her new Fae form as if he was noticing her for the first time. "You know, at first, I thought maybe you were like me. That you knew what he was to you, and you wanted to hurt him as much as I did. To punish him for working with my father, and with Arnir. But after a while, I just didn't care. You were mine, that was all that mattered."

Zylah thought she might be sick. What he'd done… what *she'd* done.

You didn't know, Zylah. Holt's voice was gentle in her mind, reassuring.

"Marcus wants you." Raif shrugged. "When this one didn't return with you like he was supposed to, I was happy to oblige."

Holt said nothing in protest, and no words, no sounds filled her head except for the ringing between her ears as her brain tried to keep up with everything Raif had said.

"You hated Marcus. Don't tell me you feel indebted to him now that you're… this," Zylah waved a hand. His eyes, his teeth. His speed and strength. Everything about him had been altered now that he was a vampire.

"I'm more than I ever was, Zylah."

And yet, something about his abilities had changed, too, or he would have turned Holt to ash the first moment they'd rolled over each other in the snow. Ash still snaked around his arms, something he'd never done when he was Fae.

"At what cost?" Zylah asked, motioning towards the ash as she sheathed her sword. They needed to leave, to get as far from him as they could. But despite everything, despite what he'd said and done, what he was, some small part of her didn't want to leave without answers, without finding out if there was any part that remained of the Fae she'd once known. *Thought* she'd known.

A gentle caress brushed against her mind. A feeling of understanding, like a quiet thank you, and Zylah knew it was Holt.

Raif had been a brother to him, a part of his life for so long, and he would have wanted answers, too.

"Are you asking if I still have a soul?" Raif asked as more of Holt's vines wrapped at his ankles. "If I can still feel? If I can still remember what that pretty mouth of yours felt like wrapped around my cock?"

Holt lunged for him again, and Raif broke free of the vines as if they were nothing. Their swords clashed; Holt's rage so thick Zylah felt it shudder against her bones. Raif's taunts were clouding his judgement, but Raif didn't relent. Holt landed a blow to Raif's sword arm, but Raif moved as if the wound was nothing, swiping his weapon across Holt's ribs. Zylah held her breath as Holt withdrew a step, the blade slicing into him and blood leaking through his shirt.

The moment her eyes locked with Raif's she knew he intended to sink his fangs into Holt's flesh. She evanesced with so much force that when she reappeared in front of him, she knocked him back, scarlet staining his mouth.

He lashed out at her, a swirl of dark ash wrapping around her neck. "Raif," Zylah pleaded, her hands grasping at her throat. Recognition seemed to flare in Raif's unfamiliar eyes for a moment, as if he realised he was hurting her, and he released Zylah from his grasp. But whatever he might have said was lost to the aether as Holt's wrist came down around hers, evanescing them away.

"Again," Holt ground out as their feet hit snow, darkness pressing in around them. She'd never seen him so angry, so rattled and untethered by what Raif had admitted. Zylah didn't hesitate, she did as they'd agreed, evanescing to another location, back up to the pass west of the Aquaris Court. There was no doubt in her mind it had been her evanescing that had led Raif to them, and they couldn't risk leaving a clear trace again.

Holt didn't release her as he evanesced them to the next location, his grip still tight at her wrist as they moved turn by turn, evanescing through the forest back towards Varda, turning back on themselves so many times Zylah's head spun. They couldn't travel anywhere directly; they'd be too easy to track.

They hadn't stopped once, hadn't uttered a word to each other, moving so quickly the world blurred into nothing but the inky darkness around them, until Zylah's nausea was all-consuming and Holt finally began to slow just outside Varda.

"Your wounds haven't healed," Zylah said, reaching a hand up to his neck.

"They're not deep. We need to find somewhere to stay for the night. What remains of it." His hair pressed to his forehead, his skin clammy in the moonlight, and with a sinking feeling, Zylah realised it wasn't her own nausea she'd been feeling, but his.

She didn't try to argue with him. She took them to the empty house she'd found after leaving Kerthen, pausing at the stone wall at the edge of the garden, her chest heaving in time with Holt's as they paused to listen for any signs of movement from inside. There were none.

They'd left Kopi behind.

He'd find them, but it didn't stop her unease at leaving him mingling with everything else she was feeling. Holt followed her inside the house in silence, swaying a little as he stepped through the door.

"Sit by the fire," she told him.

"We should check," he began. He was watching her, his chest heaving, and she knew all the evanescing hadn't been enough to burn away the lingering rage, knew he'd wanted to pull Raif apart back in the forest.

Zylah made a point of angling her head to listen. "There are only two heartbeats here, mine and yours. Sit."

The fire was still built from the day she'd left, the rug she'd pulled down from one of the bedrooms still in front of it. Holt dropped a handful of embers onto the wood pile, flames bursting to life, casting shadows across the room.

"Your wounds," Zylah said quietly, the firelight illuminating the gash at his neck, the way he pressed his hand to his ribs. He sank into the lounger in silence, the one she'd dragged from the other side of the room by herself after leaving Kerthen. She could feel every emotion rolling off him, a mirror to everything she felt inside herself. Resentment, sorrow, regret.

His eyes were fixed on her as she knelt on the lounger beside him, pressing a shaky hand to his neck where his injury still hadn't clotted over. He'd focused so much of his power on evanescing them, he hadn't spared any for healing himself, and that only made her anger flare hotter, wilder.

"Zylah," he said roughly, catching her hand in his as she pushed her magic into him. She was exhausted too, but she wouldn't rest. She would do this for him. For her mate.

His breath caught as if he'd heard her, and she looked up to meet his gaze as the wound knitted back together beneath her fingertips, saw the worry in his eyes, could hear the wild beating of his heart.

"You stopped me from accepting it, didn't you? The bond." Twice, she realised. "When Deyna removed the vanquicite. And the second time when we… were together. Why?"

"Because of what you're feeling now. Because of your reaction to the idea of mates when we talked about it back in Virian. Because I didn't want it to be another thing you hated yourself for after everything you've been through. And because I wanted you to understand that I'm in love with you before you accepted the bond when you had no idea that was what you were doing." His words were sure, steady, but he held his hand over hers tentatively, as if he were expecting her to pull away.

She remembered their conversation in Virian so clearly. *Cruel fate* were the words she'd used when they'd spoken about the concept of mates for the first time. And he'd tried to tell her what they were to each other, she realised. Several times. When he'd left her alone with Rin, and when she'd knocked on his door. Before the tomb. *I can't look at you like I'm just a friend and fine with that, no matter how hard I try to conceal this thing so that every person we meet, Fae or human doesn't see it,* he'd said.

"I tried to bury it. For as long as you needed, I would have."

"I don't want an apology, Holt. Not when you had to…" *To watch.* To have a front-row seat to her relationship with Raif. To her coming back to their room at the tavern night after night, Raif's scent all over her. *Gods.* She pressed a hand to her stomach to calm her nausea, but she couldn't sit still. She uncoiled to her feet, pacing in front of the fire.

Zylah understood why he'd done it. But it still *hurt*, and that hurt mingled with the pain she'd caused him, the absolute fucking mess she'd made of everything. "Jesper's been compelling

385

you?" He didn't reply, but she felt his confirmation in her mind. Not his words in her thoughts, just an affirmation brushing against her conscious. He didn't move, just watched her closely as his breathing subsided. Despite everything, he'd been holding back when fighting Raif, but he'd likely lost a lot of blood and then evanesced a sizeable distance. Zylah shook her head as she noticed he was still clutching the wound across his ribs. Too stubborn for his own good.

She leaned over him, one hand healing the injury, the other bracing herself against the lounger. The wound was deeper than he'd let on, and her anger spiked again at the thought of him evanescing so far before healing. That he could have bled out before they'd even made it to safety. He didn't reach for her, but she felt his eyes on hers, felt certain he could feel every last drop of her anger.

When she pulled her eyes up to meet his, the endless sadness in them quelled some of her rage. "Start from the beginning." She moved to the fire again, offering him space, giving it to herself, because she needed to hear what he had to say. "Tell me everything you can."

Panic flared in her mind. Not hers, his. But then it was gone, as if he'd snuffed it out, covered it up the moment he'd realised he'd let it slip.

"Marcus had me working for Arnir for years," he said quietly, his words flat, tired.

He'd told her as much before. But now she understood. "He had Jesper compel you into doing it?"

Another silent confirmation. So he likely knew all along that she hadn't killed Jesper, but how could she blame him for that if

386

he'd been compelled to silence? Even back in Virian, she'd known he was stuck in something he felt he had no way out of. Only here was the truth of it: he didn't.

"When Marcus realised you were Fae, he had Arnir send his men after you. The day before we met, I started to feel... I didn't know what I was feeling. I felt *you*, evanescing from the gallows, this burst of power reaching out for me, but I had no idea what it was. Who it was. I *was* bathing in the springs before I found you because I'd been trying to shake off the unease I'd felt. But then I felt something in the water." He put a hand to his chest, a far-off look in his eyes as he stared at the fire. "A pull, a ripple of something like a thread, urging me to find the end of it."

"I saw something in the water," Zylah said softly, her brow scrunching. A face, forming in the blue, as if something inside her knew he was nearby and urged her to search for him, to seek him out if only for a moment.

"I followed the thread to you. A human, tired and afraid. Rope marks at your neck. I couldn't work out how you'd escaped from the gallows, but I knew Arnir had the girl who, as far as he believed, had killed his son, so it didn't take much to figure out who you were." He was looking at her now, his eyes moving over her ears, her face, as if he were seeing her as she'd been that day.

She remembered the way he'd bitten into his brin fruit, head tilted to one side as he took her in. And then she'd evanesced away from him.

"And then you evanesced," he said quietly, as if he'd heard her thoughts, a soft laugh of disbelief curling around his words. "I told myself I'd just get you to Virian. Get you to Rose and Saphi. But I couldn't bring myself to do it. To leave you. Arnir sent his instructions to me the next day, that I was to find the girl from the posters, and I knew they'd find you by the end of the week."

Zylah pieced everything together as he spoke. "The job. At the gardens. You arranged it."

Holt nodded.

"I did whatever I could to keep you hidden. Working with Jilah. Asking the Fae and the Black Veil to look out for you. Raif was like a brother to me, I didn't think." His anger flared, and she could do nothing to ease him.

Zylah recalled Holt's words about Raif's competitive streak and hated herself all over again. *My scent all over you… it would have been like a challenge to him at first.*

"Jesper left for months after…" His words trailed off as if he couldn't finish the sentence, and Zylah knew it was the compulsion.

"After I thought I killed him."

Another brush of that feeling, the confirmation from him and a look of gratitude as he went on, "I was able to just send word back to Arnir, and that was enough for Marcus, for a while."

Zylah stared at the flames, the wood hissing and popping as it burnt. He'd thought he was keeping Marcus on his side, aiding the plan to take down Arnir. And all along, Marcus had had the upper hand. He'd had a vampire, compelling Holt to do whatever he asked of him.

"Living with you in Virian…" Holt said, "I haven't had a home in years. And for the first time, I felt like I belonged somewhere. With you. It was always you."

Zylah turned to face him, her heart beating wildly in her chest. From the start, she'd told herself he wasn't interested, that he didn't see her that way. *I won't touch you. You don't have to be afraid of me,* he'd said. But she'd never been afraid of him. She'd been drawn to him, so much that it scared her. And she'd… she'd buried it, just as he had.

"But then you came back to the tavern that night, Raif's scent all over you, asking me questions about mates. I saw how much you rejected the idea; how afraid you still were after everything that had happened with Jesper. And I told myself that if it was what you needed, if *Raif* was what you needed, I wouldn't get in the way. Even if…" Even though he'd felt something for her. His fingers curled into the fabric of his shirt over his heart as he cleared his throat. "But I'd been away from Marcus for too long, and he sought me out on his next visit to Virian."

"The night in the tunnels," Zylah murmured.

Holt nodded. "He's been using the tunnel system for years."

She remembered the all-consuming fear that had overtaken her. "I felt you," she said, so quietly she wasn't sure he could hear it. She'd had no idea where she was going that night, only a quiet certainty that whatever direction she'd been heading, it would lead her to him, and it did.

"Marcus was obsessed with you. Even now, every time I try to remember why; it's like walking through quicksand." He dragged a hand through his hair as if he could hold onto whatever memory had been compelled out of him. "The thought of him taking you… I knew I had to leave. I convinced myself it was what I wanted. Because I couldn't… couldn't breathe around you. I was going out of my mind, and I was so afraid I

389

was going to fuck everything up somehow if I stayed. That I was going to lead Marcus to you. I left Virian the next day."

For months he'd stayed away. Zylah sank into the lounger beside him, searching his face as the pieces of his story clicked together. The realisation that Marcus had been pulling the strings, all along, turned her stomach. But the way Holt was looking at her, with so much reverence in his eyes, so much love—she understood his choices, knew she would have made the same ones had it been her in his position.

"I came back two weeks before the festival with a promise of a report for Arnir, but all I could think of was seeing you. And the room at the tavern… Raif's scent was everywhere."

A fresh wave of guilt spiralled inside her. That he'd had to bear witness to that.

"I would have endured it, Zylah, if I knew you were happy." But his voice was broken as he said it, and her heart fractured for him. "I returned to Dalstead with the report Arnir wanted. Marcus always knew what I was planning in Virian, and he never tried to stop me."

"Because he wanted Arnir out of the way. And because he knew he could have Jesper compel you to do anything he wanted."

Holt's silence was all the confirmation Zylah needed.

"You looked so beautiful that night at the botanical gardens. I think I went just to torture myself." His hand dropped to the bracelet she'd given him, as if he was replaying the moment quietly to himself.

She remembered how he'd sat on her bed beside her that night when she was asleep, the way he'd been with her the next morning, braiding her hair and asking her questions as if they were having two conversations at once. *Would it have changed anything?* he'd asked her. She shifted to face him, fingers aching to reach out for him, but she let him finish. Knew he needed to finish what he had to say.

"The festival rolled around, and I knew Marcus would be there, but I couldn't do anything about it, couldn't say anything. I'd never been more relieved than when you evanesced Raif away with you because it kept you both away from him. But then he took Asha."

"And I left," Zylah said, angling her face away to look at the flames. She hadn't been able to look them all in the eye knowing Asha had died because of her, and she'd run.

"I knew you'd gone home," he said, pressing a hand to his chest again. "I thought you were safe. But days passed and I... I followed the trail of you evanescing. I went to your father's cottage and found it burnt to the ground... and I couldn't *feel* you anywhere." His voice broke on the last few words, and Zylah's eyes snapped back to his face in time to see his throat bob.

"Because I was wearing the cuffs," she said softly.

A slight dip of his chin was all the acknowledgement he gave. "I went out of my mind looking for you. Only Saphi asked me if I was okay. I should have realised then that they knew. *I* should have realised."

Rose and Raif. Zylah still couldn't quite believe it. How long had they both known? How long had they kept it secret?

"I told you it was Kopi that led me to you... but I felt you, Zylah, the moment the cuffs came off, I felt you. I evanesced to the forest and heard you calling out for help, and I think I took

391

my first proper breath for the first time in days. I saw you through the trees, and it was as if every step I'd ever taken in my life had been towards you."

He didn't reach for her, though she knew he wanted to. She could feel his hesitation, his regret at the way things had played out. His fear and his relief as if she were reliving it all with him. She took his hand, laced her fingers with his to let him know she wasn't going anywhere, let him feel her heart beating in time with his.

His thumb brushed over hers, a shudder rolling through him. "I knew what you were then. What we were. If you hadn't been injured, I think I'd have torn Raif apart the minute he arrived at the cabin."

"You were giving me time to heal."

A nod. "I'd fought the compulsion as much as I could. Being closer to you always made it easier, and in those early days, I didn't give it much thought. When Jesper showed up in the forest, part of me knew he'd been alive all along, and part of me couldn't work out how I hadn't put two and two together sooner."

"You'd been compelled to forget," Zylah said, her attention on their hands. And then Jesper had killed Raif. Or so they'd thought. Anger flared in her chest again for everything Marcus had taken from them. For the way he'd played them all.

Holt didn't linger on everything that had transpired at the cabin. "As soon as Rose told us Marcus was coming for you, it was like another part of the compulsion lifted. I knew he'd been obsessing over you for months. And all that mattered was getting you as far away from him as possible. I spent the months after you left trying to track down the spell Oz had used, and then I felt you again." He swallowed. Cleared his throat. "You were sleeping, I think. A nightmare. Night after night, when you should have been long gone from Kerthen, I felt you. And you were suffering." His eyes darkened. With anger, with regret.

"You," Zylah breathed. The voice that had been calling her name. "I heard you." Her fingers squeezed his for a moment as realisation sliced through her. "Rose didn't tell you where I was, did she?"

Holt shook his head almost imperceptibly. "I saw flashes of Varda, as if I was there with you, felt an echo of your pain. But Marcus was still searching for you and once I had the spell, the only way I could get away from him was by telling him…" He frowned, his lips pressing together.

"That you were going to bring me back to him," she finished for him when she recognised he couldn't get the words out; when she understood what he'd have had to promise in order to get away. *Her.*

Zylah thought about how he'd said he'd fought against the compulsion, if it could be peeled away the same way she could pull back the corner of wards and deceits. If all magic could be unravelled as if tugging at a thread and she tucked the thought away for another time.

"Yes." The word fell from his lips like a confession he'd been trying to tell her for months. "I could feel your pain from the vanquicite, but only the times you let me in. You're much better at shielding yourself than you know. You weren't eating, and I didn't know if it was from the vanquicite. Nothing I tried worked and the healing felt as if it were diminishing each time."

She realised now, the resentment she felt coming from him. It wasn't just at Raif, at what he'd done. It was for himself, and it shattered her heart even more. And that he'd been compelled, this entire time…

Raif had thrown that fact at them like a weapon, and she found herself sifting through all the hateful words he'd spat at them earlier that evening, just in case he'd imparted any more truths Holt couldn't. "How long have you known about Raif? He mentioned the vampire at the tomb, Caleb."

"Only then, not before. I tried to tell you, but I know how meaningless that sounds."

Zylah laughed dryly. "You were a little busy saving my life." And he'd almost given his in the process.

"You were close, Zylah." Close to dying. His lips pressed together again, but not because of any compulsion, his fear turning palpable in the air between them. "All I knew was that I was willing to do anything, *give* anything, to keep your heart beating. Even if you found out everything. Even if you could never forgive me for all of this."

"I'm not angry with you, Holt, I'm angry that this has happened to you. That Marcus has been using you. That Raif…" She choked back a sob. "I'm angry with myself. How can you say you love me after what I've put you through?"

How could a heart like his ever love something as broken and fucked up as hers?

His hand came up to her face, cupping her cheek, his eyes searching hers.

"Because I know your heart, Zylah," he said, as if he'd heard her. "How you fought with your guilt over Raif. I knew this would hurt you just as much, and I tried to protect you from it, the only way I knew how."

"By giving me time." *Time is all I could give you*, he'd told her, because he hadn't been able to give her the truth, because it was as close to an apology as he'd been able to offer her when he couldn't say the words out loud. She pushed up to her knees, pressed her hand to his chest, and she felt him sag with relief that she finally understood. "There's nothing to forgive, Holt. And I promise you, we will find a way out of this, to end Marcus, to break every last piece of Jesper's compulsion. You've fought for me, over and over again, and I want you to know that I will always do that for you. That I'm willing to do anything, *give* anything, for you." His breath caught at her words, his eyes searching hers as if he was still half expecting her to get up and walk away. But she knew, with a certainty that settled into her bones, that she would never walk away from him again.

She shifted into his lap, her hand never breaking from his chest as he wrapped his arms around her waist. "I want this, Holt. I want you, in every possible way."

This time, when he kissed her, it was soft, slow. Tender.

36

At the first tentative press of Holt's magic against hers, Zylah understood everything she hadn't before, and the gentleness of their kiss turned into something wild and demanding. Teeth and tongues and hands grappling at each other's shirts, his rock-hard arousal pressing between them, a sound of satisfaction rumbling deep within him.

His hips rolled into her as she tore off his ruined shirt, heat flooding her core. She pulled back to admire the way he looked in the soft firelight, to trace a hand along the scar running from his arm to his neck, each kiss that followed her touch a silent promise to see him liberated from every hold ever put on him. Each press of her lips to his skin was a vow to do everything she could to secure his freedom, but she wouldn't let herself dwell on those who bound him, didn't want anything but love to slip through the bond that pulled taut between them, his magic wrapping around them both.

Holt slid a hand into the waistband of her trousers as she found her way back up to his mouth, releasing the hold on her magic just a fraction and he groaned in response, hips moving against hers. She gasped into his mouth as his hand fell between her thighs, his fingers stroking and teasing her soft flesh.

Emotion poured from him, everything she felt echoed back to her, dancing along her skin: love, devotion, need and desire so fierce it was like a brand across her heart. Her magic slipped a little more with her frenzied need to touch him, to feel him, fumbling with the buttons of his trousers before he sprang free and she wrapped a hand around his solid length. He sank two fingers inside her as she slid her hand down him, his thumb moving in time with his fingers, but Zylah wanted more. Wanted everything.

His fingers moved inside her as she pulled her shirt over her head, his mouth coming down over one of her breasts, her fingers knotting in his hair. She needed him inside her. Needed every scrap of clothing between them to be gone, to feel every inch of his body pressed against hers. *Need, need, need.*

A rumble of agreement sounded from him, as if he'd heard her every thought, and as she pushed up to her knees his fingers eased out of her, pulling at her trousers and sliding them down her thighs.

Zylah stepped back to tug them off the rest of the way, and Holt did the same, a predatory glint in his eyes as his gaze raked over her body until his eyes met hers. His hands caressed the bare skin at her sides and she held his gaze as she lowered herself onto him, sinking until every glorious inch of him was buried deep.

"Zylah," he breathed against her lips. He stilled inside her with the next pulse of her magic, waiting, as if he were giving her the chance to change her mind still. This male who had always waited for her, who had been a constant presence from the moment she met him, even when she'd thought she was alone, he had always been with her, protecting her, loving her.

She ran a hand along the rough stubble of his jaw, her lips brushing his. "I am yours, and you are mine," she said softly.

His fingers dug into her hips, pushing her onto him even further. "Mine," Holt murmured against her mouth.

The last tether she held on her magic was obliterated with that single word. Their magic twined around them, inside her, over every place her body pressed against his, in her bones, her heart as she gave him everything he gave her. The thread she'd felt from him before when he'd saved her life wove into every inch of her soul, joining with everything she was and everything she would ever be.

Her best friend. Her lover. Her mate. The male she would do anything, give anything for, no matter the cost.

Holt moved in time with her, thrusting up into her as his mouth devoured hers and his fingers dug into her rear, her erratic breaths matching his as the most sensitive part of her ground tight against him.

Power seemed to flare around them, the air humming with the intensity of their magic coming together, testing, teasing, accepting, the feeling so intense it was as if Zylah had been lit up from the inside. Bright, white light burst from within her, hazing her vision as their pace quickened, Holt's breath catching as the magic rippled through them both, the last pieces of their bond falling into place.

Every part of her was his. And every part of him was hers, and the maddening, possessive tug that accompanied that thought settled something inside her. Something that had been waiting for him, for this, for the other half of her soul to bind itself to hers. Her pleasure built with each rise and fall of her hips, with each of Holt's matching thrusts, each pulse of magic tingling against her skin, her body alive with his touch.

Together. Whatever waited for them after this, they would face it together.

Together. His voice in her thoughts was her undoing. Holt's grip was punishing as he slammed her down onto him, her release obliterating her wholly until she was nothing but the feeling of him moving inside her, their magic thrumming through her, the unrelenting press of his mouth against hers as his own release quickly followed.

Holt's arms tightened around her, fingers stroking her back until she stopped shaking, his forehead resting against hers as their chests heaved against each other.

I think I knew that day you found me in Varda, she told him.

His eyes shot up to meet hers. It was the first time she'd spoken to him through the bond, the first time she'd intentionally pushed her thoughts to him, his surprise so acute she pressed another kiss to his lips.

"I felt you following me all day. I told you it was the spell that needed work. But I knew. And I…" *I was afraid*, she told him.

I know, came his reply as he kissed her back. Not just that she was afraid. But that she'd lied about the spell. *So was I.*

Zylah pulled back to look at him. Saw the flicker of fear in his eyes that was still very real for him. He'd been afraid of pushing her away with the truth. Of losing her.

Holt hummed an acknowledgement against her mouth.

Nothing would keep me from you. She pressed a hand to his heart, felt the tremor that shook through him as she traced kisses along his jaw.

His throat bobbed, and his voice was raw as he said, "I know."

She could feel his regret. His remorse over the compulsion, that Zylah knew went far deeper than he'd been able to explain, to affirm only through their bond. He'd protected her in the only way he could, by getting her away from him.

"I know your heart, Holt. I know you'll have fought every moment of it. There is nothing you could do to make me turn away from you. Nothing."

His arms tightened around her.

"The strength of your actions is what matters. The way you've fought so tirelessly for so long. The way you've never given up on your desire to see Fae and humans live freely, without fear. The greatest privilege of my life is being able to stand beside you and fight for that freedom. To stand beside you as your mate."

He swallowed heavily as the words seemed to settle over him, the rawness of his emotions causing her to choke back a sob. So much of what she knew he felt for himself was an echo of what she'd fought with since leaving Virian. The resentment. The guilt. But there was hope, too. So much hope and determination poured from him, a bone-deep gratitude that had her shuddering in his arms as he kissed her again.

Zylah couldn't help the breathy moan that escaped her, couldn't help the roll of her hips against him, the firmness of him inside her echoing her need as the bond pulled taut between them. And she didn't protest as he lifted her from the lounger, worshipping her with his mouth and his body as he took her again.

After only a few hours of sleep, Zylah had awoken sprawled across Holt, a blanket he'd summoned from somewhere draped over them both, his fingers brushing her spine in slow, lazy strokes.

She looked up to meet his bright green eyes, wondering if he'd slept at all.

A little, he told her, his voice gentle in her thoughts and yet still somehow rough with his lack of sleep. A flicker of worry, gone as soon as it was there, his hand still stroking, roving over the curve of her bottom as his hard length pressed against her thigh.

Zylah traced kisses over his chest, angling herself so that the tip of him pressed at her entrance, every inch of her body still alive with the afterglow of accepting the bond with him, already aching for more.

The threat of what Marcus and Jesper might do, the time Marcus had robbed them of sharing hung over them, but she wouldn't let this moment be stolen from them. Would do anything to ease Holt's worries, to shoulder the burden for her mate.

"Zylah," Holt rasped, tilting her chin up so that he could have access to her mouth, his lips on hers the moment she complied. *No matter what happens, I'll find you. I swear it.*

She gave him her acknowledgement down the bond, a gentle stroke of her soul against his, and he answered by pulling her down onto him, making love to her slowly, savouring every moment.

A silent vow passed between them to take whatever came next day by day. First the mine. Then Virian. But this moment was for them, and no one would take it from them. No more hiding what they felt from each other, for each other. No more disguising what they were.

Holt murmured promises against her lips, in her mind, in her heart as release found them both, and even after, between tugging on their clothes, and summoning their supplies and a clean shirt.

"We should arrive before dark," Holt said as he tossed Zylah a brin fruit. "Rin and Kej will be waiting for us. Nye and Daizin, too, depending on how fast her scouts could get them there."

"And the soldiers?" Zylah inspected the fruit and polished it against her tunic before taking a bite.

"Tomorrow morning. It'll give me some time to send updates to your brother, and to Rose and Saphi."

Zack. She hadn't let herself believe she might see him again. But now, it was a very real possibility.

Rose and Saphi, too, though she wasn't sure how she felt about the former. "Do you think she knew about Raif?"

Holt's brow pinched together. "I don't know. I don't think so. She was devastated. Although I don't know what's worse."

His death, or that he was a vampire now, like Jesper. And his father had been the one to give Jesper the order to turn Raif.

All this time Zylah had punished herself, and it had been Marcus who had been manipulating everything from the beginning.

But she knew she had to steer the conversation carefully to work around the compulsion. "We need to take Jesper out of the equation. Can you do that?"

Holt's knuckles brushed down her arm, a silent thank you for tiptoeing around the restraints placed on him. "I can't harm Marcus, but when I think about Jesper, there's no such command in place."

Zylah understood. So typical of Marcus not to bother offering Jesper the same protection he'd been afforded by the compulsion. "How long has this been going on?" But before he could answer, she said, "It started with Adina, didn't it? You tried to protect her from him."

"Tried," he said quietly. "He used her against me."

"And what if Raif told Marcus about us?"

Holt's eyes searched hers. "All I know is that the moment Marcus knows, he won't hesitate to use it against us."

"To use *us* against each other?"

A soft brush of confirmation down the bond. "The well is bigger now, Zylah. We stand a much greater chance of fighting back."

Because they could share the pool of their magic, now that they were bonded. "I can't do anything on the scale that you can."

"I don't think we've seen the half of what you can do." He tucked a stray strand of hair behind her ear as his eyes searched hers, thumb brushing her cheek, and she felt the truth of what he was saying. Had only just started to understand that there was more to her abilities, more to the little glimpses of magic she'd witnessed herself performing.

Zylah blew out a breath, unwilling to voice her next question but knowing it needed to be done. "What about Raif? Are we going to give him a second chance?" The words left an acid taste on her tongue, and she swallowed it down.

Holt's hand stilled. "Do you want to?"

Part of her, a really big part of her, wanted to hurt Raif. To make him suffer for what he'd done. What he'd put them through. But then she remembered Rose collapsing in her arms when they thought Raif had died. Remembered Saphi's words about Raif back in Virian. *He has a good heart.* Maybe he did, maybe he'd been compelled to behave the way he had. Maybe not.

She studied Holt's expression, knowing all it would take for him to rip Raif's throat out the next time they saw him would be one word from her, one hint of icy rage down their bond. But beyond Holt's blinding wrath, she felt a flicker of hope, a seed of faith that the version of Raif they'd once known was still in there somewhere. And it was all she needed to offer Holt her answer. "One chance, but not if it puts either of us at risk."

Holt nodded. Held a hand out for hers and evanesced them both to their first location.

37

The mine was located just south of Virian, built at the base of a waterfall at the foot of the Rinian mountain range. Though it was dark when they arrived, moonlight lit up the shore of the lake beneath the cascade, great wooden structures spanning from its base, the sound of turning cogs and metal pulleys carrying to them across the water.

"They're using the waterfall to power the pulley system," Zylah murmured, eyes narrowed on the small carts that tipped soil into the lake, then circled back around, disappearing back into the rock, down into the mine.

Carts were being filled by humans, even at this hour, all because of Marcus.

"We'll get them out," Holt said quietly beside her, his breath clouding in the air.

But they still hadn't figured out how they were going to get into the mine.

So far, the only one of them that could enter without being affected by the vanquicite was Zylah, and even she wasn't certain she'd survive an entire mine full of it, tolerance or not.

Across the lake, two grey shapes moved with feline grace, bodies tucked low to the snow.

Zylah held her breath as Rin and Kej made their way over, both of them already in their Fae form by the time they'd closed the last of the distance between them.

"We're the first ones here," Rin said, eyes flicking between Zylah and Holt. Kej was a step behind her, but as he approached, she held out an arm, urging him to stop. "Whatever you're about to say, Kej, I'm begging you, to please shut the fuck up. I'm not prepared to carry you out of here."

Kej's smile was immediate, his arms clapping around Holt to give his friend a hug. "Congratulations. It's about fucking time." He glanced at Rin to wait for a reprimand that never came. "Zylah," he added with a grin, but took a step back.

"Will someone explain to me what's happening here," Zylah asked, looking between her friends for an explanation. It was the first time she'd seen Kej since leaving to look for the key, the first time seeing him since she was no longer half Fae. "Why won't you look at me?"

"Because newly mated males have been known to be a little… unpredictable," Rin explained for her brother. "Congratulations, both of you." She drew Zylah in for a tight hug, a small squeal of excitement leaving her at the same time.

They can scent the bond, Holt's voice said in her thoughts, a hint of amusement in his tone.

The Fae part of her revelled in that fact, but the very small, human part of her that lingered couldn't hide the flush of heat to her cheeks. *Can all Fae do that, or just these two?*

A quiet laugh. *All.*

"Unpredictable?" Zylah asked as Rin peeled away from her. She pressed a hand to her chest in mock offence, raising an eyebrow at Holt. "On my behalf? Never."

"We've all seen precisely the lengths he'll go to on your behalf, Zylah," Kej said, his attention across the water. "But truly, we needed this good news. It's a blessing."

Zylah tried to stamp down the fear his statement pulled to the surface, a soft brush of affection from Holt accompanying it. She forced a quiet laugh, willing herself to sound lighter than she felt. "Careful, Kej, or I might think that carefully curated exterior is harbouring a sensitive soul underneath it all."

Kej grinned back at her, looking her in the eye this time. "Never."

A thrall's cry carried across the water as if it had come from within the mine.

"We didn't come across any patrols outside, but we think there's around twenty thralls and two vampires down there," Rin said in response to the sound that Zylah knew invoked more than enough bad memories for all of them. The roar of the water, the constant squeak of the pulleys and the splash of water being pumped into the lake were noisy enough to draw attention, but the area was deserted as far as Zylah could see in the darkness.

No patrols seemed unlikely, though, and from the look on Rin's and Kej's faces, they knew it too.

"How close were you able to get?" Holt asked, crouching down to inspect the water and running a hand cautiously across the surface. "They're sorting the vanquicite inside. There's only soil and rock being tipped from the carts."

A swift nod of confirmation from Kej. "We followed the carts as far as the opening in the rockface but didn't risk going in. We managed to get a message inside."

"A message?" Zylah asked.

"There are members of the Black Veil down there, posing as slaves. They're going to help us evacuate the mine before we bring it down."

Zylah's attention shifted back to the falls. "You're going to flood it."

"Fire and flood," Kej said with far too much enthusiasm.

They followed him and his sister up the rise beside the lake, deep into the trees that bordered the Kerthen forest.

Destroying the mine was just the first step in dismantling everything Marcus had been working towards, and though it was a risk, Zylah understood Holt's decision to begin here. Without the vanquicite, Marcus couldn't forge more weapons for his monsters to wield, and any advantage was better than none.

When will the army get here? Zylah asked as the trees thickened around them.

Holt's response was immediate. *The scouts can evanesce several cohorts at once, but it takes them a while with so many of them.*

That likely meant nothing would happen before dawn, and a shiver ran down her spine at the thought of stepping foot back into Kerthen.

We're not going in entirely; this is only the perimeter.

It's not Kerthen itself. She hadn't told him before. But she didn't want there to be secrets between them anymore, not any that could be helped, anyway. *I made a bargain.*

A hint of anger and worry travelled down the bond, but he was guarding it carefully. An owl cry carried through the trees before Holt could respond.

"Kopi!" Zylah whispered, holding out an arm for her friend. He seemed completely unperturbed by their time apart, no sign of the distance he'd just travelled, even though he must have flown without pause to reach them so soon.

"Don't even try to convince us he isn't Pallia's," Kej murmured.

For a moment, Zylah considered explaining. He *wasn't* Pallia's. He wasn't hers, either. He belonged to no one. But for whatever reason, he'd come back to her again, and she was grateful. She tucked him into her hood with a scratch to his head, and he responded with one of his little satisfied sounds. It was a comfort, to know that whatever came next, he would be with her, even though she knew she had no right to rely on him for that.

Another thrall cried out from deep within the mine, the noise following them as they stepped through the wards of Rin and Kej's camp. Zylah ignored the wave of magic pressing against her as they passed through, focusing on Holt's explanation as he filled their friends in on Raif's *appearance*, and mercifully, they said little about the topic. Zylah wasn't sure how well they'd known him, but she took their silence to be out of respect for her and Holt.

They met him a handful of times over the years. But you're right, it is out of respect, Holt told her.

And because you might be unpredictable? Zylah followed Rin's explanation of where the wards ended but focused on the

409

teasing, lightness to the tone of her thoughts, reluctant to let herself dwell on anything to do with Raif and eager to keep herself centred on the task ahead.

On your behalf? Always, Holt replied. There was a playfulness to his words, too, despite the weight of his admission. She caught the way his lips twitched as he listened to Rin.

Ass.

"You were right, Zylah, about the priestesses," Rin continued as they entered a large tent. It was sparse, sections split off with fabric, the area they stood in housing only a few rugs and tree stumps for them to sit on. "They're running things down there. Their acolytes are in charge of the miners."

Slaves. "That has Marcus's involvement written all over it. Using others to do his bidding." Zylah said nothing else about him, though. Kej and Rin were understanding about Holt's predicament, even though she had no idea how much detail they knew.

Enough to know I can't harm him. Holt smoothed a hand over the map Kej handed him, a layout of the tunnels beneath the waterfall.

"Is this the only mine?" Zylah asked, scanning the parchment for passages and exits. She was confident enough with her evanescing now that once she was inside, knowing the layout would be enough to get her around, regardless of whether she'd seen every part of the mine or not.

"One is enough," Kej said. "We've had reports of carts of vanquicite being hauled into Virian."

Zylah thought of Jilah and the children, the friends she'd made at the botanical gardens. The idea that Marcus might use vanquicite on them turned her stomach. "What is he doing with so much vanquicite?"

A beat of silence, and then Holt said, "Creating cells."

The thought of anyone, human or Fae, caged and frightened, waiting for whatever fate Marcus held in store for them, turning them into one of his monsters or using them for more mining only fuelled Zylah's anger. "Any Black Veil stationed out here on the perimeter with us?" she asked Holt.

"They're on their way. I sent instructions to the safe house whilst you were recovering."

When he'd been sat at her bedside, no doubt. Even then, he'd been keeping things in motion, convincing Nye to depart with the army. And though Zylah had no doubts about his leadership or the plan he'd laid out for the task ahead of them, being here, beside the mine… Zylah didn't like any of it. The lack of patrols, the absence of any presence above ground. It was a deserted area, she knew that from studying maps, but leaving it unguarded seemed… off.

"What are we missing here?" she murmured, tracing a hand across the tunnels representing the mine. A ripple pressed against her skin. "Did you feel that? I think the wards were just breached."

Kej tilted his head to listen. "It's probably Nye. I'll go check."

"I'll come with you," Holt offered. *I want to hear about this bargain when I return,* he told her. There was a hint of anger with the thought, but not for her. For himself; that she'd been pushed into the situation because of him.

"He's here, at the mine," Rin said quietly when the sound of their footsteps had long faded.

411

Marcus. Zylah willed her breaths to remain even, focused on the wall of vanquicite in her mind to shield the thought from Holt, guilt licking at her insides that she needed to keep something from him. "Does Kej know?"

Rin's reaction could barely be considered an answer, but it was enough. Kej hadn't seen Marcus, and Rin hadn't told him.

"Can we keep this between us?" Zylah whispered, as footsteps approached the tent. Holt and the others. Rin's answer was nothing but a flick of her eyes up to Zylah's and then away again as Holt and Nye entered the tent, followed by Kej and Daizin.

"Blessings," Nye said, a hand on Zylah's shoulder as her attention moved between Zylah and Holt.

"Thank you." Zylah returned her friend's smile before turning to the other Fae. "Daizin." She didn't miss the way Kej watched him closely, and though they had every reason to suspect him of working with Marcus, Zylah knew Laydan's betrayal must have stung.

"How did you all meet anyway?" Kej asked, offering a bottle to Daizin. Wine, knowing Kej.

The Fae took it with a dip of his chin. "A fighting ring in Varda. This one slipped through my shadows like they were nothing," he said, raising the bottle in Zylah's direction.

She shared a look with Holt, realisation washing over her. The deceits and wards. Daizin's shadows. Even the compulsion. The way she could pull it all back, like a layer. Unravel it. *I think I can nullify the vanquicite, or at least withstand a large quantity of it. I think…*

She didn't even want to let herself finish the thought, not if there was any chance she could be wrong.

But before Holt could reply, Nye said, "Now that my cousin has set the tone for the evening, it's probably time we told you about my research." Despite her crack at Kej, Nye's expression was serious. "The key was never for the Aquaris Court. It's for Ranon."

"What do you mean, for Ranon?" Kej asked. "I thought he was a crusty old corpse somewhere in the centre of Astaria?"

Ranon and Sira had been the first to create the monsters that wandered the continent, and Aurelia had been the one to replicate them. Zylah's skin chilled, hairs rising on the back of her neck, the last of the puzzle pieces falling into place. "The key to his tomb. Marcus's source of old magic…" The key Laydan had stolen. If he'd delivered it to Marcus, then that meant… "Aurelia… she couldn't be, could she?" She studied Nye's face, hoping she'd got it all wrong.

"Could someone please explain?" Rin asked, her attention darting between them.

Nye blew out a breath. "Ranon and Sira lost a child, though the texts were never specific. Zylah thinks that child might be Aurelia, Marcus's wife."

"His mate," Holt added.

And if Aurelia had even a fraction of her parents' magic, a far greater war than they had anticipated lay ahead of them.

38

Malok's—*Nye's* army arrived just before dawn, setting up further into Kerthen than Rin and Kej had the day before.

When Zylah asked how they'd managed to bring an entire tent and supplies between just the two of them, Kej explained how one of Malok's scouts had ferried them most of the distance; Kopi had caught up with Nye and she'd brought him along.

She'd told Holt about the bargain she'd made in Kerthen. The favour she'd promised to a stranger in return for their healing. It had been foolish, but Zylah had been desperate. And she should have known it wouldn't last. It had taken away some of her pain, exactly as she'd begged, but her condition had only worsened in the end.

And though she'd been glad for the opportunity to tell Holt, it hadn't been enough to keep her mind from wandering, to keep her gaze from lingering on the entrance of the mine during her breaks as if she could will Marcus to walk through the opening in the rock. Holt had been with the army since daylight to ensure everything went according to plan, but she could feel his concern through their bond, his flicker of warmth to reassure her that everything would be fine.

If she was right about Aurelia, Zylah suspected things were far from fine. And if Raif's mother was Ranon and Sira's daughter, what other abilities did she possess? Her power to paralyse, did it come from Sira or Ranon? Was it just the very tip of what she was capable of?

Unease settled like a stone in the pit of her stomach; the small, human part of her that lingered screamed at her to leave, to convince all her friends to leave with her, to run from this and never look back. But that wasn't who she was any more. Running wasn't an option. She wanted to fight. *Needed* to do whatever she could to stop Marcus and Aurelia. To break whatever hold they had over Holt. Zylah was beginning to understand now that this would have been something Marcus and Aurelia set into action long before Aurelia's supposed death, perhaps even before Holt's parents died.

But to what end? Did they truly loathe this world so much that they wished to refashion it in the image of their vision?

Zylah adjusted her weight, her legs starting to numb from sitting in one position for too long. She'd spent the morning preparing baylock tea for the soldiers and coating blades with a paste made from the plant until she'd run out of sources to summon it from. Some she'd had to borrow from the botanical gardens back in Virian, and she knew Jilah would notice its absence immediately. Not that he would mind, given what they were about to do.

She cast her attention to the pile of metal at her feet. There hadn't been enough baylock for even a fraction of the army's weapons, but it would have to do. Anything that gave them an advantage over the monsters waiting for them at the mine could mean the difference between an end to Marcus and Aurelia's plans, and the situation continuing to spiral out of control. There was so little knowledge about the vampires and thralls, other than bearing witness to the sheer amount of damage they could inflict. Zylah had overheard the soldiers discussing it on more than one occasion. Some had never seen a vampire, and they were afraid. She'd reassured them as best she could, offered words of comfort to quell their fears and knew that Holt had been doing the same as he'd made his rounds with Nye.

Her own blade, Zylah had coated in silence, deliberating for a while whether to cover it in baylock to give her a few seconds against the thralls and vampires, or in poisonous jupe in the hopes of harming Marcus. But she'd never seen jupe in use against a Fae, so the baylock was her only logical option.

He was just across the water, deep beneath the rock yet so close; all she'd have to do was evanesce in and out, a well-timed strike of her blade to end him. But she wasn't foolish enough to let her impatience overtake her common sense. Whilst she'd been working with her hands, she'd been working on her abilities—which was difficult, given she had no idea what she was doing. But all morning Holt had allowed her to *search* for signs of the compulsion in his mind, to look for any threads that she might be able to snag. Because if her suspicions were right, she intended to pull it apart, to untangle it from his mind herself.

Seated on a tree stump beside her was Enalla, one of the scouts who'd evanesced a large portion of the army to the forest. Zylah had tried to protest when the Fae had offered to help—

when Enalla had insisted that using her hands for physical labour would help calm her fraying mind after travelling through the aether with so many in tow.

As she'd settled into brewing the tea over the fire, filling flask after flask, Zylah had left her to it, leaving the female to lose herself in the monotony of the movements, as if the repetition had lulled her into a meditative state and eased her soul, just as she'd said it would.

By late morning, the Fae's eyes flicked up to meet hers. "The soldiers will be grateful for this liquid courage, Zylah."

"If only it were enough," Zylah said with a frown.

Enalla placed the waterskin she'd been filling in the pile beside her; canisters and skins emptied and refilled several times over since dawn, carried back and forth between soldiers by one of the scouts. "Come. Let us stretch our legs."

The Fae led them out of the forest, the wards flexing over Zylah's skin as they passed through them. She paused at their threshold, head tilting to one side as she recalled the strange feeling from the night before.

What is it? Holt asked her. He was deeper into the forest, somewhere with Rin and Kej, coordinating which units would retrieve the humans that fled the mine and where they would be taken.

I can't be certain. But I think someone is within the wards. Concealed. Someone who feels like… Zylah didn't know what the woman back in the shop had been. Fae, perhaps, but old, far older than anyone she'd met before. *Someone I met back in Morren.* She couldn't explain it, either. Just a feeling of *wrongness.* There was no feeling of irritation from Holt that she hadn't told

417

him about the encounter. There had been so much to say, and so little time to say it in.

Enalla shot her a concerned look, and Zylah quietly explained her suspicion about the breach in the wards as they made their way to the guards patrolling the shadows at the edge of the treeline, following their gazes across the lake.

"I'll go and inform General Niossa," the Fae said calmly, clasping a hand over Zylah's forearm in a gesture Zylah understood to be one of respect. She didn't wait for a response, and Zylah didn't linger in the guards' presence. She crouched low, winding her way through the reeds at the lakeshore to get a closer look across the water.

There were patrols outside the mine in the light of day, just as they'd suspected. Mostly thralls as far as she could tell from this distance, but a sizeable number of them.

And still, they hadn't received word from the humans within the mine. So much could go wrong.

So many could die.

"We won't let that happen." Holt had evanesced beside her, the reeds swaying slightly as he crouched beside her, but even if he hadn't disturbed them, hadn't spoken out loud she'd have known he was there.

Maelissa still hadn't agreed to the use of her archers, not for this, the first step in dismantling whatever Marcus and Aurelia had been planning, but Zylah trusted Holt's instincts and had faith in his ability to lead this attack. "What if Jesper's down there?" she asked him.

"Then we'll face him." Holt held out his hand for hers. "The accelerants are ready."

They were going with the scouts to start the fires, evanescing in groups of four to place Nye's custom orbs into the carts, enough to set the wood alight, but not enough to trap the humans inside. And though it would have been better to attack at night, it posed too great a risk to the humans. They'd need to be awake and alert if they stood a chance of fleeing.

Before Zylah's hand had even fully closed around Holt's, he'd evanesced them back into the forest, a short distance away from the soldiers.

"Whatever happens today," he began.

She took a step towards him, her fingers fisting into his shirt as she tilted her head back to look at him. "We'll find each other. At the end of it."

He dipped his chin in acknowledgement, his eyes searching hers before he kissed her, fingers knotting into her hair as his other hand pressed her tightly against him.

It felt like another goodbye, and Zylah resisted the urge to push him away, to tell him nothing would make her walk away from him again. She smothered the thoughts, blocking them from him, from herself, lost herself to the feel of him for one more moment before they went to join the others.

The soldiers were everywhere, preparing to move to the tree line, where some would already be making their way into the water with hollowed-out reeds to spring up onto the banks of the lake as the others moved in from the shore.

Daizin stood beside Kej as Zylah and Holt approached, shadows flickering from the Fae as he watched Kej carefully load the fire orbs into belt bags. Holt could have summoned flames to start the fire in the mine, but Nye had created the orbs to burn after rattling the ingredients inside together, with an extended burn time to allow the blazing carts to make their way into the mine's depths.

"Careful," Daizin murmured, a shadow darting out to catch an orb that was about to tumble from the pile. Whatever he and Nye were; however it was that they were the same, was no doubt something Nye would be exploring once all of this was over. And despite the way things had started between Zylah and Daizin back in Varda, the Fae's similarities to Nye cemented her trust in him. It was Laydan that had betrayed them, but she knew Daizin would have felt it the most, could see it in the way his jaw clenched tight whenever the key was discussed.

"I'm not afraid of a little heat," Kej said, flashing Daizin a grin. Daizin didn't respond, but it didn't deter Kej. Zylah was certain very little would.

Nye approached, Rin and Enalla at her side, two more soldiers following close behind them. They had the same smoky grey eyes as Enalla, but aside from that, nothing marked them as the half-siblings Zylah knew them to be.

"In and out," Nye instructed as Enalla and her two siblings each took a bag of orbs. "I need the three of you back with the others transporting humans to this side of the lake as fast as you can move." The two males beside Enalla nodded their agreement along with their half-sister.

Zylah was still trying to chip away at the compulsion, searching endlessly for something; she had no idea what it might feel like, or how she might pull it away. Holt had said it was always easier around her and at first, she'd had the same assumption he did, that it was easier because of what they were to each other, but Zylah knew there was more to it. It was the reason she'd been able to get away from Jesper the night she thought she'd killed him.

Holt reached for the nearest bag, shifting to his knees to tie a bag of orbs to her waist, his fingers sure and steady as they worked the buckles. She was reminded of the day after they first met when he'd fastened her cloak back in his cabin.

His hands lingered at her hips as he rose to his feet in front of her. *Just like old times,* he told her, the corner of his mouth dragging upwards.

Zylah smiled at him in return. She wouldn't let herself feel afraid. Not for herself. Not for him. Because she didn't want to be that frail human woman who'd run, time and time again. Didn't want to be the half-Fae who'd let herself go numb rather than feel anything at all. Learning she was Fae hadn't been enough to change her heart, and she knew there might always be that small voice in the back of her mind whispering to her, telling her over and over how much she'd fucked everything up. But she knew how to fight it now. Knew how to crush it and keep it at bay. How to accept who and what she was, even with all her imperfections.

"In and out," Nye instructed one final time.

Zylah placed a hand over her bag of orbs to steady them, before evanescing to one of the carts heading into the mine.

39

The fire started within minutes. Soldiers came from every direction; from the forest, from the lake, some came sliding down the loose chips of rock that surrounded the entrance to the mine.

Thralls screamed, but the ones standing guard were too outnumbered to put up much of a fight. The familiar robes of the priestesses were the first to surface from the mine, closely followed by their acolytes, all coughing and spluttering and gasping for air as thick black smoke billowed around them.

Shit.

If they'd caused too great a fire, the humans would be dead before they made it to the surface.

Zylah grabbed the nearest acolytes, their eyes going wide as they took in her pointed ears. A flash of red almost blinded her as she evanesced them away to the holding area Nye had set up back in Kerthen.

What was that? she asked Holt as she moved through the aether. She'd found the edges of what she was certain was Jesper's compulsion at the border of Holt's mind, as if it were a snag in a piece of clothing.

"We never wanted to go with them," one of the acolytes pleaded as Zylah handed them over to the waiting guards. She didn't wait to hear the rest of their claim to innocence.

The priestesses are using old magic. More spells, Holt told her as she reappeared beside him at the entrance to the mine, just in time to see him swipe his sword through a thrall's torso.

Ranon. Her sword was already in her hands, slashing and moving and swiping again at the thrall in front of her. A fire was blazing at the base of the pulley system, and part of the rock face had shattered somewhere above and to the side of the mine's entrance, an almighty boom following it. Miners had started to rush out, all human, panicked cries escaping them as they took in the fighting and the fires.

A vampire darted forwards, fangs sinking into the neck of a woman, tearing the flesh from her throat and shoving her aside to reach for another.

"No!" Zylah screamed. The thralls were brutal, but they lacked skill. The vampires, however, she'd seen too many times already to know what damage they could inflict, and humans would be nothing but insects to them. They'd suspected there were at least five thralls for every vampire, but they'd been wrong. There were dozens of the cursed creatures tearing at flash, rending the air with their cries as they circled the humans.

Take them, Holt told her, taking out two thralls at once. Zylah sheathed her sword and did as he asked, reaching for the nearest humans, hands grappling for hands, smoke clouding her senses as she evanesced them to safety. She kept going, sheathing and unsheathing her sword to attack the thralls, moving back and forth between the fight and the camp with as many humans as she could grab hold of, over and over until her head spun. There were so many of them.

A blast of red almost struck her as she took down a thrall, and she glanced over her shoulder to see a priestess, arms extended, palms facing towards her.

"Why are you loyal to Ranon?" Zylah asked, eyeing the priestess as she sidestepped the thrall's corpse. She needed to buy herself a little bit of time, just a moment to clear her head. There were far more thralls than vampires; Zylah had only laid eyes on two vampires since the explosions started, and one of them lay dead somewhere behind her. A small comfort, at least.

The priestess laughed bitterly as Zylah continued to move. "I am loyal to no man. It's Sira we do this for. Everything is for her. To reunite her with her daughter will be our greatest honour."

"Aurelia?" Zylah had suspected Raif's mother had been the driving force behind every step Marcus had made, and a dip of the priestess's chin confirmed it. Her light-headedness had already faded, but she wanted answers, and she wasn't going to waste this opportunity. "Why fight, then?"

The priestess's top lip curled up in a sneer. "Bringing them your blood will earn me their favour."

Bitch. Zylah didn't need to duck to reach for the dagger in her boot, and without so much as a blink it was in her fingers, then it was whistling through the air, aimed right for the priestess's heart.

The woman barely managed to stutter the first word of a spell before the dagger hit its mark, hands frozen halfway as if she'd been reaching for the blade.

There were still humans to evanesce away, but they were surrounded, and Zylah used the opportunity to attack another thrall, all the while pulling and pulling and pulling at the compulsion in Holt's mind, frantically searching for a way to obliterate it. Another vampire darted through the smoke, fangs sinking into one of Nye's soldiers.

"Zylah, we're ready!" Rin called out from among the fray, just as Zylah stepped forwards to help. She was the only one of them who could enter the mine, and Rin was part of the group in charge of flooding it.

Three more soldiers joined to help the first, and Zylah raised a hand to her face to wipe sweat from her brow. There was too much smoke to see Rin, too many snarling thralls and screaming humans to waste time trying to figure out where she was, and time was running out. Zylah didn't waste a second more on hesitating, evanescing directly into the heart of the mine to check for any remaining humans.

The minute she was inside, the hum of the vanquicite pressed at her skin, smoke filled her nostrils, and she threw a hand over her mouth to stifle a cough. There were no flames, but the smoke was pooling thick and fast above her, and though her body reacted to the vanquicite, it was nothing compared to the pain it had caused her when it had been poisoning her body. The healer had been right; she'd built up a tolerance to it, but she knew it wouldn't last long.

A cluster of humans cowered beside an upturned cart. "Help us!" one of them cried.

Zylah reached for them, evanescing them away before returning as fast as she could. She strained to listen as she moved, wood cracking and splitting somewhere in the passage behind her, but there were no humans left the way she'd come.

Movement caught her attention as she evanesced to another tunnel thick with flames, a flash of blond hair that moved far too quickly for it to be human.

Jesper.

Her eyes were watering from the smoke, her head pounding from the vanquicite, but there was one more tunnel she wanted to check before leaving, and though the temptation pulled at her to follow him, she wouldn't risk any more lives for him.

Zylah, get out of there, Holt pleaded.

He's here.

The final tunnel was a mess of debris. A supporting beam had snapped and fallen, the ceiling above beginning to cave in, a mop of red hair poking out of the rubble. And a groan.

Zylah was beside the human in a heartbeat; a boy, no older than thirteen, eyes fluttering, chest rising and falling. She pressed her hand to his, and his eyes darted open.

"My sister," he wheezed. "She's underneath. I can hear her."

Zylah paused to listen, a muffled scream sounding from the debris beyond. He was right.

Zylah.

She pulled away the shattered wood surrounding the boy, eyes darting over his cuts and scrapes. He clutched one hand awkwardly to his chest but pushed himself to his feet with determination.

"Please." He choked out the word against the smoke. "You have to help her." He was already tugging at the beam with his good hand, and Zylah fell to her knees beside him, coughing and spluttering as she heaved the wood, clawing at the rock to pull it away.

Zylah. Holt's voice was laced with panic in her thoughts, but she just needed a few more seconds to reach the girl.

Another part of the tunnel collapsed behind them, just as her fingers brushed against the girl's hand. It was all Zylah needed. She reached for the boy, sending a silent prayer to whoever was listening that his sister wasn't already dead.

Now, she told Holt, evanescing back to the surface, her lungs burning and her skin prickling from being surrounded by so much vanquicite.

For a moment, she felt herself slip into the aether, concentrating as hard as she could on where she wanted to go, the effects of the vanquicite muddying her thoughts.

An explosion split the rock, shards of it splintering and cascading over the entrance of the mine, a boom shaking the earth beneath their feet as the wall beside the entrance caved in. Rocks splashed into the lake at the base of the waterfall.

A surge of water fell from above directly onto the hole the explosion had created, pouring into the mine from where Rin and the soldiers had widened the waterfall's mouth, the roar of it drowning out the sound of the fighting.

Zylah tugged on her magic to heal the girl first, the same red hair as her brother's tangled around her face. The girl's chest heaved, and the boy was on his knees beside her, tears streaming down his face. "Anya, you're alright, I'm here."

Zylah turned to him next, the burn from her lungs fading along with the sting of the vanquicite as she healed the boy, then evanesced them back to the safety of the camp.

She felt Holt's caress in her mind as if he were checking her for any lingering injuries as her feet landed back on the lakeshore once more. *I'm alright.* Another flash of blond. "Jesper."

She darted after him, almost tripping over a corpse but she didn't dare look down. It was just as likely to have been Fae or human as it was vampire or thrall, and Zylah didn't want to let the thought deter her.

Holt appeared beside her, blocking an attack from Jesper as the vampire bared his fangs at them both.

"We really have to stop meeting like this," he said with a sneer, those endless black eyes stark against his pale skin. He wore a sword at his hip, but it wasn't the vanquicite sword he'd stolen from Arnir, Zylah noted with a small flicker of relief.

She didn't offer him a response, because she'd finally found what she'd been searching for, swiping her own sword at Jesper at the same moment she finally found a graspable edge of the compulsion in Holt's mind.

She imagined herself pulling a physical thread, tugging and tugging and tugging it as Holt swung his sword at the vampire, his vines erupting from the earth to reach for Jesper's feet. But Jesper was too fast for them.

They needed to buy some time, for the scouts to take the remainder of the humans to safety, and for their soldiers to pull back to the lakeshore if Holt was going to be able to use his magic as safely as possible.

Jesper laughed as he dodged a blow from Zylah's sword, his empty gaze raking over her. "Your Fae body suits you, Zylah."

Holt darted forwards, a vine clasping Jesper's ankle and his sword slicing flesh as the vampire twisted away.

428

Zylah clawed at the last of the compulsion, tore at it with everything she had until it cleaved away, pictured it burning to ash in her fingertips as Jesper prattled on.

She felt Holt's understanding as she moved with him in bursts through the smoke, through the soldiers, through the thralls, the world a blur around them as she followed his evanescing like an echo. He stumbled for a moment, and she reached for him, pulling him with her through the aether, feeling everything he was feeling as years of Jesper's compulsion peeled away. Felt the flicker of confusion as so many memories hit him at once, the sense of peace left behind as the coercion left him and how heavily it had weighed on him for so long.

His fingers tightened around hers, and Zylah realised he was evanescing them now, gratitude and warmth and elation flaring down the bond.

But Holt didn't break his focus away from Jesper.

"Raif was quite keen to fill me in on everything I'd missed in my time away from Virian," the vampire mused as he continued to evade them. Zylah had no time for a rebuke, too busy keeping an eye on the soldiers' retreat, on ensuring she was working with Holt to back Jesper towards the mine, beyond the line Rin and Kej had marked for them.

"He's quite descriptive you know," Jesper said on an exhale, raising an eyebrow as Zylah swapped her sword for a dagger. "I do love listening to his stories about your pretty little c—"

Holt roared, slammed his body into Jesper's with such force that he brought the vampire crashing down into the dirt, fangs bared. Holt didn't baulk. Vines erupted from the earth, wrapping around Jesper's limbs, one at his throat.

But as Holt raised a hand, flames already licking around his fingertips, a blast of lightning struck him, throwing him off the vampire and onto the earth.

Marcus.

40

Lightning crackled. "I'd been wondering where you'd got to," Marcus sneered, another blast of lightning aimed at Holt as Zylah pulled him away. Marcus shifted his gaze to her. "You've caused quite a stir, haven't you, *Zylah*?" His eyes traced over her pointed ears before meeting hers.

Holt had already healed himself, moving her behind him as he pushed to his feet. Vines snapped behind them, and they both turned to see Jesper breaking free of his restraints.

They shared a look, barely the span of an intake of breath. But it was enough. Neither Jesper nor Marcus knew the compulsion had been lifted. They still believed Holt couldn't harm Marcus, that he would simply hand Zylah over for whatever game Aurelia was playing.

They were wrong.

Holt moved for Marcus at the same time Zylah lunged for Jesper, her dagger slashing out as she slid through the dirt at the vampire's feet.

Jesper laughed, but it sounded hollow, empty, as he pressed a hand to the wound and peered at his blood-soaked fingers.

"Playing dirty? I knew you were a fighter. I can still remember the way you felt squirming beneath me back in Virian."

Zylah huffed a laugh of her own in bitter amusement that she had ever considered herself a monster after what he'd tried to do to her. But she wasn't that defenceless human anymore.

Lightning cracked and struck earth behind her, followed by a groan from Marcus as Holt deflected the attack.

Make him suffer, she told her mate as she moved around Jesper. Her eyes darted to the fires around them, searching for ways she could trap the vampire in the flames just as two wildcats crept towards him, bodies pressed low to the ground, fangs bared, silver-grey eyes reflecting the flicker of flames. Rin and Kej. And they were pushing him back, forcing him into the fire whilst Zylah blocked his only other way out.

"Play nice, kitties," Jesper purred. And then he lunged. Zylah didn't know which of the twins it was, Rin or Kej, but as fangs sank into fur and flesh, dark shadows swirled at Jesper's throat, ripping him away.

Daizin slid to the earth beside the wildcat, one hand pressed to the wound. "He'll be okay with me, I'll have Enalla take us back. Don't let the prince get away," he told Zylah as Rin joined him, licking at Kej's wound.

Zylah didn't need to be told twice. Jesper was faster than the other vampires, but he was sloppy with his sword, she could see it clearly now her skills had improved.

And with evanescing as her advantage, Zylah moved around him, faster and faster, slicing at flesh, knocking his sword from his grasp and narrowly missing the scrape of fangs as he reached for her.

Take what you need, Holt told her, as her chest heaved and sweat soaked her clothes, the air still filled with the sounds of clashing swords and cries. But apprehension twisted in Zylah's stomach.

The well is bigger now, Holt reassured her.

She spared a glance over her shoulder to see Holt and Marcus circling each other, swords drawn, and she knew he was waiting for the moment he could release the surge of power she'd only felt tremors of in the past.

Her look cost her. Jesper collapsed onto her, rolling them head over foot across the compacted earth. There was no time to think; Zylah evanesced them both high above the lake, so high they reappeared amongst the clouds, using Jesper's moment of panic to climb onto his back, spinning and tumbling and falling with him so fast she couldn't make up from down.

Jesper roared as he tried to peel her off him, but his movements were panicked, frenzied and it gave her a smug sense of satisfaction knowing that his last moments would be full of fear. Here was the monster who had started all of this; Zylah knew she was just one of many, that his other victims would not have been as lucky as she had been to escape his clutches. The fear he felt wouldn't have been even a fraction of what he'd inflicted.

His arms reached back to scratch and claw at her, but she held fast as they plummeted through the clouds, even when his head slammed back to crack against her own. She focused on her fingertips, on all the times she'd watched Holt summon flames, let herself be consumed by the feel of her magic, of *his*, and then she tugged, gently, pulled on that part of him that could create a single ember.

433

And watched in fascination as her fingers sparked against Jesper's clothes.

She'd killed Jesper once. This time, there would be no coming back for him. This time, a single ember was all she needed.

They breached the clouds, plumes of smoke drifting up from the shattered mine, Jesper's keening scream fading away into the wind. She moved her hands to the sides of his face, pressing and pushing her fingers into his flesh until the embers spread, using her healing magic to soothe her own skin where it seared against his, preventing the fire from consuming her.

Jesper's fate would not be painless. She held tight, screaming against the discomfort until she could hold on no longer, evanescing back to the shore in time to see him smash into the surface of the lake, a ball of flames consumed by an explosion of water. If the fire hadn't already taken him, the fall would.

Zylah doubled over, exhaustion gripping her as she healed the last of the burns on her hands, ruined flesh repairing itself as the water subsided, all traces of Jesper gone. Relief washed over her at the sight. Jesper had been the one to start all of this, but she'd been the one to end it, and yet the victory felt hollow. His was another death in a long list of many, and Zylah was tired of it.

A spike of pain pressed into her heart, forcing the air from her lungs. Zylah almost lost her footing as a shockwave of magic rattled the earth.

Holt had unleashed his magic. And he was injured.

She looked up in time to see power surging from him and taking out everything in its path, her mate staggering forwards a step.

She sucked in a breath as Marcus fell, evanescing to Holt's side and lacing her fingers through his. "Is he…?"

Holt didn't speak. But she knew the answer. Marcus was dead. Yet unlike the hollowness of Jesper's death, Zylah choked back a sob at the site of the Fae who had caused her mate so much harm, who had been the one responsible for so much pain.

But it wasn't just Marcus that Holt's power had obliterated. It was the thralls behind him, the remaining vampires, even the priestesses and the acolytes that had chosen to stay, each of them thrown back with the force of Holt's blast, an eerie quiet following in its wake.

Healing magic bled from her fingertips into his as she took in the lifeless bodies scattered around them in a semi-circle, her breath catching in her throat at the sight. But Holt didn't react, his chest heaving, his lips pressed into a firm line. Zylah followed his gaze, her attention falling on the cluster of soldiers he'd taken out with his magic by mistake.

She stepped in front of him, leaning up onto her toes and cupping a hand to the back of his neck to ease him to look down at her. His eyelashes fluttered, his fingers fisting into her tunic as the haze seemed to clear from his vision, emotions flicking out from him in spikes as if he were trying to keep it all locked away from her.

Zylah pressed her lips against his, grounding him, letting him know she was with him, no matter what he was feeling. Even if the guilt was laced with euphoria, she let nothing but love pass down the bond, acceptance, no matter what he'd done.

"Marcus is dead," she whispered. Jesper too. It was over. Holt was free.

He sucked in a breath, a shudder passing through him, and then frowned. "Aurelia."

But it was too late. A wail cut through the silence, and they turned to the sound, Holt's hand finding hers.

"No!" a Fae screamed, throwing herself to the dirt beside Marcus's lifeless body. Raif stood beside her, and even if he hadn't, Zylah would have known it was his mother; her black hair and her complexion, the shape of her face, just like Raif's sister, Rose. There was no doubting that this was Aurelia.

"What have you done?" she whispered, hands brushing over Marcus's face as her eyes trailed up to look at them both. The same dazzling blue eyes Raif had once possessed.

Zylah stamped out any pity she might have felt at the sight of Aurelia leaning over her lifeless mate. She would not let this female's sadness pull any remorse from her for what Holt had endured at their hands. For all that they'd done. "How could you?" Zylah asked. "How could you do all of this? And to your own son."

Aurelia held out a hand to Raif, gracefully rising to her feet. She smoothed down the front of her deep blue gown with the other, her gaze flicking from Raif's empty black eyes back to Zylah's.

"I would never do anything to harm my children. He wishes to remain this way. Being a vampire has improved the dark magic he already had." Raif was silent, his expression void of any emotion, but all Zylah felt was disgust. How could a mother do that to their child?

Aurelia's eyes cast back to her lifeless mate. "Do not try to distract me from the fate that awaits you."

Zylah tried to evanesce, but nothing happened. She pulled again on her magic, but neither she nor Holt moved.

"Which of you did this?" Aurelia demanded, taking a step closer.

"I did," Holt said immediately.

What's happening? Zylah asked. They should have been able to evanesce away, but it was as if Aurelia was made of vanquicite, as if she nullified every last drop of their power.

Aurelia took another step closer, glancing between them before settling her attention on Holt. "She will know the pain of feeling your death before she dies, and you will die knowing it was because of you."

It was then that Zylah realised the sounds around them had faded; not the same quiet that followed Holt's blast of power, but as if they were in a bubble, just the four of them, Marcus's body lying between them.

She's holding us inside, Holt warned her. *Her touch will paralyse. Don't be tempted to try and strike her.*

Zylah tilted her chin and met Aurelia's eyes as she squeezed Holt's hand. "What is it that you want with me?" She couldn't help but notice the way Raif tracked the movement, despite his stance of indifference, his hands in his pockets the way he always used to hold himself.

"I had considered gifting you to my son before you served my purpose. He was fond of you, you know. Come with me willingly, Zylah, and I will have him make Holt's death swift," Aurelia said, stepping over her mate's corpse as if it were nothing, closing the distance between them.

Gifting. Like she was a prize mare.

437

Zylah's disgust turned to ire, Holt's wrath echoing in response. She pushed against Aurelia's hold, searching and searching for a snag in the magic that she might be able to unravel, teeth clenched against the weight of it. "Fuck you."

Aurelia's laugh was cold, empty. "You have your grandmother's filthy tongue."

Blood of my blood, Pallia had told her. Kopi landed on Zylah's shoulder as Aurelia's words settled over her. Not because Zylah was Pallia's descendant. But because she was her granddaughter.

It was all her, from the beginning, Holt told her, free of the compulsion. *Aurelia's been searching for you all this time.*

It had never been about Marcus. Never been about Ranon's old magic. It had only ever been about this, about Aurelia seeking out her father. Arnir was Marcus's puppet, but Marcus had been Aurelia's all along, mate or not.

Holt's confirmation flared down the bond.

"And of course, Pallia's little companion," Aurelia added. "You were always loyal, weren't you, Kopi?"

Zylah couldn't even flinch as the Fae reached out a hand as if she might stroke Kopi on the head. But it didn't matter.

She'd found the end of the thread. And she tore at it with everything she had.

41

Zylah realised a second too late that it wasn't Aurelia's hold she'd torn away, not the magic preventing them from evanescing to safety, but something else.

Holt pulled Zylah behind him as Aurelia struck out, fingertips grazing Holt's arm instead. The Fae's eyes narrowed in confusion as she looked down at her fingers, an expectant look fixed across her face.

Not the strange shield Aurelia had constructed to trap them inside with her, but her ability to incapacitate with her touch.

Which meant they still couldn't evanesce away.

Zylah shoved Aurelia back, unable to summon any weapons to her fingertips, her sword and her daggers scattered around them somewhere amongst the fallen bodies.

She prayed none of her friends were among them as Raif moved to Aurelia's side to steady her, his lip curling back in a snarl to reveal the sharp points of his fangs.

He wishes to remain this way, Aurelia had told them.

He'd chosen.

And as if in response to that thought, Holt slammed into

Raif, as if he'd been waiting for the opportunity since Raif's confession to them near the Aquaris Court. His fist struck Raif's jaw, and Raif snarled again, staggering back from the force of the blow.

He hadn't said a word since he'd arrived with his mother, but as he swiped at the blood trickling from his mouth, he let out a dry laugh. "I knew you were holding back before."

He lunged for Holt, knocking him to the ground as they became a blur of limbs and fists, but not, Zylah realised with a small sliver of relief, any sign of Raif's magic.

As if whatever Aurelia had done with her and Holt's magic was affecting him, too.

Zylah saw the glint of her sword, but when she tried to reach it, she struck an invisible wall, as if Aurelia's strange shield around the four of them blocked out the outside world, trapping them within it.

She turned back to Holt and Raif, looking for a way to intervene, Kopi flapping his wings on her shoulder in distress.

"Stop," Aurelia commanded, and Zylah found she couldn't move. Holt stilled where his fist hung over Raif's face, dread coiling in Zylah's stomach.

She's using too much magic at once, I don't know where to start looking, she told Holt.

It'll be alright, Zylah.

But the unnatural way he lowered his fist and rose to his feet was anything but alright.

Aurelia circled him, with barely a glance at her son who brushed himself off with nothing but a smirk as he stood beside Zylah, close enough for her to feel his warmth.

She swallowed down the acid in her throat at his proximity, her eyes fixed on Holt.

I can't find the end of it, she said, her thoughts panicked and fast.

But there was no response from Holt this time.

Only silence.

He held her gaze, paying Aurelia no heed, and Zylah saw only love and sadness in his eyes.

"Jesper told me how you always fought his compulsion," Aurelia said thoughtfully. "Given she's your mate, I imagine that enabled you to fight it, whether you were aware of it or not." Her eyes slid to Marcus's lifeless body, but Zylah couldn't read the expression in them. "But like all my creations, Jesper learnt that trick from me. Where is your brother, Raif?"

"At the bottom of the lake," Zylah said, hoping to distract Aurelia from Holt, willing her tone to convey every ounce of satisfaction she'd felt watching Jesper fall to his death.

He wasn't truly Aurelia's son, but for her to refer to him as such, must have meant she cared for him.

Aurelia's eyes darkened a fraction, but she continued to circle Holt, one hand trailing a line across his chest, his arm, as she moved.

Holt didn't move, just remained still in that unnatural way, as if Aurelia was holding him there, his gaze fixed on Zylah, his eyes searching hers.

Zylah pulled and tugged and clawed at the magic binding her, a small amount of pressure releasing as she found a crack and made to move for Holt, but Raif held her back.

"Don't," Raif murmured against her hair.

A flare of heat down the bond was all she felt, Holt's expression dark as his eyes flicked to where Raif held Zylah to him.

"Holt," Aurelia sighed, seemingly unaware Zylah had found a fissure in her magic. "You always had such power; I've always been able to feel it humming within you. I've no doubt it was your magic that did this."

She stopped in front of him, gesturing to the bodies beyond their little bubble. "Do it again," she said sternly, and Zylah felt the magic in the command, even from where she stood.

I'm trying, I'm looking for a way out of this, she told him, unsure whether he could hear her, or if Aurelia was somehow blocking the magic between them.

Aurelia's quiet laugh was bitter, twisted. Under any other circumstances, Zylah might have even said the Fae sounded like she was impressed. "You've done well to try to shield yourself from me," she said to Holt, caressing the back of her knuckles down the side of his face. "So many Fae have withered away beneath the weight of my compulsion. But there are always loopholes. So I'll leave you with two choices; kill them all, or let me in."

Zylah tried to shake free of Raif's hold, but he held tight.

"Zylah," he warned behind her.

"She can't do this," Zylah pleaded.

It was a violation, what Aurelia wanted to do; what she had been doing all these years.

The Fae took a step closer to Holt, blocking his face from Zylah's view. "We both know it isn't a difficult decision for you."

And Zylah knew she was right; Holt would always put the lives of others first.

"Now," Aurelia continued, more than a hint of satisfaction in her tone. "Let. Me. In."

There'll be a way out of this. We'll find it, Zylah told her mate, Raif's grip on her arm tightening as she found another crack in Aurelia's magic, desperate to reach Holt.

"Kneel," Aurelia commanded, and Zylah watched in horror as Holt followed the order, kneeling before Aurelia in the dirt.

"Stripping your family of everything has been worth every moment," Aurelia went on. "That *she* turned out to be your mate. I couldn't have hoped for a more perfect outcome."

Zylah shredded through Aurelia's hold on her, yanking herself from Raif's grip and sliding to her knees before Holt to press her hands to his face.

But his eyes were glassy, empty, *unseeing*, and he didn't move to look down at her.

Didn't react to her touch, and no trace of emotion travelled down their bond.

Raif growled behind her, but Zylah paid him no heed as panic gripped her, her heart thumping against her chest.

She leaned up, pressing her lips to Holt's, ignoring the movement behind her from Aurelia and Raif.

I know you're in there somewhere, Holt. Just hold on. I'll find you.

"It had to be this way," Raif said with a deathly hollowness somewhere behind her.

"Do it," Aurelia commanded.

A hand clasped around Zylah's forearm, pulling her back, and all Zylah had the chance to register was Raif's empty eyes meeting hers before he slid a sword into Holt's chest.

A sword made wholly of vanquicite.

"No!" Zylah screamed, but the only sound she heard in response was Aurelia's twisted laugh as the Fae evanesced Zylah away.

Kopi's wings fluttered at the edges of her vision, but Zylah slid to her knees, pressed a hand to the cold stone beneath her, the other to her chest, pain searing through her and stealing her breath away. It was dark, but she didn't know if it was because of her shallow breaths, because of the ringing in her ears or the shadow over her eyes.

The sword had gone through his chest. A vanquicite sword. Zylah was shaking, a chill sweeping through her that had her teeth rattling together. *He can't be dead. He can't be.*

Holt, she called to him. But there was only silence. She couldn't *feel* him. Could feel nothing since Aurelia had released her magic like a web over them both, snuffing out the connection they shared.

He can't be dead. Kopi hooed in warning, and a hand clamped down around Zylah's wrist, jerking her to her feet, but she barely registered it, a sob lodged in her throat, her head pounding as she fought to suck in a breath.

I'll find you; I'll find you. I'llfindyouI'llfindyouI'llfind you, she told him over and over, praying he could hear it, but nothing but that hollow, empty quiet answered her. A sob escaped her, and she pressed a hand to her stomach, staggering forwards as Aurelia yanked at her wrist again.

"No male is worth your tears," Aurelia told her with a sneer.

"Not even your father?" Zylah asked, tears blurring her vision as she looked up into Aurelia's cruel eyes. If this was a tomb, as Zylah suspected, there was only one reason for that.

Aurelia scoffed but said nothing.

Kopi's claws dug into Zylah's shoulder as Aurelia all but dragged her along, as if he were reminding her he was there with her; that she wasn't alone. She stifled another sob and tried to take in her surroundings. It was dark and cold, a stale smell permeating the air, not unlike the decoy tomb where they'd found the key.

Holt, she tried again, clutching at her chest as if she could feel the echo of where the sword pierced Holt's. She felt the answering silence in every cell, every nerve, every bone. The *lack* of him, his presence, echoing against the absence of their magic, of everything Aurelia had stolen from her.

Kopi hooed again, just as Aurelia's grip tightened, pulling Zylah into a narrow passage. "She stole me away from my parents, you know. Pallia and the others, the ones you might have once called gods," Aurelia muttered, her other hand delicately holding her dress as if it mattered that the hem would scrape against the dirty stone beneath them. "The seven of them plotted from the very beginning. Hid me from my parents, and they from me. Made sure I would have no idea who I truly was. But then I died, or rather, I should have. And my mother came to me."

Zylah had often wondered since learning of Aurelia's return whether she'd faked her own death. But then realisation hit. "I know where your mother is," she blurted as the passage ended, orblights casting shadows on the wall of a chamber. Hooded figures stood ahead, priestesses if Zylah had to guess. "I'll… I'll make a bargain with you. Return me to Holt, and I'll tell you where she is."

Aurelia turned to her, one eyebrow raised. Her face was in shadow, but Zylah could still see the bright blue of her eyes, the paleness of her complexion so similar to Rose, Raif's sister.

"He's gone," Aurelia said flatly. "But don't worry. You'll follow him soon enough."

Every retort fell away from Zylah at that. *Holt*, she called out again in desperation.

"Aurelia," a voice said up ahead; one she recognised. Zylah looked up to see Laydan pull back a hood, a smug look across his face. Around his neck, he wore the stolen key, his robes the same as the priestesses beside him.

"Daizin loved you," Zylah told him, but the words were hollow in her ears, her thoughts a scattered mess.

"Then he was a fool," Laydan said flatly, lifting the key over his head to place it on the rock beside him. No, not rock. A tomb. Zylah's eyes widened as she took in the twist of stone, layers of it wrapping and warping over each other like petrified vines, binding the tomb within it.

Ranon's tomb.

Zylah finally looked at the six priestesses beside Laydan. *It's Sira we do this for. Everything is for her*, the priestess had said outside the mine. Zylah's attention flicked back to the tomb, to the unmistakable shape of a padlock sitting atop it.

Arnir, Marcus. Aurelia. All along it had been Ranon and Sira, recreating the world as they always envisioned it with the creatures they'd made. Even their daughter was a creation of their design.

"When Laydan told me Malok had someone who could locate the key, I didn't let myself hope," Aurelia said, running a hand over the stone plaque at the head of the tomb, the inscription long since eroded. "But when he returned with the second of my father's tomes, all that left was you."

Zylah could barely hear the Fae's words over the ringing in her ears. *Holt.* She cried out for him, her voice sounding broken in her thoughts. But it had been too long since she'd felt him. Too long with nothing but silence in her soul in the space he should have been.

A hand shoved her forwards, and she stumbled over the stone dais, hands reaching forwards to steady herself at the foot of the tomb as the priestesses began to chant. Kopi darted from her shoulder as if he'd woken from slumber, flapping his wings and clawing at the priestesses' faces, but Aurelia merely swiped a hand and he fell still, his tiny body landing on the stone at her feet.

"No," Zylah moaned. But she couldn't move. Aurelia's fingers gripped her wrist, magic passing between them. Her paralysing touch.

She lifted Zylah's wrist as the priestesses' chant grew faster, Laydan joining them, his hands rising over the tomb, pushing the key into the lock. A crack sounded, the earth rumbling beneath them.

Holt, Zylah tried. *Please. Answer me.* Tears slid down her face, her vision blurring, and then something sliced deeply into her wrist, then the other, fingers clamping at her skin to urge the blood from her veins.

The tomb began to split, the priestesses chanting faster, louder, faster, louder, Laydan's voice laced amongst them, Aurelia muttering words under her breath.

447

Zylah grew light-headed from the blood loss, her eyes beginning to close as a boom shoved them all back a step, tearing Zylah's weak body from Aurelia's grasp, her face hitting cold stone.

Her breaths were shallow. Too shallow, and from here, all she could see was Kopi's little body, lying still after he'd fought for her. "I'm sorry," she croaked, tears blurring her vision, but the words were soundless.

Stone scraped over stone, like heavy pieces sliding apart, shards smashing and showering over her face, slicing into her skin.

A strangled noise, like a heavy inhale, was the only sound that followed.

"Father," Aurelia breathed.

Ranon. Zylah couldn't see him, had no energy left to even lift her head. There would be no escaping this. No freedom this time.

"Pallia's blood has freed you," Aurelia said, but Zylah let the words pass over her.

She whispered Holt's name as the blood loss pulled her under, her eyes fluttering shut, her mind conjuring an image of her mate.

It was never about living forever, Holt. Just living free, she'd told him, when he'd pulled her back from the edge of oblivion. And he was free now, wherever he was.

It'll be alright, Zylah, the vision of him said softly. Her chest fluttered at the hope in his words, her heart swelling at the sight of him, and the thought that wherever he was, she might get to join him.

Nothing bound them now; no one held them captive. Nothing could control them like this, not even Ranon.

A soundless sigh bubbled up from her lips, wet and raspy.

To dying free.

42

Strong arms embraced her and cradled her to a firm chest. Everything was dark, and when Zylah tried to open her eyes, she found she didn't have the strength.

There were no flickers of blue like last time. No image of Pallia looking down at her. There was warmth, but all Zylah knew was that it was *wrong*.

She pulled on her magic and tried to evanesce away, but there was nothing. Just a hollow space inside her where it should have been.

Whoever was holding her was moving, carrying her with sure, steady steps. But it wasn't Holt; she knew it with a certainty that settled deep in her bones.

Holt, she called out to him, but only silence answered.

Something small stirred at her chest, a quiet, garbled sound. "Kopi?" Zylah croaked.

"Shh," the body that held her said quietly. There was something familiar about the voice, but the thought was difficult to hold on to. She still couldn't open her eyes, couldn't move her hands, could do nothing but be held.

The smallest flicker of feeling echoed in her rib cage, so quickly then it was gone. But she held onto that tiny spark of hope with everything she had. Every breath was like fire in her lungs, but she didn't have the strength to cough. A breeze blew the hair from Zylah's face, and as consciousness slowly seeped back into her veins, it brought with it a familiar scent.

Mint and lemongrass.

"No," she murmured, but she couldn't move, couldn't push away.

"Be quiet, Zylah," Raif said above her.

No. Not this. Not like this. Aurelia's words echoed in her head. *I had considered gifting you to my son before you served my purpose.*

Zylah's blood ran cold, but with no magic, no strength, not even enough to open her eyes, all she could do was let Raif carry her into the dark.

ACKNOWLEDGEMENTS

I consider myself exceptionally lucky to be surrounded by incredible humans who never cease to make my days a little brighter. Huge thanks to:

Amy Eversley: thank you, as always for the hours of back and forth writing chat, for your never-ending support, time and patience.

Belle Manuel, Jozanne Morgan and Holly Hoffmann: for the chats, calls, memes, discussions, international parcels, laughs, ADHD support, anxiety meltdowns and everything else in between.

Angie, Charli, Venetia, Megan, Kat, Esme, Kim, Kear and Rebecca: thank you for the daily laughter, the countless discussions, the hours of bookish chats, and for my exploding TBR pile.

To my cover designer Franziska Stern for creating yet another wonderful cover and for putting up with my many emails and ideas, you are exceptionally talented, and I am so very grateful to have stumbled upon your incredible work.

To my editor Melanie Underwood for your patience and diligent eye.

To Andrés Aguirre Jurado for another incredible map.

To Ellie Yatsenko, Cornelia DaVien, Flavie, Marcella and Hillary Bardin for creating such beautiful artwork.

To my beta readers Jess Hinton, Chloe Feather, Emily Withers, Shika Tamaklo, Angela and Mikaela: thank you for your insight and feedback, and for being part of this process with me.

To the many inspiring indie authors that I get to interact with, learn from, and be in awe of on a daily basis.

To the bookstagrammers, TikTokers, and bloggers who posted about Storms and Starlight, shared, liked, commented on posts, told their friends, added it to lists: thank you, thank you, thank you.

To the readers: your continued support never ceases to amaze me, and I truly wouldn't be able to keep doing this if it weren't for all you wonderful people. Thank you.

And always last but not least, to my husband Ali: thank you for the hours, days, weeks, years of love, laughs, for always being a sounding board, for your patience, your insight, your kindness and all the many wonderful ways in which you support me—I couldn't do any of it without you.

Printed in Great Britain
by Amazon

25384445R00261